The Sin War

Diablo™

The Sin War

Book Two

Scales of the Serpent

Richard A. Knaak

This book is a work of fiction. Names, characters, places, and incidents are products of the author's imagination or are used fictitiously. Any resemblance to actual events or locales or persons living or dead is entirely coincidental.

ISBN: 978-1-945683-59-6

First Pocket Books printing: April 2007
First Blizzard Entertainment printing: October 2019

10 9 8 7 6 5 4 3 2 1

Cover art by Glenn Rane

Printed in China

For all the loyal and very patient fans
of the world of Sanctuary.

Prologue

. . . The world was forever changed by the second coming of the nephalem, but changed most of all was the first among their kind, Uldyssian ul-Diomed. Wanting nothing more than the simple, worthy life of a farmer, he was now forced to become a catalyst for upheaval. Through him would be revealed some of the truth concerning Sanctuary, as the world was called by those who most vied to control it. Through him did others learn of the eternal war between the angels and demons through the guises of the Cathedral of Light and the Temple of the Triune.

And knowing Uldyssian as a threat to all they planned, both the Cathedral and the Temple in their own ways worked to either beguile him into becoming their puppet or destroy him utterly. Worse, betrayed by what he had thought love, Uldyssian became a danger to himself, for he risked becoming blind to what was happening around him even as he sought to free humans from the yoke of those believing themselves the race's rightful masters.

But although Uldyssian felt that the entire fate of Sanctuary rested on his weary shoulders, he could not know that there had been others fighting for centuries against his same enemies, fighting them despite what had seemed for centuries the hopelessness of their cause.

He could not know this, which was probably for the best . . . for they, in turn, were not certain if he should be welcomed . . . or destroyed, just as the angels and demons believed.

From the Books of Kalan
Fifth Tome, First Leaf

ONE

The city of Toraja burned . . .

While never able to approach in magnitude or glory great Kehjan to the east, Toraja had still been known far and wide for its unique sights catering to the pilgrim and the inhabitant alike. There was the vast, open market just beyond its northwestern gate, where anything from the known lands could be bought or sold for the right price. Near the city center lay the centuries-old, intricately sculpted gardens, where one could admire the spiral trees or the Falo Blooms, the fabled flowers with more than a dozen variations of bright color on each petal and a scent that perfumers could never match. Beyond that stood the towering Arena of Klytos, home of the Nirolian Games, attracting visitors from even the sprawling capital.

But all those legendary sites, often filled to capacity, were empty this one terrible eve. Indeed, there was only activity in a lone part of the city and the hint of that could be witnessed from as far as a mile away in the deep jungle surrounding walled Toraja.

Toraja burned . . . and at the center of the conflagaration lay the Temple of the Triune.

The flames illuminated the sky well above the three-towered, triangular structure, the largest temple of the sect other than the main one near Kehjan. Black smoke billowed from the foremost tower, the one dedicated to Mefis, one of the three guiding spirits. The huge red circle representing both the order and *love*—Mefis's supposed sphere of influence—hung lopsided. Cast of iron, the immense circle now threatened those below as the damage from the fire ate away at its remaining supports. The original constructors had never imagined that such a fate would ever befall the structure and so had not added additional support.

If calamity imminently threatened the tower of Mefis, it had already claimed that of Dialon, to the right. The proud ram's head—symbol of determination—still hung high, but above it the structure was a collapsed ruin. Oddly, little of the upper level had actually fallen to the streets below; most of the stone and wood rubble lay piled atop, as if the tower had somehow imploded.

Hundreds of figures swarmed the area around the steps, those nearest the entrance clad in the azure, gold, or black robes of the three orders. With them stood scores of hooded, breast-plated figures—the temple's Peace Warders—armed with swords and lances. The faithful of the Triune fought against a crush of bodies whose foremost ranks were dressed in simple peasant and farmer clothing of the upper lands far to the northwest of the great jungles. The pale skin and tighter garments of these first figures was in sharp contrast not only to the mainly swarthy servants of the temple, but also those making up most of the successive waves behind the lead attackers. Indeed, the bulk of the movement against the Triune consisted of natives of Toraja itself, marked by their loose-fitting, flowing, red and purple garments and long, black hair bound to the back.

Although it was the attackers who wielded the majority of the torches, the flames consuming much of the nearby sections of the city were not, for the most part, their doing. In fact, no one could for certain say how the first fires had begun, only that they seemed to initially work in favor of the priesthood . . . and that had been enough to turn what sympathies there had been for the Triune into anger.

That anger was all the impetus needed to urge Uldyssian to take down the temple without further delay. When he had initially arrived in Toraja—and once he had gotten over his astonishment at so many people packed into one place—Uldyssian had thought to gradually influence the citizenry into simply ousting the priests and their underlings from the city. But for such a heinous act—in which dozens of locals and even some of his original followers had perished—no remorse or sympathy remained in the former farmer's heart.

I came to this city hoping to teach, to convert people, Uldyssian bitterly thought as he strode toward the steps. *But they forced this upon all of us instead.*

Without seeing him, the crowd parted. Any of those touched by the power within Uldyssian—the power of the nephalem—could sense his nearness. The momentum of the crowd paused as they realized that Uldyssian had something in mind.

He had not been the cause of the devastation so far embracing the temple. That had been the results of the more primitive efforts by some of his enthusiastic followers, such as Romus, one of the lead Parthans. Romus was one of a handful of the most advanced among Uldyssian's acolytes. Partha had been the second place to witness the miracle of Uldyssian's gift, after his own village of Seram. However, unlike Seram, where the son of Diomedes had been cast as a murderer and monster, the Parthans had welcomed his abilities and embraced his simple but honest beliefs.

Uldyssian was not the image of a crusading prophet as fables usually went. He was no angelic, ageless youth like he who led the Cathedral of Light—the rival sect to the temple—nor a silver-haired, benevolent elder such as the Primus, whose servants now awaited Uldyssian's wrath. Uldyssian ul-Diomed had been born to be a tiller of soil. Square jawed and with rough-hewn features half-draped by a short beard, he was strong of build due to his hard life but otherwise unremarkable. His sandy-colored hair hung unkempt down to his neck, any attempt at neatness lost in tonight's chaos. Uldyssian wore a plain brown shirt and pants and weathered boots. He carried no weapon save a knife thrust into his belt. Indeed, he needed no weapon, he himself far deadlier than the sharpest blade or the swiftest, truest arrow.

Or even a squad of Peace Warders, who at this very moment charged down the steps at him. Behind them, a priest of Dialon imperiously barked orders. Uldyssian had no special hate for the fool, for he knew that the cleric simply mouthed the words of his superior, secreted somewhere deep in the temple complex. Nonetheless, both the warriors and the priest would suffer for their zealous loyalty to the foul sect.

Uldyssian let the guards come nearly within weapon's reach, then, without so much as a blink, sent the entire contingent flying in different directions. Some collided with the pillars at the top of the steps, their bones audibly cracking, while others flew all the way back to the bronze doors themselves, where they dropped in twisted heaps. A few went hurtling to the sides, landing with a harsh crash at the feet of the waiting throng, who broke out into cheers at this display of their leader's power.

An archer next to the priest fired. He could not have made a worse decision. Uldyssian frowned, the only outward hint of the terrible memories flashing through his mind. He relived again his friend Achilios's stand before the demon Lucion, who, in the guise of the Primus, had created the Triune to corrupt and control Mankind. Still as vivid as the moment it had happened was the hunter's shot, which, at the demon's desire, turned about and *pierced* Achilios through the throat.

Uldyssian now did the same for the bolt fired at him. Without hesitation, it arced around, racing back up. The archer looked aghast . . . but he was not the target.

The arrow drove through the chest of the priest as if passing only through air. It continued on, still accelerating, until it reached the door bearing the circular symbol of Mefis. There, driven by Uldyssian's will, the arrow impaled itself in the center of the circle in a perfect bull's-eye, burying deep in the metal.

It all happened so swiftly that only now did the priest's body waver. He let out a gurgling sound and blood poured not only from the wound, but mouth as well. His expression went slack . . . and then the robed figure toppled forward, rolling down the steps in a macabre tangle of loose limbs.

The archer dropped his weapon and fell on his knees in abject shock. He stared at Uldyssian, awaiting his doom.

A deathly calm pervaded the vicinity. Uldyssian strode up to the guard. Beyond the one stricken warrior, the rest of the temple's defenders grimly sought to regroup. The blood of several of Uldyssian's more impetuous converts decorated the area, giving proof to the Peace Warders' determination to let none pass alive.

Jaw set, Uldyssian placed a hand on the shoulder of the kneeling guard. In a voice that boomed as if thunder, the son of Diomedes said, "Let this one be spared . . . as an example." He glared at the other Peace Warders. "The rest can join their Primus in Hell."

His words provoked some slight confusion on the part of the armed guards, who could not know that Uldyssian had slain Lucion. This was not the first time that Uldyssian had noticed such reactions and he could only assume that word had not yet reached the outer temples of the Primus's unexplained absence. The senior priesthood had evidently smothered all hint of the calamity from their own flock, but Uldyssian would make certain that soon the truth would be known to the entire world.

Not that it would matter to those in Toraja. After this night, the Triune would be but a cursed word to many of the locals . . . as, very likely, would be his own name.

He eyed the guards and the priests. "You've spilled enough of other people's blood. Now pay with as much of your own."

One of the Peace Warders suddenly gasped. A seam opened on his throat . . . and out of it poured blood. He tried to cover it with a hand, but that hand, too, bled profusely.

Other tears spread over his body, as if invisible swords slashed him from every direction. From each gushed more blood.

The men beside him started to retreat, but first one, then another and then another suffered similar—but not identical—rips and slashes over their bodies. Blood even seeped from beneath breastplates and under helmets and hoods.

The first man finally fell, a crimson pool as large as his head already staining the once pristine marble beneath him. His collapse was quickly followed by that of another . . . and then temple guards and priests fell in numbers. They suffered a hundredfold the terrible wounds that they had inflicted upon not only Uldyssian's people but years of secret victims before them. Not one was spared among the band upon whom Uldyssian had set his baleful gaze.

And from positions elsewhere among the defenders, dark-hearted Peace Warders suddenly lost all nerve. They began to abandon the ranks and the priests did nothing to stop them, for they, too, were shaken by the unworldly might of the lone, insignificant-looking figure.

The crowd roared anew at what was surely a sign of absolute victory and surged forward again. The remaining Peace Warders were swamped, and as Uldyssian had declared, they received no mercy. Uldyssian continued on past the terrible struggle, more concerned with what lay within the walls. Peace Warders and minor priests meant nothing; the true threat awaited him deep in the sanctum of the master cleric, who answered directly to the Primus and, thus, knew the foul truth concerning the Triune's origins and goal.

The three doors confronted Uldyssian now, the ram of Dialon, the circle of Mefis, and the leaf of Bala all at eye level. The arrow he had sent flying through the priest still quivered in the middle door, the one he now chose through which to enter despite detecting that it had been barred from the inside.

A wrenching groan erupted from the door. The entire piece shook as if about to explode. Instead, though, it finally *flung* back, swinging so hard that two of the hinges tore out of the stone and the door ended up dangling lopsided.

Behind him, Uldyssian could sense several of his followers all but at his heels. He could no more stop them at this point than could have the Peace Warders. They were too caught up in the desire for retribution.

That suddenly bothered him. Uldyssian understood the reasons for their anger. When he, his brother Mendeln, their friend, Serenthia, and the Parthans had entered Toraja little more than two weeks before, it had been as weary travelers awed by the spectacle around them. Uldyssian had come with the intention of *peacefully* revealing the gift to all those willing to partake of it, but from the very beginning, the Triune had reacted as if a nest of vipers had suddenly hatched in their midst.

Two days after the crowds began to gather around him in the marketplace—most simply to hear his tale—the Torajian Guard had come to forcibly usher his followers out of the city and drag the former farmer himself to some undisclosed place of arrest. There had been no explanation given, but it had rapidly become clear that the orders had come directly from the temple.

Until that moment, Uldyssian had begun to believe that Toraja might turn out to be like Partha. Then again, perhaps the two were more similar than he had first thought, for had not the Triune struck at him there, as well? Under the command of the high priest of Mefis—sadistic Malic—friends had been brutally slaughtered and Uldyssian himself had nearly been marched off a helpless prisoner.

A scream broke out from behind him, cutting to an abrupt end his reverie. Uldyssian whirled.

Two people lay sprawled dead on the tiled floor and three others were badly wounded. Small metal stars stuck out from their throats, chests, and other parts of their bodies. The corpses were Parthans, and the loss of more of those who on their own had trailed a then reluctant Uldyssian into the deep jungles especially shook him.

With an angry gesture, he sent a wave of air throughout the chamber. His action came just in time, freezing a new mass of metal stars—their flight apparently triggered by some mechanism in the walls—in midair. Uldyssian let most of the deadly missiles clatter harmlessly to the floor, but sent a few back into the slots from which they had come in order to prevent others from launching. That done, he raced to the stricken figures.

The dying were all Torajians and one of them was very familiar to Uldyssian. Jezran Rhasheen had been the first local to approach the pale stranger speaking in the square, the dark-skinned youth the only son of a nearby prominent merchant. There had been no real reason for him to so willingly listen—much less accept—Uldyssian's words, for Jezran had obviously wanted for nothing in his life. Yet he had listened and listened well. When Uldyssian had offered to share his gift with any Torajian willing, it had been Jezran who had immediately stepped forward.

The dying boy looked up at the looming figure. As with all Torajians, to Uldyssian the whites of Jezran's eyes seemed much brighter and more vivid. He knew that the illusion was due to the latter's dark skin, but still found the sight arresting.

Jezran managed a sickly smile. He opened his mouth . . . then died. Uldyssian swore, knowing that the wounded youth had already been beyond even his skills.

But the others might *not* be. Realizing this, Uldyssian gently set Jezran's head down, then spun to the next victim, immediately placing his palm against the Torajian's forehead.

The man let out a gasp. With an unsettling sound, the vicious stars popped out of the wounds . . . which then *sealed.* The Torajian grinned gratefully.

Uldyssian did the same for the third victim, a woman,

then glanced bitterly at Jezran's corpse. *Two alive, but one dead. So much for my vaunted gift . . .*

"He holds no anger against you," said Mendeln from behind Uldyssian, his sibling's voice utterly calm even in the midst of calamity, "and now better understands the truth concerning everything than either of us."

Mendeln was slighter of stature than his elder brother and had always been more studious. Although he had accepted from Uldyssian the same touch as the rest of the converts, in Mendeln, something different appeared to have happened. Uldyssian could sense none of the same force flowing through his sole remaining sibling as through him; instead, there was a shadow growing within Mendeln, yet one that Uldyssian could not say originated from anything evil.

However, neither could he say that it had been spawned by anything *good*.

Staring into his brother's penetrating black eyes, Uldyssian snarled, "I only understand that he and so many others are dead . . . but whether it's more my fault or the Triune's, I doubt I'll ever decide."

"That was not to what I was referring—" But Mendeln got no further. Uldyssian shoved past the black-robed figure and resumed his trek into the temple. The others followed at his heels, ever leaving around Uldyssian's brother a gap akin to that which they made for their leader. However, in Mendeln's case, of late it was as much out of an unwillingness to be near the sallow figure as it was respect for his place. Even the untouched could detect the oddness of the younger son of Diomedes.

"I've shown you the gift," Uldyssian declared to those behind him, while at the same time mentally seeking out hidden dangers ahead. "Remember to *use* it. It's your life. It's you."

At that moment, he sensed *them* coming. A chill ran down his spine and he prayed that his people had listened . . . or else many more were about to perish terribly.

He turned to face the path ahead again. The vast chamber in which they stood was the central gathering place for the faithful before the sermons of the three orders began. Towering statues of the Triune's guiding spirits stood watch over the separate entryways leading to where each of the orders met. They were robed, ethereal beings with only vague countenances. Bala on the left, with its hammer and the bag containing the seeds of all life. Dialon on the right, bearing at its breast the Tablets of Order.

Mefis in the middle . . . always Mefis . . . carrying nothing but cupping its hands as if about to gently receive an innocent baby.

A baby to be slaughtered, Uldyssian always imagined.

And with such an image burning in his mind, he thrust out a warning hand to the rest just as all three doors opened and the grotesque, bestial figures in ebony armor came rushing forth. They screamed their bloodlust as they waved their weapons high, and although there were far fewer of them than the invaders, they were no less daunting, especially to Uldyssian, who knew of them best. There was that about them that did not speak of mortal flesh anymore, but rather something long overdue for the grave. Uldyssian sensed the sudden dismay among his followers and knew that he had to show them that, while sinister, the morlu were not indestructible.

But before he could strike, a brilliant, blinding light flared before his eyes. Letting out a cry, Uldyssian staggered into one of those just behind him. Once more, in his concern for the others, he had overestimated himself. He should have expected the priests to have something cunning yet planned in conjunction with this new attack.

A pair of hands dragged Uldyssian out of the way just as a heavy form collided with his right side. Uldyssian spun around, then tumbled to the floor.

As he fought to clear his vision, horrific cries rose all around. The terrifying sound of crunching bone sent renewed chills through him. He heard a deep-throated laugh and recognized the demonic voice of a morlu savoring the carnage he caused.

Uldyssian had not expected to find any of the Triune's ghoulish servants in Toraja. He had assumed that their kind was for the most part relegated to the vast temple near the capital and that those who had followed Malic had been exceptions sent out due to the Primus's interest in the son of Diomedes. Now Uldyssian wondered if each of the temples had its own contingent, which boded ill. That meant far more morlu than he could have ever imagined existing . . .

His eyes began to focus. It infuriated Uldyssian that for some reason he could not speed up the process. Too slowly, shapes began to coalesce.

And one of those shapes—filling his gaze—was a morlu reaching for him.

For his bulk, the armored figure moved astonishingly swift. He seized Uldyssian by the collar and dragged his prey up to eye level.

Black pits were all that existed physically of the morlu's eyes, yet Uldyssian knew that they saw him better than any mortal orbs. He had witnessed enough during the bitter struggle in Master Ethon's home to understand just how malevolent and powerful were the forces that animated the ebony-helmed fighters.

"You . . . are the one . . ." his assailant grunted in that voice that could not quite pass for that of anything living. "The *one* . . ."

Steeling himself, Uldyssian concentrated—but again a brilliant light flared before his eyes. Once more, he was completely blinded.

The morlu laughed harder—and then let out a peculiar grunt. He released his hold on the unseeing Uldyssian, who just managed to keep from falling and cracking his skull on the floor.

Shaking his head, Uldyssian focused his every effort on seeing. The world came into focus once more . . . and there he beheld Serenthia, a spear gripped tight in her hands, skewering the morlu as if he wore no armor nor weighed an ounce. The spear blazed silver and Serenthia's black hair fluttered as if alive. Her blue eyes, always radiant, now burned with utter determination. Her normally ivory skin was flushed and her red lips were twisted in grim satisfaction. Uldyssian did not doubt that she imagined Achilios's death as she drove the spear deeper into the twitching, armored figure. She had only just before Achilios's murder come to love the hunter after years of seeking Uldyssian's favor, knowledge that still filled him with shame.

One of the very first to accept Uldyssian's gift, Serenthia was now also among those most proficient in drawing it forth. Again, Uldyssian knew that much of that ability had to do with her loss, but even he was astonished by her amazing effort now.

The morlu clawed desperately at her, the hungry grin now replaced by something approaching fear. The spear allowed Serenthia to hold him at bay.

She looked anything but the daughter of a country merchant now. Her simple cloth blouse and skirt had given way to the wrapped, colorful dress of a Torajian woman. Indeed, with her long, sleek raven hair, she looked as if she carried some of their blood in her. The dress was designed to flow loose at the legs, and instead of boots, Serenthia also wore the strapped sandals more common to the people here.

The morlu shook violently, his massive form abruptly beginning to shrivel. Within the space of a breath, he looked even more late for the grave, only his wrinkled white skin now enshrouding his bones. Yet, still Serenthia kept him impaled. Her expression took on an unsettling eagerness . . .

"Serry!" Uldyssian called, using the childhood version of her name that he had only recently ceased favoring. He feared where her outrage was taking her.

His voice cut through the din . . . and through her fury. Serenthia glanced back at him, then, with a shiver, the morlu again. A tear slipped unbidden from her, one that had Achilios written on it.

She tugged on the spear, which slid easily out of her foe. The armored villain dropped like a puppet suddenly bereft of strings. Bones and armor scattered across the marble tile.

Serenthia looked at Uldyssian with relief and gratitude. He said nothing more to her, only nodding his understanding as he rose to see to the others.

As he feared, the trap had claimed more lives. There were bodies strewn about and although many were morlu, so, too, were there Torajians and Parthans. Uldyssian saw the slack face of a Parthan woman who had been there on the day when—near the town square where first he had preached—he had healed a young boy with a malformed arm. That brought bitter memories of the lad and his mother, Bartha, for they had both perished when the townsfolk had come to his defense against Lucion. The boy had been one of the demon's several random victims and Bartha—stalwart Bartha—had died of a broken heart soon after.

So much blood . . . he thought. *So much of it due to me . . . and their belief in what I bring to them . . .*

But then silence swept over the chamber and Uldyssian realized that the fighting was again, for the moment, over. The morlu had not laid waste to the intruders; it was the beasts of Lucion who had been utterly decimated. They had taken lives—too many lives—but not so much as their own numbers.

That in itself was a miracle, but far more important, the others had taken up both his and Serenthia's example. It had not been weapons alone that had brought the morlu to bay, but the same gift that Uldyssian wielded, albeit on a less focused scale. One warrior had been neatly severed in two, the cut so clean at the waist that it looked as if all the morlu needed was for someone to put him back together to reanimate him. Another lay far above, his corpse dangling limply over Mefis's outstretched hands. Scores more lay scattered about in all sorts of macabre conditions, a striking image that, despite their own losses, Uldyssian hoped would bring heart to his surviving companions.

Surveying the dead again, Uldyssian suddenly choked. The triangular tiles covering the floor were now splattered in black bile . . . or whatever it was that passed for morlu blood. But mixed with it was the precious life fluids of those who had either acted too slowly or had hesitated in their trust of their gift. Uldyssian mourned each and cursed once more the fact that all his vaunted might could not resurrect them.

And that, for reasons he did not understand, made him look again for Mendeln.

He found his brother hovering over not their dead comrades, but rather two morlu who had somehow become twisted around one another. Uldyssian's brow arched at this enterprising action and wondered just who among his followers had managed it.

Mendeln looked up from whatever it was he was doing. His generally unperturbed expression now took on a darker cast.

"This is not over," he announced needlessly. However, it was his next words that most set the elder son of Diomedes on edge. "Uldyssian . . . there are *demons* here."

No sooner had he said it than Uldyssian also sensed their nearby presence. The foulness of the morlu . . . themselves of demonic make, although of mortal flesh . . . had masked from him the dire fact.

Uldyssian also sensed just where they were . . . and that they awaited *him.*

He had faced other demons besides Lucion, none of them proving as much a threat as the Primus himself. Yet, that these new ones waited so patiently—something hard for all but the most cunning of them to do—further stirred his suspicions. They *knew* of him, knew what he had become . . .

He had only one choice. "Mendeln—Serenthia—keep watch on the others! No one is to follow me."

His brother nodded, but the woman frowned. "We won't let you go alone—"

Uldyssian stopped her with a glance. "I don't want another Achilios—*no one* follows, especially you two."

"Uldyssian—"

Mendeln took her arm. "Do not argue with him, Serenthia. This must be."

He said it in such a manner that even his brother paused to look at him. Mendeln offered nothing more, though, as had become typical of him of late.

However enigmatic the statement, Uldyssian had already learned to heed such comments. "No one follows," he repeated, staring down *everyone*. "Or it won't be the wrath of demons you face."

Hoping that they would listen but still fearing that some—especially Serenthia—might yet disobey, Uldyssian crossed the threshold of the door through which Dialon's followers would have gone. The moment he was clear, the door slammed behind him, just as he knew that so too did the other pair.

He had sealed the way, at least temporarily. Even Mendeln and Serenthia would find it difficult to overcome his effort. So long as he could, Uldyssian would keep the path to the underground chambers—the area where worship of the Triune's *true* masters took place—barred from anyone else. Too many had perished for him already.

He sensed the demons nearer, although their exact locations were not known. In truth, they were only a part of the reason that Uldyssian wanted only himself at risk.

Perhaps that had been what Mendeln had meant, Uldyssian suddenly realized. Perhaps with his own strange abilities his brother had also detected the more subtle yet distinctive *third* presence awaiting Uldyssian . . . a presence that was much, much more powerful than a mere senior priest and known so very well to both of them.

A presence that could only be *Lilith*.

TWO

All around Mendeln, the voices whispered. The awful truth concerning this place was best known to him, who could hear the victims' own words.

So many, he thought. *So many wrongly done in. The Balance is much askew because of this place alone.*

Uldyssian's brother did not understand exactly just what "the Balance" was, but knew that the horrible events that had taken place in the inner recesses of the temple over the past years had certainly befouled "it." That disturbed him even more than all the deaths this night, although their cumulative effect was no good thing, either.

And then there was also Lilith . . . or Lylia, as he, Serenthia, and most painfully of all, Uldyssian, had known her.

Serenthia stalked back and forth like an impatient cat, her eyes ever on the doors so effectively "locked" by his brother. The rest of Uldyssian's followers eagerly spread through the chambers, tearing apart the grand trappings as they went along despite the fact that the fires consuming other portions of the building would eventually do the same here. Mendeln, aware that victory was truly not theirs yet, paid great heed to the voices, even those of the dead priests and Peace Warders. Not the morlu, of course, for they were creatures long dead and so from them there was only emptiness. He listened very carefully, focusing on some that seemed more relevant than others.

How simple we were, Mendeln thought almost wisfully. *Farmers and brothers in a small village, destined to live out our lives tilling the soil and raising livestock.* It was Lilith's fault that it had come to all this, Lilith, who had chosen Uldyssian to be her pawn in some otherworldly struggle between demons and angels over a pitiful little rock called by them *Sanctuary*.

Mendeln's world.

He did not consider either himself or his brother to be champions of Mankind, but Uldyssian especially had been cast into a role he could now never discard. The fate of *everything* apparently depended upon what he chose to do. Mendeln could only try to be there to lend whatever questionable support that he could.

His musings were interrupted by a deep sense of foreboding. The voices cut off, save for one that did not belong with them. It was stronger, *alive,* and one that had comforted Mendeln as much as it had guided him through his own mysterious transformation.

Beware the hands of the Three . . . it said. *They grasp for everything, then crush it in their all-consuming grip* . . .

Mendeln's brow wrinkled at this esoteric comment. Of what useful knowledge was such—

"Serenthia!" he shouted with more animation than any had heard from him in days. "All of you! Stay back from the statues—"

But his warning came too late for some. As if of living flesh, the gargantuan effigies bent forward. Bala's heavy hammer came down on two Torajians, crushing them beneath it. Dialon battered away a hapless Parthan with the edge of one of the tablets.

Mefis . . . Mefis seized a woman and squeezed hard. Even Mendeln found himself nauseated by the monstrous results.

With a scraping of stone that echoed through the huge chamber like the combined moans of the dead, the statues descended among the invaders. The once confident band now retreated back to the doors through which they had come, but those doors, too, were also now shut . . . and not because of Uldyssian.

"Lilith . . ." he gasped just as massive Dialon turned a stony gaze his way. The colossus raised his hammer. "Very much *Lilith . . .*"

Through the empty worship hall he strode, eyes and other senses ever on alert. Androgynous effigies of Dialon stared down at Uldyssian, who thought that the supposedly benevolent images looked more mocking than anything else.

What great demon are you, Dialon? he grimly wondered. *What's your true name?*

In the outer chambers, torches in niches in the walls had well illuminated everything. In here, though, only a few round oil lamps dangling from the arched ceiling gave any light and that not much. Moreover, the path ahead looked even darker, finally fading into utter blackness perhaps ten yards or so ahead.

Yet still Uldyssian moved on. He passed by and under the huge statues, entering the passage that he knew would lead him to her.

Just as she desired.

The beautiful, aristocratic vision that had first graced his wondering eyes what seemed so long ago still remained strong with him even after the discovery of the dread truth and the subsequent betrayal. The thick, long blond tresses, often artfully bound atop the head as befitting a noblewoman, the glittering emerald eyes, the slim perfect lips—they would never leave his imagination.

But with them also remained the nightmarish recollection of an inhuman seductress, a creature with scaled flesh, vicious quills for hair, and a tail like the reptile she resembled.

"Lylia . . ." he muttered, the name both a curse and a yearning. *"Damn you, Lilith . . ."*

Something scurried over his foot. Startled more because he had not sensed it rather than from the thing itself, Uldyssian squinted. It was only a spider, albeit a fair-sized one. It was hardly surprising to find such a creature in this place. Uldyssian immediately forgot it, his concerns with vermin much larger and more deadly.

The last of the failing oil lamps gave way. Darkness prevailed. All this was a show for him, he realized. He had come hunting what he considered evil and so they were granting him the appropriate mood. This was in some ways a game to them and that knowledge further infuriated the human. They cared nothing for all the lives lost, not even of those who had willingly served them.

Something got into his face. He swatted at it, then felt a tiny creature crawling on the back of his hand. Uldyssian brushed it off, aware that it was a second spider.

Deciding this was a move in the game he could do without, Uldyssian summoned light.

The first time he had managed this feat, it had been due, Uldyssian later understood, to Lilith's presence. Now, it was as familiar to him as breathing. But the pale white glow he called into being now was not nearly as powerful as it should have been. The sphere barely revealed the stone corridor more than two yards ahead. He could *sense* much farther than that, but natural instinct made him want to see it, too.

While it was possible for him to increase the sphere's intensity by concentrating more on it, Uldyssian would then be able to focus less on his surroundings. This was not like the battle with Lucion, where as much of what Uldyssian had achieved had been due to outrage as it had natural ability. He needed to move with utter caution, for Lucion's cunning was nothing compared with that of his devilish sister.

The corridor stretched farther than it should have, at least according to his senses. Whether illusion or not, Uldyssian would find out soon enough. Lilith would not let him wait much longer.

He let out a sharp cry as what felt like a fork jabbed the skin at the back of his neck. His flailing hands knocked off a furred form with many legs.

The arachnid scurried out of the illumination. As he rubbed the burning patch of skin, Uldyssian noticed that the path behind him had also grown dark. The light from the chamber had been completely cut off.

The wound began to throb. Uldyssian berated himself for letting something so mundane as a spider get through defenses that morlu, and thus far, Lilith had not.

Or . . . *had* she?

Focusing his will on the wound, Uldyssian quickly expelled whatever the creature had left in him, then completely healed the location. He could thank the high priest Malic for the trick, having watched the villain eject Achilios's arrow from his back before attending to the wound itself.

But even as the son of Diomedes finished, over him flowed a swarm of multilegged creatures with sharp fangs and claws. Growing up on a farm, he was used to all sorts of insects and arachnids, but none such as these. They moved with vile purpose, attacking as quickly as they could in as many places as possible. They bit through garments and even through boots, while others crawled over them to find flesh of their own to attack.

At first, his reaction was simply human. He swore and tried to wipe them off as quickly as possible. The spiders made his attempts laughable by even clinging to the hands that sought to remove them. Within a heartbeat, Uldyssian was all but covered by the swarm.

Then, reason managed to return. Taking a deep breath—while avoiding swallowing any of the tinier vermin—Uldyssian concentrated on the floating sphere.

Now at last, the fiery ball flared bright . . . in fact, a thousand times greater than before. At the same time, heat enveloped Uldyssian and his unwanted pets.

However, where the heat only warmed the man, it *seared* the spiders.

They shriveled rapidly under the relentless scorching. Shrill cries—in some ways too close to human—assailed

Uldyssian's ears. By the dozens, then hundreds, tiny, burnt corpses tumbled to the stone floor.

Sweating more from effort than heat, he finally reduced the globe's fury to a more tolerable level. Around him rose a stench more reminiscent of decay than burning. Uldyssian kicked at one pile of vermin, which scattered into ash.

But as his foot descended to the floor again, it found no purchase. Instead, it sank into the stone as if into water.

Uldyssian suddenly sensed the immediate presence of one of the demons, but that knowledge came too late. Something snagged his sinking leg, trying to completely draw him into the floor. A thick, slow, malevolent laugh echoed in the corridor.

Something formed just at the edge of the sphere's light. It looked to Uldyssian like a grotesque, inhuman head made from the stone itself. A fissure opened, one that spread into a crude, bestial grin.

"Waant . . ." it said hungrily, then chuckled again. Whatever held Uldyssian's leg dragged him toward the ever-expanding maw. Two other, smaller fissures opened up behind the mouth, forming eyes of a sort.

"Huuuungrrryyy . . ." the demon rumbled merrily. "Waaant . . ."

Recovering from his astonishment, Uldyssian gritted his teeth and leaned forward. The demon chuckled again, perhaps thinking that its prey wanted to end this quickly. Uldyssian did, of course . . . just not the way the creature desired.

He slammed a fist into the watery stone. The power of the nephalem enabled him to send a shock wave that coursed over his macabre attacker much the way the spiders had over him. Uldyssian had not had any idea if what he intended would work; he only knew that focusing his will and determination on a goal had saved him more than once.

The demon let out a roar of outrage and pain as the wave

of pure force finished sweeping across him. The mouth twisted into a sinister frown and the eyes glared.

"Gulag kills!" it rumbled needlessly.

The walls rushed in on Uldyssian, who only now understood that *everything* around him had become part of the bestial demon.

He let out a pained groan as the stone crushed against him. Pinned and with his bones already feeling as if they were breaking, Uldyssian almost gave in to his destruction. However, once again *her* visage appeared in his mind, beautiful but also monstrous . . . and utterly mocking his failure.

Straining every muscle, he pushed against the crushing forces, pushed against them . . . and finally won. The walls receded enough for him to get his hands in position, at which point Uldyssian shoved them apart as hard as he could.

From Gulag, there was a sound that Uldyssian could only guess had to be of consternation. It was doubtful that anyone had ever escaped the beast's grasp.

Seizing upon the change in fortune, the son of Diomedes reached down and took hold of the liquid stone in both hands. It should have slipped through his fingers, but the power of the nephalem again prevailed over that of Gulag. To Uldyssian, the demon felt like a slithering serpent minus the bones. It writhed in his grip, but could not slip free.

"Is Gulag still hungry?" he mocked.

Although clearly confused, the creature was either still confident of his might or simply too dull witted to realize that he faced no mere human. Uldyssian hoped for the latter, but could not discount the former, which meant that the sooner this ended, the better.

With a titanic tug, he drew Gulag nearer. As the demon flowed toward Uldyssian, once more the man felt something clutch not only the one leg, but the other, too.

As this happened, Gulag let out another bestial roar. The walls and the rest of the nearby floor rose and poured toward Uldyssian in what was clearly a rush to smother the resisting prey. Uldyssian held his breath instinctively, then stared at the part of Gulag he held in his hands. It felt like skin or parchment . . . and that helped him decide what to do next.

As he had done before, Uldyssian pulled his hands as far apart as he could, only this time maintaining his grip on the sinister creature.

Like the parchment he had chosen to imagine it to be, the essence of the demon came apart with an awful ripping sound. Gulag let out a cry resembling the roar of a raging river. The walls and floor flailed about, finally causing Uldyssian to lose his grip and sending him falling.

But that was all that the demon could muster. Uldyssian's attack had done him in. The rip continued to spread, running quickly along Gulag's length and not even ceasing its momentum when it reached the deep maw and sinister orbs.

Gulag was literally torn in two. The halves quivered like pudding. A moan escaped both—

Then, with one last rumble . . . the demon melted.

His form lost all substance. Gulag completely liquified, puddling on the floor. A faint slime covered the walls and ceiling, but otherwise they were normal again.

The stone was once more solid beneath Uldyssian's feet, solid, if sticky. An odor akin to rotting garbage assailed him.

Something else caught his attention. Where once the corridor ahead had seemed endless, now another bronze door beckoned but a short distance away.

Stepping cautiously through the sticky sludge that had once been the demon, Uldyssian advanced on the door. He waited for the next threat to strike him, but nothing happened. The embossed image of a gentle Dialon stared back at Uldyssian from the door.

Uldyssian frowned. Another image, almost so indistinct as to be invisible, seemed to lay beneath that of the benevolent spirit. He squinted—

With a gasp, Uldyssian looked away. Although he had just stared directly at it, he could not remember any exact detail of the awful vision, only that it had horrified him as nothing else had. He thought he recalled a glimpse of curled horns and of teeth as sharp as daggers . . .

Shaking his head, Uldyssian forced the disturbing memory away. He dared not concentrate on the fiendish vision. Somehow, as faint as it had been, it yet drew from deep within him some childhood sense of *terror*. Every nightmare that had ever haunted Uldyssian as a young boy had, at least for a moment, returned as fresh as ever.

Steeling himself anew, Uldyssian raised his hand toward the door. He knew better than to touch it. Even if Lilith had done nothing to it, surely the senior priests had cast some dire spell.

As if propelled by an angry ghost, the door flung open. Uldyssian stepped through.

The chamber was vast, possibly more so than even the great hall. Much of it was shadowed, the only illumination other than his sphere being torches set to best display a marble dais upon which stood a stone platform a little more than the length of a man and tilted slightly to the right.

And on that platform—that *altar*—lay a grisly sight that had once been a man when still it had owned its flesh and organs.

Uldyssian did not try to hold back his revulsion. Although it did not surprise him to find evidence of human sacrifice, the freshness of it shook him to the core. This very day, even as he and his followers had stormed the temple, a soul had been slaughtered in order to curry the favor of a demon.

Then, he noticed a slight movement in the far upper corner above the platform, movement by something that had been hidden from his immediate detection. From what little Uldyssian had seen of it, it was a creature reminiscent of a gigantic, furred spider . . . but also . . . also somehow a *man*. The second demon? Uldyssian recalled the swarm of spiders and suspected that this was the source. If so, it was a far more cautious and cunning beast than Gulag.

He started toward its location . . . then noticed the other figures moving toward him from the dark recesses in the back of the chamber. He had wondered when the senior priest would act. From what Uldyssian had gathered about the Triune's inner workings, in all the lesser temples the three orders were overseen by one cleric chosen from either Mefis, Dialon, or Bala. Below him were three lesser priests who ministered for each the separate faiths. Only in the main temple by Kehjan could be found the three high priests—*two* now, with Malic recently dead—who governed the entire sect in the name of the Primus.

A heavyset, bald figure in gray and bloodred robes gestured almost indifferently at Uldyssian. Immediately, a dozen acolytes whose own garments represented all three orders raised their hands palm up and began chanting.

Uldyssian felt an incredible coldness surround him, but his mere desire for it to be gone quickly ended the problem. The priests faltered in their chanting, only their master seemingly unperturbed by their failure. He glanced with disdain at the nearest pair, who nervously took up the spellwork once more and were quickly joined by their brethren.

"Be silent," an impatient Uldyssian murmured.

The chanting ceased, although the priests continued for a few second more to open and close their mouths, it gradually dawning on them that their voices had been stripped away.

A curious chuckle momentarily escaped the senior priest. He drew from his robes a small, azure stone. This was apparently a signal for his underlings to do the same.

The last time Uldyssian had faced someone wielding such stones, it had been Malic and he had revealed those gems to be some manner by which to summon demons to his will. During that struggle, Lilith had secretly taken a hand, eliminating immediately what possibly would have been the most deadly and adding her strength to what he had believed strictly his own when he had battled the rest. While Uldyssian trusted more in his own power now, he saw no reason to invite threat when it could be removed quickly enough.

He made a fist.

One of the lesser priests screamed as the gem he held flared to fiery life. To their credit, the rest reacted instantly, flinging the stones from their palms. As it was, three others still suffered burns to some degree, but nothing as terrible as the first. He fell to his knees, sobbing and clutching the blackened cinder that had been his hand.

The senior priest chortled, again an odd reaction. He had not been affected in the least, having tossed away his gem even before Uldyssian had finished the fist.

Frowning, Uldyssian stared at him . . . stared at what stood there beyond mortal vision.

And then he knew . . .

The elder priest seemed to recognize this in turn. "I think they are not needed any more," the bald man announced. He looked to his lackeys. "You may die."

They stared at him, entirely baffled. Uldyssian felt some sympathy for them . . . but not much. They had willingly taken the blood and souls of the living for their dark masters.

The priests collapsed as one. They did not scream, having no time to draw another breath. There was no mark on their bodies, save the earlier burns.

For some reason, Uldyssian immediately surveyed the shadows where the spider demon had hidden. He knew instinctively that the shadows were now empty, their unsettling inhabitant having evidently fled elsewhere during the confrontation with the robed figures.

"Dear Astrogha is most obedient," the senior priest said in an oddly feminine voice. "When his Primus commands him to leave instantly, he does so without question."

"And does he realize that his Primus is no longer Lucion, but Lucion's sister?" Uldyssian stared into the other's eyes. "Does he, *Lilith*?"

She leered at him in a manner that would have likely been very seductive if not for the fact that her body was that of a sweating, corpulent man. "Fear makes many blind, as does love, my love . . ."

"There's no love between us, Lilith. Only lies and hate."

The priest pouted. "Oh, my dear Uldyssian, is it because of this poor dress I wear? That can be remedied. We are alone and the fool's served his purpose . . ."

Wild, green flames erupted around the bulky figure. Uldyssian raised an arm to shield his eyes from the intense brightness that accompanied the unnatural fire. As his gaze adjusted, he watched the priest's garments and hair quickly curl and turn to ash. The man's abundant flesh blackened and baked. Fiery gobbets dropped from him to the floor, revealing sinew, muscle, and bone.

The face burned away, in its place a mocking skull still briefly retaining the eyeballs. However, those shriveled into the sockets even as the horrific figure stepped toward the human.

"I want to look my best for you, after all," the burning skeleton cooed. By now, the flames had eaten away at everything but bone and even that was quickly vanishing. Yet, underneath the crumbling bone, Uldyssian caught flashes of emerald green cloth and ivory skin. The legs broke away, from them blossoming an elegant skirt beneath which glimpses of feminine feet became more and more obvious. The rib cage burst forward, in its place the bodice of what was a familiar, elegant gown that also revealed a very feminine form.

The back and the top of the dark skull broke as rich, golden hair flung out, then cascaded down. Last to vanish of the unfortunate priest was the burnt face. The jawbone dropped, then the rest.

Arms outstretched, she stood before him in all her glory. Despite what he had claimed, Uldyssian felt his heart wrench. Unbidden from his lips came the name by which he had best known this wondrous figure. *"Lylia."*

She smiled at him in what he recalled the exact same manner the first time their eyes had met. "Dear, sweet Uldyssian!" The beautiful woman reached forth her slim, perfect hands. "Come, take me in your strong arms . . ."

His body flinched forward before the reality struck him. The son of Diomedes swore, which amused his companion.

"How colorful a turn of phrase! That's a side you should nurture, dear Uldyssian! It adds character!"

He clenched his fists so tight the knuckles whitened. "No more taunts, Lilith! No more charades! That face isn't yours, any more than it is the priest's or the Primus's! You stand before me, then do so as yourself, demon!"

She giggled. "Whatever your tastes, my love!"

Unlike her dramatic discarding of the priest's body, the shift from "Lylia" to the true Lilith was almost instantaneous. A crimson aura momentarily surrounded the aristocratic beauty—and in the next breath the demon herself stood there.

Enough of a facial resemblance existed that no one could doubt that the two females were one and the same, but that was the only link. Lilith stood taller, as tall as Uldyssian, in fact, and moved about on splayed hooves instead of feet. Her body was dark green and hideously scaled and the lush golden hair had been replaced by the quills. Those quills ran all the way down to the reptilian tail, an appendage climaxing in wicked barbs.

Her fingers—four, not five—ended in curved claws. The hands moved tantilizingly across her torso, reminding him that she still had the ample curves that had enticed the mortal so. If anything, they were more lush and, worse for Uldyssian, unclothed. Even hating her so much as he did, he could not help surveying her body. Such was her power.

One of the hands finally led his gaze up to her face. Yes, she still looked akin to Lylia, but only in the structure. Lylia had not had sharp teeth designed for shredding or burning red orbs lacking any pupil . . .

"I've missed your touch, my darling," Lilith whispered,

her forked tongue licking over her lips. "And I know that you have missed mine . . ."

Uldyssian knew that she was seeking to keep him off his guard and the unfortunate thing was that she was close to succeeding. He had not realized just how much actually confronting her would affect him. Lilith, on the other hand, had obviously known all too well.

Then, Uldyssian thought about all the deaths instigated by her mad ambitions and most of the desire faded. To the demon, the lives lost had been minor matters. She had cared nothing for Serenthia's father, for Master Ethon and his son Cedric, or Bartha, or any of the scores of Parthans and Torajians thus far slaughtered. Certainly Lilith had not had an iota of remorse even for the priests she had slaughtered, including the missionaries whose bloody demise had begun the chain of events.

Most of all, she had cared nothing for her brother, the true Primus. Clearly his destruction had merely been so that she could seize the power base that he had created in the Triune. However, that prize was one she would not long be able to savor, if he had his way.

"This temple's fallen, Lilith," Uldyssian declared. "What those with me haven't torn down the flames your puppets set loose will consume. The same fate will befall the next and the next . . . until the great one itself near Kehjan is the last. Then . . . it'll join the rest. You'll serve as Primus for a very short time."

"Will I, my dear Uldyssian?" Her tail slapped lightly on the floor, sending odd bits of the senior priest scattering. Lilith leaned forward, letting her ample bounty display itself unhindered. "But how splendid . . . as that is exactly what I want!"

Her pronouncement startled Uldyssian. Belatedly, he realized that his mouth hung open. Face flushing, he closed it, then tried to gather his thoughts. Yet again, Lilith had proven her mastery over him with but a few words.

"Yes," the succubus said, smiling widely. Her inhuman

eyes flashed with enjoyment at his consternation. "I want you to take down the Triune! I want you to put an end to the temple . . ."

"But—" Uldyssian finally managed. "That makes no sense whatsoever. Now that *you* control the Triune . . ."

"Ahh, but it makes perfect sense, my love! It makes perfect sense! It is a sign of my affection for you that I tell you all this, which even my unlamented brother's servants do not know! Yes, my little *nephalem* . . . you *will* destroy the temple for me . . . and the Cathedral of Light, too . . ."

But if Lilith desired something of him, Uldyssian desperately thought, telling him would *surely* make the man want to do just the opposite . . .

She either read that thought—not impossible for her—or simply understood his mind better than he. "Oh, but my dear Uldyssian! *You* will not have any *choice* in the matter! You see, if you do not do your best to stir your nephalem powers to greater life—and also those latent in the fools that follow you—I will have the Triune utterly crush you! Do you think that this is all my poor brother gathered to him? There is so *much* more! My brother was very clever, his only mistake was in underestimating me—"

Suddenly, Lilith stood face-to-face with Uldyssian. How she had gotten so near without him aware of it, he could not say.

"—just as you, too, always have, poor darling!"

Before Uldyssian could stop her, the demon kissed him soundly. She had done the same in the past and so he should have been prepared for it. With as much irritation at himself as hatred toward her, Uldyssian grabbed for Lilith, but the demon slipped from his grasp.

"I won't do as you plan, damn you!" he growled. "I'm through playing your puppet! I'll not create an army of nephalem ready to do your bidding!"

That was what she truly wanted, he knew too well. She had been among those who had created Sanctuary, but for her murderous ways—including slaying most of her companions—she had been exiled by her lover . . . an angel, if Lilith could be believed about anything. Those murders had revolved around the children—the first nephalem—born through the unions of the renegade demons and angels. Uldyssian could grant her credit for wishing to save them, but now it seemed that all their descendants mattered to her was as fodder or soldiers to use in her mad campaign of vengeance.

"Will you not?" she teased. "Will you not, dear love?" The demoness pulled back. "Then, why have you not attacked me yet?"

Lilith had him again . . . but for the *last* time, Uldyssian swore. He stretched out a hand toward her—

The air around the demoness started to ripple . . . but Lilith was no longer there. Instead, Uldyssian felt her materialize behind him.

"Much improved, my darling Uldyssian . . . much improved."

He did not turn to face her, instead merely concentrating on where she was.

But . . . again, he was too late.

Now Lilith's voice echoed throughout the chamber, though she herself was nowhere to be seen. "However, you still need a little more practice, I think! After all, you must be your best when facing the power of the Triune . . . much less sweet, treacherous *Inarius.*"

Try as he might, Uldyssian could not sense Lilith anywhere and that told him just how insufficient all his might was. He had expected to be able to face her much better than this, but, as before, both emotionally and physically she had played him perfectly.

"Come and face me, Lilith!" Uldyssian shouted as he turned in a circle. He sought her in every dark corner, but there was *nothing,* absolutely nothing save her voice, projected from far, far away.

"All in good time, my love. A little more practice first.

Why, you can start by perhaps still saving some of your *friends*! You have so few left already . . ."

Her voice faded away. Caught up in his anger, he did not at first pay heed to her last comments. Then . . . then Uldyssian felt the terrible threat without, a threat he could only assume that Lilith's cunning skills had shielded from his "vaunted" perceptions.

Rather than keeping Mendeln, Serenthia, and the rest safe, he had left them right where the demoness had wanted them.

Three

In a place that was not a place, the black-shrouded figure stared beyond his empty surroundings into that realm called Sanctuary by the knowledgeable few. He noted the terrible strife overtaking the city of Taraja and had already begun calculating the possible repercussions.

"He is moving too quickly," the shadowed man said to the emptiness. "Too irrationally . . ."

He moves as he must . . . as do we . . .

The voice would have stilled the heart of most, for it was as much presence as it was sound. Yet, the one to whom it spoke merely nodded, for he had known the speaker so long that even its uniqueness had become too familiar.

Failure had also become too familiar, and he did not want to face it again. Failure threatened the Balance and despite centuries of learning to focus his emotions inward—where they could be controlled—a deep frown slowly spread across his marblelike countenance.

"Then . . . we must become more active . . ."

As he spoke, above him there suddenly glittered what seemed to be stars. Yet these stars moved, gradually forming an immense, serpentine figure, a creature half-seen, half-imagined . . . and to most, completely myth.

A dragon . . .

More active than the initiating of his birth brother? the stars asked, the tone invoking irony.

"More . . ." the shrouded figure returned defiantly, "although Mendeln ul-Diomed is far exceeding my expectations. I would almost swear that he . . ."

Is directly of your blood, yes . . . it would also explain why she chose the elder sibling for her goals. You sensed the strength slumbering in them. So would she.

"My mother would, you're correct. So, too, would my father . . ." His frown deepened. "Yes, so, too, would my father."

The stars swirled, briefly losing resemblance to the fabled beast. *Of whom we have heard nothing . . .*

The man nodded, his focus once more attuned to Sanctuary. "Yes, and that troubles me more than anything."

As it should . . . The shape coalesced again. *Yes . . . a more active role must be taken, just as you have said . . .*

Wrapping his voluminous cloak about him, the hooded figure prepared to leave. "As I said," he murmured more to himself than to his vaguely seen companion. "Even if it means revealing my survival to both my parents . . ."

Mendeln expected to die. He watched as the hammer fell, knowing that he would never move swiftly enough to escape it. None of the words in the strange tongue that he had begun to learn in his dreams came to him. A crushing death was to be his imminent fate, and although he tried to be as detached to that realization as he had become to so many other fateful moments of late, Mendeln nonetheless felt an overwhelming bitterness. He had believed that some other destiny awaited him—

Someone collided with him. Both figures tumbled to the side just as Dialon's hammer smashed into the marble floor, creating a fissure of broken stone more than half a dozen yards in length.

"Next time don't dream. Act," muttered Serenthia in his ear. She leapt to her feet before Uldyssian's brother could offer any kind of thanks . . . and with good reason. Dialon's effigy turned on her, almost as if, despite the unreadable expression, the statue was furious at Serenthia for taking from it its prey.

Serenthia took aim with her spear, throwing it with accuracy enhanced by her powers. It drove through the giant's chest much the way Uldyssian had earlier sent the arrow through the priest's.

At first, Mendeln thought her heroic action had been all for nothing, for Dialon moved unperturbed by the gap in its torso. After all, it was only animated stone . . .

But then fine cracks quickly spread forth from the hole, racing along until they covered the statue's body with what looked almost like a web. As the effigy raised its hammer, portions of the giant began breaking off.

Serenthia gave out a warning cry to those in the vicinity of Dialon. They backed away just in time, for the hand wielding the murderous tool chose that moment to break off. As even the statue itself watched, both dropped to the floor, shattering in pieces that spread throughout the chamber.

No sooner had Dialon lost its hand, then the rest of the limb followed. That opened the floodgates, huge chunks of the stone goliath dropping like rain. The effigy looked down at its crumbling body—and the neck snapped.

As the head crashed in front of Mendeln and Serenthia, what was left of Dialon joined the wreckage.

But there were two other giants with which to contend, two giants making savage sweeps across the chamber as they hunted the tinier figures. However, Mendeln gave thanks to whatever watched over the humans, for despite their attempts, the behemoths were having little good luck since the initial slaughter. He wondered at that until he saw the hand of Mefis bounce off of the air just before Romus and a small band of Parthans and Torajians. The bearded man—a villain reformed by Uldyssian—looked to be the guiding force of this group. He stared at the menacing figure, almost seeming to defy it to break through.

There was still a good chance that it might just do that. Mendeln decided that it was time he lent his hand to the matter rather than stand around gaping while others merely struggled to survive. The shadowy gift that *he* had been granted had to be of some use now . . .

Words finally flowed through his head, words in that archaic language first glimpsed on the stone just outside Seram. They were the ones Mendeln knew that he had to speak and so Uldyssian's brother did just that.

Hands formed into fists, the statue battered at the invisible barrier. Yet, as the first blows struck, the giant was repelled. Cracks materialized in the giant body and chips broke off as if something unseen had fought against the effigy with the same violence with which the latter had attacked Romus's band.

Mendeln allowed himself the ghost of a satisfied smile. Undeterred by the damage to it, Mefis renewed its assault. Yet, each hit caused more and more damage. Driven by whatever dark force had animated it, the giant would not cease. It did not understand that the magic Mendeln somehow knew was making it the instrument of its own destruction.

Romus, on the other hand, evidently understood. He gestured for those with him to remain calm and wait out the situation. The statue of Mefis was strong and that tremendous strength—turned on itself—quickly reduced the giant to a precarious state. At last, great portions of the statue already piled around its feet, Mefis collapsed.

That left only Bala . . . or, it would have, if the third of the great statues had not suddenly frozen. The robed figure—in the act of leaning down to swat three Torajians with the tablets—teetered, then tipped over. But Bala did not fall in the direction his balance would have demanded. Rather than plunge forward—toward his would-be victims—the effigy went against common sense and dropped *backward.*

Only as it smashed to pieces on the floor did the reason for its sudden and peculiar destruction become obvious. Uldyssian, his aspect even more grim than Mendeln's, stepped through the immense pile of shattered stone, the path ever clearing ahead of him.

Mendeln did not like what he read in his older brother's eyes. He had not made it clear to Serenthia that Uldyssian faced not merely a pair of demons, but Lilith herself. Had she known that, the merchant's daughter would have attempted to plunge in ahead of even the demoness's former lover. After all, Lilith was as guilty, if not more so, in the death of Achilios than Lucion—who had merely been the physical cause. Lilith it had been who had drawn all of them into this.

Lilith, whose memory would no doubt tear at Uldyssian's heart until he was dead.

Mendeln's brother glared at the losses caused by the statues. "Damn her . . ."

Fortunately, Serenthia had turned to help one of the injured. That gave the siblings a moment to confer.

"Nothing was resolved . . ." Mendeln offered.

"Nothing . . ." Uldyssian continued to survey the dead. "Too many . . ."

The younger brother refrained from making any comment. He understood that his own recent opinions concerning death did not always sit well with Uldyssian.

What sounded like a great rumble of thunder shook the temple. Uldyssian glanced up, his expression hardening yet further.

"The fires and other damage have taken their own toll. The temple's about to collapse." He stepped past Mendeln. "Leave now!" he shouted to the rest. "Our task is done here!"

It was a measure of the utter command Uldyssian had that no one even hesitated. The dead were left where they were. It was not that they were so readily forgotten, just that the survivors knew that their leader would not have ordered them out without good reason. Some helped in carrying the wounded away, whom Uldyssian would surely attempt to heal later.

Mendeln turned his gaze back to his brother . . . and his studious gaze noted a sudden strain in the other's expression.

"Uldyssian—"

"I said that we all need to leave now." Uldyssian's voice remained even, but the vein in his neck had begun throbbing.

There was a second rumble, but much more muted. Mendeln noted an increase in the throbbing.

"As you say," he finally replied as calmly as possible. "But the doors are sealed—"

"No, not anymore."

Mendeln took his brother's reply as truth and, sure enough, he turned just in time to see the formerly sealed doors fling themselves open just as the first of Uldyssian's followers reached them. None of the others questioned this; they had the utmost faith that he would see them through anything.

"They need to move faster . . ." Uldyssian growled under his breath.

Nodding, Mendeln increased his pace. "Do not lag," he called to the rest. "Be wary but swift."

From farther on, Serenthia caught his eye. Her own gaze informed Mendeln that she understood the truth concerning the situation. Like Uldyssian's sibling, she did her utmost to quietly usher out the others.

Another rumble briefly shook the temple. Cracks appeared in the walls and ceiling, but otherwise the edifice remained fairly intact. The only fragments on the floor were the result of the earlier conflicts.

Mendeln felt the warm night air rush at him as he neared the outside. Aware of what they faced, he counted each step as if they were as important as the beats of his heart. It would have been simple to tell the others to run, to flee from the area before it was too late, but that would have only caused more calamity.

Flames illuminated the outdoors. In their awful light, Mendeln glimpsed some other parts of Toraja. The tree-lined streets were most obvious, their foliage the home of the serka—small simians revered by the populace. There were also the tall, rounded buildings with their columns carved to resemble one powerful beast standing atop another. The work was so intricate that some of the animals almost seemed to be gazing in concern at the conflagration surrounding them. In truth, there would be no stopping the fire from consuming the immediate district, not that Ulydssian would have cared. The serka had long fled the area and everything else here bore the mark of the Triune.

The mix of Parthans and Torajians spilled out beyond the temple grounds. Mendeln finally took a glance back at the giant structure.

Only to his eye was the constant quivering evident in the dark. Flames now covered most of the roof. Crevasses ran over the face of the building and no doubt lined every other part of it as well. Some columns farther on had cracked in half and fallen down. A major fault ran across the base on the western side.

It should have collapsed by now, he decided. *It should have collapsed on our heads . . .*

But it had not and the taut-faced figure coming up next to him was the sole reason why. Sweat poured over Uldyssian and his breathing came in rapid gasps. His gaze darted left and right, as if he sought to take account of everyone.

"No one remains behind," Mendeln assured him. "No one living, that is. Even the last of the brethren have fled."

"Into the . . . jungle . . . if they know what's good for . . . them," Uldyssian managed to grate. He stood there, obviously weighing his decision.

"It is safe to let go," his brother softly assured.

Nodding, Uldyssian exhaled.

With a terrible roar and a wrenching of stone from stone, the Torajian temple caved in on itself. Massive blocks of marble tumbled into the courtyard. Bursts of flame shot up into the night as the open air fed their fury. Gasps arose from several of Uldyssian's followers. Romus let out an oath.

Huge chunks of marble continued to spill over the area,

yet none of them came close to where the band stood. Even now, some part of Mendeln's brother kept the devastation in check.

Finally, it began to settle down to a mere catastrophe. The fires continued to burn, but the ruins now surrounded them in such a manner that they would not spread much farther. Again, Mendeln knew that this could be no coincidence.

Uldyssian looked past Mendeln, who at the same time sensed what lay behind him. As he turned, the rest became aware of the mass of figures filling the streets. The bulk of Toraja's remaining citizenry stood before Uldyssian and his flock and in that crowd Mendeln noted a variety of emotions.

A grand figure in flowing red and golden robes separated from the crowd. He wore a scarf over his long, bound, silver-colored hair and an intricate gold ring in one nostril. The sunburst design of the ring indicated his high status. The man was lanky and appeared old enough to be the brothers' father. In his left hand he clutched a tall staff with markings etched in silver running along its length.

"I seek the stranger from the high lands, the Ascenian called Uldyssian." "Ascenian" was, Mendeln's party had discovered early on, the term the jungle folk used for the pale inhabitants of such regions as Seram and Partha. The actual meaning was lost even to the locals, but it had come to mean anyone with skin and looks akin to the sons of Diomedes.

Uldyssian did not hesitate to reveal himself, although a few of his converts gave verbal protest at this. Their fear for him was not unwarranted; in addition to the leather-padded soldiers Mendeln noted among the newcomers, there were certainly representatives of the mage clans in the vicinity. They were keeping discreet, though, for although Mendeln knew that they were there, not once did he see anyone who resembled one of the powerful spellcasters. They had their own, internal matters with which they sought to deal; Uldyssian was not yet a problem to the jaded masters in Kehjan.

But after tonight, Mendeln suspected that they would be reaccessing their stand.

"Uldyssian, son of Diomedes, stands before you with empty hands," Mendeln's sibling replied, with the same respectful formality.

The elder nodded. "I am Raoneth, Councilor Senior of Toraja. Speaker for the people—" He paused, obviously noting the many darker faces among those following Uldyssian. "—but not for all, it seems. There are many known to me among those who stand with you, Ascenian, a fact that is a marvel and a concern. I was told that only the lower castes found your word of interest and that you promised them the riches of those whose stations are well above . . ."

"I promise the same thing to everyone," Uldyssian interjected, his tone only slightly hinting of the anger Mendeln knew he held against those who had spread such rumors to the Councilor Senior. "The chance to achieve what we were meant to be, regardless of our birth! I offer something more than even kings can attain, Lord Raoneth, if one will just listen! I offer what the Triune—and the Cathedral—would never desire for their flocks . . . independence from their utter mastery!"

Raoneth nodded again. His thin lips pursed and it was evident that he did not entirely like or dislike what he had heard. "The Triune has these past nights been accused of dire crimes, the least of which are too horrendous for me to declare openly here, Ascenian! I have proof from sources as well that you are a danger to the lives of those over whom I watch—"

"You want more damning proof of the Triune's crimes, Councilor Senior? It lies within those ruins, preserved despite the collapse."

For the first time, Lord Raoneth looked uncertain. Mendeln, too, was impressed. If he understood his brother as the other did, then even though Uldyssian had let the temple finally fall, he had still shielded the inner chambers from the tons of tumbling stone. An astonishing feat and one done for good reason, it now seemed.

"Perhaps that may be the case," Raoneth finally went on. "But that does not in itself excuse the case against you, Uldyssian, son of Diomedes."

"Uldyssian's no villain!" came a voice that sounded much like Romus's.

Something flew out of the dark, aiming right for Lord Raoenth's unprotected forehead. The Councilor Senior had only time to gape as the projectile reached him—

And halted just before it would have shattered his skull.

"I'm sorry, my lord," Uldyssian muttered, sounding incredibly exhausted. The makeshift missile—a sharp, apple-sized fragment from some corner of the temple—crumbled. A pile of soft ash formed at Raoneth's sandaled feet.

"By the—" the elder man began, then clamped his mouth. Mendeln suspected that, like many Torajians, he had likely been about to call upon the Three . . . Mefis, Bala, and Dialon. It had been pure reflex, though, Lord Raoneth not radiating any of the darkness that *true* converts of the Triune would have. He had been an innocent dupe like the rest . . .

"I'm sorry," Uldyssian repeated. He turned toward his followers. Although his eyes swept over the entire throng, his brother had no doubt that the one who had used his power to hurtle the missile now felt as if Uldyssian's entire focus was upon him. "Let that never happen again. This isn't the point of the gift we have. To fight for the truth, yes, to fight for our right to be what we are destined to be, yes, but not for mayhem and murder . . . then we're no better than the Triune."

He returned his gaze to the Councilor Senior, who only now looked up from the ash. To his credit, Lord Raoneth's momentary gaping when he had seen his death approaching had given way again to determination to protect his city and his people.

Uldyssian spoke before the other man could. "We're leaving Toraja, my lord. For the rest of the night, we'll camp beyond the walls. Tomorrow, we'll be gone. I came here to try to do some good, but that good's now mixed with something you and I both find distasteful. That's not what I want . . . that's not what I ever want."

The Councilor Senior bowed his head slightly. "You are beyond my power, Ascenian. For you to leave Toraja in no more devastation than what has been wrought this night . . . I can only thank the stars. No soldier shall raise a weapon to you or those who choose to follow you out, not if they do not wish to answer to me. I will brook no more bloodshed."

"One thing only, Lord Raoneth."

The man looked wary.

"The Triune is no more here. If it grows in Toraja again—like a weed can—I'll return."

Once more, Raoneth pursed his lips. "If the evil is as you said, that weed I will personally pluck clean from my city's soil."

That appeared to satisfy Mendeln's brother. Uldyssian did not look at his followers. He merely started toward Lord Raoneth and they, in turn, flowed behind him. The larger mass that had accompanied the Councilor Senior quickly gave way, hundreds of eyes watching with as many emotions as the converts—several of them once friends, neighbors, and family—passed through. The Torajians among Uldyssian's flock eyed their fellow locals with equal intensity, although in their case they radiated the determination of the newly converted. No one was going to tell them that they might have chosen wrong.

The Councilor Senior bowed his head again as Uldyssian reached him. The latter nodded in turn. Neither spoke, words now past use. Mendeln surreptitiously eyed the Torajian leader. Raoneth was an interesting figure himself; ghosts flocked around the man, but whether family or foes, there was not time enough to determine. That so many did was all that mattered; it bespoke of Raoneth's strong presence. Had the man chosen to follow so many of his citizens in accepting the gift within, Mendeln suspected that Raoneth would have quickly become one of Uldyssian's most promising candidates so far.

And perhaps that is good reason to be glad he did not join, the younger brother considered. Raoneth had been a leader; he might chafe at having to follow.

The crowd continued to give way. Even among the soldiers, there was a mix of expressions. Some looked full of distrust, others full of curiosity.

We will grow in numbers, it occurred to Mendeln. Likely, Uldyssian knew this as well. *We will grow in numbers even before we leave this throng behind.* There would be others, too, who would sneak out during the night to join the camp beyond the walls. Mendeln calculated that not only would all the lives lost tonight be gained back, but that ten times that quantity would be added yet.

"So many," he murmured.

"Yes. So many," Uldyssian replied. At that moment, whatever their own personal changes, the brothers understood one another absolutely. They both acknowledged the growth of what Uldyssian had started, acknowledged that each day would bring more and more into the fold.

And both knew, as well, that all those added souls might yet not be enough . . . that everyone here and everyone to come might simply end up *dead.*

FOUR

There was no flaw to the Prophet, not that any could see. He looked so young to his followers, yet his words were wiser than those of any ancient sage. His voice was pure music. He had not the trace of stubble on his young countenance, one barely seeming out of childhood. Those who had the privilege of seeing him close always came away with the impression of handsome, almost beautiful features, yet, their descriptions would have varied based on their own preferences. All would have agreed, though, that his hair, which fell well past his shoulders, was the gold of the sun and that his eyes were a luminescent mix of blue and silver.

He was slim and athletic in the manner of an acrobat or dancer. When the Prophet moved, it was with such grace as even a sleek cat could not match. He was clad in the silver-white robes of the Cathedral of Light, his feet sandaled.

At the moment, the Prophet stood in his glory, having just completed a sermon to more than three thousand eager pilgrims. Behind him, a choir of some two hundred—all of them as perfect in face and form as humans could be—sang the closing praises. The audience remained enraptured, as always. Although the sect had other locations elsewhere, the prime cathedral just north of the capital had a constant flow of newcomers mixing with the local worshippers. After all, here was where the Prophet himself lived. Here was where one could hear his personal words.

I must change that, he thought as he accepted the homage of his followers. *All should know my words personally.*

Perhaps through a sphere held high by the priests of each location during sermons . . .

He locked away the notion for another time, his own interest on a matter far removed from his present circumstances.

The mortal Uldyssian ul-Diomed and his ragtag followers were on the move again.

Long, golden horns blared as he finally turned from the dais. The choir shifted their singing to mark his departure, never once missing a single note. The members were from all castes, all races, but in their joyous harmony one would have had great trouble telling any of them apart.

He was met by two of his senior priests, Gamuel and Oris. Oris had her hair bound back and although she looked old enough to be his grandmother, her expression could not hide her attraction and love for him. The Prophet could see still how the oval face had once rivaled any of the young ones in the choir, but as with the singers, he had had little interest in the female priest then or now. He was also certainly not inclined toward any male aspect, such as broad-jawed Gamuel's. No, only one being—one female—had ever stirred his passions so . . . and she was now anathema to him.

"A rich, magnificent speech as usual," Oris cooed. Despite her demeanor around him, she was one of the most able of his servants. Besides, the Prophet could hardly blame her for her admiration. She was only human, whereas he was so much more.

"It sounds so terribly redundant to agree with her on this subject, but, I fear I must again, Great One!" added Gamuel, bowing low. He had once been a warrior and stood half again as wide as his master, but no one doubted which of the two was the more powerful. The Prophet had chosen Gamuel for his role because, in the remotest manner possible, he had been the one mortal most reminding the Prophet of his true self.

"It was good," their master conceded. By the priests'

standards, all of his speeches were perfection, but even he had to admit that there was a bit more to this one than many previous. Possibly that had something to do with the current flux; the status quo of which he had become used to suddenly no longer existed. In truth, that both infuriated . . . and *enticed* . . . him.

"One sensed the mood shift when you spoke of the Triune," Oris went on, her mouth wrinkling as she pronounced the last word. "There are new rumors of trouble concerning them and some fanatic from the Ascenian regions."

"Yes. His name is Uldyssian ul-Diomed. He has caused the temple much trouble in Toraja. We should hear official word of that very soon."

Neither priest registered much surprise at this knowledge. They had both been around long enough to understand that the Prophet was privy to things that they could never even imagine. Still, he always had them report whatever they heard just as a matter of form. There was always the remote chance that *something* might escape his notice.

Gamuel shook his head. "So near. Will this . . . this Uldyssian . . . seek to war against the Cathedral, too?"

"You may assume that, my son."

"Then, we should move against him—"

The Prophet gave the priest the sort of look that a father gives a naive but favored son. "No, good Gamuel, we must move *with* him."

"Holy One?"

But the Prophet said no more. He strode away from his top acolytes toward his private quarters. No one followed in his wake, the glorious master of the Cathedral of Light insisting no servants ever attend him unless summoned. No one questioned this quirk; they were all too enthralled by his holy presence.

For ceremony and the sake of his acolytes' concerns, helmed guards kept watch at the elegantly carved, twin doors. The six stood as statues as he neared.

"Be at peace," he told them. "You are dismissed for the evening."

The senior guard immediately went down on one knee. "Holy One, we shouldn't be leaving our posts! Your life—"

"Is there anyone here who could possibly threaten it? Is there anyone *I* should fear?"

They could not argue with him there, for all knew that the Prophet wielded powers unbelievable. He could defend himself far better than they could. Even the guards understood that they were for show, yet their devotion always made them hesitate to leave.

"Go with my blessings," the ivory youth declared, adding a beatific smile to encourage them to depart. "Go, knowing that you are all in my heart . . ."

They flushed with pride even as they grudgingly obeyed. The Prophet did not watch them leave. He walked directly to the doors, which flung open by themselves to admit him and then swung tightly shut once he had passed through.

There was little in the way of furniture in the otherwise sumptuous chamber the robed figure entered. A plush, down couch was where his followers assumed the Prophet slept . . . those who assumed that he slept at all. Beyond that stood several crested, marble stands atop which perched an enviable collection of the finest vases and glass sculptures from throughout the world of Sanctuary. Fresh garlands of flowers draped the walls and vast, tapered rugs with the most intricate, handcrafted patterns covered much of the shining marble floor. The walls also bore magnificent paintings of the natural beauty of every imaginable land, each *personally* dictated to the various artists by the golden-haired figure.

But above lay what most of those with the rare privilege of entering the Prophet's private sanctum thought the true focus. An immense mural covered the ceiling from end to end, each portion of it filled with fantastical images. Creatures thought only myth, landscapes almost surreal, and most of all, a host of exquisitely rendered, ethereal beings flying about through the use of vast, feathered wings sprouting from near their shoulders. The figures were male and female and all clad in gossamer robes; each had features that would have been the envy of the most beauteous princess or dashing prince. To the careful onlooker, it was evident that they were not merely part of the scenery, but rather that they were the ones *molding* it.

They were angels, as humans portrayed them at least. The Prophet, more the wiser, acknowledged the artisan's exceptional attempt, but an attempt was all it truly was. A mere mortal could not have grasped the true essence of such beings. A mere mortal could not conceive of creatures who were not exactly physical in nature, but instead harmonic resonances.

Yes, a mere mortal could not conceive of angels as they truly were, but the Prophet could.

After all, was he himself not among the greatest of angels?

It happened in a flash of brilliant light a thousand times quicker than a blink. The chamber shook and it was as if a violent wind current erupted from the very spot upon which the gold-tressed figure stood. Gone in an instant was the Prophet, who, for all his perfection, was a mere shadow of the awesome truth. In his place stood a looming, hooded figure with vast wings of flame. Within the hood there was no face, instead a radiance—formed from the blending of both light and sound—so wondrous that it would have been almost blinding to most humans. What appeared to be long, silver hair draping around it was also no more than pure light and sound mixing together.

He was clad in breastplate and robes, the former a shimmering copper, the latter as if sewn from the very rays of the sun. In mortal terms, what had been the prophet seemed now some divine warrior, and in truth, he had faced many a harsh battle against the demons of the Burning Hells.

So many, in fact, that the angel, *Inarius,* had finally

spurned the eternal war between the High Heavens and their monstrous foes and set about finding a place for himself far from the struggle. With him he had taken others of like mind, all weary of winning this victory and losing the next, over and over and over.

I SEARCHED FOR PEACE AND WAS GRANTED ITS ILLUSION . . . Inarius thought bitterly. *I FOUND MY SANCTUARY AND NAMED IT THUS . . .*

But his mistake had been, long before founding Sanctuary, to ever accept the entreaties of a pack of demons also no longer caring which side won. He had compounded that error by falling for the seductions of their leader, whose every words had mirrored his own resolution. It was because of the comingling between the two—and among their followers as well—that Sanctuary had become not only a refuge, but a *necessity*.

Because of her . . . all this had become . . .

WOULD THAT I HAD NEVER MET YOU, LILITH . . . WOULD THAT I HAD NEVER SEEN OR TOUCHED YOU . . .

But he had and all his regrets were simply that . . . regrets. Even he could not go back and alter the past. The flight from the High Heavens and Burning Hells, the search for a place for the renegades to live, the creation of Sanctuary . . . they were all an indelible part of history.

As was Lilith's betrayal.

Inarius gestured and a fiery line split the ceiling down the middle. The chamber shook as a gap opened in the center of the mural.

Without hesitation, the angel soared up into the air and out through the gap.

He had no fear of being noted. The mortals were naturally blind to his presence and his power shielded him from any others who might have been otherwise able to detect the celestial being. Inarius no longer even had to worry about the High Heavens sensing either him or Sanctuary, for he felt at last that his powers were vast enough to keep even the Angiris Council oblivious, especially with the everlasting war to further distract their attention.

And so, for the first time in centuries, Inarius soared high into the sky. He let his wings spread wide as he soaked in the sensation of being utterly free. It had been foolish of him to wait so long to finally fly again. Certainly, it had not been due to fear. No, Inarius realized that Lilith's betrayal of him—even more so than the heinous slaughter of the other angels and demons—had struck him to the very core. Only for that reason had he kept himself confined to such mortal cloaks as the Prophet and others.

NO MORE . . . NO MORE . . . AFTER THIS FARCE IS AT AN END, ALL HERE SHALL KNOW OF MY GLORY, AS IS RIGHT . . . After all, if not for him, none of this would have existed. It was his right, his duty, to keep Sanctuary on the course he had planned. Lilith would be punished, the demons would be ousted, and the troublesome mortal would become nothing but a fading memory. Sanctuary *would* be as he envisioned it . . . or he would destroy it and begin anew.

The angel arced suddenly, soaring past the gargantuan cathedral and within seconds over the capital. Kehjan the city was vast enough to be a land unto itself and there were some who argued that the surrounding regions had been named for *it*, not the other way around. Such trivial matters were of no interest to Inarius, but he did find the lights from the capital interesting in a crude fashion. They vaguely reminded him of the brilliance of the High Heavens, a place of eternal illumination.

I WILL MAKE OVER SANCTUARY ONCE THIS INCIDENT IS AT AN END, he swore. *I WILL MAKE MY OWN HIGH HEAVENS, ONE THAT WOULD BE ENVIED BY THE FIRST!* It would require much sacrifice, especially by his mortals, but it would be done. He had too long suffered silently in squalor when, by rights, he could have lived as more befitting his role. He would create a paradise untroubled by petty feuds—

Without warning, a sensation of familiarity struck him so hard that, for a moment, the angel veered off course. Inarius corrected his flight instantly, then immediately turned about.

He had thought it *her* at first, but her presence was already known to him. No, this was another. Inarius felt what to a human would have resembled a fast pounding of his heart. First Lilith . . . and now one once nearly as close to the angel as she had been.

Above the cathedral again, the glorious figure paused to survey the dark lands surrounding him. Yet, a thorough survey of every direction revealed nothing. The brief glimmer was the only hint of this new return.

BUT, THEN, HE IS CLEVER, EVEN IF EVER MISGUIDED . . . AFTER ALL, HE MAY BE OF HER CREATION . . . BUT SO, TOO, IS HE OF MINE . . .

The resurrection of yet another old—and apparently *living*—memory would change nothing, however. As Inarius descended into the chamber and the ceiling began realigning itself, he already knew that, when the time came, he would treat the other just as he intended his former lover.

Even if it *was* his errant son.

Uldyssian rose from the simple blanket upon which he slept to a sea of new faces staring apprehensively in his direction.

"I couldn't get them to stay any farther away," Serenthia apologized as she came on his right. Her dark hair was bound back and she walked more like a soldier than a merchant's daughter. Despite her growing proficiency with her powers, she continued to carry her spear in an aggressive grip.

"It's all right, Serry," he replied automatically, only afterward realizing that he had slipped back to her childhood name.

Her expression tightened and moistness appeared around her otherwise stern eyes. Only three people had consistently called her by that name once she had grown up. Two of those were dead, the last Achilios.

Rather than try to correct his error and likely compound the situation, Uldyssian focused on the newcomers. They were of all castes and ages and, as he knew would be the case, there were many children with them. The last greatly concerned Uldyssian just as it had when the Parthans had brought along their own offspring. Children had already died and those deaths more than any tore at his heart. Yet, no matter his entreaties against such, families still joined him.

I should be better able to protect them, he thought bitterly. *If not for the children, then who most am I doing this for?*

He never delved deeper into that question, for the answer ever revolved around *him*. He did this for those who followed his path, true, but also because of outright vengeance. There was no denying that at all, no matter how base such a reason was.

And that made seeing the new children only worse.

Straightening, Uldyssian accepted a water sack from Serenthia. He drank some of the cool liquid, then poured more of the contents over his head in order to wake himself up. Uldyssian did not care what the newcomers thought of his actions; if such a little thing turned them from him, then they were not ready.

But no one left. They all stood patiently waiting. He hid a frown, having secretly hoped that some of the parents would take their young and ease his guilt a little.

"You all come to me for the same reason, I hope," Uldyssian declared. "You know what the gift means . . ."

Several heads bobbed up and down. Uldyssian estimated more than a hundred newcomers. They filled most of the clearing where he slept. His own followers had blended back into the jungles, watching both hopefully and warily. Each convert was to the others a new miracle.

He saw no reason to waste more time with speeches. He had promised the Councilor Senior that he would take his followers away from Toraja, and Uldyssian had always been a man of his word.

The son of Diomedes stretched forth a hand to the nearest, an older woman whose head was protected by a multicolored scarf. Uldyssian sensed her wonder and fear warring with one another and realized that she had come here alone.

"Please . . ." he murmured, recalling his own long-dead mother. "Please come to me."

She did not hesitate, which was a credit to *her* more than him. The woman was thin and had a pinched face, but her eyes were a beautiful brown and he suspected that in her youth she had been quite alluring.

No one questioned what an elderly person was doing among the rest. Age did not seem to matter much when it came to the gifts, save that those below ten years seemed to take longer to develop any sign of success. Possibly this was some natural factor to keep them from harming themselves or others, as could sometimes be noted with some animals.

"What's your name?" he asked.

"Mahariti." Her voice was strong. She did not want others to consider her a foolish old crone unworthy of this moment.

Nodding his approval, the former farmer took her left hand in his. "Mahariti . . . open your thoughts to me, your heart to me. Close your eyes, though, if you wish . . ."

She left them open, as he had expected. Again, Mahariti rose in his estimation . . .

A peculiar buzzing filled the air.

Uldyssian had but a single breath to react. He glared at empty air.

A moment later, three spinning objects converged on his location—and crashed against an invisible barrier as if against walls of iron. The deadly objects tumbled to the ground, where they were revealed as arced pieces of metal with small, glittering teeth all along the edges. Had they struck Uldyssian, he had no doubt that he would have been dead in an instant . . . and possibly with his head lying unattached to his body.

From among the waiting figures burst two unkempt, insignificant-looking men. Yet, as they charged Uldyssian, their forms shifted and they became Peace Warders.

From nowhere, one produced a short lance that he threw at the son of Diomedes. The sharp tip had an odd red tinge to it. At the same time, the second cast another of the savage metal weapons.

But before Uldyssian could act, the whirling weapon abruptly turned and headed back to its wielder. It caught him in the chest, cutting through the metal breastplate, then the cloth, flesh, and bone underneath. The Peace Warder went flying back among the Tarajians, who just managed to avoid his bloody body before it crashed in an ghastly pile.

Uldyssian concentrated on the lance, but although it slowed, it did not stop. The red tip could only be demonic in origin. Serenthia leapt forward, using her spear to knock it off course. It went spinning past him.

Before the other Peace Warder could do anything else, some of the new Torajians seized him. He let out an oath, which turned into a cry of pain as the crowd began to tear him apart.

This was not what Uldyssian had in mind. This was not battle, but butchery. "Stop!"

As he spoke, he used his abilities to gently move aside those holding the Peace Warder until only the villain himself remained. The Peace Warder tried in vain to regain his limbs. He stood at an angle that should have made him fall on his back, only Uldyssian keeping that from happening.

The warrior's every muscle strained as Uldyssian loomed over him. One hand twitched and the son of Diomedes noted that a dagger hung near the fingers.

"I can let you take that dagger, if you like," he said without emotion. "But it'll do you no good."

Yet, still the man struggled for the feeble weapon. With a

sigh, Uldyssian straightened the Peace Warder, then let the one arm move.

The hand immediately grasped the blade. The Peace Warder raised the dagger up—and to Uldyssian's startlement, slashed his *own* throat.

A hush fell over the throng, but as Uldyssian—stupefied by the suicide—let the bleeding man drop, he saw that they assumed that their leader had caused the warrior to slay himself. They thought that the fatal strike had been Uldyssian's punishment and proof of his power over such assassins.

Still managing to hide his shock, Uldyssian stared at the Peace Warder. The man gurgled twice, his body twitching . . . then stilled.

All the while he wanted only to kill himself! He'd failed and knew no other course . . . Such fanaticism astounded Uldyssian. Perhaps the man had believed that he would suffer some more terrible fate, but somehow, that seemed doubtful. In fact, Uldyssian had been toying with the notion as to how to let the assassin live. Enough had perished last night, and now with the coming of the new day, more bloodshed had happened. He was sick of it all.

But you chose this course, he reminded himself.

"Master Uldyssian! Master Uldyssian!"

Uldyssian gratefully looked to Romus, any interruption welcome. The former criminal pointed behind himself, where two other Parthans were dragging a limp form toward the rest.

A third Peace Warder. Only now did Uldyssian think of the fact that the first attack had come from farther back.

"We found him just within the jungle," explained Romus, rubbing his bald pate.

As the other Parthans dropped the body, the cause of death became very evident. Someone had expertly cut down the assassin with an arrow to the base of the neck, apparently relying on honed talents rather than still questionable powers.

It was yet another death, but one that could not have been avoided. The Peace Warder had brought it on himself. "Good work, Romus."

"Wasn't my doin', Master Uldyssian."

The other two also shook their heads. Uldyssian digested this for a moment. "Then who?"

But no one took credit.

Frowning, Uldyssian knelt by the body. The shot had been an excellent one, as he had earlier noted, the work of a obviously skilled archer. A slight shift in direction and either the shot would have missed or the armor would have deflected it.

There was a dark substance on the shaft. Uldyssian rubbed some of it off. His brow furrowed in perplexity.

It was moist dirt . . . moist dirt covering most of the arrow, as if someone had once *buried* the bolt.

FIVE

He was cold. Even in the steaming jungle, he was cold. In fact, he was never warm anymore except when near them . . . or perhaps *her*. Yes, he thought it was likely her. Who else could it be?

It had been a risk, taking such action, but the Peace Warder might have otherwise escaped. Whether that counted for something, his dulled mind could not say, but he had decided it was best not to take a chance. An arrow through the neck had done the trick.

But now he had to move away as quickly as possible from the others. He dared not be seen. They would identify him as a threat . . . and he was not so certain that they were wrong.

The bow slung over his shoulder, the figure pushed through the thick plant life. Now and then, when he was forced to lean against a trunk, he left in his wake fragmented handprints of dirt. Soft, moist dirt. It seemed no matter how much he tried to wipe his hands clean, there was always more.

He suddenly tensed, aware that he was no longer alone. Something large but lithe slipped through the jungle, aware of his own movement even though he had thought his steps silent. One hand slowly went for the bow—

A savage, feline countenance with two long saber teeth thrust through the brush ahead. The jungle cat snarled.

But just as quickly, the snarl turned into a hiss. The beast recoiled.

He lowered his hand. He should have known that there

would be no danger. Like all animals, the cat could sense the wrongness of him.

As much out of disgust for himself as it was impatience to end this little farce, he took a step toward the great feline. The cat immediately retreated an equal distance, spitting as it moved.

"I have no . . . time . . . for you . . ." It was the first words he had spoken in days and the croaking sound of it repelled him as much as it seemed to the animal. Without any more pretense, the massive cat spun around and fled, his tail between his legs.

The bowman stood there for a moment longer, drinking in the creature's reaction. It only verified his own thoughts of what would have happened if anyone had seen him.

But he *had* to stay near. Not only because he wanted to, but because something *compelled* him. Even now, the urge to turn about grew stronger. It would not be too much more before he would have to turn back. He could even count the number of steps left, but still he knew that he would try his best to add just one. An innate stubbornness demanded that much independence of him.

The cat was long gone. Shoving aside a broad leaf the size of his head, he moved on.

Behind him, on the leaf, he left yet another dirty print.

It took well into the morning to deal with all the new converts, but despite his promise, Uldyssian refused to leave until everyone understood just what it was he had awakened in them. That did not mean that they would be able to wield any power, but at least there was a chance that it might somehow serve them should danger rear its head . . . which he felt it would soon enough. Fortunately, other followers, especially the Parthans—who had been able to practice longer—would be constantly trying to encourage their Torajian brethren.

"Nephalem" had been Lilith's word for what they were becoming, but that word not only left a bitter taste in

Uldyssian's mouth, but also did not fit right . . . at least where he was concerned. From the Torajians, he had come across another title, an ancient one that even sounded a little like the first.

"Edyrem." It meant "those who have seen" and to Uldyssian that was a perfect description of him and the rest. He had already used it this very morning and seen how easily it slipped off the tongue. Already, many were using the term rather than the old one . . .

They left the vicinity of the city the moment he was done. Despite the sun being high in the sky, it seemed almost like dusk. The foliage was so thick that the light came for the most part in minute shafts. That was not entirely undesirable, for the jungle already sweltered. The Torajians did not mind it so much, but most of the Ascenians—Uldyssian included—were already covered in sweat.

The one obvious exception was Mendeln, naturally. He trudged through the jungle as if more comfortable in it than even the locals. With his dark garments, Uldyssian's brother should have been dying under the sweltering heat, but not one drop of moisture had so far formed on Mendeln's calm countenance.

Uldyssian's gaze shifted to Serenthia. She, like him, showed signs of the heat, albeit not quite so severely. He looked at her closely, seeing for the first time how beautiful she was as a woman, not simply a friend he had always thought of like a sister. How he envied now Achilios's place in her heart, a place he had once held, but had squandered. Any thought of making an advance toward Serenthia Uldyssian quickly crushed; he still felt directly responsible for the archer's terrible demise.

Serenthia paused to drink from her water sack, but as she lifted the opening to her lips, her grip slipped. The sack fell, its contents spilling all over the ground.

He reached for his own. "You can drink some of this."

Retrieving the sack, Serenthia shook her head. "Save yours. We passed a stream just a few yards back . . . and besides, this'll give me a chance to deal with some private matters."

"Someone should go with—"

She gave him a grateful smile. "I'll be fine. You'll probably be able to see the top of my head most of the time."

That still did not satisfy Uldyssian, but he knew better than to argue with her. Signaling the others to keep moving, he stood firm where he was. "I'll be right here. I won't go anywhere."

Again, Cyrus's daughter smiled. Uldyssian found he liked when she smiled at him.

Serenthia rushed off. A few of the others wanted to stay with Uldyssian, but he politely refused their company. Despite the shifting greenery and the shadows caused by the thick foliage, Uldyssian did the best he could to keep some part of her in sight at all times. As she had said, the stream was right beside them; in fact, others had used it before Serenthia. There was really no reason to be concerned . . .

But then, that was not the first time that he had thought that . . . and been proven horribly wrong.

Serenthia bent down, for the first time vanishing from his field of vision. Uldyssian held his breath . . . then exhaled as she rose again.

She glanced over her shoulder and with a wave of her hand, commanded him to look away. Despite his trepidation, he finally obeyed.

There was a rustling of leaves, then silence. It occurred to Uldyssian that he could use his powers to check on her location, but suspected that Serenthia would, with her own, notice him doing just that. However, considering her present circumstances, the former farmer shied away from doing so.

There was a muffled sound from Serenthia's direction. Uldyssian peered around for her. With relief, the dark-haired woman's head reappeared. Seconds later, Serenthia slipped back to join him.

"I was worried . . . for a moment," he admitted.

Much to his surprise, her eyes brightened at this comment. Serenthia put a hand to his cheek. She smiled almost shyly.

"I like that," the merchant's daughter finally murmured.

Then, her face reddening, Serenthia rushed on, briefly leaving a befuddled Uldyssian to try to understand just what the incident meant, if anything. Then, forcing such dangerous thoughts from the forefront, he hurried after the rest of the party.

They did not head toward the capital, as some thought, but rather, farther south, toward where the main temple lay. It was not what Uldyssian would have chosen, but Lilith had forced his hand. Despite her acting as if she *wanted* him to destroy the Triune, he somehow felt that if he went directly for their supreme headquarters, it would be more than the demoness expected. Uldyssian hoped in that manner to throw her off guard.

Unfortunately, he also suspected that he was still playing into her hands.

The makeshift army paused near a river that, according to the Torajians, flowed between the southern gates of the city and the lands owned by the Triune. Uldyssian saw the river as the perfect guide for the rest of their journey. Romus and some of the others located the best area for the camp and the nephalem started to settle down for the night.

Recalling the river reptiles that Achilios had caught, Uldyssian made certain that not only did his followers steer clear of sleeping too close to the water, but that no one went alone to it for any reason. Even then, those small groups who did head to the river were to alert other people of the fact first.

"We should be able to fear nothing," he remarked sarcastically to Mendeln. The two sat alone near one of the many fires. "That's what these powers should mean, but look at us . . ."

"They are learning rapidly, Uldyssian. Have you not

noticed that the more converts you gain, the more of your followers increase their abilities and quicker?"

"They need to! I'm marching them into a war with demons and magic and who knows what else!" He buried his head in his hands. "Will they be ready for that, Mendeln? You saw how it was in Toraja . . ."

"The lesson of Toraja is burned into all of us, brother. The next time will be different."

Uldyssian looked up, his eyes narrowing. "The next time. What did the Torajians call the place?"

"Hashir. It is smaller than Toraja."

"But somehow I doubt it'll be any easier."

Shrugging, Mendeln replied, "What will be will be."

The younger brother stood up, and with a pat on Uldyssian's shoulder, walked off. Uldyssian sat there, watching the flames and recalling the ones engulfing the temple and parts of Toraja. Would it be like that all over again? How many would perish this time? He had felt so determined after Lucion's destruction, but Toraja had taken much of that from him, not that he let anyone other than Mendeln truly know that.

"You shouldn't fret so, Uldyssian. It's not good for you or for those who follow you."

He looked up to see Serenthia step into the light of the fire like some night spirit. Her hair flowed loose and Uldyssian was surprised at just how long and lush it had gotten.

"I thought you were asleep," he replied.

"Sleep . . ." Brushing back some hair, she sat down next to him. "I don't sleep as much as some think, Uldyssian."

That was something that he could understand, often suffering it himself, but to hear that Serenthia shared the problem worried him. "You should have said something . . ."

Her eyes glistened in the light of the fire. "To you? How could I bother you, when you've got so much with which to deal?"

As she spoke, she leaned against him. Her nearness both stirred him and added to his guilt.

"I always have time for you," he heard himself say.

Serenthia touched the back of his hand. "If there was anyone I'd turned to, you know that it would be you, Uldyssian. And you know that I would be there for you, also. I've always been there for you . . ."

He remembered all the years that she had followed him around, waiting for the farmer to notice the young girl who had become a woman. Uldyssian had, but unlike most of the other men in Seram, not in the manner in which Serenthia had hoped.

But now, at a time when he least wanted to, he was noticing her as she had once dreamed.

She leaned closer . . . too close. "Uldyssian—"

Caught between desire and loyalty to a lost comrade, Uldyssian tried not to look directly into her eyes—

And, in doing so, saw something all but shadowed by the nighttime jungle.

With a gasp, he leapt to his feet.

"Uldyssian! What is it?"

He instinctively looked down at her, then quickly returned his gaze to the wilderness. However, all that met his eyes were darkened trees and vines. Nothing else. Nothing remotely resembling a human shape.

Nothing, certainly, resembling a figure with a pale face draped by blond hair, a figure whom he had taken for someone long dead.

"*Achilios . . .*" Uldyssian whispered. Without thinking, he took a step toward the jungle.

"What did you say?" asked Serenthia, suddenly standing in his path. "Did you see something out there?"

"No . . . nothing . . ." He could not tell her that he had just seen a ghost, a dead man walking. After all it had only been his own guilt that had manifested the vision. They had left Achilios buried far, far behind them . . .

To his further dismay, Serenthia put her palms on his chest. She looked up at him. "Uldyssian—"

"It's late," he interrupted, backing up from her.

"We should do the best we can to sleep, Serry." He purposely used the other name this time, hoping it would douse the volatile situation.

She frowned, then nodded. "As you say."

Uldyssian expected her to say more, but she suddenly turned and headed deeper into the encampment. He watched her vanish among the others, then sat down by the fire again.

Staring at the jungle, Uldyssian suddenly probed the shadows. There was nothing, though, and he had not thought that there would be. It had been his own regrets, nothing more.

Achilios was dead...and for that reason alone, Uldyssian could *never* allow things to grow between Serenthia and him.

Mendeln jolted to a sitting position, the sensation of something awry filling him. He hated when that particular sensation occurred, for it usually presaged imminent disaster for all. Quickly peering around, he saw no reason for his concern, but that did not assuage him in the least. His brother and he dealt with far too many dangers that kept themselves hidden until ready to spring upon the pair.

Moving silently, Mendeln rose from his blanket. Unlike most of the others, he did not sleep near the fires, preferring somehow the quiet dark of night over the protective light of the flames. Another change from the young boy who had always huddled closest whenever the last glimmer of day had passed.

His first concern was Uldyssian. With catlike movements, he stepped among the sleeping edyrem—as they were now apparently to be called—until he located his brother. Uldyssian slept fitfully and alone, Serenthia nowhere in sight. Mendeln felt mildly disappointed about the last. With Achilios dead, he had hoped that the two would find one another. Certainly, they deserved a little bit of happiness. Of course, his brother likely still felt too much at fault over the hunter and Serenthia had long ago given up trying to catch Uldyssian's eye.

Would that my concerns would all revolve around something so mundane as love, Mendeln finally thought. *Matters would be so much more simple.*

But if it was not any imminent danger to Uldyssian, then what troubled Mendeln so? As he wended his way back to his sleeping place, he considered the event again. No dream of significance came to him. No sound had touched his ears. By rights, he should still be fast asleep.

Mendeln looked about and only then noticed that the area was devoid of his own companions. There was always a ghost around, some shade who could not immediately detach itself from his presence. The party had left Toraja not only with new converts, but also several dozen specters who, for the most part, had perished in the struggle. Many had disappeared along the way, but a few new ones had joined during the day's march. Most of those had been unlucky hunters or travelers who had fallen victim to the dangers of the jungle. Like the rest, they appeared to be wanting something from Mendeln, but when it became clear that he would not give it to them, gradually faded away once more.

But rarely did *all* of them disappear.

Curious, Mendeln headed to the edge of camp. He could see far better than anyone else in the dark, but still all he noted was more and more shadows.

And yet . . . was there a slight movement well to his right?

"Come to me . . ." he whispered. The first time he had spoken such words, it had summoned the ghosts even closer to him. Normally, Mendeln kept from summoning them, but if this specter had significance to him and his brother, it behooved him to find out.

But the shape did not drift forward, and in fact, the more Mendeln eyed it, the less certain he was that he had seen correctly. Now it *did* resemble some fern or other plant, not a man . . .

But the sensation continued to press at his mind.

Exhaling in exasperation, Mendeln entered the jungle. He knew that he took some risk, for while the insects that plagued most of the others stayed clear of him, he did not know if the same held true for the huge carnivores of whom the Torajians spoke.

In his eyes, the jungle at night was lovelier, like a beautiful, mysterious woman. The dangers hidden by the dark made that woman only more thrilling. As he forayed deeper, Mendeln marveled that such imagery would occur to him. Yes, he was definitely no longer the frightened child he had been even after growing up.

The shape Mendeln had noticed had to be near, but now nothing he saw even remotely resembled it. Had it been, after all, his imagination or had whoever he had seen retreated once discovered?

A hand touched his shoulder.

He spun about . . . and found nobody behind him.

"Who are you?" Mendeln whispered.

The jungle remained steadfastly silent. Too silent, in fact, for a place where the calls of the daylight were often but a murmur compared to those beginning once the sun was gone. The jungle held more life in it than a thousand Serams, yet none of that was apparent now. From the smallest to the largest, the fauna was conspicuously absent.

But no sooner had Mendeln thought that when the leaves to his left rustled . . . and a form moving on two legs slipped by at the edge of his vision.

"Spare me your tricks and games!" he growled. "Show yourself or else!" Mendeln had no idea exactly what "or else" might be. In past circumstances of danger, he had suddenly spouted words in an ancient tongue he had never known, words of power that had saved him more than once. However, whether those words would protect him from the lurker, he was not so certain.

It moved again, this time to his right. Mendeln automatically spouted a word—and a brief, gray glow filled the immediate vicinity.

But what he saw was not at all what he expected.

"No . . ." Uldyssian's brother rasped, refusing to accept what that momentary glow had revealed. "No . . ."

It had to be a delusion . . . or a trick, he thought. Yes, that made sense and hardened his resolve. Mendeln could think of only one being who would do such an obscene thing.

"Lilith . . ." And here he was alone, a fool overconfident in his feeble abilities. No doubt the demoness was readying the fatal blow. How would it come? Mendeln would perish in some monstrous manner, naturally, his death drawn out.

Oddly, death itself did not disturb him. It was the part just before that which Mendeln wished to avoid.

He would not show her any fear. If somehow he could use his demise to help or at least warn Uldyssian, then that was something. "Very well, Lilith. You have me. Come and do what you wish."

Words formed on his tongue. His hopes rose slightly. He knew that the words' power would give him some chance to at least stave off the inevitable . . .

Something whizzed past his ear. There was a grotesque, bestial howl, followed by a dull *thunk,* as if something had collided with one of the many trees.

Mendeln peered in the direction of the howl and saw something sinister standing against one of the thick trunks. When he saw that the thing did not move, he finally approached it.

It was a morlu . . . a morlu with an arrow through the throat just where the helmet and breastplate left only half an inch of space. Mendeln started to reach for the arrow, its presence stirring another nightmare—

The morlu lifted his head, the black pits staring at Mendeln. The warrior grasped for Uldyssian's brother.

The same words that he had earlier used on one of these fiends in the house of Master Ethon spilled from Mendeln. As they did, the morlu's grasping hands twitched wildly. A gurgle escaped the pale lips.

The morlu slumped again, only the arrow pinning him to

the tree keeping the bestial figure from falling at Mendeln's feet.

Without hesitation, Mendeln put a hand over the monstrous warrior's chest. Other words, again first used in Partha, sprang easily from the lips of Uldyssian's brother.

Most would have been unable to see the small, black cloud that rose from the morlu. It hovered over Mendeln's palm. He stared at the foulness for a moment, then snapped shut his hand.

The cloud vanished.

"No more will you be raised to do evil." Whatever darkness animated a morlu, gave it semblance of true life, would not be able to resurrect this particular corpse. Mendeln had made certain of that.

But there still remained whatever had initially rescued him from the Triune's servant. Mendeln finally touched the arrow, noting with mild dismay that there was dirt all over the shaft. Just like the arrow that had slain one of the Peace Warders.

"It cannot be . . . he is dead . . ."

But life is only a robe which all wear but fleeting . . .

Though the thought flowed through his mind, Mendeln by no stretch of the imagination believed it his own. He had felt that other presence in his head before. It had always guided him, yet, now what it said only made Mendeln more anxious.

"No!" he growled at the darkness. "He is dead! To think otherwise is evil! He is buried! I was there! I chose the spot! I chose—"

He had chosen to bury the body very near an ancient structure bearing the same sort of markings as the stone near Seram. Mendeln gaped at his own naivety. Why did he think that he had chosen that very location? Something had urged him to do it and he had blithefully acquiesced.

Shaking his head, Mendeln backed up—

And collided with another form.

Uldyssian's brother spun around . . . and stared into the pale, dirty face of Achilios.

SIX

Astrogha was a demon of ambitions. He had sat near the taloned hand of Diablo, the greatest of the Prime Evils, and had learned well. It had always chafed him to be subservient to Lucion, but then Lucion had actually been the son of Mephisto so there had been little he could do about it.

But Lucion acted strange of late. In his persona of the Primus, the archdemon had always done things in a certain manner, but since his return from some mysterious foray, that had changed. Had Astrogha not known better, he would have sworn that it was no longer the son of Mephisto who sat upon the Primus's throne. That was impossible, surely, for who could ever masquerade as Lucion?

The demon shifted in his shadowed web, located now in one of the high towers of the Triune's supreme temple. Astrogha had chosen the one dedicated to Dialon, naturally, that being the spirit who was, in fact, his master, Diablo. Around the brooding demon crawled his "children," sinister black spiders of every size, some as big as a man's head.

Astrogha was a demon of many incarnations, many shapes. For this moment, he wore a form both arachnid and human, a macabre mix of the two. He now had eight limbs, broader and thicker than any spider, which could be used as arms or legs, depending on circumstance. All ended in clawed digits perfect for rending soft flesh, the better to stuff it into a maw with not only fangs, but jagged teeth that looked as if they had been filed. Astrogha's torso was generally humanoid in design, but rounder and broader at the shoulder. He could make it otherwise, should the mood suit him.

Atop his head were eight more smaller limbs, each ending in human hands. They were good for dragging prey closer to his mouth and for plucking tiny vermin from his black-furred body for the occasional snack in between.

His eyes were crimson orbs clustered together, each lacking any pupil. With them, Astrogha saw in almost every direction and beyond the sight of most mortals or even demons. With them, in fact, he could see back somewhat into the Burning Hells, where he would now and then report to his lord and master.

Astrogha was overdue to give such a report. He did not like stirring Lord Diablo's ire, for it would be a simple thing for the great demon to reach out from beyond to squash Astrogha like a bug.

The arachnid had hesitated to report because he was still trying to assess the change in Lucion. If Lucion was no longer fit to command, then someone would rightly have to step in and take his place . . . but that would prove difficult, considering Mephisto's role in this. The other Prime Evil would not take kindly to his offspring's role being usurped . . . unless the results of that proved most promising.

And so Astrogha was debating plots of his own. This human, this Uldyssian, represented both tremendous potential and threat to the cause of the Burning Hell. Humans could become the weapon the demons needed to at last seize total victory from the sanctimonious angels, yet the tendency toward good in them might make them ally themselves with the High Heavens . . . until the piousness and rigidity of the winged warriors sickened their stomachs as much as it did the demons'.

Astrogha lifted the limp arm from which he had been sipping and drank what was left of the blood within it. The children hungrily scurried over the rest of the emaciated corpse, a young acolyte of the temple no one would miss. Lucion had always permitted him to take the occasional innocent, for did not a demon have to eat, too?

But as he drained the last, a sudden, intense *fear* overtook Astrogha. The demon flung away the arm, at the same time as the children were rushing for the deepest recesses of the corner—not that *any* shadow could conceal either him or them from the cause of their terror.

Barely audible voices filled the chamber. There was a frenetic tone to them that raised the bristled fur covering his grotesque body. Astrogha could sense their pleading, their hopelessness. Their torments were such that he, who had caused so much terror himself over the centuries, shook hard.

Then, eyes that could see beyond Sanctuary now beheld a huge form seemingly halfway between realities. At first, it flowed toward him like an inky shadow, but as he caught better sight of it, he made out faces both human and demonic and all in midscream. The faces constantly melted into one another and none were ever perfectly defined, but rather more as if out of a nightmare.

As the hideous specter neared, Astrogha then caught glimpses of a fiery red shape, huge fists with black talons, and a horrific countenance that was in part a rotting skull with blazing eyes that burned into the arachnid's own. Monstrous, curled horns—like those of a ram's gone amok—topped the thick-browed, scaled head. That shape vanished, to be replaced by a skeletal form in rusting armor and in whose arms it carried rotting organs covered in maggots. Then, that was without warning replaced by a reptilian beast with a maw like a huge frog and a tongue four times forked. The mouth looked wide enough to swallow a man . . . or an arachnid as big as one . . .

The reptilian visage slipped into and out of his eyesight, mixing constantly with the shrieking heads. Yet, at last there came a powerful voice, with each word sounding like the crunching of a spider's tasty flesh. *"Astrogha . . .*

Astrogha . . . I have awaited your word, you pathetic worm . . ."

The demon in the web took hope at the mildness of the summoner's anger. "Forgive me . . . forgive me for my lateness, my lord Diablo . . ."

The murky form shifted, most of it fading into shadow. Even Astrogha never cared to see his master in all his terrible glory. Some demons had been driven mad by such an audience. Astrogha was stronger than most, but the one time he had been granted a full visualization—and that for only a few seconds—it had left him shivering for years.

"What of this little mud ball you call Sanctuary?" Diablo demanded without preamble. His voice touched every nerve in the spider's body, each syllable like a thousand tortures. *"I grow impatient for results from my nephew . . ."*

There was the opening that Astrogha needed! "Great and glorious Diablo, whose very name sends nightmares to the angels, this one has at all turns your desires followed as best can be done! Ever have I offered noble Lucion my word, my advice, but he listens not! True, the son of Mephisto has so *many* pressures upon him! It is so hard for him to direct all, to constantly plan alone . . ."

There was a harsh grating laugh that made Astrogha wish that he had ears to cover. Even then, though, that would not have kept the laugh from causing him to quake.

"The little bug has notions of his own on how the worms of this mud ball should be persuaded to our just cause? Notions my nephew would not hear?"

"Yes . . . they have gone unspoken. It is . . . difficult for this one or any other to understand what noble Lucion thinks and so offer advice to him. His planning grows erratic. He sets a trap for the leader of these mortals, then leaves myself and Gulag—who is but a stinking puddle now—to fend for ourselves against might both angelic and demonic . . ."

"So powerful . . ." Diablo's tone left no doubt as to his interest. The destruction of his brother Baal's minion was of

no significance save that it gave some credence to the belief that the humans would prove very useful soldiers.

"This one would have continued the struggle—Astrogha fears only his master—but Lucion then cast me out and sealed from my view his confrontation with this Uldyssian!"

"And the mortal is not ours even then?"

"Nay! He even just this last eve as Sanctuary counts time ravaged another temple! Yet Lucion not only seems not to care, but this one has not seen him of late . . . a second inexplicable absence! Our mortal servants are left to their own minds—no good thing coming of that—and this one must sit and wait and sit and wait, when there is much that could be done!"

He expected Diablo to comment, but only silence met the arachnid. That silence stretched longer and longer and the more it did, the more anxious Astrogha became.

At last . . .

"You have something in mind, little bug?"

"Yes, my lord Diablo . . . if this one may be permitted to act freely . . . and possibly beyond what the noble Lucion would prefer."

There was another silence.

"Tell me, crawler in the shadows, tell me, my Astrogha . . ."

And, with barely concealed glee, the arachnid did just that.

Mendeln was unusually silent even for him, enough so that Uldyssian noticed. He glanced at his brother as they trudged through the jungle, noting how Mendeln kept his gaze fixed directly ahead. It was as if he feared that he might see something undesired if he looked anywhere else.

Unfortunately, there was too much troubling Uldyssian's own mind for him to continue to concentrate on Mendeln. It only partially had to do with the dangers ahead. There was also the incident with Serenthia.

She had been open to his advance, that much had been obvious, and he realized more and more that he wanted to pursue the matter. Yet, that meant trampling on the memory of his best friend . . .

With a grunt, Uldyssian tried to dismiss the subject from his mind yet *again*. There were too many threats merely from the land around them, much less the Triune, to become so distracted. Constantly, he probed ahead, seeking anything that might endanger the others. More than once, Uldyssian had mentally fended off predators. He had also sent several poisonous snakes and one huge constrictor slithering in other directions. It was a constant task; the jungle held so much potential danger that he could scarcely believe it.

At times, the trail turned as dark as night. Footing often proved tricky even for Uldyssian, who was better able to detect the shifting ground. Despite his own powers, he found he had to also rely on a pair of Torajians, Saron and Tomo. They were cousins, Saron the elder by five years, and had ventured farther in this direction than any of their fellows. They were nearly as skilled hunters in their environment as Achilios had been in his and were chief among those securing food for the rest.

"Watch for the jagged leaf of the tyrocol bush, Master Uldyssian," Saron told him, pointing to the thick, reddish plant to their left. "To cut yourself on them is to invite its strong poison . . ." To emphasize that fact, the elder cousin used a spear to lift the lower leaves. The rotting corpse of a small, furred creature lay underneath. Tiny, crimson lizards who had been snacking on the remains darted for the safety of the underbrush.

"Kataka," Tomo offered. "They resist the poison, but it fills their skin. They can eat the tyrocol's victims and are poisonous to others because of what they ingest."

Uldyssian had sensed some threat, but discovering that it was a plant he had to avoid and not some creature made him vow to double his efforts. He believed that he could reject the bush's poison, but what about those not yet coming into their powers?

"Let all know of the tyrocol," he commanded Romus and several others. It was not the first such pronouncement that Uldyssian had made and he knew that it would not be the last. It seemed that *everything* in the jungles had some hidden—and ofttimes malevolent—aspect to it.

Their intended destination remained the smaller city of Hashir. As they marched along, they kept a special eye out for any trace of the Triune's servants. Uldyssian was certain that the three assassins had not been the only ones left. In fact, he somehow felt that the Triune had some part to play in Mendeln's behavior, but trusted that, if it was necessary, his brother would certainly let him know the truth.

Certainly . . .

"You seem so lost in thought."

Uldyssian glanced to his side, startled by Serenthia's sudden nearness. That he had not noticed spoke volumes concerning the state of his mind. "I have to keep all of them safe and there's so much here in the jungle compared to home."

"Yes, Seram seems so peaceful in comparison." She frowned. "Or at least, it used to be."

That stirred up his guilt again. "Serenthia . . . about Cyrus and what—"

"Go no further, Uldyssian. What happened was not your fault. You were hardly aware of the powers within you, much less how to control them."

Her attempt to placate him did nothing to help Uldyssian. Nevertheless, he nodded gratefully.

"Nor do I blame you for Achilios," the woman went on, her glittering eyes snaring his. "Achilios was a good man, but independent. He chose to do what he did. He wouldn't blame you any more than I."

"Serenthia—"

Her hand slipped over to his, touching the back so very softly. "Please don't worry about me so much, especially where Achilios is concerned. I mourn him as a lost friend . . . but perhaps not the lover I thought he was."

This admission nearly caused him to stumble in his tracks. "What are you saying? The two of you—"

"Uldyssian, Achilios always cared for me, but you know I"—she glanced away for a moment, her cheeks red from other than the heat—"had other feelings. When I thought that there was no more hope . . . I think I turned to him for comfort . . . for . . . I feel so *guilty* . . ."

He waited, and when she did not go on, he murmured, "Now you're the one who shouldn't." Uldyssian shrugged, not certain if his next words made sense or not. "You brought happiness to Achilios. He died thinking that you and he were one. That's something, isn't it?"

Her hand slipped closer, tightening on his. Uldyssian did not draw back. A part of him felt like he once again betrayed his friend, but another was pleased by what he had heard.

But before matters could go any further, Mendeln interjected himself into their presence. Uldyssian's brother wore an expression that boded no good.

"There is something in the jungle," he quietly announced. "Can you feel it?"

His attention brought back to their current situation, Uldyssian now did. He could not fathom what it was, but it was very close. He signaled Tomo over to him.

"Do you know this region? Is there anything we should beware?"

The Torajian considered. "We are beyond where my cousin and I hunt, Master Uldyssian, but I recall a little about the area. It was said that jungle spirits frequent this location, but those are only stories our grandmothers told us!"

"Jungle spirits?" Mendeln seemed to find this of particular interest. "Why here? What is so different?"

"There are ruins here, Master Mendeln." As with many of Uldyssian's Torajian followers, Tomo seemed uncomfortable speaking directly with the younger son of Diomedes. "Ones so old the markings are all but washed away. They are nothing but curiosities . . ."

"We should avoid them, anyway," suggested Serenthia. "They're away from the river, aren't they, Tomo?"

"Oh, yes, mistress." Serenthia was treated with nearly as much reverence as Uldyssian. Tomo and some of the other younger converts also seemed quite smitten with her. "Two or three hours through dense jungle! Not worthy of the time!"

Mendeln looked disappointed. "So far as that?"

"Well . . . perhaps not so far as that," the Torajian reluctantly admitted. "But far enough!"

Unless they had something to do with the Triune—which evidently they did not—Uldyssian had no use for the ruins. He gestured ahead. "We keep moving. Hashir's our goal. Nothing else."

Yet as they started on again, Uldyssian continued to sense *something* from the general direction of the unseen ruins. He had no idea exactly what it was, but it felt very, very old and somewhat dark of nature. Curiously, there was also a feeling of . . . of *fury* . . . that seemed to be growing with each passing moment.

Almost as if whatever it was had taken notice of them.

Uldyssian tried to ignore what was happening, but the fury continued to swell with each passing breath. He finally pulled aside Serenthia and Mendeln and was not at all surprised to discover that they felt it, too.

"We have attracted its attention," his brother agreed. "It is awakening from its death . . ."

"And what does that mean, Mendeln?" Uldyssian demanded, suddenly growing weary with the mysteries surrounding his sibling. "Just what do you understand about this?"

"More than you, it seems," the other snapped back, his abrupt vehemence matching Uldyssian's own. "I do not walk around oblivious to everything but myself!"

"No, you walk around speaking to shadows and making vague comments, all the signs of madness—"

The eyes of both brothers went wide as they both noticed their odd anger at one another. Uldyssian glanced around them and noticed that many of his followers had paused to stare aghast at the unexpected confrontation.

"It is feeding us its fury," Mendeln declared. "and in the process feeding from that . . ."

"Get everyone as close to the river as is safely possible," commanded Uldyssian to Romus and others. "Everyone must keep their thoughts calm and if they feel any anger—about anything—they'll keep it smothered or answer to me!"

He was not certain if any of the others would be affected, but did not want to take the risk.

Serenthia brightened. "Tomo! Is there anywhere to cross the river? I thought someone mentioned an area ahead."

The Torajian frowned. "I know of none, mistress, but there could be . . ."

"I'm certain that I remember right." She looked to Uldyssian. "I'm sure of it. The sooner we find it, the better!"

Uldyssian was glad for her suggestion. A crossing would let them better get to safety. The intensity of the ancient fury was still growing. In fact, he had some slight worry that even the other side of the river would not prove sufficient to escape it.

But at the moment, Uldyssian had no other choice for his people. He waved them on, staying his ground and staring in the direction of the ruins and their malevolent inhabitant. Uldyssian kept his will focused, determined not to let the dark thing play with his emotions.

Mendeln stepped up next to him. "Go on with the rest, Uldyssian. I will stand watch here."

"You take Serenthia and lead the others on," the older brother demanded in turn.

"There is no time for argument—" Mendeln snapped his mouth shut. Uldyssian knew that they had both nearly started another fight. Perhaps it would have been wiser for the pair to retreat, but he felt that so long as the inhuman fury concentrated on them, then the others were in less danger.

Evidently, Mendeln was of a like mind, for he said almost at the same time, "We will stand together, as shields for the rest, then."

They said no more, both shoulder-to-shoulder, staring into the jungle.

But Uldyssian noticed a subtle shift in the monstrous rage. While part of it still focused on the brothers, some of it yet followed along with the fleeing band. He concentrated . . . and knew exactly why.

"Serenthia!" Uldyssian gasped. "It's turning its evil toward her!"

"But why—" Mendeln began.

Uldyssian did not know why and had no interest in wasting time discussing the devastating discovery. More and more, the dark force turned its attention to the vicinity of their companion.

He knew of only one way to prevent that from continuing. His aspect grim, Uldyssian strode toward the distant ruins. At the same time, he pushed his will ahead, demanding that whatever lurked out there concentrate on him and him alone.

The jungle darkened as he bore toward the hidden site. The cries of the animals and insects faded into the background. As Uldyssian progressed, he noticed that the trees and other plant life took on a shrouded appearance, as if some shadow other than that cast by the foliage above now settled over them. Limbs took on the appearance of skeletal arms and all the leaves suddenly reminded him of the poisonous plant Tomo had pointed out.

He stumbled over a protrusion in the ground. Glancing down, he saw that it was a piece of stone, but one not naturally formed. Uldyssian extended a hand and the stone flew up into it.

It was from some shattered carving, part of the upper

face of what looked to be a woman. What there was to view had an ethereal beauty to it—

A harsh force struck him full, sending Uldyssian flying against a nearby tree. Only his abilities kept his back from snapping in two. The stone went tumbling from his hand . . . but where he had hit hard, it landed *gently* on the soil.

At the same time, Uldyssian sensed that he was not alone. However, whatever stood with him was not any mortal being. It was not, he knew, even alive in any normal sense.

And this close, Uldyssian understood that it was demonic in origin.

He had slain demons before, but never had he thought what might happen to them after they were dead. He had supposed that they simply ceased to be. Yet, what Uldyssian faced was more akin to a ghost or angry spirit, not a living demon.

How was that possible?

That was not important, though. Protecting Serenthia *was*. "You'll leave her be!" he abruptly growled, standing. "You'll leave them all be!"

There was a feeling of immense bitterness and hatred . . . but not aimed directly at Uldyssian. For him, there was more of a sense of irritation, as if he was merely in the way from what needed to be done.

He decided to become more than that to the angry essence. Staring at the trees before him, Uldyssian pointed.

The jungle exploded, trees collapsing and bits of plant raining down on everything save Uldyssian. Where once the landscape had blocked his way, now a perfect, oval path lay open.

And at the end of it, just visible, was a stone structure tilted at a precarious angle. The roof—once angled, Uldyssian thought—had been crushed in as if by a huge fist. The windows—three in all—were odd in their design, having five sides to them. It appeared as if the building had been carved from stone the color of bone . . . the same stone as the fragment of face.

Tomo had severely miscalculated the distance of the ruins from Uldyssian and the edyrem. They had virtually been on the very doorstep.

Uldyssian squinted. Near the left side, the side from which the structure tilted away, was a small gap in the ground that he realized was another window. If that was the case, then at least another floor lay buried beneath. That bespoke of not only the great age of the building—for it must have taken centuries to bury the rest—but also some powerful catastrophe that had initially befallen the area.

Every muscle taut, Uldyssian closed in on the building. Tomo had described it as a place with markings all but worn away by the elements, but to the former farmer's heightened senses, there were still symbols and illustrations quite evident on the face. What the language was, he did not know, but the images were at least somewhat recognizable. Many looked as if they were of the same ethereal female, only now on a few she was accompanied by a tall, almost menacing figure. Yet, between the pair there was no sign of menace . . . but something more resembling *love*.

The two never looked quite the same in any relief, but there was just enough to make Uldyssian certain it was always the original duo. Recalling how easily Lilith could wear other guises, he finally assumed that, if these were anything like her, they probably had a thousand shapes from which to choose. These had likely just been *favorites*.

At that momenet, a voice whispered in Uldyssian's ear, but its words were unintelligible. He hesitated, then took a step forward.

An image flashed through his head. A beauteous woman with wings—of *fire*?

The face had looked familiar, but only after a moment did he recall it as the one from the reliefs and the shattered carving. None of the works had done justice to what he had just seen, though . . . and again Uldyssian knew that even the vision had only shown him a shadow of her true glory.

Uldyssian took a cautious step forward . . . only to be met by a second vision. Here was the winged woman with the male who, while strikingly handsome, had skin of absolute white and two ice-blue orbs without pupils. They stood together in what was clearly a scene of deep affection, despite obvious differences between them.

Again came the whisper, the words no more understandable than before. Suspecting what would happen next, Uldyssian nonetheless moved on.

It was the unearthly couple again . . . but now the winged woman lay torn to shreds on the ground. The male, his legs ruined and his back cut open so deep that he should have been dead, crawled toward her. A green ichor poured from his wounds. He bared teeth that were as sharp as those of the river reptiles. The male pounded the ground in growing rage and the tears dropping from his face sizzled when they touched anything else.

Behind them, fallen at the angle that he had first seen it, was the white structure . . . all four stories of it. Something had crushed in the roof, as Uldyssian had already noted, and then had demolished the base on the right as well. The landscape beyond was also in ruins, but in place of the jungle, trees akin to those of which Uldyssian was familiar from Seram dominated . . . or had until their destruction.

The vision . . . the longest of all . . . faded. As Uldyssian shook his head to clear it, he felt the presence that he had been combatting suddenly reach far past him . . . for Serenthia.

Recalling himself, Uldyssian sought some manner by which to redraw the thing's attention to himself. On a hunch, he eyed the ancient building. It did not take much of his power to start the edifice shaking. Bits of stone quickly began breaking off.

But no sooner had he started than he was battered to the ground by what could only be described as pure rage. Uldyssian cried out from pain, realizing that he had obviously underestimated the malevolent force's determination. In his head, he heard howling and more words he could not understand. There was also a sensation of terrible loss, which under the onslaught, did not in any way cause him to sympathize with his attacker. Uldyssian had no idea what had provoked the spirit, wraith, or whatever it was, only that he had to stop it from hurting Serenthia . . . and him, too.

Straining, Uldyssian lifted his head. Through his tearing eyes, the land took on a surreal effect. In it, he almost imagined that he saw the male figure—a demon, he felt sure—standing over the ruins like a protective and enraged guardian.

And a moment later, that guardian reached a giant hand toward him.

It did not take imagination to know what might happen if that hand enveloped Uldyssian. The human focused on shielding himself.

But the giant vanished, replaced by a savage onslaught of broken branches, loose stones, and more . . . the refuse of Uldyssian's own earlier action to clear the path. The pieces struck at him from all sides, guided by such force that they pressed closer and closer despite the human's tremendous efforts. The jagged ends of branches scraped the air within an inch of his face. Rocks flung past Uldyssian's eyes at a speed far greater than that of the swiftest bird and more than enough to crack a skull. He felt the ground below shake up and down, as if something beneath sought to reach up and take him . . .

He had demanded that the demonic essence pay heed only to him and now Uldyssian had been granted that demand. All he had to do now was survive . . . if possible.

But if he did not, then surely it would pursue Serenthia again. Uldyssian had to assume that, in its madness and outrage, the demon had somehow left some part of itself behind after it should have died. That part now evidently wanted Serenthia to replace its lost mate.

He had to end this. If Lucion, a powerful demon, had been unable to stop him, then surely Uldyssian could defeat this undead presence.

Again, he concentrated on the ruins. They seemed a distinct link to the demon. Forcing one foot forward after the other, Uldyssian tried not to notice how much closer the attacking fragments got despite his efforts . . . not even when one branch caught him over the brow, leaving a minute but telling trail of blood that he had to blink away while never losing sight of his own goal.

The ancient building shook anew, this time harder than ever. A portion of the right wall cracked off, sending what little remained of the roof into the trees. One of the windows lost all definition as portions of the border crumbled.

The voice shrieked in Uldyssian's head. Something grasped his ankle, jarring Uldyssian's attention despite his best efforts.

A fleshless hand—human-looking save for the fact that it had four digits and long, long nails—tore at his skin. Only then did it flash through Uldyssian's mind that the male figure in the visions had had hands just so. A demon's hands.

A second hand thrust out of the soil, this one still covered by a bit of ragged skin as pale as the bone. Uldyssian pulled away from the first, only to fall backward over some unseen obstacle.

Out of the ground burst a misshapen thing, the demon who was and was not dead. His bones were not bones as humans knew them, for they were segmented differently and what should have been the rib cage was solid. It amazed Uldyssian that this demon had bones at all—the hideous beast Gulag apparently having none—but his ilk seemed to come in a monstrous variety with no two alike.

The head tilted at one angle and the jaw hung slack. There was nothing handsome about the creature anymore, the carrion eaters—a centipede made a hasty retreat into an eye socket—still working after so long.

Then, to Uldyssian's greater surprise, Mendeln—whom he had assumed had wisely stayed with the rest—stepped past him. There was an unsettling aura about his brother.

Mendeln stood before the macabre creature, arms spread wide. He shouted something in a language that Uldyssian did not understand . . . but suddenly realized was close in tone to what the demon had been spouting.

The ghoulish figure hesitated. Although the eyes were gone, he gave every indication of staring at Mendeln in something approaching surprise.

But if the demon radiated surprise, so, too, did Mendeln, who clearly expected something more to happen. He shouted out another word, one that, despite being unknown to Uldyssian, sent chills down the older brother's spine.

This had more of an effect, but still clearly not quite what Mendeln had hoped for. The macabre figure teetered like a drunken fighter, then righted himself. The sense of menace grew, but also one of uncertainty, as if the demon was not quite sure what to do, either.

"He still lives . . ." murmured Mendeln more in fascination than anything. "No . . . he clings between life and death fueled by a desire for revenge . . . and a loss so great he still cannot accept it . . ."

Uldyssian did not care for the reason, only that they had to stop the fiend. Steeling himself, he glanced at the ruined structure yet again.

The walls cracked apart. The building let out a groan . . . and finally crumbled much as the temple in Toraja had.

But even then, the demon did not fall.

Uldyssian rose, but before he could prepare anything more, Mendeln put out a hand to stop him.

"Wait! See!"

Suddenly ignoring the intruders, the skeletal figure slowly turned toward the rubble. He raised his monstrous face skyward and let out a roar that Uldyssian recognized as deep anguish.

A small object shot up from near Uldyssian and Mendeln. It flew directly into one of the demon's outstretched hands.

It was the shattered female face.

The demon held the sculpture up and the empty hand reached to caress the piece . . . and then, to the astonishment of the brothers, both simply faded away.

Expecting some trick, Uldyssian leapt forward. Yet he could now barely sense the demon's presence. It was as if the creature had retreated beyond the mortal plane.

"He has gone back to that place between places," Mendeln muttered. "It is over."

"But why did it *begin*? What stirred that thing to life—or whatever you'd call that?"

His brother shrugged. "As I said. Vengeance . . . and loss."

Uldyssian recalled the visions that he had had about the otherworldly couple, both so distinctively different from one another. A demon and . . . and an *angel,* perhaps?

But that was ridiculous. Uldyssian could not imagine a more unlikely scenario. He dismissed the notion, more concerned with another aspect of the situation. "Serenthia. She's safe now, right?"

"It would seem so. You protected her well, brother."

That reminded Uldyssian of something else. "Yes, and you protected me—"

"But not so well."

Waving that aside, Uldyssian growled, "You know what I mean, Mendeln! I've been patient, but something's touched you that has nothing to do with the gifts I've shown the rest! You've changed! Sometimes, I'm not even certain to whom I'm talking!"

The younger brother bowed his head. "Neither am I," he whispered. "Neither am I."

"We've got to have this out between us," Uldyssian persisted. "I've got to know what's happening to you . . . and how it might affect those with us. There are too many things at stake!"

"Yes . . . I agree." Mendeln glanced back at the crushed building. "But not here. Not now. Tonight. When all others sleep."

"Mendeln—"

Uldyssian's brother raised his hands palm forward. Almost pleading, he added, "It *must* be in the night . . . and only the two of us."

Mendeln clamped his mouth shut. Uldyssian knew that he would get no more out of him. Still, "Tonight, then. Tonight and no later. I mean that, Mendeln."

The other nodded, then turned and walked back. Uldyssian stood for a moment, watching Mendeln's retreating form. Then, without effort, someone else invaded his thoughts.

Serenthia . . .

And with her gently smiling face burning into his mind, Uldyssian forgot about demon spirits and mysterious brothers. All that mattered was returning to the others and making certain that she was all right.

After that? Uldyssian could only pray that Achilios—wherever he was—would forgive his friend's weakness.

SEVEN

As the sun settled over the horizon, the edyrem began to look for a place to camp. Mendeln, who had steered clear of his brother after the ruins, studied his many companions with an unusual anxiety. He lagged behind as they pushed toward the chosen location—a relatively clear area about ten minutes' walk to the river—then paused by a trunk as if taking a breath.

They had found the crossing of which Serenthia had earlier claimed to have heard about from someone else. A convenient crossing it had been, wide enough to enable several people to simultaneously move to the other side. By the time he and Uldyssian had reached the others, more than a third had already made it, Serenthia apparently leading the way.

She had been most delighted to see Uldyssian, delighted enough to run into his arms. If not for Mendeln's presence, he suspected that the embrace might have led to something more right there. The battle against the creature in the ruins had obviously changed Uldyssian's mind about her and it seemed Serenthia had no more qualms concerning the late, lamented Achilios.

And that now bothered Mendeln more than the danger that they had this day faced.

The last vestiges of daylight had given way to the torches and—more and more—glow lights many of the fledgling edyrem were now able to cast. Some of those Mendeln watched looked much too confident with their minor success; a glow light would scarcely fend off Peace Warders, morlu, or demons.

At last his opportunity came. All eyes were focused on other matters and Uldyssian could only see Serenthia. Mendeln slowly backed into the jungle.

He went headed not toward the river, but rather back along their trail. Despite his heightening anxiety, Mendeln's breathing remained calm. It was as if he were two men in one body, the newcomer adapting to whatever change around him as necessary.

Mendeln counted each step. Twenty. Fifty. A hundred . . .

At precisely that many, the figure he had been expecting to meet appeared from around a tree as if by magic . . . which very likely was the case.

"Always . . . timely . . . Mendeln . . ." The voice, so familiar, carried with it now a raspiness, as if the other constantly needed to clear something from his throat.

Mendeln suspected that what needed to be cleared out was *dirt*.

"I promised I would meet you at the appointed time . . . Achilios."

A short, harsh chuckle escaped the half-seen figure. The archer took a step closer.

Mendeln did not gasp, having done enough of that the first time he had been confronted by the dead man. After all, before him stood his good friend, even if that friend had a gaping hole in his throat, the edges of which were lined with congealed blood and more dirt. Uldyssian's brother did not bother to wonder how the blond hunter could even speak, considering that awful gap. Achilios existed now because of some force beyond mortal ken, a force surely powerful enough to give voice to the cold corpse it had animated.

But that description seemed cruel to Achilios, Mendeln suddenly decided. Achilios was no shambling ghoul nor a fiend like the morlu. The spark that was the archer did indeed still make house in his remains; there was no doubting that. True, the flesh was as pale as the whites of Achilios's eyes—which were *completely* white now—and there always seemed to be bits of fresh ground spilled over him, but it was still the man the sons of Diomedes had always known. Achilios even showed embarrassment over his condition; even now he tried to wipe his hand clean so that he could clasp Mendeln's.

Rather than let the archer continue a useless task, the black-clad figure reached out and seized the grimy hand. He shook it as he would have if both were still back home and nothing had changed for either. Not even death.

The shadow of a smile escaped Achilios. Even in his present state, he was a handsome man, lean like the prey he had so successfully hunted . . . until Lucion. Mendeln had always envied the blond hunter his looks, although the latter had never been vain about them. It had been the perversity of fate that he, who could have had so many women, had desired the only one who had not wanted him . . . until just before his slaughter. "Braver than . . . you used to . . . be . . ."

"You are my friend."

"I am as dead as these tree dwellers I caught." Achilios reached behind him and brought forth a brace of tailed beasts the size of cats and obviously related to them. He set his catch by Mendeln.

The scene both amused and saddened Uldyssian's brother. Even in the state that he was, Achilios could not keep from his calling. Perhaps, Uldyssian's brother thought, it was because it allowed him to play at his former life, to pretend that terrible events had never happened.

"And how may I explain this bounty when I return?" Mendeln gently joked. "All know my prowess with hunting. I am fortunate if I can catch a mushroom, as quick and cunning as they are."

Achilios grimaced. "I . . . thought of . . . that . . . but . . . I hunted, anyway . . ."

Again, he attempted to brush himself clean. Yet, although even in the dark Mendeln could see the dirt fly from the archer's pants, boots, and shirt . . . it almost immediately seemed to be replaced by more simply forming from nothing on Achilios's very body.

"I have spoken with Uldyssian," Mendeln finally interjected, as much to put an end to Achilios's perpetually futile effort as it was to bring the conversation around to the matter at hand. Not the original conversation that they had planned, but the one he now felt superceded all others. "and I have come to a decision. It is time he was told of your presence. I will bring him out here to—"

"No."

Mendeln had expected argument and while he respected his friend's awful position, this was something that could not be avoided. "Uldyssian is your friend, just as I am. He will see beyond what has happened to you—"

The archer's expression tightened, the white eyes narrowing dangerously. "No . . . Mendeln . . . it can't . . . be that way . . . don't say . . . any more . . ."

There was that in Achilios's tone that suddenly made the hair on the back of Mendeln's neck rise. Nevertheless, he grew defiant. "I will not keep this any longer from him—or Serenthia, for that matter! At the very least—"

"At the very least," intoned another voice behind him. "Doing that might cause great catastrophe . . ."

Mendeln spun around. He knew that voice. It had haunted him long enough, after all . . .

The tall figure was clad in a dark, cowled cloak that emphasized a face nearly as pale as Achilios's. At a glance, he otherwise looked like any man . . . save that his features were, despite their angular structure, far too perfect.

"Who *are* you?" Uldyssian's brother demanded. "I know you, but not your name!"

The newcomer nodded. "Yes, we have come to know each other quite well, son of Diomedes . . . and I thus apologize for what I must do. Unfortunately, you leave me no choice."

"What are you blathering about?" Mendeln backed away

from the figure, only to collide with Achilios. Grimy fingers seized his arms, holding him in a literal death grip. "I say again! Who are you? Who?"

"A stubborn fool, that is what I am," returned the other with a grimace. He raised a hand toward Mendeln.

In it was a dagger . . . a dagger that, to Mendeln's eye, seemed not to have been forged from metal, but rather something akin to ivory.

Bone?

His tormentor uttered three short words and although Mendeln did not understand them, he still knew the language, of course. It now constantly flowed through his head.

The dagger flared bright, illuminating the cowled face yet more. It was as Mendeln always dreamed it, yet seeing it now, he saw just how *ancient* it was despite a general appearance little older looking than his own.

"As for a name, once I was called else by my mother, but now I am known as . . . *Rathma.*" He gave Mendeln an apologetic nod. "And now, we must be going."

"Going? Where—"

But before Uldyssian's sibling could finish, both he and the being called Rathma vanished.

Only Achilios remained, just as the archer had known would happen. He stared at his empty hands, empty of the man he had gripped, but not of the infernal dirt.

"Sorry . . . Mendeln . . ." he finally murmured to the empty jungle. With some reluctance, he took up his catch again. "It had . . . to be . . . done . . ."

Suddenly, a sound in the distance made him look toward the camp. Moving in utter silence, Achilios vanished into the dark. He could not let anyone see him, especially Uldyssian, whom he suspected was the approaching figure.

And even more than his old friend, he dared not let *her* know he was near . . .

Uldyssian stopped suddenly, aware that something was wrong. He had come in search of his brother, who had promised answers, and had been directed by one of his followers in this direction. Uldyssian had immediately sensed Mendeln's nearness . . . and then the next moment had *not*.

At first, he wondered whether this was some trick of his sibling, some new ability. Uldyssian had no idea what sort of powers Mendeln had nor their cause. He recalled how Lucion had tried to make Mendeln seem like a demon himself or at least someone corrupted by one. Those memories haunted Uldyssian, for despite knowing better, he wondered whether there had been some truth to them after all.

Resuming his trek, Uldyssian finally located just where he had last sensed his brother. However, there was no trace that he could detect of Mendeln's abrupt departure and that made Uldyssian worry even more. Mendeln was not the sort to play games, especially not of this type.

Unable to find his sibling through his abilities, Uldyssian resorted to a more basic approach. He called out Mendeln's name, first as a whisper, then more pronounced when the initial attempt failed to garner results.

But still Mendeln did not appear.

Recalling the dangers of the jungle—both natural and otherwise—Uldyssian's anxiousness grew. Yet, he noticed no hint of anything out of the ordinary.

Bending down, Uldyssian ran his fingers across the soft earth. At the same time, he finally summoned a sphere of soft blue light. Under its illumination, Uldyssian looked for any prints.

He found two that were certainly not his own. They seemed paused just a yard to his left. The stance seemed that of one person waiting for another . . . but then why was it facing *away* from the camp? Surely, Mendeln would have faced the other direction instead.

Then, another area just to the side of the first caught his eye. Only now did Uldyssian notice that the ground had been turned up as if someone had moved about much in a very short space. He could not tell with any certainty which way the feet had faced here, but the disturbance of the soil made him suspect that here was where something had gone amiss.

Here was where Mendeln had suddenly vanished from his brother's supposedly superior senses.

Standing again, Uldyssian took a step deeper—

"Here you are!"

He glanced over his shoulder as Serenthia emerged from the jungle behind. With the light away from his face, she could not possibly see the brief look of consternation that he quickly buried. Mendeln had just disappeared; the last thing that Uldyssian wanted was to have the other person dearest to him in the vicinity. Who was to say that the same danger did not remain, waiting the chance to steal her now, too?

"Serenthia . . . what are you doing out here?"

"Looking for you, naturally." She took hold of his arm, the pressure of her fingers sending his blood racing. "And I'm going to ask you the same question . . . this is no place to be alone."

"I thought I heard something," Uldyssian responded lamely. "I was wrong, I guess."

She leaned close to him, staring into the wild. "You were afraid it was that—that demon—from across the river, weren't you?"

He knew that he should not lie, but nonetheless, he answered, "Yes. I thought that."

At first, that seemed to satisfy her, but then the merchant's daughter suddenly asked, "Uldyssian, have you seen Mendeln?"

"Mendeln?"

"When I went looking for you, I also asked about him. I assumed that the two of you might be together." Her grip tightened as she continued surveying their dark surroundings. "I thought . . . I thought I sensed him here . . . but I must've been wrong."

Uldyssian smothered a curse. Of course, of all the

others, Serenthia had come the closest to matching his abilities. Why would she not then be able to do as he? But the fact that she had gained that gift meant that it was harder—no, *impossible,* Uldyssian decided—to keep her from the truth.

He put his other hand on hers. "Serenthia . . . I did come out here looking for Mendeln. We were supposed to meet. He wanted to tell me about . . . about what he's been having to deal with. The changes *he's* been going through . . ."

She did not press him on those details, more concerned with the most immediate one. "Then, where *is* he?"

"I don't know."

Her fingers squeezed his arm with astonishing strength. Serenthia quickly looked left and right, as if Mendeln would suddenly appear. "But he has to be nearby! I was *right* when I thought I sensed him! You did, too, didn't you?"

"I did . . . and then he simply wasn't . . . there." Stating that now, so bluntly, shook Uldyssian to his core. His brother—his only *surviving* family—was nowhere to be found.

Her voice firm, the dark-haired woman declared, "We'll search the entire area! He can't be far! He knows he can protect himself, too! We'll find him, Uldyssian . . ." She touched his cheek. "I promise that we'll find him . . ."

But although the two of them spent the next several minutes utilizing their abilities as best as Uldyssian knew that they could, they found not the slightest trace. By this time, other voices began rising from the direction of the camp, foremost among them Romus's.

"Master Uldyssian! Master Uldyssian!" The onetime brigand—a low, silver light drifting before him—stumbled into their presence. The bald Parthan exhaled in tremendous relief. "Praise be! We'd feared the worst, we did! Jorda noticed you absent and when no one could find you—" He suddenly stopped short as he drank in the nearness of the two.

Despite the Parthan's conclusion being not entirely amiss, Uldyssian did not want such an image to overshadow his search. "We're looking for my brother," he informed the man. Then, in what was clearly to him evidence of his desperation, Uldyssian actually asked, "Have *you* seen Mendeln?"

"Nay! I can't fathom when last I did, either," Romus replied with a low bow. "Perhaps . . . perhaps he merely walks to enjoy the night, him being the way he is—" The Parthan faltered when Uldyssian gave him a reproving look. Most of the edyrem assigned to Mendeln a host of bizarre and mysterious activities, the vast majority of which were the product of their imaginations.

Unfortunately, the few that were not were enough to disturb most folk, even Uldyssian.

But that had nothing to do with finding his brother. As others igorant of the situation gathered behind Romus, Uldyssian feared that their presence would only further complicate the situation. If something had taken Mendeln—and that thought shook Uldyssian far more than even he could have ever expected—then who was to say that it might not grab others as well. Mendeln was, in truth, stronger than any of the edyrem, yet apparently he had not had a chance . . .

"I want everybody back in the camp," he commanded. "Go! Now!"

"But Master Uldyssian!" protested Tomo, now standing near Romus. "We must not leave you alone out here!" That Uldyssian likely could defend himself better than a thousand of his followers did not seem to occur to the Torajian nor any of the rest, judging by the many heads bobbing in agreement with Tomo.

"Return to the camp . . ."

Romus shook his head, blurting, "What of your brother, Master Uldyssian? If he is lost as you fear—"

Now the newcomers knew why their leader was out in the jungle during the night. No matter how great their uneasiness around Mendeln, they knew his importance to Uldyssian.

"They'll not go now," murmured Serenthia. "The only way to get them to return to the camp is to do so ourselves . . ."

"I can't! Mendeln needs me!"

She put a soothing hand on him. "I know that, Uldyssian. I know that better than anyone else! But think . . . can you really help him right now, with everyone distracting you?"

Serenthia had the truth of it; all that his legions of followers did right now was to keep him from concentrating.

"We're all heading back," Uldyssian suddenly ordered. "Make sure that everyone is accounted for, Romus."

The Parthan nodded, although obviously still perplexed. "But, your brother, Master Uldyssian—"

"Will be found, Romus." Uldyssian put an end to any more questions by striding past his lead acolyte, Serenthia accompanying him on his arm.

But although he took up a stalwart aspect in front of the others, Uldyssian dearly wanted to turn around and rush through the jungle calling Mendeln's name until he found him. He could not imagine what might have happened. He had sensed nothing amiss. Surely . . . surely Mendeln was merely lost, somehow, and would turn up before long.

But what if he did not?

"Calm yourself," Serenthia whispered reassuringly. She leaned her head close to his. "When all have settled down, we can work together to find Mendeln."

"Work together?"

"Combine our powers together in a manner we haven't tried yet . . . I think it possible . . ."

He took hope from her suggestion. They might be able to amplify the effect of their search. Surely then, they would locate Mendeln.

But would whatever she had in mind work?

"We can only try, Uldyssian," she murmured, as if reading his thoughts. "You and Mendeln worked together to help me, didn't you?"

He nodded, glad that she did not know how close the demonic presence had actually come to reaching out to her.

Once they returned to the encampment, it was all Uldyssian could do to wait for the rest to finally go to sleep. The sentries he did not concern himself about; they would not see what he and Serenthia attempted. The two had moved off to a secluded side of the camp. They would still be vaguely noted by those on duty, but not their actual activities. He wanted no one interfering, not even if only to volunteer their help.

Serenthia sat across from him. Both had their legs folded, and as touch had always worked when Uldyssian had introduced new people to the gifts within them, they held hands. Uldyssian felt some guilt at how much he enjoyed such closeness to her. He had not felt this way about anyone since . . . since *Lilith*.

Smiling at him, Serenthia said, "I've no idea how to start . . . except maybe I could reach into you the way you did me and the others the first time."

"Try that." He would have been willing to do it himself, but so far Serenthia had made perfect sense with her suggestions. Considering his state of mind, Uldyssian was more than happy to let her take the lead throughout this.

Serenthia shut her eyes. Uldyssian did the same. He felt her briefly squeeze his hands and returned the action.

Suddenly . . . it felt as if he were two people in one.

The swiftness with which the merchant's daughter successfully touched his mind—and his soul—startled him. There was a momentary hesitation, then Uldyssian sensed her invite him to do as she had. His thoughts, his emotions, reached out to hers. For a breath or two, it was as if a pair of animals sized up one another. Then, growing more confident, Uldyssian pushed forward.

He and Serenthia melded together. It was not a perfect blending of their selves, for Uldyssian kept up certain barriers—especially those concerning his feelings for the woman before him—and sensed that Serenthia likewise barred some access to her inner thoughts. Yet, they were still linked strongly enough to now attempt what she had proposed.

Let me . . . came what, to his imagination, sounded like her voice. *Let me try to guide us . . .*

No sooner had Uldyssian given his silent agreement, than suddenly it was as if his eyes were open again. Yet, now he soared through the surrounding jungle . . . and in *several* directions simultaneously. Moreover, it was as if day had arrived, only day lit by a golden sun. Everything was a glorious yellow . . .

And with him . . . very much part of him as he was of her . . . raced Serenthia. Their speed was greater than that of the swiftest bird. As one, they coursed mile upon mile around the region, not only backtracking the previous day's trek, but moving well beyond what they would cover tomorrow. Uldyssian noted important points along the journey ahead that he hoped to recall well enough to pass on to his followers, while at the same time seeing how if the edyrem had made certain changes, they could have covered more distance earlier.

He saw creatures of the forest, night dwellers now uncovered by the golden illumination. Yet, they neither sensed his approach nor even knew that they were no longer cloaked. Some he had never seen before, and their exotic nature fascinated the son of Diomedes despite the present circumstances.

But even after what was the most meticulous hunt imaginable . . . Uldyssian discovered no trace of Mendeln.

Finally, despite the headiness of their success, he could stand it no more. Uldyssian felt Serenthia's surprise when he began to withdraw to the camp. The scenery flashed by and although Uldyssian continued to watch and study, yet again he discovered no clue.

And then . . . the former farmer once more sat across from

his companion. Uldyssian did not know when he had opened his eyes, but both he and Serenthia sat staring at one another as if having done so for hours. Very reluctantly, he disengaged one hand in order to rub his brow. She did the same.

"I'm sorry," Serenthia finally said. "I thought we'd find Mendeln for certain."

"So did I." However, despite that terrible failure, Uldyssian was not altogether sad. It was not only because he and Serenthia had discovered a new, fascinating ability . . . but also because they had been drawn together as no two people surely ever had. One glance at her face was enough to tell him that she felt much the same.

Uldyssian immediately shook his head, angry at himself for becoming distracted by such things when his brother was in terrible danger. The attempt, however successful in itself, had failed. That was *all* that mattered.

Serenthia leaned forward. "Uldyssian—"

He wanted to stay with her, but knew that to do so would keep his mind from fully focusing on Mendeln. With an abruptness that made Serenthia gasp, Uldyssian jumped to his feet and left.

He regretted the action almost immediately, but did not even consider turning back. Uldyssian dared not let himself become distracted again. Only Mendeln mattered . . . providing it was not *already* too late.

That thought made him shiver anew. Mendeln *gone*. First Achilios, now this.

Uldyssian looked up to the dark, shrouded sky, raising a fist at the same time. He wanted to shout, but aware how that would stir up the others anew, forced his voice down to a virulent hiss.

"Damn you, Lilith! Damn you for beginning all this!"

The jungle remained silent, but somehow Uldyssian was certain that she heard his bitter oath . . . heard it and laughed merrily.

"Don't . . . give up . . . hope . . ."

The voice was barely a whisper, yet it pierced the fog in his brain. Uldyssian turned about, seeking the speaker . . . and finding no one.

Brow furrowed, he stared at the emptiness for several seconds, then grimaced. Now, on top of matters, he was imagining voices . . . or rather, one voice in particular.

Achilios's.

"Damn you, Lilith . . ." Uldyssian repeated, seeing in his mind both his brother and the dead archer. "If Mendeln's gone, too . . ."

But he had no threat against her in which, at the moment, even *he* believed.

EIGHT

They remained in the area the next day . . . and the next after that. Uldyssian did not sleep once, fearing that any respite would lessen his chances of finding Mendeln. The longer his brother remained missing, the longer the odds that Mendeln was still alive.

Saron and Romus, accompanied by Tomo and a small mix of other Parthans and Torajians, finally dared approach him late on the succeeding day. They found Uldyssian where he often was, standing at the edge of the camp with eyes shut and hands curled into fists. Around him, noticeable only to the eyes of edyrem, glowed a silver aura.

The aura vanished before either of the first two could summon the courage to speak. Uldyssian turned to face the group.

"Tomorrow . . ." he muttered. "If nothing by then . . . I promise it'll be tomorrow."

Saron, thin and wiry, bowed low. "Master Uldyssian, it is not that we wish to abandon your brother . . . if Tomo, who is like a brother to me, were missing, I would search just as you do, but—"

"But searching the same ground over and over and over is futile. I understand, Saron. I can't risk everyone else by forcing them to wait here." He looked among those who had come, both men and women. These were many of his most promising, with enough control now to be a threat to the majority of human foes. Even perhaps a morlu or a lesser demon. Yet, they were lost without him.

"Tomorrow," he repeated, starting to turn back to the jungle. "Thank you for understanding."

The Parthans nodded while most of Saron's people bowed. As they trudged off, Uldyssian refocused his efforts. There *had* to be somewhere or something that he had missed. Some clue that whatever had taken Mendeln had left behind.

But continually he came up empty-handed. Finally, as the sun set, Uldyssian retired to eat. He did not even notice of what his meal consisted, his attention entirely on seeking some new course of action.

Belatedly, Uldyssian noticed that Serenthia sat across from him. Since his wordless departure from her, they had stood apart. He knew that she would have liked to have been with him, even comforted him, and the fact that he felt the same ripped at his heart. Yet, for more than one reason, the son of Diomedes refused to give in to such things.

He went back to searching as soon as his food was gone. Taking his cue from the effort he and Serenthia had put in together, Uldyssian let his mind reach out far beyond what his eyes could see. Alone, he could not survey the jungle in quite so dramatic a fashion as the two of them had, but still Uldyssian felt certain that he covered the areas that he studied as thoroughly as possible.

But *still* he did not find even so much as a hint of what had happened.

In the end, there remained only one other hope, something that he had not wanted to attempt for it endangered not only him. However, it was the single possibility that Uldyssian thought at all yet likely.

And so, stretching himself to his limits, he reached out to the distant ruins . . . and that which lurked among them.

The effort proved not quite the strain Uldyssian had believed it would be. He could only assume that perhaps his efforts with Serenthia had further unfettered the potential of his abilities. Uldyssian marveled at this, even as his thoughts propelled him within range of the demonic presence's ancient abode.

But once there, Uldyssian immediately noticed the lack of any sign of Mendeln. More curious, he also noticed how faint the *specter's* trace was, so much so that at first he could not even sense it. If the presence was the source of his brother's disappearance, surely Mendeln could have easily fought back against such paltry power.

Nonetheless, Uldyssian continued to probe the ruins. As he did, he finally sensed the presence stir somewhat . . . but without radiating any of the violent emotion from the first encounter. In fact, it was almost as if the demon now wished to *relay* something to him.

To enable it to do that, though, would require Uldyssian to let down some of his guard. He studied his adversary as best he could, sensing only weakness . . . and urgency. There was no hint of threat. At last, desperate to find some clue, however remote, Uldyssian relented.

But as he began to open himself up, someone suddenly shook his physical form. Immediately, the ruins—and their malevolent inhabitant—receded into the dark . . . and Uldyssian found himself once more poised at the edge of the camp.

Serenthia stood beside him, her eyes wide with fear. "Uldyssian! Are you mad? I nearly didn't break the link between you in time!"

"I finally had some hope!" he snapped back, registering what she had done. "A clue to Mendeln—"

"Not from *that* evil thing! Think! Why would it tell you anything to help you? *Why?*"

He started to reply, then hesitated. Uldyssian had no good explanation and the more he thought about it, the more he knew that Serenthia's point had much merit. Why *would* the creature do anything to assist in the hunt? In his desperation, it was very likely that all Uldyssian had been doing was giving the demonic presence a chance for vengeance against him.

And, after that, surely it would have once more tried for Serenthia . . .

Running his fingers through his hair, he muttered, "You're right. Damn it, you're right, Serenthia . . ."

"I'm sorry. Really I am." She looked deep into his eyes. "You've done everything for Mendeln that you could . . . that anyone could. What more is there?"

Again, Uldyssian had no good answer.

"You're tired," the merchant's daughter continued. "You need rest."

He nodded. Suddenly, it was all Uldyssian could do just to stand. Even he had to admit that nothing good would come of attempting any more searches today.

"I promised the others that we'd leave tomorrow," he informed her. "Tell them that we'll do so at first light."

"I should stay with you—"

"No. Please tell them, Serenthia." With that, Uldyssian purposely retreated to a spot near the closest of the fires and immediately laid down. He eyed the flames, noticing belatedly that Serenthia still watched him. Finally, her expression masked, she walked away to do as he had requested.

Uldyssian shut his eyes. Even though he was so very tired and had agreed to get rest, he knew that he would not sleep. How could he? His brother was very likely dead. Uldyssian already knew that he would spend the entire night going over every search for the hundredth time, seeking some error he had made. Over and over he would analyze *everything* that he had done—

A soft hand on Uldyssian's shoulder gently shook him awake. He stiffened and a grin started to cross his face, for he had just been dreaming that Mendeln had returned unharmed. However, glancing up, his smile faltered, for he saw that it was Serenthia awakening him . . . and that above her, light had begun filtering through the foliage.

"I had them let you sleep as long as possible," she quietly told him. "The others are nearly ready to depart."

An intense feeling of guilt washed over him, as if he had somehow betrayed his brother by actually sleeping. "You should've woken me much sooner!" Uldyssian blurted, his anger unreasonable even to himself. After all, the woman leaning over him was almost as concerned about Mendeln as he was. "I need to do one more search! I think that this time I can find—"

His companion frowned sadly. "If I thought you had any chance at all, Uldyssian, I'd be there at your side. You know that. I can see it in your face, though. You don't have any new idea, do you? You just want to search and search, isn't that right? Search until you find him . . ."

"Yes . . . no . . . but . . ."

"You've done all you could for Mendeln . . . just as you did for Achilios. We *have* to move on, even if I don't want to any more than you. For the sake of all the rest . . . and you, too . . . there's no other choice. Mendeln would be the first one to tell you that. You know he would."

There was nothing more he could say. Uldyssian rose, took one look at the jungle, and then summoned Tomo to him.

"Can we make it to Hashir in four more days?"

"If we walk long and hard, Master Uldyssian. I would prefer to say five, if you please."

"We make it in four."

Tomo bowed. "Yes, Master Uldyssian."

"We make it in four and we lose no one else along the way. I want that understood." The son of Diomedes fought to keep his tone even. "No one else."

"Yes, Master Uldyssian."

Uldyssian looked at Serenthia. She gave him a determined smile and repeated his oath. "No one else."

With her at his side and Tomo in his wake, he marched to the head of the already waiting throng. Tomo rushed to Romus and Saron, whispering animatedly to the pair. What Uldyssian had demanded would quickly spread to the rest, just as he wanted.

Once in the lead, Uldyssian nodded back at his followers, then continued on. Silently, the edyrem flowed after.

They made great distance that day, driven for the most part by Uldyssian's determination to now get as far away as he could from where his brother had vanished. By the end of the trek, even he felt every muscle scream. Guilt at how some of the others, especially the women and children, had probably suffered made him promise to the weary group that the next day would go much easier.

But it did not. Barely had they begun their trek when a storm swept across the jungle, a violent storm that forced Uldyssian to finally call a halt.

"It looks to last the whole day!" shouted Romus, shielding his eyes from debris torn up by the wind. The rain coursed down like a thousand battering rams, forcing people to take what shelter they could. Those with a better sense of their abilities created invisible barriers above themselves and others, but the longer and harder the rain fell, the more those weakened or dissipated entirely.

"Keep everyone together!" Uldyssian cursed the storm, certain somehow that it was working in league with Lilith and the Triune.

Serenthia struggled to hold on to his arm. "Something must be done about it! *You* must do something about it!"

Her words brought back undesired recollections. Lilith—as Lylia—had at one time suggested much the same thing. Then, it had concerned the storm clouds over Seram and its surrounding region. That storm had been dispersed, but he had later discovered that it had been more due to the demoness's work than his own.

"No . . ." Uldyssian growled, not wishing to relive that time in any way. "No . . . I can't . . ."

A nearby tree creaked ominously. Leaves and jagged branches flew through the air. A woman screamed as a terrible gust tossed her back into her companions. Children cried. Despite all that they had been given, despite all that they had learned, even the most talented of the edyrem began to give in to their fears and exhaustion.

Uldyssian knew that he *should* attempt something, even if only to remind the others of what they were capable. The band was not long from Hashir. They had to be ready to face what might be a more terrible foe despite the temple's smaller size, for surely Hashir would be forewarned.

Yet, his will was weak, worn as it still was by Mendeln's loss. He shook his head, fighting with himself—

Without warning, Serenthia let go of him. Uldyssian grabbed for her but missed. To his surprise, she stepped into the most open area around them, where the storm threatened worst. Although already drenched to the skin, Cyrus's daughter stood proud and tall. She held high the spear, brandishing it at the sinister black clouds.

"Away with you!" Serenthia shouted at the top of her lungs at the dark sky. "Away!"

Seeing her there, doing futilely what he might actually be able to accomplish, filled Uldyssian with incredible remorse. Mendeln would not have wanted him acting this way because of him. If there was any hope that Uldyssian could stop this raging tempest, then it behooved him at the very least to make the attempt—

But that thought died as something incredible unfolded. Like some warrior goddess, Serenthia continued to not only defy the elements, but demanded that they bow to her. She waved the spear as if ready to toss it into the heart of the storm . . .

And then . . . and then the rain slowed, finally *ceasing* altogether. The wind died down to a mere whisper. The black clouds faded to gray and then began to disperse.

The others—Uldyssian included—stood awestruck by this miracle. An aura surrounded Serenthia, a brilliant golden aura. Yet, she stood as if unnoticing of this or any of the other phenomena. Instead, she continued to demand obedience from the sky . . . and received it.

The last of the clouds melted away. A hush settled over

the dense jungle, not even the multitude of insects usually present letting out so much as a single sound.

Arms dropping to her sides, Serenthia let out a gasp. Her body shook and the spear dropped from her grip. At the same time, the aura disappeared.

Slowly, very slowly, Serenthia looked over her shoulder at Uldyssian. Her face stone white, her breathing rapid, she managed to blurt, "I . . . did it . . . didn't I?"

He nodded, feeling both shame and exhilaration. Serenthia had done what he *should* have instinctively chosen to do. In the process, she had revealed a level of power that only he had so far exhibited. She should not have had to put herself through so much . . . but the fact that she had just proven what Uldyssian had always preached finally stirred him to life.

"Yes . . . you did it," he said proudly and so loud that all those around them could hear. "You did what *any* of us are capable of!" He faced the edyrem. "And I, who claim so much, offer my deepest apologies that I did nothing—*nothing*—at all . . ."

But Serenthia was the first of many to protest his failure. No one said why they bothered to defend him, but to Uldyssian it obviously had to do with Mendeln. He felt grateful for the care and support and swore that he would not let himself fall again, if only for *their* sake.

Still, he could not feel but thrilled by Serenthia's triumph and advancement. There had always been a hint of disbelief among his followers whenever Uldyssian had insisted that he was no more mighty than any of them. Now, even the least among the Parthans and Torajians knew that they could achieve so much more. Even Serenthia, for all that she had done this day, had not yet reached his level.

"The storm is gone!" Uldyssian shouted. "And, in honor of that, it'll be you, Serenthia, who gives command for the rest of us to continue the march! You!"

A wide smile spread across her still wet countenance.

Serenthia plucked the spear from the ground, then pointed in the direction of their goal.

"Onward to Hashir!" she called with gusto.

A cheer erupted from the others. Serenthia looked Uldyssian's way once more. He nodded, indicating with his chin that she should begin the trek. If anything, her smile grew wider yet. Shoulders proud, she started walking.

After giving her a few paces, Uldyssian followed. Romus and the other edyrem joined after. The mood of the makeshift army rose to new levels. Uldyssian sensed their confidence; here was now the force that had taken Toraja's temple and would do the same to Hashir. Here was the beginning of something that the Triune would now truly fear. Here was something, he started to believe, that even *Lilith* would be unprepared to face.

And perhaps . . . perhaps . . . here was something that somehow might help him yet find Mendeln . . .

Arihan had not lived half as long as his late counterpart, Malic—who himself had supposedly had not one, but more than *two* lifetimes granted him by the master—but he looked almost old enough to have been the dead high priest's father. Arihan, who had once been a thief, a liar, a cutpurse, and a murderer—and now used those skills more often as high priest of Dialon—did not believe in the vanities that Malic, partly Ascenian by birth, had so often displayed. Malic had been a peacock, wearing not only fine clothes but maintaining a face and form not truly his for many, many decades.

Born of low caste in the deep recesses of the capital, the gaunt, thick-bearded Arihan had expected that one day the lead cleric of Mefis would, in his arrogance, overstep himself. That prediction had recently come to pass, but Arihan wisely kept his glee hidden from the others. It was one thing to maneuver for position in the hierarchy, another to be pleased with a failure that affected the Triune even more than it had the fool who had perished because of it.

This Uldyssian ul-Diomed was of significance to the sect's ultimate objectives and Malic's tremendous debacle had ruined any chance of ever seducing the peasant to the cause. Now, a more harsh course of action would need to be taken.

Arihan had been ready to offer his services in pursuing the matter immediately after Malic's demise, but something strange had happened that had caused him to hesitate. The Primus, ever predictable in his perfection, of late acted as if not quite himself. He had grown very reclusive and subject to lengthy, inexplicable absences. More confusing, he gave commands to his followers that seemed just as likely to create havoc among the priests as they did to better enable them to coordinate their efforts.

Yes, there was something amiss . . . but Arihan had no idea how best to approach that difficulty. He certainly was not about to register his concerns with either of his counterparts, especially Malic's novice—but highly ambitious—replacement. If only—

A particularly ugly Peace Warder suddenly stood in the high priest's path. So caught up in his thoughts, Arihan nearly collided with the dolt.

The Peace Warder was obviously mad, for he seemed unconcerned about his transgression. "The Lord Primus wishes to speak with you, High Priest Arihan. Immediately."

"Where is he?" the bearded elder asked, his monotone voice belying his sudden anxiety.

"Awaiting you in his chambers, venerable one."

Arihan gave the man a dismissive nod and strode down the long marble hallway at a pace that indicated confidence but not disrespect. He passed several more Peace Warders standing at attention along the way, the guards as resolute as statues. For some reason, that stirred his concerns more.

The sentries at the doors to the Primus's inner sanctum gave way without any preamble, which made the robed figure feel as if he was already late. The Primus did not like tardiness; Arihan recalled at least one incident when such a sin had left the sinner bereft of his beating heart.

All was darkness as he entered the chambers. The doors slammed shut behind him with a harsh finality. Arihan blinked, trying to accustom his eyes to the black rooms. He knew in which he would find his master, but what was the reason for having no light whatsoever along the path? Generally, there was at least an oil lamp or dim torch.

The priest took a step forward . . . and something about the size of a cat scurried over his sandaled foot.

Arihan let out an uncharacteristic yelp, which only served to add to his tensions. How did it look for the high priest of Dialon—or rather, *Diablo*—to be startled by something so small and unseen? He served the master of terror! Arihan hoped and prayed that something had distracted the Primus's attention at that moment . . .

He could now see just enough to wend his way to the innermost chamber. It occurred to him that perhaps he could have conjured a light, but the Primus wanted darkness for a reason, whatever that might be.

As Arihan reached the doorway to his master's sanctum, it opened by itself. A dim, unearthly illumination greeted him. Arihan glanced down at his narrow hands, which were now the green of decay.

"Enter, enter, High Priest Arihan!" the Primus called, his voice oddly excited.

Doing as commanded, Arihan stepped toward the throne. As he neared, he saw the Primus, a giant, bearded man both younger and older in appearance than him, study the newcomer with a strange fascination. Again, Arihan wondered about the recent changes in the personality of the figure before him. He had always known what to expect . . . but not this time.

As was custom, the priest went down on one knee just before his master's feet. He knew that the Primus was indeed the scion of Lord Mephisto, but always thought of him by his mortal title, not his name.

Never as Lucion.

"Great and powerful Primus, son of the most regal Mephisto, your loyal attendant, Arihan, is here at your request. How may I serve thee?"

A short, erratic chuckle escaped the vicinity of the Primus. Arihan fought not to look up in surprise at this disconcerting sound. He had *never* heard the master laugh so . . . so madly.

Almost as quickly as he thought it, the priest smothered the blasphemy. It was not proper to think ill of the Primus, not proper and not wise for one's health.

"Rise! Rise, High Priest Arihan!" the seated figure commanded almost jovially.

Arihan obeyed. He tried to keep his expression and gaze respectful. Perhaps this was a test. Perhaps his master wanted to see how dedicated and loyal Arihan was.

"I am yours to command, most glorious one."

"Yes . . . yes, you are . . ." The Primus leaned against one of the armrests of the throne. "This—*I* am the Voice of the Triune, am I not?"

"But, of course, most glorious one." Arihan felt his brow begin to furrow in concern and perplexity, but fought the action away. He would keep a face of calm adoration, no matter what peculiarity the Primus next exhibited.

Yes, surely this was some sort of test . . .

The Primus fidgeted. Then, as if aware of how he looked, his aspect grew stern. "High Priest Arihan! Do you have *anything* to say?"

"N-nay, most glorious one! I but await your word on what it is you wish of me!"

"Very good . . . very good . . ." A small, black form—a spider, Arihan realized—crawled up out of the Primus's collar. The leader of the Triune paid no mind to the vermin, even when it began making its way up his neck. "This—I have a plan to bring the mortal to our cause, High Priest Arihan. A masterful plan! But it must be implemented quickly, for it involves our brothers in Hashir."

"Hashir?" repeated the priest, trying in vain to keep his gaze from shifting to the arachnid. It now crawled on the Primus's jaw, still apparently undetected.

"Hashir . . . yes, Hashir will be the perfect place to turn this all around . . ."

Arihan bowed to the Primus's wisdom. If he had a plan, then surely it would come to wondrous fruition.

The spider now crawled near the ear, two legs even probing within. Try as he might, the high priest of Dialon could not help but stare at it.

Spiders . . . there was something about spiders that Arihan had once known. What was it—?

With astonishing reflexes, the figure on the throne suddenly snatched the arachnid up. The Primus clenched his hand, crushing the creature within.

"There is something wrong, my Arihan?"

It was the first time since the gaunt man had entered that his master had not used his title. Although unsettled, Arihan managed to shake his head.

"So good . . . so good . . ." The hand remained clenched. The Primus smiled wide . . . something he had never done before. "You are to be my agent! This is what you will do that will bring the human Uldyssian to our side . . . whether he wishes to come or not."

Arihan bowed his head and listened as the Primus outlined his intentions. He listened and all thought of the master's recent quirks were quickly buried deep in his mind. After all, Arihan lived to serve the Primus; in the end, that was all that mattered.

That . . . and the knowledge that even if there might now be a hint of madness in the son of Mephisto, the Primus could still *crush* Arihan as simply as he had the spider.

NINE

Darkness surrounded Mendeln, darkness that felt as if it went on forever. Uldyssian's brother suspected that if he ran and ran as hard as he could for as long as possible, he would find no change in things. It would still be dark and empty. A part of him was unnerved by that . . . but another part was morbidly fascinated.

Still, his concerns for Uldyssian overrode that fascination and the longer Mendeln stood alone and silent in the darkness, the more impatient he became to return . . . if such a thing was possible. He was, after all, very likely a prisoner.

Why this betrayal, Achilios? he asked himself. *Why steal me away when I only wanted to reunite you with the others? What reason could you have for stopping me?*

"Because what you would have done would have had very unfortunate repercussions," replied the voice he knew so well from his own mind.

A shape emerged from the darkness, a shape that yet still seemed very much a part of it. The tall, very pale man with the features too perfect. The cowled figure stood a full head higher than Mendeln, something the younger son of Diomedes had not earlier noticed.

"What repercussions? What? Speak some sense! What repercussions?"

But instead of answering those questions, the other turned from him and looked up . . . not that Mendeln saw anything different when he, too, stared in that direction. There was simply more of the darkness.

The stranger—no, he had called himself *Rathma*—quietly asked the emptiness, "Well? Can you sense what she is about?"

And the emptiness *answered.*

No . . . she is well shielded in this regard. There is perhaps only one who knows best how to infiltrate that shield and learn the truth . . .

Rathma frowned. "And we cannot exactly expect my father to be of assistance . . . as he is more likely than even her to try to reduce me to dust."

There is that small matter . . .

Mendeln's head throbbed each time the second voice spoke, as if his mind was not strong enough to fully accept its presence. He clutched his temples, trying to regain his balance.

Forgive me . . . the voice said, its intensity much reduced. *I will endeavor to keep within your bounds . . .*

Rathma helped Mendeln straighten. "The first time he spoke to me, I thought my head would split open."

"Did not mine do so?" Mendeln blinked, again seeking the source of the voice. "Who is it who speaks to us? I have heard him before, too!" To the darkness, he suddenly railed, "Show yourself! I'd know *all* my captors!"

"But we are not your captors," Rathma quietly returned. "Hardly that. Nor, definitely, your enemies."

"Not my friends, to be sure! Or else why take me from Uldyssian's side, where I should always be?"

Because, if you wish to be there for him when you most need to be, you must be with us now . . .

"More riddles? Who are you, speaker in the shadows? Cease hiding from me!"

Rathma tsked. "There can be no going on with explanations until he sees you, my friend," he said to the emptiness. "But recall that he is mortal."

He is not so much less than you, Rathma . . .

"I never said otherwise."

Listening to the pair, Mendeln sensed how long they had

clearly known one another. There was a bond here as great as that between him and Uldyssian . . .

Know me, then, Mendeln ul-Diomed . . . the voice declared, keeping its intensity to a low booming in his head. *Know me as Rathma here does . . .*

And suddenly there were stars in the darkness above, a blazing multitude of stars that swirled about as if caught up in a tempest. They filled the area above to the point that Mendeln had to shield his eyes. At first there seemed no rhyme or reason to their movements, but quickly they began to spread apart and settle into certain areas. As they did, Mendeln noticed that a shape began to form, a shape only half-seen, yet seen enough to finally identify it.

It was a creature of myth, a thing in fairy tales and stories, but never truth. Uldyssian had cheerfully frightened Mendeln with tales of such when the latter had been a small child . . . and Mendeln had savored every story.

But now . . . now to see such a giant, especially one composed of *stars* . . . Mendeln stood gaping and speechless.

It was a *dragon*. A long, sinewy, serpentine dragon *beyond* epic proportions.

The dragon has chosen you . . . those words or ones very close to them had been etched on the stone in the ghastly cemetery Mendeln had found himself in while staying in Partha. *The dragon has chosen you . . .*

The celestial creature shifted, its "eyes" a startling array of smaller stars. *Know me . . .* it repeated. *Know me as Trag'Oul . . .*

"The One Who Is Forever," added Rathma, almost blandly despite the astounding spectacle. "At least, that is one meaning. There are several."

But Mendeln barely heard that, for as the dragon spoke, he constantly shifted . . . and in doing so, revealed a more stunning facet. Within each of the "scales"—the stars—Uldyssian's brother beheld short glimpses of life . . . *his life*. There he was as an infant, in his mother's arms. Mendeln cried out at the sight of her, the pain of her loss—of his entire family's loss—suddenly renewed.

He forced himself to look beyond that moment and thus witnessed one scene after another as the years of his pitiful little mortal existence raced along in what was for Trag'Oul surely the blink of an eye.

Trying to shake free of his feelings of insignificance, Mendeln beheld the fantastic entity as a whole . . . and in doing so noticed that not only was his life displayed before him, but so were hundreds, no thousands more.

We are all there, Mendeln realized. *All of Humanity, from the first on . . . each scale . . . each scale is a measure of some part of us . . .*

And among those lives, his eyes somehow fixed upon Uldyssian. In fact, the images of the brothers intertwined constantly, which made sense, of course. Whether together or alone, they were bonded by more than simply blood.

Yet . . . as the years of their lives swiftly progressed down the "body" of the giant, the two lives grew more separate. Mendeln saw the discovery of the stone near Seram and his brother's seduction by Lilith as Lylia. The images flashed faster and faster. Partha. Lucion. Achilios's death. Toraja. Serenthia. And on and on until—

Trag'Oul shifted again and the lives of the sons of Diomedes became lost among the sea of other existences. The human let out another cry and stared at what passed for the face of the dragon.

No more should you perceive, Trag'Oul told him. *For beyond that is the realm of possibilities, where what you see are the paths that choices not yet made determine. It would be a danger to yourself and to this world to try to choose from them before life has assisted you in the decision . . .*

He was speaking of the *future.* The dragon not only reflected the past and present, but what could be. The incredible immensity of the being stretched above him only now struck Mendeln. He sensed that Trag'Oul only revealed to him—and even Rathma—a most minor portion of himself. Turning to the cowled figure, Mendeln blurted, "What—?"

"What is 'he,' you want to ask?" Rathma gestured at the ever-shifting form. "Even Trag'Oul does not entirely know.

He has existed since just after the beginning of creation, although not quite as we sense him now."

No . . . that came later . . . Whenever the dragon spoke, the scales flowed and shifted, constantly displaying other lives, other times. *That came with the finding of the Shards . . . with the molding of Sanctuary by the renegade angels and demons . . .*

Mendeln had no idea what the leviathan was talking about save that it had mentioned demons. He glared at Rathma, whose features had, for the past few moments, greatly reminded him of another . . . too much of another, in fact.

And then it struck Mendeln like a bolt through his heart. He knew exactly who it was.

"You and she!" Uldyssian's brother grated, anger exploding. He pointed a condemning finger at the figure, who stood as motionless as death. "You and she! I can see it in you! You are *hers*! Hers!"

Mendeln summoned words of power, words that he was well aware he had gained from the very one he sought to attack.

Rathma raised a hand. In it materialized the ivory dagger that Mendeln had seen before his kidnapping. As the last of the words escaped Mendeln's lips, the dagger flared bright.

So near the unnatural illumination and with his eyes now accustomed to the darkness, Mendeln was instantly blinded. He let out a cry and stumbled back.

He has adapted to your teachings well, Rathma . . .

"Almost too well. I was nearly too late. But his mind . . . his spirit . . . are not yet utterly in tune with the Balance."

Discovering yourself before the offspring of Lilith can be rather disconcerting. You must consider emotions, Rathma. Sometimes I believe you have taken my teachings too much to heart, my friend . . .

Mendeln paid no mind to their discourse, his only concern recovering his sight. He continued stumbing back, somehow hoping to escape the demon before him.

"I am no demon . . . at least not in the full sense, Mendeln ul-Diomed," Rathma declared, again seeming to read his thoughts.

"Get out of my head!"

The cloaked figure began to coalesce before Uldyssian's brother. "We are beyond that, my student. You proved yourself receptive to what I offered that day when you were shown the stone near your village, the stone that was the first of your tests."

"Tests for what? To see if I would become servant to a demon?"

Above, the stars abruptly shifted. Looking up, Mendeln thought that the face of Trag'Oul seemed almost . . . reproving. *You are much too absolute at times, Rathma. Explain more. Tell him of his bloodline. Tell him about Lilith . . .*

"I was going to." For the first time, there was a hint of emotion—irritation?—in the cloaked figure's tone. "You know I was."

Eventually . . . More reshaping of the stars, more displaying of different lives. Never the same ones. *Always eventually . . .*

Rathma suddenly sighed. "Yes, perhaps I do hesitate, despite what I have said about the need for haste." To Uldyssian's brother, he calmly explained, "Mendeln, son of Diomedes, who himself was son of Teronus, who was the son of Hedassyian . . . I tell you now that you are of my *own* blood, my own offspring . . . and, thus, in turn, the one you know as Lilith . . ."

And Inarius, too, recall . . .

"He will know of Inarius soon enough." Rathma watched Mendeln closely, the dagger held ready.

But there was neither a renewed attack or even protest from Mendeln. The skills he had gained through Rathma were enough to enable him to gauge the truth of the other's words. "You do not lie . . ." rasped Uldyssian's brother. "You've made certain that I would know it!" He shook his head. "Uldyssian and I—we are of *her*?"

"As are so several others, the generations that have passed being of great number. And as I said, you are also of mine," Rathma pointed out, finally lowering the ivory blade. "Which number far, far less . . ."

Mendeln sought to put this all together. "Is that why she chose him and you me? Because it was easier to play games with those closest to your infernal blood?"

Irritation once more crossed Rathma's face, but before he could speak, the stars once more briefly swirled, then re-formed into Trag'Oul. *Peace,* the dragon murmured as best as he could. *If Rathma can be called a demon, so, too, can you and every human. Theirs is where in part all of you come . . . but also there are the angels to consider . . . and their role is no less significant in your creation . . ."*

Demons and angels . . . The notion that he—that everyone—was descended from such sounded so ludicrous. Yet once again the abilities with which Rathma had imbued him made it impossible for Mendeln not to see that all of this was truth.

It all only verified what Lilith herself had revealed in the course of matters. Mendeln had always secretly denied her claims, believing them lies used to undermine Uldyssian's defiance somehow. *But the only lies involved were to myself, it seems . . .*

"Very well. You know that I must believe you. What does that matter? I will be your pawn no more than my brother will be hers!"

Rathma let out an exasperated sigh. For him, Mendeln realized, these small slips represented major displays. "We seek no puppets. That is my mother's way . . . and my father's, it appears, also. No, Mendeln ul-Diomed, what we seek is nothing less than any who can stand against what has been destined to come to pass since the very beginning . . ."

Above, the dragon stirred. In some ways, Trag'Oul was to Mendeln a far more emotional being than the man with whom he trafficked. Therefore, when the leviathan spoke, Mendeln had no trouble sensing the urgency Trag'Oul sought to relay.

Rathma speaks of his father's folly, the dragon explained.

The folly of keeping Sanctuary secret from those beyond. The Burning Hells know already . . . and thanks to Lilith's insanity, the High Heavens will also soon discover this realm . . .

Through Lilith, Uldyssian—and thus, Mendeln—had learned the name given their world by those who had founded it. The demoness had also mentioned something of its earliest, highly turbulent history, too, yet she had never spoken much, as far as he could recall, of what would happen if those from whom the refugees had fled would all come to know of Sanctuary's existence. He had supposed that not an important point, anymore, but it was obviously a very, very vital one. Indead, dread spread through Uldyssian's brother, so much so that he was barely able to blurt out, "And so?"

And so, even if Lilith is foiled and Inarius offers peace . . . an improbable thing . . . it is very likely that Sanctuary and all within it—being that which not even the most powerful of either side could have once imagined—will still be destroyed.

"But why?"

There was that in the shifting of Trag'Oul that hinted to Mendeln how disturbed even the great creature was concerning what they discussed. *It is what the demons and angels do whenever they come across a potent potential advantage. They fight over it until they destroy the very thing they desire . . . a fate, sadly, that is better than becoming the fodder for either . . .*

"That is why we need you, Mendeln ul-Diomed," added Rathma, nodding to the mortal. "That is why we truly need you to stand with us . . . of your own free will, naturally."

Mendeln swallowed.

Hashir came into sight near noon on the last of the four days that Uldyssian had demanded of his edyrem. They had crossed the vast jungle with a swiftness that no one before them surely had. So Tomo, Saron, and many of the other Torajians claimed . . . and Uldyssian had no reason to doubt them.

Distant Hashir, as seen from his vantage point, could be

no more than half the size of Toraja, but Uldyssian felt that taking the temple there would require a hundred times the effort. Still, he hoped to avoid unnecessary bloodshed . . . if that was at all possible at this point.

"I want to enter the city in peace," he told Serenthia and the others. "I want them to see as Toraja did that we mean no harm to those not seeking to harm us. That's essential."

"The Triune knows we're headed this way. They've had time to work on the populace. It could be that the people've been poisoned against us," the merchant's daughter pointed out. "Our greeting might not be so gracious as in Toraja."

Romus and several others nodded. Nevertheless, Uldyssian was steadfast in his decision. "We're not the Triune nor the Cathedral. We show empty hands to Hashir . . . but fill them if need be."

Uldyssian had the majority of his followers wait in the jungle just out of sight of the first settlements near the city. He chose a party of fifty to come with him, Serenthia and Tomo among them. Romus he left in charge, trusting most in the reformed villain.

As with each time that Uldyssian had shown such faith in him, Romus fell to both knees and took the other man's hands. Touching his forehead to Uldyssian's fingers, the Parthan tearfully said, "Master Uldyssian, I'll not be letting you down. Not ever. By you, I've been saved from myself. That's a greater gift than I've ever been given."

"You've earned what you have." Uldyssian bade the Parthan to rise. "If we're not back by tomorrow morning, you know what must be done."

Romus gritted his teeth and his hands formed fists. "But you'll be coming back, Master Uldyssian! You'll be coming back . . ."

Uldyssian wished that he felt so confident. The closer that they had gotten to Hashir, the more he had considered leaving Serenthia and everyone else in the jungle and merely walking into the city by himself. Then, if there *was* some plot afoot, at least none of the rest would be caught in it with him.

But Uldyssian knew that Serenthia would never have allowed him to make her stay behind. Nor, for that matter, would the rest of his edyrem have permitted him to go without someone to watch his back. They were as possessive about his safety as he was about theirs regardless of how much stronger Uldyssian was than the whole of them combined.

The whole of them save Serenthia, perhaps. By the time they had reached the vicinity of Hashir, she had become true second in command and her word was nearly as respected as his own. Her counsel had become invaluable to him . . . just as she herself had.

And that was why, the night before reaching Hashir, he had finally given in to his emotions and hers.

Even Achilios's shade could no longer keep him from her. Their coupling had lasted long, the pent-up fury as much for what had been lost as what was now found. There had been comfort, too, in the familiarity between them, the only familiarity that Uldyssian had left in his life.

She stood at his side as he led the smaller band toward the city gates. Uldyssian had purposely mixed his party half Torajian and half Parthan. The Hashiri, as Tomo said the locals were called, eyed the lighter-skinned members with something approaching awe, many possibly never having seen an "Ascenian" before.

Whether that was true of the guards at the arched gate was not evident, for they stood with wary faces and taut muscles even as the newcomers approached. Other traffic flowed in and out through the gates—wooden carts pulled by oxen, robed pilgrims on foot, and well-dressed merchants on horseback, just a few examples noted in passing by Uldyssian. All got short but studious glances by the sentries as they crossed the threshold. One, a plumed figure who had to be the officer in charge, eyed the foreigners but said nothing until they were next to step into Hashir.

"Do you carry goods for the market?" he asked, even though it should have been obvious that they did not. When Uldyssian answered for everyone with a shake of his head, the officer then peered at the various individuals. "Pilgrims, then. Where is your town, Ascenian?"

"I'm from the village of Seram. Others here are from the town of Partha and the city of Toraja."

The man grunted. "Torajians I can recognize, Ascenian. Partha and Seram . . . these are places I do not know." He finally shrugged. "Obey all laws and Hashir will always welcome you."

"We thank and respect Hashir for its generosity," Uldyssian returned, having learned the reply from Tomo. Lowlanders, as Uldyssian and the Parthans thought them, always expressed gratitude to a new city upon arrival in it.

His knowledge of the proper response took some of the stoniness out of the guards. The officer waved them past.

Hashir was similar in style to Toraja and from what Uldyssian had learned the former was actually the foundation of the larger city. At some point in the past, Hashir had sent out the explorers who had built Toraja, named after a hero in lowland epics. Uldyssian found it ironic that Toraja had outgrown its birthplace despite its seemingly remote location.

The tree-lined streets were there, but lacking the small creatures so venerated in Toraja. Instead, a variety of colorful birds appeared to have staked claim to the rich foliage, some of the avians exotic even to Tomo's people.

"The Hashiri are said to bring back whatever beautiful birds they find on journeys, the better to color the skies of their home," the Torajian explained wide-eyed. "I always thought that was bragging of theirs, for Hashir now lives in Toraja's vast shadow . . . but *such* marvels! See that one?"

Uldyssian had to admit that the birds made for a wonderful, ever-shifting tapestry, but the noise their combined voices made—not to mention the tremendous amount of residue they left in their wake—did not overly enamor him of them. Instead, they made him yearn once more for the soft sounds of the more singular songbirds back home.

Their party continued to gather stares from the Hashiri and among the men Serenthia was a noticeable choice of views. Uldyssian felt a mild jealousy come over him. He managed to quell the desire, but constantly watched in case someone tried to become too familiar.

The Hashiri were dressed very similar to the Torajians, save that many wore silver sashes around their waists, and for the upper castes, nose rings of that very metal. There were other travelers as well, including a few yellow-skinned merchants from east of Kehjan. With their narrow eyes and unreadable expressions, they seemed almost feline. The Parthans among his group were especially fascinated by them, not that the Torajians did not also express interest.

The jungle lion was the patron symbol of Hashir; stylized versions perched atop many a column or gateway. The artisans had given the lion a savage grin that reminded Uldyssian too much of a demon, even though the stone creatures were supposed to be guardians against such.

Then there came into sight that which made all else in Hashir fade from Uldyssian's mind.

Above the rounded buildings ahead loomed the familiar triple towers of the Triune.

Uldyssian wanted to go directly there, but striking at the temple would only alienate the citizenry against him, who, so far, appeared not to have been warned against them. The last meant that what had worked in Toraja could still work here after all.

The market was an oval region situated at the main thoroughfare in the city. Twin fountains set on opposing ends bubbled enthusiastically. Tents and carts filled the vicinity, their exotic wares even briefly taking some of Uldyssian's attention from the temple.

He finally spotted that for which he had been searching. In the center of the market was a raised stone platform used for public gatherings and where even now would-be prophets preached to any who would listen. Most had audiences numbering only in the handfuls, if that much.

"On the right," he told the others. "That'll be our spot."

Even some of the ragged speakers paused as he neared, although Uldyssian was certain that it was due to his pale appearance, nothing more. He nodded politely at one, who rewarded him with a sneer.

The edyrem took up positions that Uldyssian had arranged in advance. A few, such as Serenthia, stood with him, while the rest became his initial audience. Uldyssian had learned the last part from Toraja, where some of the preachers there had secretly supplied their own cohorts as "converts," the better to attract others wondering what drew the "crowd." He did not consider his choice having anything to do with fakery; the edyrem, after all, were true believers who had joined him because of his previous speeches.

One or two locals drifted close even before he could clear his throat, no doubt merely interested in his foreignness. That suited Uldyssian fine. Tomo and his cousin had done the same in their city, as had others.

"My name is Uldyssian," he began, his voice amplified by his powers. From every direction, heads turned toward him. Uldyssian kept his voice even and friendly—one man to another. In his case, he knew it was more him than his speechmaking that would attract people. "And I ask only that you listen for a moment."

A few more Hashiri trickled toward him. The edyrem in the audience subtly shifted positions, enabling the locals to better view Uldyssian. As more and more newcomers added themselves, his followers pulled back. They would speak to the listeners only if asked questions. Uldyssian wanted his presence alone to be the reason anyone chose to gain the gift.

He started to tell them about his simple life and how he had been no greater a man than any of them. Even before

Uldyssian reached the part where he had discovered his powers—leaving out the detail of Lilith—those listening numbered more than his party, with others constantly streaming toward the area. Serenthia glanced at him, her smile giving him more confidence. Hashir started to promise to be like Partha, a place full of acceptance, not fear and hate.

Not like his lost Seram.

The crowd in the market was now mainly his. Uldyssian gazed out at the faces, many of them clearly ready to learn of the gifts within themselves. Giving the throng a cursory search, he also detected no enmity, no treachery. He had expected there to be at least one servant of the Triune among his listeners, but could find none. Perhaps, he thought, they had holed themselves up in the temple, preparing for battle.

If so, they would find it coming soon enough.

Nearly every other activity in the market had ceased. The rest of those preaching had long fallen silent and at least one stood among Uldyssian's audience, his expression as rapt as several of the others.

As he neared the conclusion of his speech, Uldyssian created a glow light. Gasps arose from the crowd. He dispersed the light, but the point had been made. What he spoke of was not mere fantasy nor trickery. Magic, yes, but one that he now pointed out was possible for anyone there, if only they would see.

The city guards who had been patrolling the market when first he had arrived now stood at the outer edges. They watched the proceedings with what were supposed to be disinterested faces, but Uldyssian noted a couple who seemed caught up in his words. The others merely did their duties and he saw no threat from them. Uldyssian continued to keep watch out for the Triune, but they remained absent.

At last, he finished, offering, as he always did, to show any who desired what their potential might be.

As expected, there was a moment of hesitation and then the first brave soul—a young woman whose face was half-concealed by a veil—stepped forward. Uldyssian repeated the same steps he had with his converts in Partha and Toraja and was not at all surprised when the woman gasped with delight and immediate understanding.

Her reaction caused a sudden flow forward by most in the front of the throng. The edyrem standing with Uldyssian moved to create some sort of order. Even then, he faced a sudden sea of outstretched hands, each supplicant wanting to be next.

They all imagine it differently, Uldyssian thought as he chose one. *But they all see it the same once it's been awoken. No one looks at it as if it were a way to take advantage of others.* He had wondered about that more than once. Was it because *he* was the messenger? If it had been someone like Malic, would the edyrem now be a force willingly embracing the evil of the temple?

Uldyssian could not believe that. As he greeted the man before him, he sensed nothing evil. Surely, the gifts could never be tainted.

But then, Lilith, Malic, and Lucion had all thought otherwise . . .

The crowd continued to swell. It was suddenly all Uldyssian could do to concentrate on his efforts. People were clearly spreading the word, for there were more in front of him than there had been in all the market at the beginning. Not even Partha had shown such eagerness. There, it had taken the healing of a child. In Toraja, it had needed more. But with Hashiri, it was almost as if the populace had expected his coming.

Uldyssian choked back any sign of his dismay. He quickly searched the crowd again, something that, with so many potential converts with which to deal, he had ceased doing.

He found them immediately. They were mixed into the crowd, especially among the later arrivals. They had waited for his concentration to be pushed to the brink before joining.

Peace Warders.

Without their uniforms to mark them, they were as any of the rest in the crowd. Once again, Uldyssian had grown overconfident. He had dared the Triune to act and they had obliged him.

But getting assassins close and enabling them to succeed were two different matters. Uldyssian easily picked out the foremost three. However, when he probed for weapons, Uldyssian found none. Did they hope to strangle him? Why send unarmed men against him, who could easily strike them down?

Or could he? Doing so would make it appear that he was attacking simple pilgrims. He noted two more behind the three. Five men and still their purpose was unclear. They pushed as hard as possible to reach him, even though they had to assume that he now kept an eye on each. What was the Triune hoping to achieve?

And suddenly, he knew.

Uldyssian pulled back from the eager supplicants. Even as he turned, with his mind he sought out Serenthia.

She was there, but not alone. Two figures, a small girl and an elderly man, held hands with her. Likely, Serenthia had sought to bring them to him. However, her expression—mostly puzzlement—indicated that she was just becoming aware of something amiss.

To his own heightened senses, there was *very* much wrong. He could see them for what they were even though they wore the semblances of others and seemed impossibly small and weak in comparison to their true, foul selves.

Morlu.

Uldyssian reached out for Serenthia, his power simultaneously rising up to strike the disguised creatures.

But in the next second, the morlu vanished . . . and with them, Serenthia.

TEN

Not again! Not again!

Those two words repeated themselves over and over in Uldyssian's head. First Achilios, then Mendeln, and now, Serenthia. One by one, those nearest to him had been lost. It in no way eased his pain that he now suspected what had happened to his brother. Surely the morlu, using some spell, had materialized around Mendeln and stolen him away just as they had done to Serenthia.

But *what* had happened did not matter. Only somehow trying to save Serenthia. The temple had plotted well; most did not even notice that she was missing. The edyrem were all too busy trying to maintain some order without using their powers . . . a command given to them by Uldyssian. Even they would not have noticed anything amiss around Serenthia.

But now, alerted silently by Uldyssian, they straightened in disbelief. Eyes turned to where the raven-haired woman had stood.

And to Uldyssian's astonishment, Serenthia and her kidnappers *reappeared*.

She stood as if some mystical spirit summoned to the mortal plane. Around her there once again glowed the aura. Her hair flew about, as if caught up in a storm. A grim smile crossed her face.

The glow about her shot without warning toward the figures holding her hands. Hissing escaped both the young girl and the elderly male, an inhuman hissing. In the blink of an eye, their skin *burned* away and as it did, both their shapes and height severely altered . . . until the two morlu stood revealed before the masses.

"Behold the true face of the servants of the Triune!" Serenthia shouted. "Behold the evil hidden from you all these years!"

The morlu that had been a child shifted one hand behind it, the bestial warrior's reflexes like lightning. The hand came forward again, in it a curved blade as long as Uldyssian's forearm.

But Serenthia merely eyed the hideous creature as he attacked. The blade dissipated to ash as it reached her chest, leaving the dust to blow back in the startled morlu's black eye sockets.

Serenthia let go of the undead warrior . . . who suddenly flung up and over the crowd as if a leaf caught in a tremendous gust. He rose higher and higher, finally crashing into the roof of a building some distance away.

While this had gone on, the second morlu had remained oddly still. The reason for that Uldyssian knew was again Serenthia. Her aura continued to surround the hapless fiend, who could do nothing as she pulled free his own weapon—and then, with one smooth strike, *beheaded* him.

As the corpse toppled, she looked to Uldyssian. "The Triune has declared itself! They leave no choice! We must move against them immediately!"

He felt her determination mingle with his own. Well aware of the things that the priests might have had in mind for Serenthia, Uldyssian's anger grew by the second. Still, he swore that he would keep control. Uldyssian wanted no repeat of what had just happened.

"People of Hashir!" he shouted. "This is the truth of the temple! This is—"

His head suddenly filled with what he quickly realized was sinister *whispering*. At the same time, Uldyssian felt a pressure in his skull, as if something sought to squeeze it to pieces. There came unbidden the brief image of a gaunt, bearded man who, despite his elderly appearance, radiated a darkness akin to that of the late, unlamented Malic and was surely another high priest of the Triune.

Summoning his strength, Uldyssian managed to force the pressure away. Far in the temple, Uldyssian sensed the high priest's consternation.

Serenthia was suddenly at his side. She placed a hand against the back of his head, cradling it. "Uldyssian, my love! What are they doing to you?"

He could not speak, for just then a violent pain coursed through him, so sharp that his heart nearly ceased beating. Vaguely, he registered that Serenthia was still calling to him. Farther away, there were concerned shouts from others.

Shouts . . . and then *screams*. Despite his own dilemma, Uldyssian yet managed to sense that there were more morlu in the immediate vicinity. He tried to rise, but the pain was too intense. Uldyssian managed at least to look up at Serenthia—only her face looked distorted, out of sync.

His ears filled with more shouts, more screams. At some point, the sky had turned *red*. Uldyssian could make no sense of it—

Then, Serenthia cried out as something dark briefly covered her gaze. She fell back from Uldyssian, who would have tumbled to the stone street if not for another pair of hands seizing him tight.

"I have you," promised a voice in his ear.

Mendeln's voice.

Before he could react, the world spun around. The cries and other sounds receded, as if Uldyssian now heard them from the end of a vast tunnel.

At the very last, he heard Serenthia call his name—and then darkness swallowed him.

Darkness and stars.

Arihan had absolutely no idea what had gone wrong. Everything had been in place and all the servants had known their roles.

Capture the woman, the Primus had commanded. *Capture her and you place a yoke around the male.* Arihan had immediately seen the wisdom of that. One glance through a scrying globe had been enough to reveal just how much the fool cared for his companion. To keep her from harm he would give his soul . . . exactly what the Triune desired.

But all accounts had indicated the woman far weaker than she had just revealed. In Hashir, she had displayed abilities that even Uldyssian ul-Diomed had not. Arihan would have sworn that she was actually even *more* powerful than the man the sect had been battling. Two morlu had not been enough, even cloaked as they had been by a spell given to him by the Primus.

Through the scrying globe, the priests from Hashir's temple were frantically asking what was going on. They had no idea yet that the plan had turned into an utter disaster for them. The morlu were evidence enough that the Triune had a darker side than it exhibited and with passions as they were at the moment, Arihan foresaw a violent rush upon the temple that would only end with a bloodbath.

A painful noise in his head finally made the high priest return to the globe. A harsh exhalation escaped Arihan when he saw what those in charge of Hashir had now wrought. Some fool had decided that, since *he* had not reacted to the unfortunate turn of events, then they had better do something themselves.

And so the cretins had sent out the rest of their morlu after the peasant and his followers, not thinking how the Hashiri would react to this further revelation of the Triune's true calling.

They are deserving of their fate, the imbeciles! Ignoring any further contact with the priests, Arihan instead surveyed the damage their attempt was causing. Twenty morlu had materialized as if out of thin air among the populace, accompanied by twice that many Peace Warders. However, given orders by those without any good sense, the warriors of the temple were not simply seeking Uldyssian ul-Diomed and his core followers, but anyone near them.

The high priest frowned, noting a sudden absence of one particular subject. Where *was* the peasant leader? Where *was* Uldyssian?

Arihan could certainly see where the woman was. She stood at the center of things, reveling in the carnage and looking as if an angel reborn. A blazing aura continued to surround her and seemed to spread to other followers even as he watched. They began to beat the morlu and Peace Warders down.

Hashir is lost! Lost! The bumbling fools had done it, not Arihan. He had followed the plan to the letter, the perfect plan of his master.

Now . . . if only the Primus would see it that way . . .

No sooner had he thought that than Arihan tried to smother the thought.

Too late.

My Arihan . . . I would see you before me . . .

The high priest of Dialon stifled a shiver. He had served the Primus well these many years. There might be some pain involved, but the Primus would certainly not waste such a valuable servant.

Arihan rose from the stone floor of the meditation chamber he had usurped for his efforts. He dismissed the scrying globe and doused the oil lamps in the walls with the wave of a hand, then, uncharacteristically, rushed from the room. Now would not be a good time to let the master wait, even for a moment. Let him see that the high priest did not fear to come to him.

The same stolid guards let him pass into the private chambers. Arihan tramped bravely through the darkened outer room, ignoring little sounds around him that he had never noticed in the past. What he could not ignore, however, was a silky material that draped his face just before he reached the inner door.

The high priest spit out what was in his mouth and

wiped away the rest. The gauzy material reminded him of a spider's webbing, but that could not be. The Primus had always been very fastidious, even in his torturing. Whatever the filmy substance was, it surely had a logical purpose.

As Arihan wiped the last away, the door opened to admit him. He stepped through immediately.

"My Arihan . . ." came the Primus's voice. "So good it is that you have come . . ."

His face a perfect mask, the high priest bowed toward the voice. "Ever I am at your service, most Holy One."

"Ahh, yesss, but how good is that service?" An unsettling green light materialized above the throne, at last revealing the Primus. Although the figure on the throne smiled, there was what Arihan took for strain in the effort.

"All you've asked, I've done," the high priest cautiously returned.

"And where is the female? Is she on her way to me at this very moment?"

"Nay, my lord. She is lost because of the *fools* in Hashir. They underestimated her. It was no fault of mine that the plan did not succeed, Great One."

The Primus's gaze grew terrible. The smile reversed itself. "And is it mine, then?"

Arihan caught himself. "Of course not! Never could such a thing be! The priests in Hashir were inept in their execution of your grand plot! They misused the morlu and their guards and have brought worse havoc down upon themselves. I fear, most holy lord, that the temple there is lost."

"This one is most, most disappointed, my Arihan." The Primus rose. As he did, the high priest noticed a spider on the wrist of the right hand. It was at least twice as large as the one he had seen on his last visit and *surely* should have been noticeable by his master. "Most disappointed. Assumptions were made. Promises were made . . ." Arihan's master shivered and looked up. "Promises were made . . ."

"The female . . . she was stronger than expected," the priest offered. "At least as strong as the male. That was something no one knew."

Much to his relief, the Primus brightened. "Yesss . . . that could be useful. He would understand that this could not possibly have been foreseen."

Exactly who this other was of whom he spoke, Arihan did not know, but the Primus's reaction sent a chill through the high priest. There were only three beings that the son of Mephisto would fear . . . his father and the other two Prime Evils.

To assuage them, even the Primus would need a scapegoat. Arihan suddenly wondered how best he might flee, well aware that his chances of success in that direction were likely nil.

Another spider appeared, this one crawling out of the Primus's collar just as had the one during the previous audience. Arihan belatedly noticed other small and very agitated forms scurrying over the throne . . . and even over his own feet. What were all these *spiders* doing here and why did his master react with such indifference to them?

"My Arihan . . ." the figure before him murmured. The Primus reached out to the high priest, who had no choice but to step nearer.

So close, though, Arihan now noticed something wrong with the Primus's eyes. He had seen Lucion's true eyes . . . and these were not them. In fact, so near, it was possible to tell that each was actually composed of *three or four* separate ones . . . and all were as crimson as fresh blood.

"Most Holy One," he began, seeking some word that would mean his salvation. "It is possible that this woman—"

But the Primus shook his head. "No, my Arihan. No. The plot—my glorious plot—should have triumphed! *He* will demand the reason why and she may not be enough—"

"'He,' O Great One?" the human blurted, trying to stall for time. The many spells he knew were unlikely to work here, but Arihan had to attempt *something*. Unfortunately, it was impossible to concentrate for another reason. There were too many spiders, either crawling on the throne, the walls, the Primus—and *himself,* Arihan discovered—or dangling from the ceiling. Some of them were as large as the high priest's hand or even larger.

And at last Arihan recalled what those spiders indicated. He knew what stood before him, disguised as his master. He had never seen the demon, but had, as a young priest, read of him and heard the rumors that the creature dwelled deep in the recesses of the grand temple.

"Our lord *Diablo,* my good Arihan . . ." the false Primus answered to his question. "He it will be that demands not only a reason why, but the one who failed!" As he spoke, the figure's handsome face began to rip away. Loose threads erupted where the flesh split, threads of silk.

Spiders' threads.

And underneath, was a hairy monstrosity that once Arihan would have gladly summoned, a demon who served the true lord of the high priest's order.

"Great One!" he gasped. "Let me go with you to speak with the wondrous Diablo! Together, we can—"

The robe tore apart as a huge, somewhat manlike shape with eight limbs expanded. Arihan's desperate suggestion was cut off as four clawed hands seized him and pulled his face within inches of a savage pair of mandibles. Saliva dripped on the high priest's immaculate garments.

"Together we shall go, yes, my Arihan, but to present your head on the platter! The head only, yes . . . for the *rest* of you this one will need for strength when facing the grand and magnificent Diablo!"

The mandibles sank into the high priest's throat, ripping out everything. Arihan had no chance to utter even a gurgle. His head flopped to the side, barely held by some bits of bone and sinew.

Astrogha swallowed the mouthful, then shifted the body to begin sucking out the precious fluids. What the human did not understand was that the demon had actually done him a tremendous favor, killing him so quickly. Lord Diablo might have made him suffer longer, torturing the puny mortal until he was satisfied that he not only knew everything, but had put Arihan through all that entertained the master of terror.

But in the process of that, the high priest might have implicated Astrogha in the failure. Even despite having prevented that scenario, the arachnid would have to do some quick thinking to save himself.

And as he supped, one notion already formulated. Lucion was still absent, Lucion who should have noticed what was afoot and come to add his power to the effort. Yes, somehow this would be steered again toward Lucion . . . and the female with Uldyssian ul-Diomed, also. Arihan had spoken the truth when he had said that she had revealed more than even the demon had expected. She would become the other focus of Astrogha's defense . . .

At last satiated, he threw the carcass down for the children to finish. Already, Astrogha could sense Diablo awaiting word of his success.

The demon glanced down at the high priest's grotesque corpse, already covered by spiders. "Consider yourself fortunate, my Arihan . . . consider yourself fortunate . . . this one may yet envy your fate . . . yes, envy and plead for it to be so merciful . . ."

With that, Astrogha opened the way between places, reaching forth into the Burning Hells . . .

I have awaited you . . . came the dread voice.

The edyrem looked up as one, sensing the call. It was not from the master, but from she who was closest to him. That was enough. Romus waved his hand and they surged toward Hashir. Even those minding the smallest children followed, for the edyrem did not leave anyone behind. The weakest among them would be better protected staying with the rest, even if that meant following them into a struggle . . .

And so, there was left only one figure standing in the jungle, one figure who wished with all his might to join the stream of bodies flowing toward the city gates. However, Achilios could not do so, not without creating greater catastrophe.

It's . . . as they said . . . she'll take up the reins if he's gone. The archer had not wanted to believe that, but he should have known that Rathma and the dragon were correct. They seemed to be correct about all things.

No . . . not all. They had been wrong about him. They felt that he would be utterly obedient to what they said. Not because they demanded that obedience, but because they assumed the rightness of their decisions made no objection possible.

But even if a dead man now walking, Achilios was still Achilios. He had considered other courses of action that skirted the choices made by Lilith's son and the thing called Trag'Oul.

He had Serenthia to consider . . . and that was the most important matter of all.

Achilios looped his bow tight over his shoulder, then started running. Death had not slowed him, and in fact, he could cover ground much, much faster now. He left little if any trail and could avoid nearly all obstructions.

From Hashir came screams and the clash of metal. Rathma had granted him abilities necessary to the cloaked one's demands and so Achilios knew what was going on inside even better than Uldyssian's edyrem. He also knew very well who was leading the struggle. That made the hunter increase his already astounding pace.

Around the outskirts of Hashir's territory he ran, pausing only to avoid the homes of those who lived beyond the city's walls. At all times, Achilios kept one sight in focus; the three towers of the temple. As with Toraja, the Triune preferred a location that gave them access through a separate gate. To Achilios, that should have been enough to warrant suspicion from anyone concerning them, for what reason would a noble and loving sect have need of a path of escape?

Of course, to be fair, before his own slaughter, Achilios doubted that even he would have paid much attention. Life had a way of blinding people. Only death seemed to truly open the eyes . . .

The gateway he sought finally came into view. One side was already open. The senior priests obviously did not trust their chances at this point. He wondered if they actually thought that their masters would welcome them with open arms after this fiasco. Then again, perhaps the Triune's true lords *would* . . . and then promptly flay all of them alive.

Achilios decided to save the demons the trouble. Freeing his bow, he reached for an arrow—and found himself staring at a startled Hashiri woman carrying a basket.

The moment she registered him, the woman shrieked. Achilios could imagine her shock and self-loathing filled him. However, for all he hated how he was, there remained greater priorities.

"Run . . . home . . ." he rumbled. "Go!"

She did not need more coaxing. Spilling the basket and its contents on the jungle floor, the woman rushed away.

The incident already forgotten, the undead archer notched an arrow—

And was promptly tackled by a heavy, armored form.

The dagger that sank deep in his chest would have killed him, if he had not already been dead. His attacker started to lean back, clearly confident of his strike. The vague outline of a morlu filled Achilios's gaze.

The archer grinned, a sight he was certain would have been ghastly to any living person. "Too little . . . too late."

With a strength now as inhuman as that of the morlu, Achilios threw the bestial warrior high into the air. The morlu collided with a tree, cracking the latter in two.

Achilios, well aware how little that would stop his adversary, was already on his feet. The bow came up and a shaft went flying even as the armored assassin rose from the tangle.

With utter accuracy, the bolt hit one of the black eye sockets. As the morlu grasped for it, Achilios fired at the remaining socket.

Grunting, the helmed creature batted away the oncoming missile. However, Achilios had already expected that. His shot had only been to distract. The bow fell to the ground as the hunter pulled free a long knife. He leapt toward the morlu as the latter finally pulled free the one bolt, a sucking sound accompanying its removal.

The knife, honed sharp and wielded by an expert, severed the armored creature's head from the neck.

Achilios kicked the twitching body aside. He grabbed the head even as one of the morlu's hands sought for his leg.

Hefting the head, the archer threw it deeper into the jungle. Turning back only long enough to retrieve his bow, Achilios raced past the torso, which sought in vain to regain its footing. The foul magic animating it would last only a short time longer, too short for the morlu to save himself by retrieving his head. Achilios wondered if the same thing would hold true should someone remove *his*. Perhaps, if somehow the crisis passed and the others no longer needed his questionable aid, he would test it out himself. After all, what was there left for him? No love, no life . . .

The hunter grimaced. As an animated corpse, he had become very maudlin. All that mattered was fulfilling his mission and then dying again. Everything else he could leave to Uldyssian, Mendeln . . . and, if there was still hope, Serenthia.

If there was still a Serenthia.

The morlu had been a warning that the woman's scream had alerted some of those he sought. Achilios stuffed the knife in his belt, then readied another arrow.

By this time, four wary figures had emerged through the gate. Three were guards, the last a priest he estimated somewhere in the middle of the hierarchy. The guards faced different directions, evidently checking the safety of the immediate area.

The priest—his robes that of Bala—stared in the direction of Achilios.

The hunter let the bolt fly. With darkness to shadow it, it should have cut down the robed figure. Instead, the priest raised a hand—

Achilios's arrow exploded in midflight.

But the archer had already expected that something might happen. Barely had he let fly the first than he shot a second. As Achilios had surmised, the priest had quick reflexes, but not *that* quick. The second arrow burrowed deep into the robed chest, its momentum sending the prey falling.

The guards turned in his direction. One shouted something and two more came through the gateway.

Achilios fired three more bolts in rapid succession. One bounced off the breastplate of his target, the second caught a guard in the arm, and the third pierced the throat of its quarry.

The two survivors retreated to the new pair. They looked convinced that they were being attacked by more than one person, exactly as he had wanted. Achilios retreated from his location, blending into the darkness in a manner that he could only do by being dead.

There was no sign of another morlu, which possibly meant that the rest were involved in the chaos. That increased Achilios's chances of finishing the special task he had set upon himself. All he needed now was to continue pressing those seeking flight from Hashir.

But at that moment, he sensed something else in the jungle, something as unsettling to it as he was.

The ground below him heaved up, as if about to erupt. What at first he mistook for the upturned roots of the nearby trees shot up and around him. Only after the first had snared his leg did the archer see them for what they actually were.

Tentacles . . . the tentacles of some huge, grotesque creature burrowing through the soft dirt.

A creature that was not of Sanctuary.

As a second tendril snared his bow arm, Achilios cursed himself for forgetting the true patrons of the Triune. The priest he had shot had been a servant of Baal, the Lord of Destruction. Foolish of the archer to forget the man might have summoned another servant of the Prime Evil, a servant not in the least human.

Still, whether or not the dead priest had summoned this denizen of the Burning Hells was a moot point. What was important was escaping it; no easy task. It already had both of Achilios's legs and one arm and he had still not seen more than the tentacles. Instead, the only measure he had of his foe was that the ground everywhere around him continued to shake, as if whatever lurked below it was *gargantuan*.

Reaching the knife would have driven a living man to terrible wrenching pain, but Achilios was thankfully beyond such mundane sensations. Thus, he was able to grip the blade just as another tentacle sought his wrist. Twisting, Achilios slashed at the tip, watching with satisfaction as the faithful edge cut through.

A low, thick thundering arose from beneath him. The jungle shook violently. If not for the very tentacles holding him, Achilios would have fallen on his back.

"Hurt you . . . did I?" he rasped triumphantly.

In response, another, thinner tendril shot out, wrapping like a whip around his throat. The appendage constricted.

Fortunately, unlike most, Achilios no longer breathed. He did not actually even draw breath when speaking. The power that animated him also gave him voice. Hence, while having his neck snared did slow Achilios further, it did not incapacitate the hunter as it would have a living being.

He took immediate advantage of the demonic creature's misconception, slashing with the knife at not only the tentacle snaring his throat, but his other arm, too. Both times, Achilios struck true. A black substance resembling tar dripped from the cuts. The two appendages were instantly withdrawn.

Achilios wasted no time in assaulting the others. One received a shallow line across its width, but before he could do more, both retreated below the soil.

The hunter allowed himself a brief smile as he righted his balance. No beast had ever had the final laugh against him; that triumph, however short-lived, had been the arch-demon Lucion's alone.

Still, it was best not to simply stand there. Achilios plucked up his bow—

Again came the thundering that the archer had decided was the demon's roar. A quake that toppled most of the trees near him also sent Achilios tumbling. This time, he lost not only the bow, but his knife.

"Damn!" he gasped. "Damn!"

And out of the ground burst a dozen tentacles of varying length and size. Whether they belonged to one monster or another did not matter, only that suddenly they snagged him by the legs, the arms, the torso, and the throat.

There was nothing he could do. Against their combined might, Achilios might as well have been a newborn baby. At this point, there was only one question as to his fate. Would the beast tear him to pieces—which might or might not actually finish the undead hunter, although it would certainly make him useless—or instead drag him down into the ground, a much more daunting prospect. Achilios had been buried once; he found the idea of a second interment frightening.

The tentacles tightened. Achilios felt his body strain. Dismemberment was the decision made by his captor. The archer perversely wondered if he should thank the demon for that choice.

A brilliant *golden* light suddenly turned the jungle brighter than day. Achilios felt a warmth such as he had not known even before death and which, because it actually *did* warm him, stunned the archer that much more.

But if it warmed Achilios, the light did much more to the beast. Now the thundering reached an ear-splitting crescendo. The tentacles shook and Achilios noticed burning flesh.

The demonic appendages shot back into the ground. The jungle shook . . . then stilled.

The golden light vanished . . . leaving a puzzled and very disturbed Achilios. He lay there for a moment, uncertain if either would return. When neither did, the archer stood.

However, no sooner had he done so, than Achilios experienced an odd sensation. Had he been living, he would have thought it vertigo.

His legs gave out. The world swam. Achilios tried to reach his bow—

And then all was blackness.

ELEVEN

Uldyssian had heard the voices for several moments now and although a part of him sought to react to them, his body would not obey.

"He has still not opened his eyes," came what he vaguely noted as Mendeln's voice. But that was not possible; Mendeln was lost to him. Uldyssian recalled thinking that he had heard Mendeln earlier, yet that, too, had to have been his imagination.

Have patience, young one. Her strike was as subtle as it was heinous . . .

Even unconscious, Uldyssian jolted the moment that the second speaker voiced himself, for the words resounded in both the head and soul of the son of Diomedes. He must have moaned at the same time, for that which sounded like Mendeln suddenly grew excited.

"Did you see? He stirred! Uldyssian! Listen to me! Come to me! By our father and mother, you'll not leave me like this!"

Mention of his parents finally caused Uldyssian to actually wake. He remembered how he had felt when Mendeln had vanished; if this was indeed his brother, he could not very well let him suffer so, not if it was in his power to do anything.

And then there was Serenthia . . .

That proved more than enough. With a cry, Uldyssian struggled free of the last vestiges of unconsciousness. Immediately his body was wracked with terrible pain. He rolled about and perhaps might have hurt himself in the process if not for hands grabbing him by the shoulder in order to keep his body still. Yet again he heard Mendeln.

"Be at ease, Uldyssian! Be at ease. It will pass . . . most of it, anyway . . ."

There is much within that will take longer. The demoness is a poison deep in his blood . . .

"And I could have stopped her, if only you'd all have let me!" snapped Uldyssian's brother. "I could've prevented so much!"

Not then. You would have been slaughtered and Uldyssian more in her grip . . .

"But you said that she went in unsuspecting of the betrayal! That alone—"

A third voice intruded just as Uldyssian forced his eyes open. Vague shapes and much darkness greeted the battered man's gaze.

"My mother is very adaptable, Mendeln ul-Diomed. You saw how quickly she turned potential defeat of her plan into a new and possibly more terrifying path toward her ultimate goals. Now she is nearer than ever to victory . . . and Sanctuary that much nearer to cataclysm."

Some of the agony subsided, enough so that Uldyssian could finally focus. The first thing he saw gladdened his heart, for it *was* his brother. Mendeln wore an uncharacteristically broad grin and Uldyssian knew that he wore the same.

"I thought you lost forever," the older brother told the younger.

"As I you."

"Your sibling was always safe," the third speaker interjected. In some ways, his voice was very similar to Mendeln's in both tone and speech, yet there was something about it that bespoke of great age and a person who was not entirely human . . . if at all.

And when the figure joined Mendeln in gazing down at Uldyssian, the latter saw that this was no mere mortal. The face was too handsome, the features too perfect. Most of all, though, the eyes held more than great age . . . they were so ancient that Uldyssian immediately suspected the worst.

"He is no demon," Mendeln quickly stated, recognizing his brother's reaction.

"Although Lilith *is* my mother," added the stranger.

With an animalistic growl, Uldyssian sought to grab the speaker. However, his body was too weak. Worse, intense pain coursed through him again, forcing him to lie back.

Only then did he notice the stars. Their positions were so different from what Uldyssian was familiar with, that he momentarily forgot the demoness's offspring.

"Where—where are we, Mendeln?" Uldyssian finally asked. "I don't recognize any of those."

It was the son of Lilith who responded. "You are somewhere and nowhere."

Such answers only served to stir Uldyssian back to anger. He did not trust being in the vicinity of a being who claimed Lilith as the one who had begat him. "And *who* are you? If not a demon, then *what* are you?"

"My name is Rathma," the stony figure answered without preamble. "Although that is not the name given to me at birth, but rather the one placed upon me by another after parting from my parents' ways. It means 'keeper of the Balance' which is also my function and duty."

Uldyssian had no idea what Rathma spoke about and cared less. "But Lilith *is* your mother . . ."

"And Inarius is my father. Yes, I see that name also fills you with dread. I bear no grudge for that, for both have become anathema to me as I am to them. As to *what* I am, I am a nephalem . . . one of the very first, in fact . . ."

The revelation should have struck Uldyssian harder than it did, but quickly he realized that it had not because, horribly aware of who Rathma claimed for his lineage, there was no other possible answer.

"You . . . you are like us . . ."

Rathma shook his head. "No, I am unlike you or any of those who follow you. I cannot explain, but what you call the 'gift' has metamorphosed. There are abilities that I have that you do not just as you bear some I am lacking. I suppose this should not so surprise me since I am from the very first generation birthed on Sanctuary . . ."

So long ago as all that, Uldyssian thought in awe.

Lilith's son nodded as if having read the mortal's mind, then added, "There are few of us remaining, for when only my father was left of the original refugees, he was strict in his punishment of those who used their powers. He insisted that his perfect world, his Sanctuary, would remain as *he* desired it . . ." Rathma shook his head. "But for one who is eternal, my father should have known that nothing stays static."

That is enough for now, came that other voice from both within and without Uldyssian. He pushed himself up, seeking the source . . . and his eyes for some reason looked to the stars above. For the first time, Uldyssian imagined that he even saw a shape formed by the celestial lights. Not a complete one, but enough to give the illusion of a vast, half-hidden beast. A reptile—no—something more than that. It was long and sinewy like a great snake, but the head reminded him of another creature straight out of myth—

A dragon . . . yes, it looked like some sort of serpentine dragon . . .

The stars shifted . . . and it seemed to Uldyssian that the half-seen behemoth now stared *back* at him.

Though we would all wish it otherwise, you are not well enough yet for more strain . . .

Uldyssian swallowed, unable to believe his eyes, his mind, and his heart. "What—what are you?"

"He is *Trag'Oul,* brother," Mendeln explained quietly. "Born in creation, defined when the angels and demons who came here formed Sanctuary. He is more its guardian than any other can claim."

A simplified description, albeit most accurate . . .

Oddly, the introduction of this celestial creature was not what most demanded Uldyssian's attention. Hearing the dragon, then his brother, and recalling how Rathma had spoken . . . he felt as if he were listening to three extensions of the *same* being. Uldyssian looked from one to the other and the feeling only increased.

"Mendeln," he muttered. "Mendeln, I want to leave here *now*. Both of us, I mean."

"But we cannot, Uldyssian . . . at least not yet. There is so much to learn and you need recuperation."

Rathma stood next to the younger son of Diomedes. "He speaks the truth. It would be unwise at this juncture."

Uldyssian swallowed. Rathma and Mendeln looked more like brothers than he and his sibling did. The dark garments, the pale faces—and the nearly unblinking *gazes*—added further to the horrific effect.

Forcing himself to his feet despite the torture to his body, Uldyssian growled, "Mendeln! Look at you! Look at him! Listen to him and that—that thing!—and then yourself! They're doing something to you!"

He felt his power rush through his body, fueling his emotions and strength. They had been wrong, his kidnappers. He was more than fit despite their games.

Raising his hands toward his brother, Mendeln replied, "No, Uldyssian! You must not do that—"

It was too late. Certain that not only were he and Mendeln trapped here for dire purposes but that his sibling was being turned into something to serve the dragon's and Rathma's needs, Uldyssian unleashed the raw forces within.

"You said he was too weakened by her to do this!" Rathma shouted, evidently to Trag'Oul.

He is different! They would all be different! They are no more nephalem than you are human! They are more—

But the fantastic creature got no further, for then it was that the dragon's empty realm shook as if some giant hand sought to turn it upside down. Uldyssian knew that he was the cause but did not care. He had to free Mendeln and him from this black prison—

As if responding to his thought concerning his dark surroundings, the elemental forces bursting from Uldyssian took on a blinding brightness. Above, Trag'Oul roared. Rathma uttered something in a language unknown and momentarily the brightness lessened. But Uldyssian, fearing that if his effort failed then all was lost, threw his will into restoring the light.

Around him, the very blackness suddenly began shredding as if torn cloth. Utter white at first replaced it . . . then a mountainous landscape erupted full-blown.

Mendeln called out to Uldyssian, but the two looked now to be separated by miles. Fearing to lose his brother again, Uldyssian attempted to draw back within him the energies he had released, but it was as if they now fought against him. The new landscape began to shiver and shake and seemed as ready as the blackness to shred apart.

But finally, Uldyssian managed to contain his powers. The effort sent him to his knees. His heart pounded and for a time his breath came in short gasps.

Then, slowly, he registered colder, drier air and soil much harder than that of the jungles. After having grown accustomed to the hotter climate near Kehjan, the change left him shivering. Only belatedly did Uldyssian finally regain enough control over his abilities to adjust himself to this new environment.

And new it was. He had thought at first that he had returned to the vicinity of his village, but nowhere around Seram were there mountains so great. In fact, nowhere that he had been looked like this region.

The sky was overcast, but Uldyssian could still see far enough to marvel at the landscape. No, definitely not near Seram, Kehjan, or anywhere else of which he had heard. Perhaps Mendeln might have—

Mendeln! How could he have forgotten about his brother? Spinning in a circle, Uldyssian looked for any sign.

But he was alone in the strange land.

"Mendeln!" Uldyssian roared. "Mendeln!" When he

received no answer, the son of Diomedes switched tactics. "Rathma! Where are you, damn you? You want me—you and that thing—well here I am! Me for my brother! What say you?"

His voice echoed throughout the mountains. Without at first realizing it, one particular peak caught his attention. It was taller, vaster than the rest, almost as if a king among kings. The more he looked at the mountain, the more he felt drawn toward it.

With a colorful curse at Rathma and Trag'Oul, Uldyssian turned his back on the peak. Nothing good could come of it, not if it somehow sought to call to him. He trod up the sloping land, glad that he had not switched to the garments of the Torajians. They were thin and airy, not suitable at all for this region. Even though he could keep himself warm, just wearing shirt, pants, and boots gave him additional mental comfort.

Uldyssian reached the top of the hill upon which he had found himself and searched both with his eyes and power for any nearby settlement. However, if there were any in the region, they were hidden from him. All he saw or sensed were trees, hills, and the mountain again.

Uldyssian stiffened.

Yes, there it was. Not *any* mountain, but the very same peak from which he had been retreating.

"More games!" He glared at the overcast sky, seeking the dragon. "I told you! Stop this now! Come for me if you want me!"

Again his voice echoed over and over, but still there was no reply. Uldyssian finally decided to get their attention.

Mustering his will, he clapped his hands together as hard as he could.

The resulting sound was like thunder, so loud, in fact, that it shook the trees and ground. Over and over it repeated, as if some massive but invisible storm swept through the area.

He waited, this time certain of success . . . but after several breaths, Uldyssian still stood alone.

"Damn you, Rathma!" Uldyssian roared. This time, though, his fury was spent. The echoes perished after only three or four repetitions.

Defeated, he knelt down by a rocky growth and buried his face in his hands. Each time Uldyssian began to believe he could face those arrayed against him, he was proven wrong.

Without warning, the ground shook again and for a moment Uldyssian thought that his efforts had caused some collapse or tremor. He leapt to his feet, not certain exactly what he planned to do, and saw that the shaking was confined to his immediate location.

More to the point, centered directly beneath the outgrowth.

He started to back away—only to find the ground rising up *behind* him as well. Ahead, the outgrowth swelled. It stood almost twice as tall as Uldyssian and nearly as wide. One part jutted above the rest, giving it some resemblance to a head.

And then two *eyes* opened up in the "head," two eyes a deep rich brown and almost human. They glanced left, then right, then down at Uldyssian, who stood awestruck.

There was shifting in the dirt and grass that made up the mound. The outgrowth took a *step* toward him, huge chunks of stone and more breaking away. Another step . . . and more collapsing dirt and rock.

The thing now had two thick, solid legs. It paused, then began shaking itself like a wet hound. More dirt and stone flew away, some of it toward Uldyssian, who awoke from his astonishment just in time to deflect the most dangerous ones.

First one arm, then the second, formed. The earthen giant looked at the blunt end of the initial appendage. Stony fingers suddenly cracked through, a full hand created less than a breath later. The same then happened with the other arm.

Uldyssian backed up against the dirt wall behind him,

but did not otherwise act. If a demon was about to attack him, then this thing was a slow-witted one. It seemed more like a sleeper waking than any threat.

The giant flexed its fingers, then surveyed its body as if seeing it for the first time. The eyes shifted and Uldyssian could have sworn that there was a tremendous sadness in them.

It *spoke*. Through a crevasse suddenly forming near the bottom of the head, the creature spoke.

"Wwwho arrre yyyooou . . ." it began slowly, each syllable sounding as if the thing was clearing a throat of centuries of disuse. "Whhooo are you . . ." it repeated stronger. "That calls a name . . . that calls a name I haven't heard for . . . so very, very long?"

As the voice cleared, Uldyssian recalled what he had noticed about the eyes. The voice, while still very gravelly, was also almost human.

"Who are you," the being said a third time. "Who calls the . . . name of *Rathma*?"

"My name is Uldyssian ul-Diomed and if you are a servant of Rathma's, then beware, for I've no love for your master!"

The giant studied Uldyssian, who now stood in a battle stance. Yet, something held Uldyssian back, prevented him from striking the first blow.

A grating, rumbling sound suddenly issued forth from the bizarre creature. Slowly it evolved into something recognizable . . . *laughter*.

"So glad I am . . . to have awakened for a time . . . if only to hear this . . ." The thing shook his head, sending more fragments flying. "*Rathma!* No sense of humor . . . in that one! He would be . . . offended . . . and for *me*! No, little Uldyssian ul-Diomed! Ha! Such a . . . long name for my . . . dry throat! I am no servant of . . . the dour one . . . I was . . . am . . . *Bul-Kathos* . . ."

He announced this as if Uldyssian would know the name and marvel at it. But as the former farmer failed to react, Bul-Kathos lost some of his own humor.

"The name . . . the name means nothing to you . . . has it been . . . has it been so long . . ." He studied hard his earthen and stone body. "Yesss . . . there is little of me and . . . much more of the world! What I dreamed for . . . what I decided must befall . . . me . . . is working well . . . even the forgetting . . . by mortal men . . ."

The wall behind Uldyssian collapsed. Uldyssian expected some sort of trick, but instead the giant sat down on a patch of ground that rose up to create a seat for him. Bul-Kathos eyed the empty area between him and Uldyssian.

"The years . . . they must number a thousand . . . or more." He glanced up at the intruder. "Tell me, little Uldyssian ul-Diomed, know you . . . know you the names *Vasily* . . . and *Esu*?"

"The names mean as little to me as that of Bul-Kathos," Uldyssian admitted. "But all would be preferred to be known by me than that of the monstrous *Rathma*!"

It initially appeared that Bul-Kathos did not hear the last, for he looked to the ground once more and muttered to himself. "No Vasily . . . where are you . . . my brother?" A slight, sardonic chuckle escaped the giant. "But no Esu, either! How that would irritate . . . her . . ." As quickly as the humor came, it disappeared. "If even she . . . still rages . . ."

Uldyssian cared little for the creature's ramblings. All that mattered was that this Bul-Kathos—whatever he was—knew of Rathma. Perhaps somehow this could aid Uldyssian in rescuing Mendeln.

He focused on one comment the other had made. "Bul-Kathos, you speak of a lost brother. I've one also missing. His name is Mendeln and he is a victim of Rathma! If you could in some way aid me—"

Bul-Kathos looked up. "Rathma has . . . no victims. He is not . . . Esu . . . never Esu . . . if she still lives . . ."

Uldyssian finally gave up. Bul-Kathos had obviously long ago abandoned touch with others . . . and perhaps even himself. If the strange being was no threat, then it was time for Uldyssian to move on.

And again, his eyes shifted to the towering mountain. This time, Uldyssian wondered if he should go to it.

But as if reading his intention, the macabre figure, suddenly animated, leapt up. "Your path . . . lies *elsewhere* . . . young one . . . not there . . ."

That only made Uldyssian even more determined to reach the peak. "And why not there?"

"Because . . . it is forbidden . . . for you."

To be told that further infuriated Uldyssian. Thrusting his chin out defiantly, he returned, "A good enough reason to journey to it, then."

Bul-Kathos *swelled* in size and an ominous shadow crossed his earth and rock face. Even the eyes—the almost human eyes—now held a threat. "No. You will *not*."

The giant moved toward Uldyssian, and as he did, more stone and dirt fell away. Now, although he still looked as if created from the very ground, Bul-Kathos wore the vague semblance of a bearded warrior. His skin was the brown of the soil and his hair the green of grass. There was nothing hesitant anymore about his movements—

Nor about his intentions toward Uldyssian.

Bul-Kathos raised a fist and in it formed a huge, stone club. He swung at the mortal's midsection.

But the club deflected off an invisible barrier quickly created by his target. Uldyssian already sweated from effort; the giant's strike had nearly penetrated.

"You are more than you seem," rumbled Bul-Kathos. "A nephalem I would call you, young one, if not for the fact that I and Rathma may be the last . . ."

"The last of your age, maybe," retorted the son of Diomedes. "But time has long passed you just as you've pointed out."

"But no matter how many centuries, I yet recall my duty well! And so Mount Arreat will remain forbidden for you and all else who would desecrate its interior!"

He struck the ground with the club and the land shook so much that Uldyssian toppled. More and more the earthen creature gave way to an ancient warrior. Clad in kilt and sandals and with a golden band around his head, Bul-Kathos resembled some barbarian deity . . . a barbarian deity who radiated raw force such as Uldyssian had never faced, not even from Lucion.

"We swore that the way to the mount would be forever sealed from those like Esu," continued a furious Bul-Kathos, "who would've used that within to further ravage a weakened world! And though the others may be more of the soil than even I desired to be, in their memory and our oath I'll continue to fulfill my sacred duty!"

He struck the ground again and Uldyssian, who had nearly gotten to his feet, fell back. Uldyssian turned that tumble into a roll, a wise maneuver as the club next shattered the stones atop which he had just lain.

"I am not the master of the elements that Esu was, young fool, but Bul-Kathos wields much might of his own!"

"And speaks about it even more!" snapped Uldyssian in turn. From his awkward position, he still managed to focus on his adversary. The giant made for a hard-to-miss target . . .

There was a sound like a thunderclap. The area between the two exploded, as if the very air had caught fire. Both combatants were thrown far from one another.

Uldyssian struck a tree, jarring his bones so hard he thought that they were all shattered. Despite that, he managed to immediately fall forward into a crouching position and seize a handful of dirt. He threw the handful high in the air and concentrated.

The dirt broke apart, becoming a whirling, blinding force that assailed the giant just as he regained his own balance. However, Bul-Kathos did not recoil, but rather inhaled . . . and sneezed. The whirlwind broke apart and the dust formed in a tight ball that landed in the warrior's brown palm.

With a bellowing laugh, Bul-Kathos raised his hand and the dirt stretched two directions, creating in the blink of an eye a spear with a tip that gleamed like a diamond. He threw the spear at Uldyssian.

Again, the former farmer raised a shield, but this time it was not quite strong enough. The spear slowed, yet did not halt. Uldyssian pressed, but the missile caught him in the left shoulder. He cried out as the point penetrated—

Bul-Kathos was suddenly before him, the giant gripping the spear with both hands. He obviously intended to drive the spear deeper, for Uldyssian had managed to keep the wound fairly shallow.

"You were warned! If only you'd not refused to turn away, young one! I'm sworn to do what I must now!"

Uldyssian clutched the upper edge of the spear.

Lightning crackled along the length of it, racing to where his foe held the weapon. Bul-Kathos let out a roar as the powerful energy engulfed him.

Gritting his teeth, Uldyssian shoved the spear from the wound. Falling back, he touched the bloody opening, which immediately sealed.

The pair paused. Both Uldyssian and Bul-Kathos gasped for air as their gazes met.

"A fine battle!" the giant almost cheerfully called. "It breathes new life into me, recalls me the magnificent challenges I once faced daily . . ."

"You may find amusement in this, but I don't!" Uldyssian snapped. "A friend is dead, my brother is lost, and the woman I love and those who trust in me might all be dead now while I waste my time on *this*!" He suddenly straightened. "Continue with your game, if you wish, Bul-Kathos, but I'm done with it all! Very well! Keep whatever foul secret you guard in that mountain to yourself!"

"I can't trust that you'll not be returning, young one, and though 'tis in part my own folly that you know of Arreat and that she houses something, I cannot let you live!"

The giant clasped his fists together, but before he could do whatever it was he planned, a figure materialized between them.

"But you will let him live, old ox. Not only live, but come with me to the depths of Mount Arreat . . ."

Bul-Kathos blurted the name before Uldyssian could. "Rathma!" Then, as the other's words registered, a scowl spread across the giant's gravelly features. "Inside the mount? Am I mad from isolation and only dream you? You'd never suggest such a thing!"

"I am as real as you, Bul-Kathos." To prove his point, Rathma thrust a gloved finger into the taller figure's chest. "And, perhaps, even more so," he added, his glove coming away covered in ground and grass. Rathma shook his head. "I thought you would outlast even me . . ."

"I may yet, if you persist in this! How does this one come to need to visit the mount?"

"Because my mother has returned."

It was all Rathma had to say. Bul-Kathos's face changed utterly. He spat, but instead of water, *mud* landed on the ruined ground. Uldyssian realized that Rathma had the right of it concerning the giant; Bul-Kathos looked much more like them now, but what the son of Diomedes had first seen was the truth. Bul-Kathos existed more as spirit; his true body had long ago been replaced by the soil in which he had lain.

It bespoke how very old the giant was and how very long he had likely stood sentinel over this mysterious peak.

"Lilith . . ." Bul-Kathos spoke her name like someone who had just discovered that they had swallowed poison. "She still bears the murders of my parents on her shoulders! They would've never let Inarius slay us, as she said he would, Rathma! I'm sure of it—"

"And I am not . . . but that is neither here nor there. My mother saved us only to become hers, a fate that would have been worse than death, trust me. As for my father . . . in the name of his sanctimony, he is capable of things just as terrible . . ."

That stilled the huge warrior completely. "Aye, I know that too well . . ."

"Then you understand why I shall now take Uldyssian to see Mount Arreat's secret."

Bul-Kathos nodded. "Aye . . . and no one else'll stop you. If they still stand, that is. I've let any who can hear me know that the way must be clear for you and yours . . ."

With a swirl of his cloak, Rathma turned to Uldyssian. "Well, son of Diomedes, you wanted to see what lay in the mount. Come and I will show you."

But something else concerned Uldyssian far more. "Where is my brother? Where's Mendeln?"

"With Trag'Oul. It must be so for now. Events are rushing forward even swifter than I had imagined that they could and he, too, must be ready to aid in the struggle."

Despite Rathma's indifferent tone, Uldyssian felt every fiber of his being go taut. "What is it?"

"It is," the ancient being said with a sigh, "what it has been. My mother. Lilith. I underestimated her. She has adapted once again . . ."

"What? What has she done?"

Rathma's gaze shifted to Mount Arreat. "She has gained control of your edyrem, of course."

And before Uldyssian could respond . . . they both vanished from Bul-Kathos's side.

TWELVE

Mendeln worried about his brother. He had no idea where Uldyssian had vanished to and the being called Trag'Oul was of no help whatsoever.

He is where he must be, just as you are where you must be, the dragon had each time answered to his question.

Where Mendeln was bothered him almost as much as the location of his sibling. He no longer stood in the empty darkness that seemed Trag'Oul's domain, but rather in a wasteland, a place where there had been much carnage long, long ago.

The landscape and sky were utterly gray and not the slightest hint of wind graced his cheek. Dust covered what Mendeln assumed were ancient buildings of some sort, buildings scattered far from one another. They all bore some similarity to one another, though. Some stood nearly whole, others were barely skeletons. In addition to the buildings, there were also signs that this place had been rich in tall trees and other flora as well. Now, though, there were only the petrified traces of that once lush time. Every plant, however, great or small, had perished at the same time that this settlement had come to ruin.

As had the inhabitants. Mendeln sensed the dead. They had died long, long ago. Longer than even legendary Kehjan had existed, yet they were not fully at rest.

He awaited some word from Trag'Oul, but the celestial creature was as silent as the grave. A frustrated Mendeln finally stalked toward the nearest of the ruins, where he began dusting off the upthrust corner of one.

Not at all to his surprise, the archaic words of the language Rathma had burned into his head were just barely visible. These, however, meant nothing to him, not even after Mendeln sounded them out. He understood the "letters," but they added up to nothing comprehensible.

Straightening, he muttered, "And so what do we have here, then? What?"

The legacy of the demoness's previous crusade . . . came the answer immediately.

Mendeln shuddered, but not only because of what the dragon had said. Since Uldyssian had pointed it out, even he now recognized the similarity between his voice and that of the leviathan . . . not to mention Rathma, also. How long ago and how deeply had they infested his mind?

That question almost made him rebel against any further movement here, but the threat of Lilith and his concern for Uldyssian overrode the hesitation. In truth, thus far Mendeln had not experienced anything actually sinister at the hands of those who claimed that they wanted to be his mentors. In fact, if he recalled his own mind, they only acted on desires already stirring within him for the past few years.

And if learning from them could help save both his brother and his world . . . it behooved Mendeln to do whatever was necessary.

He stepped to the next ruins, the trek taking barely more than a heartbeat. Mendeln was aware that this was not right, that the distance should have taken much longer. However, he was grateful that he would not have to take what would have possibly been hours just to traverse his immediate surroundings.

The second structure was much more intact than the first. A quick dusting revealed more unknown words. This time, however, Uldyssian's brother did not so quickly give up. He repeated each rune with care, trying them in different vocal variations. Perhaps pronunciation was the mistake, he wondered. Perhaps—

Suddenly, the word before him made sense. A name, or at least a noun. *Pyragos.*

Quite pleased by his success, Mendeln spoke the word out loud. "Pyragos!"

Instantly, the ground around the ruined building shuddered. Mendeln stumbled back, already regretting his rash action.

From below burst a grotesque, fleshless form with wings stripped of the membranes that had once given them the potential for flight. The head was shaped like a bull's, even with two savage horns that interlocked in the middle. The fiend leaped up, dry dirt and what might have been drier skin dropping from it. Mendeln was immediately put to mind of the demonic presence that he and Uldyssian had fought in the jungle.

But something concerning this situation was not quite the same. First and foremost, the skeletal form rising up from its grave was shorter than the one in the jungle and its frame was much more petite overall despite the vast wings. Staring at it, Mendeln would have sworn that it was—or had once been—*female.*

Less certain than a moment before, he yet again repeated the name. "Pyragos?"

In reply, the ground to his *right* shook. In fact, the entire *landscape* suddenly convulsed. He cursed himself as he leapt back. Once had been ignorant; twice had been utterly foolhardy.

Out of the wasted landscape rose a *legion* of monstrous corpses, none of them completely human and all nearly bone . . . or some equivalent to it. In fact, there were many that to his eye seemed more merely empty garments or shadowy images. They came in all shapes, all sizes, to his eye registering as once male, female, and . . . simply *other.*

But there was something about them that did not seem right. Mendeln had faced ghosts before and these were not such. He put a hand to the foremost, a winged thing with horns that, from its slight size and certain characteristics,

Mendeln judged once female. The hand went through, not so great a surprise, but the sense of former life was not there.

They are the memories of angels and demons, came Trag'Oul's voice. *Their deaths so terrible that their shadows are forever burned into this place . . .*

Not real spirits. Mendeln wondered if either group had what he would have called a soul, but suspected not. Perhaps that was another reason they both coveted and distrusted humans . . .

Then . . . among them he sensed the coming of others. Misty forms milled around and even *through* the macabre memories, misty forms with which Mendeln was more familiar. These were true spirits, true souls.

But . . . of whom?

Show yourself to me! he demanded. *Show yourself!*

They did. A legion of men and women, many of them astonishingly perfect even in death, overwhelmed the visions of demons and angels. Mendeln recognized them for who they were, for their perfection was as Rathma's.

The children of Sanctuary's founders. The first nephalem and the immediate generations after.

The ghosts of the nephalem stood motionless, as if awaiting *his* next action. Mendeln had no notion as to what that might be and Trag'Oul appeared silent on the subject. Evidently, it was up to Mendeln to make his own path.

But with an endless array of dead before him, what *was* that path?

He looked to the foremost of them, a woman of such dark beauty that she made his heart beat faster. Her silver eyes stared into his without blinking.

Hoping that he was not making a fatal mistake, Mendeln reached out a hand.

The female nephalem immediately bowed her head so that the top of it hovered directly before his fingers.

Acting on a hunch, Mendeln let the fingertips graze the lush, black hair. Immediately, he felt a force surge through him and a voice—a distinctly feminine voice—said to him, *I was Helgrotha . . .*

He pulled the fingers back. The nephalem raised her head, the silver orbs again staring into his own.

Curiously, although he had only heard the name—*her* name—Mendeln discovered that he now knew much, much more about her. He could imagine her as she had once been, from her birth to her death. Once, she had been nearly as powerful as Rathma and had watched over those creatures who lived during night as opposed to the day. She had been kind, but also firm in her protection of those for whom she had cared.

He stood there, wondering what next to do. The dead waited with him, forever patient, even if he was not.

"And what am I to do with you?" Mendeln demanded. "Will you march against Lilith for me? Will you? Will even one of you do this?"

The woman raised her left hand to him. The action startled Mendeln, who took another step back. But the specter did not attack. Instead, in her hand materialized a long, narrow object. A *bone.*

She offered it to him.

Having no idea what he should do with the grisly gift but certain that it would be folly to refuse it, Mendeln gingerly gripped the piece of bone.

"Thank you?" he blurted.

But even as the last word slipped from his lips . . . what had once been a nephalem called Helgrotha faded like a dying wisp of smoke suddenly caught in a breeze. Mendeln looked around and saw the rest of the ghostly legion vanish in like manner.

No sooner had they faded away, than the ruins, the visions of demons and angels—the *entire* wasteland—followed suit.

A moment later, Mendeln did the same, suddenly reappearing in the dark emptiness with which he was starting to become too familiar.

Say the word again. Say it, son of Diomedes . . .

"Pyragos?" Mendeln instantly felt a coolness in his hands, an almost refreshing coolness. He glanced down and saw the bone shimmer. It took all his will not to drop the fragment.

It is the first word of summoning and this the item that will better bind you to the powers involved in such an act.

The nephalem's bone twisted, reshaped. It grew slightly shorter and much slimmer. One end narrowed to a point, then flattened. The edges grew sharp.

The shimmering dulled but did not completely fade. Mendeln stared at what he held.

A dagger . . . an ivory dagger such as he had seen Rathma wielding.

They have accepted you who hears them—the children of angels and demons slain so foully—accepted that you will keep Sanctuary from becoming either the fury of the Burning Hells or the oppressive order and worship of the High Heavens. They who were the first birthed in Sanctuary and are, because of that, still more of it than either Lilith or Inarius can understand, forever open the link between the phase of afterdeath and that of living . . .

"'Afterdeath'?" Mendeln repeated, but the glittering stars did not further explain that term and Mendeln finally understood that he should define it as best he could on his own.

Take up the dagger in one hand, Trag'Oul then commanded. When Uldyssian's brother had done so, the celestial leviathan added, *Turn it point down to your palm.*

Mendeln did not like where this was going, yet he still obeyed. "Great Trag'Oul—"

Prick your palm, son of Diomedes . . .

"But—"

It must be done . . .

He had come this far, Mendeln thought. Besides, all the dragon asked of him was a slight jab, nothing more. What harm could come of that?

What harm, indeed . . .

Mouth grimly set, Mendeln did as instructed. He pulled the point away almost as soon as it touched, so swiftly, in fact, that at first he wondered whether he had actually punctured the skin.

But a tiny red dot did form, so miniscule that Mendeln expected Trag'Oul to command him to try again. The dagger still hovered an inch or two above the palm . . .

Then, to his shock, a thin stream of blood rose from his hand to the blade's tip. Only magic could explain this defiance of nature. The tiny stream covered the point . . . then continued to flow up, covering more and more of the narrow end of the blade and heading slowly but inexorably toward the hilt.

Mendeln could only imagine how much blood it would take to reach that point and started to pull his hand away.

Leave it . . .

Mendeln wanted to disobey, but did not. It was not that Trag'Oul had just cast some spell over him, merely that he yet trusted in the dragon that no harm would come to him.

But when did I start to trust him? Before he could answer that question, the first drops touched the handle.

The blood already flowing continued its journey, but no more rose from Mendeln's palm. In fact, when he sought the small wound, he could find nothing.

Watch . . .

His gaze returned to the dagger, where the blade was now colored crimson. Yet, the crimson grew more faded with each passing moment, until finally it disappeared.

The dagger is bound to you and you are bound to the dagger. Through it, you are bound to them and through them, the Balance.

"What is this *Balance*?" Mendeln called to the stars. "You speak of it and I think of it, but I have never known what it truly means!"

The stars moved, briefly erasing any semblance to a beast. When they returned to their proper positions, Trag'Oul replied, *The Balance is the even distribution of Light and Dark. Its essence is most significant to Sanctuary, but it goes beyond, to all of creation. A world where Dark rules would burn itself up. A world where Light commands would eventually stagnate. If either gained enough control of Sanctuary so that the other could not match it again, then that would be the end of all things . . .*

There was sense to what the leviathan said, or at least Mendeln saw it that way. Yet . . . "But should we not ever strive for good over evil?"

Light and Dark are not necessarily good and evil, son of Diomedes. Yes, good must outshine evil, but if the knowledge of evil is erased utterly, even good may turn on itself . . .

"Even still, I would never side with any demon!" Such a notion seemed incredulous.

What almost appeared mirth touched Trag'Oul's "voice." *"Never" is a word rarely attained in fact. And would you ever join the cause of an angel . . . such as Inarius . . . who would keep Humanity bent low in prayer to him?*

The dragon had him there. From all he had learned, Inarius's notion of what was right meant absolute obedience to him.

Mendeln shook his head. "I cannot believe that we must suffer two such forces without any hope . . ."

Did I say there was not? The High Heavens and the Burning Hells create their own notions of their absolute might. The dragon paused, then added, *They will someday find that they are far from the ultimate masters of all things created . . .*

Uldyssian's brother seized upon the other's words. "Are you saying that there is something more, something greater?" He recalled something that he had wondered about earlier. "The spirits of the firstborn; they have not moved on, but where do all others go? Where do the souls of my people go?"

To their rightful place . . . to beyond the reach of both the High Heavens and the Burning Hells and this universe of tragedy they have wrought . . .

"What does that mean? How do you know all you say?"

We know because we know . . .

Mendeln noted the "we" and somehow felt it did *not* include Rathma. Were there others like Trago'Oul? Was that possible?

But the celestial beast said no more on the subject and Mendeln knew that, if he asked such questions, Trag'Oul would not answer him. Still, some of what the dragon had said just prior gave him hope again.

"Then, there is truly a chance for Sanctuary to be more than what they would have of it . . ." Mendeln clutched the dagger, which felt so right in his hand. It was not a weapon—although it could easily be used as such—but one key toward freeing Humanity's destiny from the angels' and demons' perpetual war.

However, that was only if he and Uldyssian managed to somehow help prevent Lilith and the mysterious Inarius from succeeding with their own plots.

The angel bothered him most. "This Inarius . . . Rathma's father . . . what does he do now?"

For the first time, Trag'Oul radiated uncertainty. *Lilith is a creature of many plots and although difficult to always ferret out, her mark is generally quite noticeable. Inarius, on the other hand, plays the game more subtly. It may be that we are already destined to fail against him, for he may have moved to defeat her and us simultaneously. Rathma can judge him better, but even he is uncertain as to how well . . .*

Which was a lengthy way to tell Mendeln that the angel was as much an enigma to his mentors as he was to the human. "But we know he acts as the Prophet, whose face stands unveiled for all to see! Surely, we can calculate his actions thus—"

Inarius stands utterly veiled even surrounded by a multitude of eyes. What is seen of the Prophet is never necessarily what he is, even more so than the Primus, who has been not one but at least three . . .

And here he brought up another point that had troubled Mendeln even before Rathma had whisked him away.

"The demon Lucion was the Primus and he is no more. It is Lilith who wears that mask, surely."

But would Lilith have created such chaos in Hashir?

She would not have and Mendeln knew that. He had wondered at what had seemed irrational even for the demoness.

"Another commands?" Uldyssian's brother finally asked. "Another demon? That could work in our favor! If even indirectly this third interferes with her plots—"

It does not . . . in fact . . . it has accelerated it.

That did not bode well. With both him and Uldyssian gone, that left only Serenthia to watch for the demoness. Still, in many ways, Cyrus's daughter was likely far more capable than Mendeln. "Serenthia will guide the edyrem. They trust her. They will follow her in all things—"

The stars yet again shifted, then resettled. Mendeln had learned quickly that this was a sign of the dragon's displeasure. *Yes . . . they will heed the commands of your companion in the absence of your brother . . . and thus become Lilith's more and more . . .*

Mendeln let out a growl of frustration. "What are you not *telling* me? What is it you know?"

There was an unusual hesitation . . . and then Trag'Oul replied, *Uldyssian's edyrem believe that they follow your friend, but in doing so, they actually follow the demoness.*

"Follow—no!"

Yes . . . it is Serenthia of Seram that they see before them, but she is in truth Lilith and has been so since some days ago as Sanctuary counts time . . .

"Serenthia . . ." Mendeln fell down on one knee, so struck was he by the news. His mind raced back to Partha and Malic, who had worn the skin of another. "No . . . Serenthia . . . no . . . it cannot be . . ."

The skin of another . . . Lilith wearing Serenthia's skin . . .

Hashir might have been far smaller than Toraja, but the mark the edyrem left upon it—especially within the temple—far exceeded what they had done in the first city. The temple still stood, but it was awash in blood. The high priests had been made special victims, their bodies now hanging from the ruined pillars standing at the building's front. The power of the edyrem had allowed bolts a foot long to drive into the thick marble . . . after going through the soft flesh first.

Each of the priests had their arms held directly over their heads. The metal bolts had pierced the back of the hands, which had been first clasped together. Bolts had also been driven through the throats and torsos.

The suggestion for such a visual display had come from the woman now leading the edyrem. The priests had stolen away Uldyssian, Serenthia had vehemently claimed, and one by one they would be hung so until some voice among those remaining revealed where he was.

But all the priests perished, each swearing that they did *not* know what had happened to the mob's leader. Serenthia had seized upon that to further scour the area for supporters of the sect, especially among city leaders.

Three days after Uldyssian and his followers entered the city, Hashir was, in many ways, little more than a scar.

The populace hid while this happened, fearful of both the temple and the newcomers. However, on the fourth day, Serenthia—her long hair flowing wildly in the wind—went to the market center and proclaimed in a voice that echoed throughout the city that she had now brought peace and hope to Hashir. This was naturally met with some wariness on the part of the locals, but the edyrem ushered many out of their homes so that they could see that she spoke the truth.

To her captive audience, Serenthia offered the same as Uldyssian, but not immediately. The Hashiri had witnessed the might of the foreigners and so not a few were tempted. Yet, Serenthia did not show even those the way, although she among all the edyrem should have been able to do so.

Instead, in the very temple they had conquered and even

as the bodies of the priests fed some of the local birds, good Romus found himself summoned for an audience with the master's first acolyte. He had no idea what Serenthia wanted of him, save that, if Uldyssian *were* no more—as was the rumor vilely spreading through the ranks—then she was their only hope of not only continuing on, but even merely surviving.

Serenthia had taken for her temporary quarters those of the local high priest. Romus, who had always been poor even when he had been a brigand, could only marvel at the silken wall coverings and gold-laced tapestries as he entered. Some of the regret that he had had for the harshness of the edyrem's actions in Hashir faded as he considered the Triune's massive, ill-gotten wealth.

A moment later, he stopped short. Serenthia lay stretched across a reclining couch, her gaze on a parchment in her hands. Her long, lush hair cascaded down her shoulders and even enshrouded part of her face. She was a breathtaking sight to behold even in her battle-worn garments, especially to Romus, who had been infatuated by Serenthia almost since the first he had seen her in the Parthan square.

He finally managed to clear his throat, which made her immediately glance up.

"Romus!" The smile that lit up her face kindled the fire in his heart. Had Serenthia asked him to singlehandedly fight a pack of the savage creatures called morlu, he would have willingly leapt into the fray. "I feared you wouldn't come!"

"How could I not, mistress? Anytime, for anything, all you need do is call and faithful Romus will rush to obey . . ."

She sat up. "How poetic! But come! Why are you standing all the way over there by the doorway?" Serenthia patted the couch. "Join me here!"

Bowing low, he hastened to approach. At the couch itself, the onetime thief hesitated, but again Serenthia smiled and patted it.

He seated himself, leaving a respectful space between them. Romus looked at his mistress and immediately found his gaze captivated by her glittering green eyes. A small part of him vaguely wondered why he had once thought them blue. Surely, he could not have been so mistaken . . .

"Romus . . . you were one of those closest to Uldyssian besides myself."

It took him a moment to notice the past tense. "We'll find him, we will, mistress! Have no fear of that!"

She shook her head. "No, dear, loyal Romus . . . even though I've said so to the people, I don't think we will. Like his brother, I fear Uldyssian's lost to us forever!"

It was unthinkable. The master had defeated terrible demons and legions of warriors! Nothing could take him so easily . . . and yet . . .

"Some say . . . mistress . . . some say that they saw his brother near him just before he vanished . . . perhaps . . ."

"A disguise, like that worn by the two monsters who attacked me." Serenthia shuddered, which made Romus want to comfort her in his arms. "No, a demon took Uldyssian, of that I'm certain." Her green eyes bore deeper into his. "One almost took *me* even. Before Hashir."

He was aghast. "Mistress! When?"

"In the jungle. When Uldyssian ordered us across the river. You recall?"

"Aye . . ." Romus gritted his teeth. In some ways, it bothered him even more that she had nearly been taken than it did that Uldyssian was now missing. He found it impossible to imagine the edyrem without her.

"Uldyssian . . . and even Mendeln . . . protected me then. Since they vanished, I've worked as hard as I can to protect everyone else, but . . . I must tell you something, for your ears alone, dear Romus."

"What? What?" Without realizing it, he slid closer until they were nearly touching.

"I am afraid. *Afraid*. I can protect the others, but who is there now to protect *me*?"

The answer escaped him before he realized how it sounded. "Me! I'll always be there to protect you, mistress!"

Before his face could redden too much from shame, Serenthia suddenly put a soft hand to his cheek. She smiled. "You would? Would you *really*, Romus?"

It all began pouring out. "I'd give my life and soul for you, mistress! I'd stand against all the powers of the Triune! I could never let anything happen to you!"

He expected her to throw him out for daring to speak so when it was evident to all how much the master had meant to her.

And yet . . .

"Romus . . ." Serenthia whispered, her lips so close that he was nearly ready to sacrifice his life just to kiss them once. "Romus . . . you've no idea how much that means to me . . ."

She caressed his cheek again, then, almost reluctantly, leaned back. The former brigand was unable to stop himself from exhaling sharply.

"If you mean what you say . . . and I so very much hope that you do . . . this gives me another idea . . ."

Still recovering from before, Romus managed only a grunt of inquisitiveness.

"You know how Uldyssian introduced others to the gift. But with me, he delved deeper . . . and that's why I think that my abilities grew faster than anyone else's."

"Very likely, very likely," he replied, glad to have a safe subject to discuss.

"I think . . . no . . . I *know* . . . how he did it. They were private moments, when he could focus on me alone. You did notice that there were times when he and I were gone for hours?"

Romus recalled some such periods and felt for the first time a jealousy that the master had been able to partake in them with the woman before him. "Yes . . . mistress . . ."

"Good!" Her eyes seemed to glow brighter than the torches in the chamber warranted. "Will you do me the honor of doing as Uldyssian did with me? It'll mean hours together, for which I apologize, but with both him and

Mendeln gone, someone else must step up . . . and I suppose you could better protect me while I protect you . . ."

He could hardly deny her. "I'm yours, mistress. To my very soul, I'm yours. Teach me, if you think me worthy . . ."

"I find you *very* worthy," Serenthia returned in what from any other woman would have sounded coy to Romus. Not the mistress, though. Not her.

Steeling himself, the brigand finally tore his gaze from hers. She wanted him merely as a fellow comrade, nothing more. Everything that she had suggested made perfect sense; Romus should have felt honored for that alone. If the master was indeed never returning, as she clearly believed, the least that his loyal follower could do was to see that his legacy lived on.

Feeling better about his decision, Romus bowed his head. "When shall we start, mistress?"

Her smile curled higher. "Why not now?"

"Now?" He thought quickly. "Saron and some of the others'll need to know, mistress, so they can do without me . . ."

"They are capable of that already. You need go and tell them nothing . . . not even after tonight . . ."

Her hands went to his and when she touched them, a flush went through Romus. Trying to recover, he looked to the doors and only then noticed that they were shut.

"I want us alone . . . the better to concentrate," Serenthia explained. "You understand the need for privacy, don't you?"

"Yes . . . yes, mistress . . ."

She giggled, which caused his face to again flush. "And one more thing, dear Romus . . ." Her fingers intertwined with his. "*You* need never call me 'mistress' . . ."

THIRTEEN

It sounded to Uldyssian as if something immense was breathing.

The cavern in which he and Rathma stood stretched so high that the stalactites forming above had managed to grow many times the length of a man. The stalagmites had done fair, too, rising like squat giants from the floor.

Ulydssian felt as if he stood in the mouth of a hungry beast. The "breathing" only added to that disconcerting sensation.

It was the stalactites and stalagmites that were also the source of illumination for the tremendous chamber, for radiating from deep within each was a ghostly crimson light whose source he could only imagine. While he was grateful for their brightness, they, too, contributed to Uldyssian's overwhelming sense of unease.

"This is as far as I can risk bringing us by other than physical means," Rathma commented with his usual detachment. "You can sense why, I think."

But now that he was getting over his astonishment at where he and his undesired companion had just materialized, what Rathma had proclaimed just before their arrival once more seized hold of Uldyssian.

Lilith had control of the edyrem . . .

Stirred anew by anger, he seized Rathma by the collar of his cloak. "What did you mean by what you said before?" Uldyssian growled as he shook the demoness's son. "How did it happen? How did she do it?"

"You refer to my mother and her usurping of your followers," the other said needlessly. "She is cunning and keeps herself well shielded, but I have gradually considered that she must have possessed the woman Serenthia at some point when she was out of your sight in all ways. From there, it was a simple task to—"

Head pounding, Uldyssian roughly released Lilith's son as he thought of just when it might have been that the demoness had taken the merchant's daughter. One incident immediately came to mind. Serenthia had gone to get water and for once, he had not used his abilities to monitor her. She had bent behind the lush plants and . . . and a moment later had *gasped*.

And fool that he had been, Uldyssian had taken her response to his concern at face value. He had forgotten the twisted ways of Lilith . . .

"Serenthia . . ." he whispered. "It can't be . . . she can't be dead . . ."

"And she is not."

Confusion, hope, and distrust warred for mastery over Uldyssian. "What do you mean? It's Master Ethon and his son all over again! That foul witch wears Serry's skin like a damned dress! She slaughtered her then stripped her of her flesh!"

Rathma shook his head. "No . . . for the game my mother's chosen to play, she cannot disguise herself so. Such a technique, while definitely demonic in nature, allows only a limited ability. Enough to fool some priests or household servants for a time, but not for extended periods and needs. For this, Lilith required a more careful, more delicate touch. She has literally had to make herself and the woman one. My mother is like a haunting spirit that now guides each movement of the body, yet your Serenthia is still within, but very, very deep asleep."

Uldyssian's heart, which had felt to him a moment before as if it had ceased beating, now pounded with renewed life. "Then, she's all right? If we can cast out Lilith, Serenthia will be herself again?"

"That, I cannot promise, son of Diomedes. Her slumber must be very strong, so that Lilith can also have some access to her memories and thus better perpetuate the lie. Even if my mother is ousted, I cannot in full honesty promise that your friend will be restored."

"I should've never been taken from Hashir! I've got to go to her immediately, then! Send me from this place or show me how to do it myself!"

But Rathma remained steadfast. "Had you been left in the situation from which we took you, you would have at this point been nothing more than a shell acting on Lilith's behalf. She is constantly altering her plots as the moment invites, hence the difficulty of predicting her next move. Having taken the woman's body and seeing the foolish attack by whoever in turn played her role as Primus, she obviously decided that you could not be trusted to lead as she wanted. In fact, my mother is the reason that you were so weakened at the last moment. Clad as someone so dear to you, you let her through much of your guard. She infiltrated your body and soul, manipulating your thoughts and actions. If we had not taken you when we had, Hashir would have proven the point where Lilith took utter mastery over you, as well, Uldyssian."

"So, instead she has it over Serenthia and the others," Uldyssian retorted. "Your help seems more trouble for me than it's worth . . ."

Rathma acknowledged his comment with a slight tilt of his head, adding, "I have erred much too much. I agree. But alone you would have fallen quickly to her. There is still opportunity to remedy this, if you will just listen."

"Serenthia—"

"Will be lost forever if you try to separate her from Lilith at this juncture. As distasteful as I, too, find it, my mother must be given her free hand for the moment. But only for the moment."

Such a vile thought did not sit at all well with Uldyssian. He could not imagine what would become of Serenthia and the rest under the wicked guidance of the demoness. Yet, he had to admit that confronting Lilith would be a monumental task; how could he keep from injuring or possibly even slaying Serenthia?

"What can we do?" he finally demanded of the pale figure. "Tell me that, at least!"

Rathma gestured ahead to where a passage at the far end beckoned. "We can go on to where we should."

It was the sort of answer that Uldyssian had unfortunately expected. Still, as much as possible, he intended that matters would from here on go as he wanted. With that in mind, he strode off at a quick pace past the other.

Taller and longer of leg, Rathma quickly caught up to him. Lilith's son then kept pace, perhaps trying to make Uldyssian not feel so guided.

They journeyed through a mazelike series of corridors that someone had meticulously carved out long, long ago. The corridors had no illumination, but Rathma pulled free his dagger, uttered a word in the strange tongue he had used previous, and suddenly the blade shone. Because of that alone, Uldyssian finally fell back a step behind his companion.

As they made their way, Uldyssian could not help but feel that someone or something watched them. He did not broach the subject with Rathma, for fear of the answer that the other might give. Uldyssian had enough with which to concern himself already.

After what seemed the dozenth meandering passage, Rathma finally looked back at him. "We are nearly there. I ask that you pay careful attention to yourself . . ."

The black-clad figure did not clarify what he meant. Uldyssian resolved to continue to keep on his guard. What else could he do? The breathing sound that he had first heard in the outer cavern was not so loud it pounded in his ears. Whatever it was that they sought, it was very likely also the source of the ominous sound.

Then, but a few steps after Rathma's warning, what felt

like a wave of intense heat washed over Uldyssian. Yet, the heat rolled through him from *within,* not without. He felt his pulse quicken and all his concerns—Serenthia, Mendeln, the edyrem, and the rest—magnified at least a thousandfold. His step faltered and it was all he could do to smother a moan.

Ahead, Rathma continued on as if unmindful of his plight. That only upset Uldyssian more. How could the fool not see that they wasted their time, that they faced insurmountable hurdles? How could he—

Rathma's warning came back to him. Shaking with effort, Uldyssian forced away the rising fears, the worries . . . and suddenly the heat within dissipated.

"You are better again?" the cowled figure asked without looking back.

"You could've given better warning than you did!"

Still facing the path before them, Rathma shook his head. "No, regrettably, I could not."

Uldyssian might have argued that, but then a faint red gleam arose from the far end of the corridor. At the same time, there came a sound like shattering glass that reverberated through the passage. Uldyssian stepped up next to Rathma, who slowed his own pace.

"Stay near me when we enter the chamber. Our way is not completely clear."

"Not even for you?"

"This place is of my father's making."

His words were punctuated by another loud crash. Keeping wary, Uldyssian did as he was bade. His pulse raced again and although he knew that it had to do with what lay farther on, he was unable to calm himself.

"What is it?" Uldyssian finally had to ask.

"The making and unmaking of us. Inarius's ultimate yoke for humanity. You shall see . . ."

As they drew closer, the crimson gleam—and the slow but incessant *breathing*—grew even more pronounced. Whatever lay within the chamber glittered as bright as a sun. Rathma muttered something and his dagger dulled. However, Lilith's son did not put the weapon away.

"Be wary . . ." Rathma warned as they reached the end of the corridor. "Take each step slowly."

Together, they entered the new cavern. However, immediately the light became so glaring that even when Uldyssian shielded his eyes, it was impossible to see beyond his own feet.

And then—"We are under attack!"

The warning from Rathma barely came in time. A high-pitched squeal almost deafened Uldyssian. Acting on instinct, he immediately created a barrier above him.

There was a heavy thump and an angry shriek. Uldyssian heard the flapping of wings. It was swiftly followed by scratching and more squealing. He was under assault by more than one of the foul creatures.

Uldyssian spun around so that he faced the tunnel. That enabled him to just barely see. Out of the corner of his eye, he caught a glimpse of a leathery wing.

From elsewhere, Rathma called out. Uldyssian did not understand him and so assumed that the ancient figure was casting some sort of spell. That reminded him that he, too, supposedly had fantastic abilities. Swearing under his breath, Uldyssian listened for the next approaching attacker.

The sound of wings from his left was all that he needed. He thrust a hand in that direction.

Whatever flew at him let out another squeal. Whether this was designed to shatter his eardrums or for some other reason, Uldyssian now used the cry against the creature. He repelled the squeal, letting it strike back with several times its original intensity.

From the direction of his foe came another shriek, followed by the thumping of a body against what Uldyssian believed rock. The shrieking continued, but with a pained tone to it. Thumping accompanied the cry, as if the winged beast was going through convulsions.

Rathma somehow cut through the multitude of squeals. "Uldyssian! Back up to my voice!"

Uldyssian obeyed. An anxious breath later, he collided with what he hoped was the pale figure.

The ivory dagger flashed before Uldyssian's pained eyes. Before he could react, he heard Rathma chant something.

The dagger flared, blinding Uldyssian. He wondered if he had been duped all along, that Rathma had brought him here at Lilith's request so that she could humiliate him one last time before he perished.

Yet after that moment of blindness, Uldyssian's eyesight not only returned, but became *normal* . . . something even he, with his powers, had not been able to accomplish. Now he could see well enough to turn from the tunnel.

And what he saw left him dead in his tracks.

The cavern he stood within dwarfed the previous one. It dropped deep below as well as rose high above. Rathma and he stood on what was actually some wide, ancient platform carved from stone. It was several yards long and at the end stretched to each side. Uldyssian realized that if the creatures had driven him much farther to the right, he would have fallen to his doom.

A low wall lined the platform and at the corners were small constructions built like step pyramids. Atop each glowed a tiny—and in this chamber—insignificant light.

The chamber's own color reminded Uldyssian of a living heart fresh with blood. He only studied that aspect for a moment, though, for that which was the focus of this place now demanded his absolute attention.

It resembled some of the crystalline formations that, as a boy, Uldyssian had found in the small caves at home, but none of those had stood well over a hundred feet high—perhaps even more than *two* hundred, since the base was too deep down to view—consisting of several monoliths jutting in a dozen different directions. Unlike the formations he recalled, this behemoth had a harshness to its look, with its jagged appearance and frightening crimson color.

Each facet of the gargantuan formation contained thousands of minute ones. From within it emanated not only the illumination that had so burnt Uldyssian's eyes, but, deeper yet, flashes of multicolored lightning. The overall light from the great crystal not only extended the entire length and breadth of the cavern—itself vast enough to fit the village of Seram and its surrounding lands within at least twenty times over—but looked as if it seeped through the very stone walls.

With each burst of lightning, the formation pulsated and at last Uldyssian understood the source of the "breathing."

There came another ear-tearing, shattering sound. Uldyssian looked up and for the first time noticed that smaller fragments of the crystal—"smaller" as in only two or three times his height and width—floated around much of the cavern in seemingly random directions. The harsh noise had come from two such pieces colliding. The broken fragments spilled around—and then began to re-form in different designs.

All this Uldyssian drank in in only a few scant seconds. Then, a more immediate and highly grotesque sight took Uldyssian's attention from the astounding crystal. Four winged furies with heads resembling skinned hounds dove down at him from various points above. The creatures had savage teeth and ears long and wide. Their snouts were fat, with wide nostrils. The only thing the heads lacked were eyes. There were not even gaps where the eyes should have been. It was almost as if whatever had created them had forgone such on purpose.

Perhaps that was not far from the truth. Of what use were eyes in this place, where only Rathma's magic had enabled Uldyssian to see *anything*. Of better use were the huge ears and the nostrils, which could ferret out any prey entering.

Each of the beasts had a wingspan of at least six feet, and like the bats they somewhat resembled in shape, those wings were also their hands. Yet, unlike bats, the claws of these aberrations were each longer than Uldyssian's hand

and so razor-sharp that to be cut by them even once would surely cause a gaping, dangerous wound.

Uldyssian cupped his hand. A blue energy formed over his palm. He threw it at the nearest of the fiends.

The blue energy engulfed its target . . . and vanished in a puff. The winged fury shook its head, stunned but otherwise unhindered. Certainly not turned to ash, as Uldyssian had assumed it would be.

Startled by this failure, he barely recovered in time to re-create the shield. Even that was not as strong as it generally was, and with three—then four—assailing it, Uldyssian began to sweat.

It was Rathma, naturally, who supplied an answer. From farther in, Lilith's son—his vast cloak seeming to provide him with the same protection as Uldyssian's barrier—shouted, "Your powers are dampened here! It is the effect of the crystal! You must focus harder, whatever you attempt!"

Cursing the other for not having told him this before they had entered, Uldyssian concentrated more on the barrier. By now, seven of the bizarre beasts fluttered about him, each seeking to shred his flesh. Up close, he saw that they had no true bodies whatsoever. There were the shriveled remnants of a torso and what might have been vestigial legs. The creatures were essentially composed of wings and head. Uldyssian wondered whether they even ate . . . then decided such a question was one for which he would prefer not to have an answer.

Mouths snapped at his face, sometimes coming much closer than he desired. Forcing himself to calm down despite the frenzied efforts of his attackers, Uldyssian wondered how best to defend himself. What he had assumed a deadly attack had failed miserably. Uldyssian had to choose well, for when he struck, his shield would also weaken. Even with his recuperative powers, he doubted that he would survive long should even one beast manage a slash.

In the end, there was only one strategy that came to mind, a variation on something he had done earlier.

Drawing himself up, Uldyssian took a deep breath . . . and whistled.

To his own ears—and hopefully to Rathma's as well—all he did was let out a long, loud, single note. Certain that his efforts would again be muted by the massive crystal, the son of Diomedes concentrated as much of his will as he dared—possibly even more—into the whistle. As he did, he felt a wing brush against his shoulder . . .

But in the next instant, just as what felt like a claw touched his arm, *every* winged monster around Uldyssian let out a bloodcurdling shriek. They pulled back from him, then whirled around as if entirely mad. Two immediately collided, but instead of merely separating, tore at each other as they had at the human. Another crashed into the rocky wall of the cavern, then repeated the accident over and over until it finally crashed on the floor.

Three others simply *dropped* to the ground, where they screeched and shook their heads as if trying to remove something.

"I would not have believed it if I had not witnessed it," Rathma called in his ear. The cowled figure stepped up next to Uldyssian. "What you did should not have been possible for you in this of all places."

"I just followed your advice. I just concentrated harder. It worked."

"It should *not* have . . . especially not to this degree. Look around you, Uldyssian ul-Diomed. Look around you and see the truth of that."

Uldyssian did as he was bade . . . and his eyes widened at the results of his desperate attempt.

More than three score creatures either flew or lay in states of chaos. Two collided with floating fragments. Several fought furiously with one another, while others on the ground twitched wildly. At least two were savagely biting themselves to such a degree that their deaths were certain.

Then, two in aerial combat dropped. A moment later, some of those on the floor stilled. As Uldyssian looked around, the cavern's denizens one by one simply fell to the ground . . . and *died*.

"I don't—I don't understand . . ."

Rathma shrugged as if it should all make perfect sense to anyone. There was a red scar on his chin and a tear in his garments just above where Uldyssian supposed his heart should be. The creatures had gotten closer to slaying the ancient being than they had the son of Diomedes. "You recalled their similarity to bats, obviously. You imagined that, if you whistled loud and used the power within to amplify it, you would at least injure or confuse some . . . yes?"

"Yes . . . but . . . I thought I might succeed with those before me, but . . ."

"You should have been fortunate to do that, even with my warning." Rathma shook his head. "Uldyssian ul-Diomed, you are not what you should be." He looked over his shoulder. "And the reason for that *must* have to do with you . . ."

That to which Lilith's son referred was none other than the vast, menacing crystal. Even with bat creatures perishing all around them, Uldyssian could not help but again stare in fascination at it. Never could he have imagined such a thing existing.

"What is it?" he at last asked. "Why is it here?" Rathma gestured at the floating giant. "It is the reason why no nephalem or anything akin to it has risen lo these many centuries, my friend. It is the reason why you and yours should *not* exist! You stand before the curse of all the descendants of those angels and demons who forged Sanctuary! You stand before the *Worldstone* . . ."

Merely hearing the name sent an involuntary shiver through Uldyssian, as if some part of him should have always known of this incredible artifact . . . known of it and rightly feared its existence.

Even with the aid of Rathma's spell, the Worldstone was hard to eye directly. Uldyssian discovered that he could best observe it by glancing slightly to the side. Even then, it sparkled as if reflecting a hundred red suns.

"Inarius thought the nephalem a disease, a disgrace to what he was. To him, we should have never been. He only agreed to consider our fate as opposed to erasing us from existence because of the protests of the others. I feel that he would have yet chosen to follow through with his original intention if not for my mother murdering the other refugees. That act altered everything. Had Inarius exterminated us afterward, then he would have been all alone, something which even he could not stand. Yet, the notion of the nephalem disgusted him and that is why he took the Worldstone—which had been created in great part as a manner by which to hide Sanctuary from the eyes of the High Heavens and the Burning Hells—and *altered* its resonance."

Uldyssian had been trying to follow Rathma's tale as best as possible, but did not understand the last at all. "What does that mean? What would that do?"

"What it means is thus; in addition to secreting this realm, the Worldstone also began a steady and subtle dampening process. Each succeeding generation of nephalem became far less powerful than the previous, until, in very short order, those next born were bereft of *any* ability. Soon, only a few from the first generation—myself and Bul-Kathos, to name the obvious—survived. The gifts—or curse—of our forebears was forgotten. Inarius began reshaping Sanctuary to his satisfaction . . . and to his iron rule."

Uldyssian could feel the Worldstone's radiance and did not doubt that it had the ability to utterly smother his powers. Yet, why was it not doing so now?

"This is the work of Lilith," Rathma quietly declared.

"Do you read my mind?"

The demoness's son shook his head. "I read . . . *sensations*. It is almost like reading thoughts, but far more accurate, for thoughts can be filled with lies."

Once again confused, Uldyssian turned back to the subject at hand. "What's she done?"

"Clearly, my mother altered the resonance of the Worldstone again, so that now its effect is minimal and limited more or less to Mount Arreat, if that. Even in its presence, you were able to overcome it. With the Worldstone no longer a hindrance, the natural process enabling the nephalem powers could now flourish. You are the result of that . . . the first, anyway."

The more he stood near it, the more Uldyssian sensed the Worldstone's emanations. He imagined them a thousand times greater . . . no, a thousand thousand times. What Rathma had said made more sense. With such mighty forces sweeping over Sanctuary, his kind would surely never have come into existence. Only Lilith's interference had changed that.

He suddenly cursed the artifact, hating it for having smothered the potential of all humans, hating it for failing that duty and forcing him and his followers into their current desperate situation.

Then, something occurred to him. "Rathma . . . could it be altered again?"

"A question I have pondered and the true reason we are here, son of Diomedes." The black-cloaked figure gestured toward the Worldstone. "What would you have of it? Would you return to what you once were? Make yourself somehow more mighty? Tell me, Uldyssian ul-Diomed . . ."

Uldyssian would have liked desperately to unmake all that had happened to him, to somehow return to the day before Lilith had entered his life and begun his trials. Yet he doubted that even the Worldstone was capable of that. At most, it would remove from him and the others the nephalem gifts. Unfortunately, it would not remove the threat of the Triune, now surely determined to deal with those defying its will and existence. Moreover, he doubted that the angel Inarius would let things be, either.

Which left only one option . . .

"Can the Worldstone really be altered to make us more powerful?"

"No, not directly, but it can be altered to encourage the gifts' growth. That would, in essence, result in much the same of what you desire."

To Uldyssian, that was all that mattered. "Tell me what I can do."

"This is the Worldstone. For you to achieve what you desire, you must think it. The crystal will either accept your will or deny it."

"That simple?"

Rathma grimaced. "No . . . not in the least."

Tired of his companion's murky and often contradictory statements, Uldyssian turned his complete focus on the huge crystal. The Worldstone pulsated almost hypnotically.

You must think it . . . Rathma had said. Uldyssian tried to clear his thoughts, then concentrated on what he wished.

We need to be stronger, he told the Worldstone. *We need our powers to grow faster . . .*

The Worldstone did not outwardly change in any way, but Uldyssian felt something within start to shift in response to his probing. He repeated his desire, emphasizing the need for more power and quickly.

But the slight shifting of—of the *resonance?*—went no further. Try as he might, Uldyssian could not do more. Although he forced every iota of his will upon the Worldstone, in the end it was he who fell back gasping and defeated.

Rathma's gloved hands took hold of his arm. Sweating and furious, Uldyssian glared at his companion.

Lilith's son wore an expression of utter shock.

That, in turn, left Uldyssian momentarily gaping. He had never seen such a show of raw emotion from Rathma.

"What's wrong?" he finally managed to ask. "Is there danger?"

"The Worldstone . . ." the pale figure whispered almost reverently. The narrow eyes darted from Uldyssian to the

gleaming artifact and then back to the human. "I wanted to see . . . but I never *expected* . . . it was a theory . . . no more than that . . . no more . . ."

Again, he made no sense to Uldyssian, especially after a glance at the gargantuan crystal revealed nothing changed. "What're you talking about? I *failed.*"

"Do not look with your eyes . . . look with your mind and soul."

Brow furrowed, Uldyssian stared again at the Worldstone, but this time also delved into it using other senses. He still found nothing different; the Worldstone reverberated as it had before, not even the slightest—

No . . . there was a hint of a change, so intricate that it was no surprise that he had earlier missed it. But such an alteration could hardly cause any worthwhile effect . . . could it?

"I did something after all. Not much. Will it mean anything?"

Rathma uttered a sound, then murmured, "Observe the structure of the artifact, Uldyssian. Observe it at the very core. You can do that . . ."

Uldyssian concentrated more . . . and found himself staring deep within the Worldstone. He saw the fine, crystalline pattern that made up the fantastic formation and marveled at the minute details. Tiny, five-sided segments multiplied endlessly and formed the stone's most basic structure. Uldyssian could not help but admire their perfection. That the artifact had been *created* as opposed to being a natural formation astounded him so much that he briefly forgot the trouble it had caused him.

But none of this had to do with his search. He was about to give up when one small area near the heart caught his attention. There was something not right about it. Immediately, Uldyssian knew that this was the source of the alteration in the Worldstone's resonance. He thrust his mind deeper, seeing more detail—

Seeing where the rest of the Worldstone was composed of a five-sided pattern, this one part had *six* edges.

What had been perfect, was now flawed . . . impossibly so.

He withdrew immediately. "Lilith's work—"

"No, son of Diomedes . . . your work." Rathma's gaze burrowed into him. "My mother altered the resonance through a spell, which affected outcome but not structure. I expect you to do the same, or more likely, fail. It was a desperate chance, but one I felt worthy. You had been cast this near the Worldstone for a reason, I thought . . ."

"It was an accident that I came here."

"Have you not discovered yet that there are no accidents?" the shrouded figure returned. "I did not know what to expect, but certainly not *this*. Uldyssian ul-Diomed, you have altered the very *essence* of the Worldstone, something that should not be possible . . ." Rathma frowned. "And whether that means good or ill for our hopes, I fear that we can only wait . . . and pray . . ."

FOURTEEN

Achilios stirred. He did not wake, for the suggestion of waking itself referred to sleep, which was an impossibility for one in his state.

Yet he had not been conscious. As the archer slowly pushed his face from the muddy jungle soil, he wondered what had happened to him. Achilios recalled the tentacles of the Triune's demonic servant starting to pull him asunder, but after that, it was all a blank.

Thinking of the beast, he leapt to his feet. Achilios gave thanks that, despite the lurid tales he had heard as a child, he was at least a very *agile* dead man. He supposed he should be grateful to the dragon for that, but in some ways being so near to alive, and yet not, left a bitter coldness inside. Near to alive was not the same as *being* alive.

Then, memory of what he was actually doing in this part of the jungle came back to him. Achilios spun around to face Hashir.

But the edge of the city closest to his location was in ruins.

He stared without blinking—another habit of the living he no longer required—trying to decipher just how long it had been since the destruction. The gates, the walls surrounding them . . . those had been smashed as if by giant fists. Within, two of the triple towers had been destroyed, one not even visible anymore from his point of view. The sole remaining tower—Dialon's, if Achilios was not mistaken—leaned precariously. A hint of smoke rose from the area below the towers.

This destruction happened at least a day, maybe two, Achilios estimated. *Hopefully, no more than that.*

Yet, even that was too long. *She* would not be here. At first chance, she would have ordered Uldyssian's followers on . . . but to where? He no longer understood her plan, not that any of it mattered that much to him now. Only one thing was of importance to the hunter, no matter what Trag'Oul or Rathma might insist otherwise.

Serenthia—*his* Serenthia—had been possessed by the damned demoness.

At the thought of what Lilith had done, Achilios seized up his bow. He imagined Uldyssian's treacherous lover in his sight. An arrow through the heart. An arrow imbued with the magic of the serpentine dragon . . .

But that would mean slaying Serenthia as well.

Despite what he knew *they* would insist, Achilios felt that there *had* to be another way. Serenthia was not dead, her flesh peeled off so neatly by demonic magic so that Lilith could parade in it. No, the woman he loved was still there, albeit deep asleep. Somehow, she had to be stirred awake so that she could battle Lilith from within while others fought the demoness from without.

Somehow . . .

First, you've got to track her down, you dolt! He had no idea how much of a head start Uldyssian's followers had or whether they were proceeding to the same destination as originally intended. All Achilios could do was what he did best. Follow his target.

It was daytime, which meant that the living were about. However great the devastation on this end of Hashir, the common folk would still need to eke out a living, be it hunting, farming, or fishing. Achilios was grateful that no one had come across his body, lest he find himself forced to dig out of yet another grave, or worse, trying desperately to douse the fires of a pyre. His lone encounter with one of the locals had been enough to make Achilios wary of any repeat. He was too recognizably dead even on his feet.

Equally frustrating was the fact that, thanks to his collapse, he had more dirt than ever caked on his body. A quick attempt to brush some of that away had proven nearly as futile as removing the original coating. It seemed that the soil in general believed that Achilios belonged to it and refused to give up attempting to put him under again.

He would not allow it to do that until he had done everything he could for his beloved.

Like a shadow, the hunter slipped through the jungle around Hashir. Twice, he came across some of the inhabitants, but they were slow of wit compared to him and Achilios readily avoided detection. He finally managed to reach the area beyond the ruined gate, where he hoped that he would find clues to those he sought.

That actually proved easier than he thought. The edyrem had grown in numbers again, so much so that the trail they left was like that of a herd of the giant animals with the snakelike noses that the lowlanders used for some chores or rode almost like horses. Even a blind man could have followed the mass exodus he confronted.

But what surprised him was that they were not headed, as they should have been, on the route that would take them to the main temple. Instead, they were veering even farther south, to an area he knew nothing about.

What was Lilith up to?

Achilios shoved on. Whatever it was did not ultimately matter. He would catch up to them no matter where they journeyed.

Hopefully, by then he would have some plan . . .

They are returning . . .

Those three words cheered Mendeln more than he could have imagined. He looked up from the task the dragon had set for him, learning how to even better focus his will through the astonishing dagger. It had been going surprisingly well. He was amazed at his inherent ability to manipulate the tool, especially considering how short a time it had been his.

But now, all interest in the blade vanished as he stood up and looked around. "Where? Where?"

And suddenly, Uldyssian and Rathma stood before him. His brother appeared as relieved as he. The sons of Diomedes hugged one another while Rathma gazed on stone-faced and a sense of amusement radiated from the celestial serpent. The many images of life continually flashed into and out of view as the creature undulated.

Be not so disdainful of familial affection, my good Rathma, Trag'oul remarked so that all could sense him.

"My experience with such has not been the best and you should know that."

Mendeln and Uldyssian separated. The first thing out of Uldyssian's mouth was, "Serenthia . . . Lilith's possessed her . . . it happened before Hashir . . ."

"As I also understand it, although at first I feared that she had been slain like Master Ethon." Mendeln gave the starry being a short look of frustration for that temporary shock. Still, Serenthia's current situation was not all that much better. "We must find a way to force the demoness out . . ."

"That will not be so simple," interjected Rathma. "I know of old how tight my mother can cling to that which is of use to her . . . as you might also recall, Uldyssian ul-Diomed."

Uldyssian bared his teeth at the tall figure. "I don't give a damn! I've got to save her . . . and the others, too! At the very least, they need to be warned!"

Rathma looked to the dragon. "Trag?"

Her influence is already mounting. Uldyssian is weakened in the eyes of his edyrem.

"And whose fault is *that*?" Mendeln's brother roared. He shook a fist at the stars. "Who took me away? Who *kept* me from going to her?"

Had you returned immediately, in the condition that you were in, she would have easily subdued you . . .

"He speaks the truth," Rathma added. "She had already infested you with her darkness. A return to Lilith at that time would have only served to allow her to complete her spell."

Mendeln understood just what they were saying, but felt the need to defend his sibling. "Why could we have not done more, then?"

"You should understand better than that," returned Lilith's son bluntly. "Trag'Oul cannot be known to exist, neither by my dear parents nor the Burning Hells or High Heavens. For the greater good of all Sanctuary—and for its very survival—he must always be hidden from their sight in order to help make certain that the world remains in Balance." Rathma took a breath, then added, "As for me, my fate lies elsewhere, as I have known all along. I can say no more."

It was hardly an answer to satisfy Mendeln, much less Uldyssian, but both had come to know that they would get no more from Rathma.

In fact, Uldyssian was clearly growing impatient to do something . . . *anything*. Mendeln had seen his brother like this on a few rare occasions and feared what would happen if they delayed further.

"All is not without hope," he started to tell Uldyssian. "There is another who is even now—"

But he got no further. Uldyssian blurted, "Small wonder that Inarius and the demons have been able to play with our world for so long! You do nothing but interfere with those who're no danger to you and stand idle against those most of a threat!"

Mendeln put a calming hand on his brother's shoulder. "Uldyssian . . ."

But the older sibling ignored the younger. "Tell me, Rathma! Did we accomplish *anything* with the Worldstone? Has anything changed?"

"Most certainly, but how much must be deduced by careful observation—"

"I've observed enough! I—"

HOLD!

Although Trag'Oul's outburst happened only within them, it was as if thunder had just exploded. Even Rathma clutched his head in pain from the loudness.

The angel is active.

Those words brought the three others to attention. Uldyssian glanced at Mendeln, who indicated he should instead study Rathma.

The pale figure was, if anything, more pale than ever. Yet it was not fear that Mendeln sensed in the other. Rather, he believed it something more akin to *resignation*.

"It is settled, then," Rathma said.

That is your choice. I have always said that . . .

"No . . . it is my father's choice . . . never mine . . ." Rathma eyed the two mortals. "But perhaps . . . perhaps I have been overanalyzing . . . perhaps . . ." His narrow eyes narrowed further as they focused on Uldyssian.

Mendeln's brother *vanished*.

"What did you do?" Mendeln demanded. He could not sense Uldyssian anywhere.

"I sent him where he needed to be."

Loyalty stirred within the younger brother. "Then, I shall go with—"

"No . . . I will need you for the confrontation." Rathma's resignation grew more pronounced. "I trust you've been educating him swiftly, Trag?"

As much as can be done. You are not bound to this . . .

"Aah, but I am. Come, Mendeln."

Well suspecting that he had no choice in the matter, Mendeln still wanted to know into what he was being forced. "And where do you take me when I would be at my brother's side? Where?"

Rathma spread his cloak wide, his look now that of death itself. "I would take you to the place I would rather be farthest from. I would—no—I *must,* I am sorry to say, bring you with me . . . to stand before my loving father . . ."

Uldyssian stood in the jungle.

At first, he welcomed the sight. Rathma had finally given in and sent him where he needed to be.

Then, Uldyssian noticed that he was once more missing Mendeln.

He shook a fist at the thick canopy above. "Damn you again, Rathma! You're no better than those you disclaim as your parents!"

But neither Lilith's son nor the great beast responded. Uldyssian concentrated on Mendeln, trying to first draw his brother to him, and then when that failed, attempting to return to the emptiness that was Trag'Oul's domain.

But still nothing happened.

Before he could consider what else to try, Uldyssian sensed something that completely took his attention from his brother.

Serenthia—Lilith—*both* of them—were nearby.

Aware that for the moment there was nothing that he could do for Mendeln, Uldyssian immediately focused on the new situation. Trust Rathma to throw him into the thick of things. Why was Lilith's son not here to deal with his mother? What could be more important than that?

But that could not be a concern for Uldyssian. What mattered at the moment was to make certain that the demoness did not sense his presence. Throwing everything he could into shielding himself from her sight—and hoping that he knew what he was doing—Uldyssian cautiously moved on. If it was to be him alone against his former lover, then so be it. He would not let her continue her evil . . .

It was now nightfall, something that at first disconcerted him. Time in the dragon's realm seemed to pass oddly; he had expected it to be much earlier in the day. Still, the cover of darkness would surely assist Uldyssian, who wanted to stay out of sight of his followers until he could gauge what influence Lilith might have already had on them.

While it was tempting to confront her in front of the others, Uldyssian doubted that such a maneuver would work in his favor. With Lilith it was best to render her harmless first . . . somehow. Only then could he worry about the rest of the problem.

As he approached the encampment, it was evident that the ranks of the edyrem had swollen since Hashir, something that did not please Uldyssian as it might have once. Most of the newcomers would be of Lilith's making, although he wondered how she had accomplished that. The fact that the demoness had chosen him for her dupe had made him assume that she needed him to easier awaken the gifts within other humans, but the large number of new edyrem Uldyssian sensed gave the lie to that . . . so it seemed.

Uldyssian circled the area, surreptitiously seeking evidence of Lilith without her noticing him in turn. He did not have complete faith in his ability to stay hidden from her for very long.

The jungle sloped down, giving him at last a fairly good view of the main part of the encampment. He gazed with only the barest interest at the hodgepodge of tents, blankets, and lean-tos. Somehow, he doubted that Lilith would deign to sleep in one of those. Still, he knew that she had to be close—

A structure in the very midst of the edyrem made Uldyssian freeze. A large stone building illuminated by torches stood before him. At first he thought it some old hunter's lodge, but as Uldyssian eyed the building further, he noted more than just the sharply pointed door frame and the oddly angled roof. The fluted columns, the scrollwork on the door, they all added up to one thing. Albeit smaller and more ancient than any he had seen before, this was obviously some sort of temple.

Even as that registered, his eyes—augmented by him to see well in the night—caught sight of something that further chilled his blood.

There was a relief of Serenthia's face atop the entrance.

Her expression was that of a glorious and understanding goddess, not a human woman. Even though the face looked as if it had always been a part of the building, clearly it was new.

He understood immediately what it meant. Through Serenthia, Lilith was creating a cult focusing on her. In fact, although Uldyssian could not be entirely certain from his vantage point, it seemed that the more he studied Serenthia's face, the more there appeared subtle hints of another mixed with her features.

And then he recognized to whom they belonged. *Lilith*. It was obvious that she already intended to make herself their mistress in body as well as spirit. At some point, she could then cast off Serenthia's form, perhaps even return as "Lylia" somehow.

Fighting his smoldering anger, Uldyssian wondered about the ancient temple. It could not be coincidence that had brought Lilith to it; she did not work that way. This structure had been her intended destination.

That realization further sent a chill running through Uldyssian. Something was to happen here, something integral to the demoness's desires . . .

Most of the edyrem began settling down for the night, no doubt exhausted from their arduous trek. There were more sentries than ever, far more than should have been warranted. More disturbing to Uldyssian was their manner, which seemed colder and wary of even their slumbering comrades. The guards were a mix of Parthans and lowlanders, some recognizable by face to him. Most were male, but a few women—equally dark of expression—also walked among them.

Even without trying, Uldyssian could sense a shadow over their souls, a taint that bespoke of Lilith.

Without warning, one of the sentries glanced in his direction. Biting back an epithet, Uldyssian strengthened his shield and backed deeper into the jungle. Frowning, the guard took a step toward his hiding place.

You see nothing, Uldyssian thought at the man. *Merely the jungle. It was all your imagination . . .*

He had never attempted to influence another in such a manner and hoped that by attempting to do so he did not give himself away. The sentry stood looking for a moment more . . . then grunted and returned to his post.

Slipping farther on, Uldyssian berated himself for his carelessness. He had come too close to revealing his presence . . . and to a guard. Had it been Lilith, surely Uldyssian would have been discovered.

Was Lilith inside the temple? Unable to sense her properly, Uldyssian could only assume so. Taking the utmost precautions, he tried harder to probe the structure.

Tried and quickly failed. There was a shroud of sorts around it, making whatever was going on inside undetectable by anyone, even him. That only served to make Uldyssian even more anxious. What would Lilith desire so much to hide even as she insisted that it took place surrounded by those with the potential to sense it?

He feared he had some idea . . . and that forced a decision upon him. Lilith surely could not act until most of her "followers" were sleeping. If Uldyssian could reach the building undetected—

There was a sudden movement to his left. He barely secreted himself in time to avoid being seen by a figure passing by. Uldyssian caught his breath as he recognized the bald man striding at the edge of the camp.

Romus.

Uldyssian dared not let the moment slip away. Concentrating, the son of Diomedes reached out to the Parthan.

Romus smothered a gasp. With casual movements, he turned toward the jungle, then slipped out of sight of the camp.

A breath later, the two men faced one another. Romus could not hide his startlement. "Master Uldyssian? We thought you dead! Where were you?" He hesitated, then added, "It *is* you and not some phantom, yes?"

"It's me. Praise be, Romus! You of all people I could use now!"

The former brigand blinked, then returned, "I am at your service, Master Uldyssian, surely!"

Nodding in gratitude, Uldyssian pulled his companion farther away from the camp. "First, I must know something, Romus . . . how did the edyrem fare in Hashir?"

"It was a bloody thing! The temple had magic and might greater than we could've imagined! Aye, there were some lost, Master Uldyssian, Tomo among them."

Tomo. Uldyssian mourned all those slain, but he had come to know eager Tomo better than many. "How fares Saron?"

"He's sworn to avenge his cousin's death with a hundred of the Triune's when next we come upon them . . ."

The blood kept flowing. Uldyssian blamed himself, but he also blamed beings like Lilith, Inarius, and Rathma for thinking so little of mortal life.

They would pay. They would all pay . . . with Lilith first.

That brought him back to another question that had to be answered quickly. "That ancient structure. How does it come to be that you're all here, near it, and not on your way to the main temple?"

Romus's face lit up. "'Twas Serenthia! She had a vision and saw this place! Such a new and wonderful power! Even you've never had that, have you, Master Uldyssian?"

"No." Uldyssian doubted that *any* of the edyrem had experienced such an ability or possibly ever would. "No . . . and I fear that neither has Serenthia."

"What do you mean?"

"Romus, has she . . . has Serenthia seemed *different*?"

"Different?" The bald man shrugged. "When you vanished, she took up the struggle and saved many of us who might've joined Tomo! She brought *spirit* back to us, Master Uldyssian, when we thought you were no more!"

Lilith had done her work well, judging by Romus's rapt expression and marveling tone. Uldyssian had returned just in time.

He took the man by the shoulders. Romus had come far from the disreputable figure that had watched him from far across the Parthan square. "Listen to me. Nothing is what it seems. You believe that Serenthia's been guiding all of you since my disappearance—"

"Aye, of course—"

Vehemently shaking his head, Uldyssian went on, "You're all being tricked, Romus! That is Serenthia in body in there, yes, but what you hear and see is the work of a demon, the sister of the foul Lucion! You know of whom I speak!"

The edyrem's visage clouded. "You speak of Lilith, of whom we've all heard, aye. Can it be true that you're saying Serenthia's her in disguise! It can't be!"

"She possesses Serenthia. Serenthia is there, deep in slumber. What you've seen, what you've experienced, I promise you, Romus, that the true Serenthia would have had nothing to do with it . . ."

"Nothing . . . aye . . ." Romus looked down in thought.

Uldyssian could not give him the luxury of digesting all of this. "Romus . . . Romus, is Serenthia inside that place?"

"Aye. She should be."

"Do you know what she plans there?"

The edyrem shook his head. "Nay, but I and some others are to come to her near midnight. Ser—She says that there is a matter of import for us to discuss."

"The sentries I saw. Have they had special contact with her?" After Romus nodded, Uldyssian explained, "We must be wary of them. They may be under her spell."

"It's to be us two alone, then, Master Uldyssian? You can be trusting in me!" Romus's tone all but pleaded for Uldyssian to believe in him.

Uldyssian not only believed in him, but Romus, unfortunately, needed to play a pivotal role. He could still get near Lilith without being suspected. Uldyssian required the former brigand to distract Lilith enough so that he could then strike at her while her defenses were down.

He explained such to Romus, then asked, if the man was still willing, what he knew of the building.

"'Tis an old chapel or monk's abode, she said," Romus

answered. "Serent—She told us that it was a sign that we were directed to it. Said it would mark the beginning of a turn for all of us . . ."

Again, Uldyssian felt a cold chill. "Would she see you before the time she requested?"

"I could find reason, Master Uldyssian." The Parthan shivered. "Poor Serenthia . . ."

"If you can keep the demoness from noticing, I'll make my way in. Then, you leave."

"But what about you?"

For what Uldyssian had in mind, he wanted no one else near. It was possible that forcing Lilith from Serenthia would wreak destruction on the immediate vicinity. "Just get as far away as possible. Understand?"

Romus reluctantly nodded. They talked over the details a minute or two more, then, with a short bow, he returned to the camp. Uldyssian had kept their plan as simple as possible, aware how even the slightest complications could worsen the situation several times over.

Romus did not immediately go to the temple. As dictated, he first found reason to speak with the nearest sentries and direct them elsewhere. Uldyssian did not wish to be forced to injure any of them simply because they had been entranced by Lilith.

By the time Romus had dealt with the guards, night had well established itself and from most corners of the encampment there came only silence. Many fires had all but died down. A few glow lights hovered around the area, a hint of the growing proficiency of the edyrem. Fortunately, most of the lights were dim, the better for their creators to sleep.

At last, Romus headed toward the ancient structure. The two edyrem standing duty hesitated only a moment before admitting him. As one of the most senior of Uldyssian's followers, Romus was probably now second in command. That made his inclusion in Uldyssian's plan invaluable.

The thick, wooden door creaked closed behind the bald

man. Uldyssian counted under his breath, giving Romus time to establish his conversation with the false Serenthia. According to the Parthan, until tonight's impending gathering, she had intended to be alone.

Finally, Uldyssian deemed that enough time had passed. Any longer, and he risked Romus's life. There remained only the two guards, both of whom eyed the area before them with a distrust amplified by Lilith's hold over them.

Not wishing to hurt anyone unnecessarily, Uldyssian concentrated on the two men, then slipped toward them. The guards continued to stare ahead. They now neither heard nor saw anything. Even when he hurried past them, they did not move.

There was no other entrance to the building—the only other openings being small air slits well above—but Romus had explained that there was an outer chamber before the one in which Lilith had arranged her sanctum. All Uldyssian needed to do was reach it. Then, there would be no more reason for stealth . . . only for swiftness. He would have one chance and one only.

At his direction, the door opened just enough to admit him. Uldyssian muffled any creak, lest the demoness be warned by even that.

The chamber he entered was utterly empty, whatever decor or artifacts likely long removed by thieves or the departing builders. Uldyssian cared not for what use the edifice had been, only that voices rose from the room beyond.

Romus's . . . and Serenthia's.

" . . . and yes, Romus, we'll soon be on our way to the Triune's main temple. I swore by Uldyssian's death that I'd complete his quest. First the Triune, and then, definitely, the Cathedral of Light . . . who may be an enemy worse than those we now fight."

"I apologize again," the Parthan responded to her. "But I, too, wish to fulfill Master Uldyssian's legacy. I thank you for reassuring me."

"Not at all. Is there anything else?"

Uldyssian dared risk Romus no longer. Aware that he also did not wish to harm Serenthia's body, the son of Diomedes threw all his will into repeating what he had done to the guards outside. He fixed on the feminine voice . . .

A silence enshrouded the building, a silence finally broken by a gasp from Romus. "Master Uldyssian! She does not move! She stands as if a statue!"

Uldyssian entered. The first thing he noted was Serenthia, as beautiful as he remembered her, poised like a goddess with one hand extended to Romus. A beguiling smile that had never been worn by the merchant's daughter gave ample proof that Lilith was in truth within the woman.

Then, a second, more awful sight behind her attracted his attention.

An altar.

An altar stained by centuries-old blood.

He might have thought it merely macabre coincidence, but atop the gray, stone slab had been set a long dagger and a goblet. Worse, there were also runes drawn on the stained surface, runes freshly made.

Tonight, the altar would have drunken for the first time in generations.

Despite the risk of Lilith escaping his power, Uldyssian could not help but look up. Above the altar, the face of whatever spirit or demon that had been carved there had been artfully replaced by that unsettling combination of the two females, with a bit more of Lilith recognizable.

"Master Uldyssian?"

Romus's pensive voice finally brought him back to the present. The Parthan stepped back as Uldyssian faced the frozen figure.

Up close, Uldyssian could see the tiny hints that the woman with whom he had grown up was not truly there. Besides the smile, the eyes had a harsh cunning that he recognized too well.

"It's over, Lilith . . ." he breathed. Uldyssian put his palms on the woman's temples. He was not certain what he needed to do, but if he could reach Serenthia, somehow, he felt that she would help him force the demoness out. "It's all over . . ."

Something hard cracked against the back of his head.

The world spun about. Through blurred eyes, he saw Romus leaning toward him, the Parthan with a fanatical expression and a heavy stone apparently taken from somewhere in the chamber in his hands. The fresh blood on one end of the stone belonged to Uldyssian.

"You'll not harm my Lilith!" Romus snapped, his face twisting into something evil. "You'll not!"

And as Uldyssian collapsed, he heard Serenthia's voice . . . and Lilith's all-too-familiar laugh.

"Well done, my love . . . just as we planned . . ."

FIFTEEN

Uldyssian awoke to find his limbs bound to the altar stone. That in itself was unnerving enough, but when he attempted to use his powers to free himself . . . nothing happened.

Then, he heard the familiar laugh again.

"My dear, dear sweet Uldyssian," Serenthia cooed. Only, it was not Serenthia, the son of Diomedes reminded himself, but Lilith. "So naive. So trusting."

A face appeared over him, but it was not the one that he expected. Rather, Romus glared down at his former friend. "You should've never come back, Master Uldyssian. Never."

"Romus! Are you mad? This is the demon, Lilith, here, not Serenthia!"

The Parthan shook his head. "No . . . you're wrong. It's both of them. My Serenthia and my Lilith. I've both of them . . ."

Footsteps presaged the appearance of the demoness. Brushing aside some of Serenthia's long, dark hair, she leaned lovingly against Romus's shoulder. "And I have *you,* dear Romus! How much more a loyal lover than you, Uldyssian, who could not see all that was offered! I could have been anyone you desired, including what you see . . . but you spurned my love and my offer . . ."

"All you wanted was a puppet to lead the creation of your magical army so that you could take Sanctuary from Inarius!" Uldyssian looked to Romus. "When she finds someone even more useful, you'll be tossed aside! Think, Romus! This isn't you! This isn't!"

"You know nothing of my life before your coming to Partha, Master Uldyssian! I answered to no one! I was feared by all! You took that away from me and made me one of your sheep! But she's reminded me of who I really am"—he leaned close, his eyes wide and deadly. His expression was manic—"and I adore her more for it!"

There was no hope talking to the Parthan. Lilith had completely seduced him, seeking deep within that lingering darkness that had once entirely engulfed Romus . . . and now did so again.

Uldyssian tried to pull his left hand free, but the bonds held. Romus smirked. Lilith pouted her lips in mock sorrow for their prisoner.

As Uldyssian fought for time and some manner of escape, he asked, "So, has she been using you to bring forth the new edyrem? That's all she really wants! She can't do it so quickly herself. It's the nature of the gifts; they're a human thing and she's not, Romus!"

His words fell on deaf ears. "She chose me. She chose me from all of them because she saw how powerful I was and that I could be stirred from the illusions you cast upon us. Since, Hashiri, I've shown others, both new and old, the same, and each day, there's more." He grinned. "They treat me like a god . . ."

Lilith leaned close, first kissing Romus on the cheek, then licking it. He responded to her action like a cat, rubbing his face into hers. The scene sickened Uldyssian on more than one level; not only for Serenthia's sake, but the Parthan's, too. This was not the Romus he knew.

"And after tonight," the demoness murmured to Uldyssian as she continued her seduction, "they will *all* see the truth, dear Romus! Isn't that so?"

"Are you going to use *him*?" the former brigand eagerly asked.

She chuckled at his question. "Now *that* would be marvelous, but no. His blood would be no good. In fact, it might have the opposite effect, adding his taint. No . . . I need someone whose life force would magnify that which I desire, dear, sweet Romus . . . and there's truly only one person in my mind for that."

The Parthan suddenly gaped. His eyes widened even farther, to the point that they looked like those of a frog.

With a shiver, he slumped forward, sprawling over a stunned Uldyssian. As he did, his back became visible.

A long, crimson puddle oozed out of the wicked hole in his back.

Lilith held up the dagger that Uldyssian had noted before his betrayal. Romus's blood dribbled down the blade and over the hilt. Lilith paid no mind as red spots formed on her hand. Instead, she used her free hand to stroke the Parthan's bald head.

"He was a delight . . . I'm sure Serenthia enjoyed it, too. Pity he was so perfect for the role."

"You're mad, Lilith!"

Her expression tightened. "No . . . I am *justified,* dear Uldyssian! Justified! I saved the children and for that good deed I was cast out into emptiness! Inarius thought that I would *never* find my way back . . . but I did, I did!" She returned to caressing the dead Romus. "He was so determined to prove himself to me and her. He came right in and told me how you'd called him into the jungle and that he'd pretended to still be your friend!" Lilith smiled. "I will admit your timing startled me, my love. I smell another's work in that. Have you been talking to my darling Inarius? Hmm?"

Even though Uldyssian had more than once thought Rathma no better than his parents, something made him hold back from telling the demoness the truth. "I had a short conversation with him. He misses you and begs your forgiveness. Then, he wants to kill you."

The face above him contorted into one that held no sanity whatsoever, a spectacle made all the more terrible by the fact that it was Serenthia's.

Then, as quickly as it had appeared, the madness once

again vanished behind a mask of seduction. "Such a jest, dear, sweet Uldyssian! No, I don't believe that Inarius would ever have use for you! He thinks himself without flaw, and thus, in need of no one but himself to set things as he sees them!" Lilith grinned. "And so he shall sit oblivious on his throne even as the walls of his glittering cathedral come raining down around him!"

Uldyssian doubted that the angel would be so complacent, but Lilith clearly shared Inarius's megalomania. She could not imagine her plots unraveling, especially due to the interference of any mere mortal.

The trouble was, in that last case, it seemed that she was correct. Uldyssian could feel the power within him trying to burst free, but something held it in check. He could not sense any spell on him, but the work of the demoness could be very, very subtle.

"Still struggling," she commented. "How admirable is your determination . . . or is it that you just wish to one more time hold me in your arms?" Lilith leaned close enough to kiss him, and although once Uldyssian had wanted those lips against his, he was now revolted. Not for himself, however, but for Serenthia, whose body was now the demoness's plaything.

The lips moved to his ear, where Lilith whispered, "Not too long, my love, and you *will* hold me again. When I cast the spell using poor Romus's blood, you shan't be immune, either! You'll finally see matters as I desire, then . . ."

He wanted to spit in her face. "Why didn't you do this in the beginning?"

A throaty chuckle. "Because a dupe who thinks he is doing good is the best cover for my plan! But we've gone far past that point and you've gathered so many followers! When the opportunity arose, how could I resist? Now, you'll gather new converts knowing exactly what is demanded of them—allegiance to *me!*"

Uldyssian tried to grab her, but his struggles remained futile. Lilith laughed again and backed up the better to admire his efforts. She brushed against Romus's body, still half-sprawled over her prisoner.

With a weak growl, the Parthan abruptly pushed himself up. He grabbed Lilith by the arm that held the dagger. Blood splattered on Uldyssian.

Any hope by Uldyssian that the Parthan's startling act would save both of them quickly died as the demoness twisted around and grabbed Romus by the throat. To his credit, the former brigand, his eyes bearing none of the fanaticism of her control, tried to burn her with his power. His hands glowed bright and smoke arose where they touched Lilith.

But she only laughed, and with one squeeze of her hand, *crushed in* his windpipe.

Already suffering a massive wound, Romus perished instantly. This time, Lilith let his still form collapse on the stone floor.

Both hands now awash in the Parthan's life fluids, she turned back to Uldyssian. Her ghastly smile made even Serenthia's countenance too terrible for Uldyssian to behold and he turned his gaze away.

"Such strong life! Yes, poor Romus's blood will do spectacularly, my love." Moist fingers forced his gaze back to her. "Don't you think?"

When Uldyssian only glared, she patted his cheek—leaving more of the Parthan's blood—and laughed again.

At that moment, Uldyssian sensed someone else in the chamber. He had no hope, though, that it was someone who had come to help him and sure enough the newcomer turned out to be one of the guards that he had earlier frozen.

The edyrem eyed Uldyssian like a vermin discovered in his food.

"The others are here, Mistress Serenthia." He seemed unsurprised to find Romus's body.

"They may enter. Then you and your friend keep the doorway sealed until I am done."

The guard nodded, then vanished through the entrance.

Lilith stood over the Parthan as she spoke to Uldyssian. "You've no idea how many there were so easily turned to my desire, dear love! You were so gracious, accepting all who came to embrace what you offered, but even though your will buried what they were, it did not erase it. Turning them was even more simple than Romus here." Dagger still in hand, she performed a mock curtsy. "For arranging things so well for me, I thank you!"

Still attempting to stall, Uldyssian looked around again. Despite there being only signs of Lilith in the chamber, he suspected that once the walls had been covered with markings dedicated to beings equally vile. "What is it about this place? You sought it out."

"This? This place is a nexus, my love, important to the making of Sanctuary, all those centuries ago! Here was set one of the first points of reality—you might say hammered down—that allowed this world to hold together! There is power beyond belief here, the contribution of every angel and demon who built this refuge, including *him*. So strong are the forces inherent here that you see that even your kind sensed them and built this." Indicating herself, she merrily added, "And this . . . more than three of your lifetimes ago . . . is where I found my way back to Sanctuary!"

It startled him to hear that Lilith had been in his world for that long without ever being noticed. That raised anew his fear that the demoness just might be able to accomplish all that she planned. If even the angel who had cast her out had not sensed her in all this time . . .

But before he could discover more, Lilith's turned edyrem began filtering inside. So many of the faces—male and female—were known well to Uldyssian, which pained him further. He saw both Parthans and Torajians and assumed that a few Hashiri were also among the gathering. All told, there were at least a couple dozen.

"Stand along the edge of the room," Lilith commanded.

Uldyssian used her distraction to try one last time to free

himself. He had little hope of success, but could not bring himself to merely accept what appeared inevitable—

Then, to his surprise, he sensed the magical forces binding him weaken in a few places. Managing to cover his pleasure at this, he focused on those points . . . and then noticed that they were where Romus's blood had splattered him.

Cautiously, Uldyssian sought to exploit them. He worked at the spell holding him, gradually feeling it unravel here and there.

But the effort went too slow. Lilith already had most of her pawns in place for whatever ceremony she had planned and now the demoness again positioned herself above the dead Parthan.

From her lips erupted sounds that no mortal creature could utter. They were evidently words of power, for he sensed the chamber immediately fill with invisible but potent forces rising from deep beneath.

Something else rose . . . blood from Romus's wounds. It streamed up into the air, reaching at last the dagger. This time, Lilith desired far more than just enough to cover the blade; Uldyssian suspected that she would drain the corpse completely before her task was finished.

As she did this, her edyrem turned their palms up. Energies from within each sparked to life over the palms. The edyrem moved with such perfect coordination that he wondered if Lilith now utterly controlled them.

He felt her spell upon him fade more, yet still not enough to enable him to fight her, much less her followers, too. Time was against him. Lilith was nearly done with her grisly task.

At last, she held up for all to see the insidious dagger. Even though it was drenched in blood, there should have been far more of the crimson fluid present. Uldyssian did not want to even think where the rest had gone.

The binding spell continued to weaken. All he needed was a minute or two longer . . .

But it seemed that Lilith had no intention of giving that to him. She strode to where he lay, paying no mind to the droplets left in her wake.

"Now it begins, my love," she whispered, reaching to the side to take the goblet. "Retribution begins . . ."

Her mouth contorted as out of it again issued those inhuman sounds—

One of the edyrem let out a cry and fell back.

Uldyssian at first thought it Lilith's doing, that she had intended from the start to use her other puppets as she had Romus, but then he saw that which had slain the man.

An arrow through the throat. An arrow encrusted in dirt.

Before the first body stilled, a second follower also collapsed, a shaft through his chest exactly where the heart was located.

Lilith's followers broke ranks as some sought shelter while others looked for the source of the seemingly magical bolts. Uldyssian was the first to recognize their point of origin, the narrow slits above. How the archer had managed to avoid the guards outside or to be sensed by Lilith was a much more major question.

But the answer to that was something with which he could concern himself later . . . if possible. The momentary interruption had given him the time that he needed to at last extinguish the spell keeping him bound and helpless.

One of the nearest edyrem saw him rise. The dark-skinned figure started to point at Uldyssian, but the latter, not needing to focus, sent his would-be attacker flying up into the wall. Uldyssian then glared at two more just registering his freedom. They suddenly flung against one another with such force that both were knocked unconscious.

Another of Lilith's followers screamed. The arrow that had slain him stuck out of his back, which meant that it had come from another direction. Whether that meant more than one bowman, Uldyssian had no chance to consider, for Lilith, face monstrously contorted, had resumed her chanting. Uldyssian could only assume that meant that she still had hope of fulfilling her plan and turning the rest of the edyrem to her cause.

Whatever the cost, he could not let that happen. The chamber shook as pure force radiated from him in every direction. Edyrem went tumbling, some crashing into each other and into walls. Uldyssian did not care if they lived or died, for they had likely been forever tainted by Lilith. What was important was saving all the rest.

Lilith, too, had been thrown back by his brutal assault. But as he leapt off the altar, he saw her rise. Serenthia's blood dripped from a wound near the mouth and a dark bruise discolored the forehead.

Unfortunately, the demoness was far from defeated. She raised the dagger as if to throw it, but instead uttered another of the incomprehensible words. Uldyssian swore, fearing that Lilith had yet succeeded . . .

To his shock, though, it was her followers who cried out, then fell still all around them. Uldyssian sensed Lilith quickly draw something from them into herself.

"My foolish, foolish love . . ." the demoness rasped as she stood up. "Always a little shortsighted. Always not doing quite enough. From these I'll still have my way with but a moment more. You can't stand against me enough to keep me from taking the rest of your precious flock with what I've grasped from these fools! A greater sacrifice than I planned, but their loss is paltry compared to what I gain!"

He did not speak, answering instead with a force that should have pounded her to the ground. However, although she shook, Lilith remained standing.

They both knew the reason why. As much as he wanted to, Uldyssian could not bring himself to slay Serenthia, the only certain method to stop the creature possessing her body. That hesitation meant that, despite the shift in circumstances, Lilith would still in the end win.

And Sanctuary would surely be doomed.

"Poor, sweet darling," she cooed. "Always seizing failure

at the moment of victory! Still, I promise you some delights with this body, once I've made you mine again . . ."

Something struck the blade of the dagger with such force that it ripped the weapon from the distracted demoness's grip. Blood splattered the area around Lilith as the dagger and what had hit it clattered against the back wall.

And as both pieces stilled, Uldyssian saw that what lay near the dagger was another arrow . . . again covered in dirt.

"Serenthia . . ." a voice called from the entranceway, a voice that despite its grating, was so familiar to Uldyssian that it made the hair on his neck stiffen. "Serenthia . . ." it called again, closer now. "Come back . . . to us . . . to me . . ."

Despite Lilith still free, Uldyssian had to turn to the newcomer, had to see if he was dreaming . . . or living a new nightmare.

It *was* Achilios . . . Achilios, who was very dead.

The hunter's too pale eyes gazed only momentarily at Uldyssian, as if just to acknowledge that the latter saw the truth. Then, Achilios, bow drawn for another shot, continued forward. Behind him, he left a trail of slightly moist dirt, the same which seemed to cover much of his form.

"Serenthia . . ." the dead man repeated. What little remained of his ruined throat twisted and shifted as if actually drawing the breath needed for speech. "You can . . . hear me . . . you . . . know me . . ."

Lilith had been oddly silent, but now she snapped, "There is only Lilith, dear decrepit Achilios! My! Love can be foolishly strong, can it not?" She spread her arms. "Would you like me to warm you for her, archer?"

"Spare . . . spare me . . . your pathetic . . . seductions," Achilios replied, raising the bow to fire. "If I . . . can't . . . free her one way . . . I'll free her . . . another . . . she would . . . want that . . ."

"And perhaps when she, too, is dead, you'll have the chance to win her again? How macabre and wonderful at the same time!" She leaned so that he had a clear shot at her breast. "Fire, then!"

But Achilios did not rise to her bait. "When I am . . . ready, witch . . . first . . . I still want . . . her . . . to come to us . . ."

Seeing that Lilith was focused on the walking corpse, Uldyssian readied his own attack. However, Achilios shook his head.

"No . . . this is not for you to . . . do . . ."

There was that in the rasping voice that made Uldyssian listen. He watched as the archer lowered the bow.

"Serenthia . . ." Achilios murmured. "Serenthia . . . please awaken . . ."

Lilith stood as if frozen. Uldyssian thought that she planned some new mischief, but then the demoness's hands clutched at her throat as if to choke herself.

She screamed. She screamed so loud and with such raw agony that it would not have surprised the son of Diomedes to see the rest of the dead in the chamber rise up to join Achilios. Lilith screamed without pause, the very building shaking from her effort.

And then . . . and then . . . something monstrous emerged from her upturned mouth. They initially looked like a pit of small serpents, but Uldyssian finally recognized them as *fingers*. Taloned fingers.

Serenthia's face distorted, her mouth growing twice, then three times the size of her head. The hands pushed it wider, wider . . . and only then did it become apparent that the scream was issuing forth from whatever was emerging, not from the woman before them.

Fearing for the merchant's daughter, Uldyssian started forward, but again the archer forbade him. "Do not . . . do not stop this . . . if we are . . . to have any hope . . . for Serenthia . . ."

If it had been any other—no, if it had even been a *living* Achilios—Uldyssian would have paid the command no heed. Yet, somehow, he realized that his dead comrade understood the matter more than he could ever begin to. Nerves taut, Uldyssian forced himself to watch things unfold.

A grotesque array of red quills erupted from Serenthia's monstrous maw. They pushed upward. Upward . . .

And with one terrible push, the demoness Lilith burst full-blown out of the dark-haired woman's mouth.

Still screaming—but from what seemed more rage than pain—the green-scaled siren flew around the chamber several times. Below, Serenthia—now normal again—teetered dangerously.

"Fools!" bellowed Lilith, suddenly hovering. "Little-minded mortal fools! Do you think this means *anything*? Do you think you've won at all?" She laughed wildly, then thrust a taloned finger toward Serenthia. "Careful, dears! She's about to drop!"

With that, the demon flew up to the ceiling, vanishing just before she would have crashed into it.

Neither Uldyssian nor Achilios dared watch to see if this were another trick, for Lilith had at least spoken true when she had warned them about Serenthia. Nearly as pale as the archer, Serenthia let out a slight gasp, then fell over.

Uldyssian intended to use his abilities to keep her from striking the stones headfirst, but somehow Achilios moved even faster. Gritty arms caught Serenthia mere inches from disaster. The archer gently set her down as if she were made of fragile glass.

Serenthia exhaled . . . and her eyes fluttered open. She gazed up at her savior, who himself looked to Uldyssian as if he suddenly wished that he were anywhere else at the moment rather than in her sight. The archer quickly put one hand over his throat in a futile attempt to cover the monstrous sight.

"A-Achilios . . ." she mumbled. "Achilios . . ." A smile started to spread, but before it could go very far . . . Serenthia passed out.

"Praise . . . be . . ." muttered the dead man. He stepped back from her, only then looking at Uldyssian.

The son of Diomedes could still not believe what he was seeing. "Achilios—"

"Take . . . take better care . . . of her . . . next time . . . if only so I won't . . . be back . . ."

The archer turned to flee, but Uldyssian seized him by the arm. Ignoring both the dirt and the cold he felt, Uldyssian growled, "You can't leave!"

This brought a harsh laugh from the dead man. "And . . . how could I . . . remain?"

Before Uldyssian could answer, yet another scream resounded in the ancient structure. Both looked to the entrance . . . where, unnoticed in the heat of things, a crowd of startled edyrem had gathered.

A crowd now seeing their mistress as still as death, their master returned as if from the dead . . . and a man the Parthans in the group knew had been slaughtered by a demon.

SIXTEEN

Mendeln had never stood atop a mountain before.

He did not like it in the least.

The wind howled and snow covered everything. However, nothing, not even the chill air, really touched him much. He supposed that he had Rathma to thank for that, if gratitude was the proper emotion for being dragged off to this desolate spot to face a figure whose very name filled Uldyssian's brother with dread.

"And what assistance am I to be against an angel?" he asked not for the first time. Mendeln had to raise his voice to be heard over the wind.

"Whatever it turns out you can supply," was Rathma's response, the same one he had used to answer the prior questions.

Mendeln folded his arms tight, if only out of habit, not from being cold. "Where are we?"

"Near where I brought your brother. Near to the vicinity of the Worldstone."

What little Mendeln had learned of this "Worldstone" had filled him with new awe and not a little uncertainty. To have created such a thing, the angels and demons must have utilized fantastic magic and energy.

He was about to ask Rathma another question when the ancient nephalem raised a hand to cut him off.

"My father approaches. Be wary."

To Mendeln, it was an unnecessary warning. How could he deal with the arrival of an angry angel with anything but wariness?

The wind suddenly picked up, so ferocious now that it nearly shoved Mendeln from his position. He did not like the thought of tumbling down the mountainside, no matter what he had learned from the dragon and his companion about the many states of life. At the moment, Mendeln still preferred the "living" stage too much to abandon it just yet.

The snow also increased. A storm raged about them. Rathma pulled free his dagger and muttered something, but the storm remained intense.

Then, an ear-splitting thunderclap shook them further, a thunderclap immediately followed by dead silence. If not for being able to hear his own breathing, Mendeln would have believed himself now deaf.

And then he noticed in their midst a golden-haired youth.

"I am disappointed in you, my son," the robed figure stated in a voice of pure music.

"As you ever have been since my birth, my father," Rathma replied, his generally bland tone with a hint of an edge in it.

The newcomer looked away from the pair, instead seeming more interested in the general landscape. "And have you seen your mother of late?"

"No. I have been fortunate in that regard. I wish I could say the same concerning *you.*"

Now Rathma had his attention again. "Your insolence is unbecoming. Be grateful that I have not deigned to punish you for your past sins."

Mendeln watched the pair, still uncertain, despite what he had heard, that this was indeed Inarius. He knew that the angel was master of the Cathedral of Light and had heard of the Prophet's general description, but to actually see the young figure was disconcerting, to say the least.

As if sensing this, Inarius turned his gaze to the human. Suddenly, Mendeln had no more doubts. The eyes were enough to stop him in his tracks. He could not even say what color they were, just that to have them look his way made Mendeln almost wish to drop down on his knees in worship. That made him again wonder just how much help he would actually be, should Rathma truly need him. If he was this weak merely because of a *look* . . .

To his surprise, a slight chuckle escaped Rathma. "Not so insignificant, are they?"

"And that may be their downfall," returned the angel coldly. "You and your kind had no place here. Nor do these. If they cannot be contained, they must be removed . . ." He turned from them as if they were nothing to him. His sandaled feet left no impressions in the snow. "Sanctuary must be purified . . ."

Rathma was uncharacteristically emotional. "For *who,* Inarius? For who? All there would be then is you! Must all else in this world bend to your will or be expunged for their defiance?"

"They exist by my will, therefore, yes . . ." The Prophet turned to them again. As he did, Mendeln noticed that he momentarily left the edge of the mountaintop, yet did not fall. "This is a debate we have had before, Linarian . . ."

Rathma pulled his cloak tight around him. "That name I have rejected, as I have you and my mother."

The Prophet shrugged. He glanced briefly at Mendeln, then again at his son. Without warning, Inarius suddenly said, "You know why I am here."

"Of course."

"You were forbidden."

"Fate decreed otherwise," Rathma returned.

The angel spread his arms and his face contorted. His hair stood on edge and he grew larger and larger. Fire radiated around him. "*I* am Fate here. I am the yea or nay for all that exists in Sanctuary—"

"Beware!" Mendeln's companion warned, not that Uldyssian's brother needed to be alerted. The son of Diomedes drew his own dagger, a thing seemingly so insignificant in the sight of Inarius's abrupt and staggering transformation.

I AM THE ULTIMATE JUDGE OF WHAT IS AND WHAT SHALL BE! declared the angel, his mouth no longer moving. The words struck Mendeln much as Trag'Oul's had, but without the dragon's consideration for their effect on a mortal body and mind. It was a struggle to maintain his stance, but Mendeln knew he dared not falter.

From the angel's back burst what at first Mendeln took for magnificent, fiery wings. Yet as they spread wide, he saw that they were more astounding than even that. The wings—so different from the feathered ones that Mendeln had most of his life imagined on angels—were actually *strands of light* that moved almost as if with animation of their own. They writhed and shifted like serpents or tentacles, a very contrary suggestion to what the angel represented. Inarius's body and face contorted. A breastplate formed over his torso. The handsome, youthful visage sank into darkness beneath an immaculate hood, once within, finally transforming completely into shadow. It was as if there was no true physical substance to him. All vestiges of Humanity vanished as a heavenly warrior suddenly hovered beyond the mountain's edge, one gleaming, gauntleted hand pointing accusingly at the angel's rebellious offspring.

I SPOKE WITH YOU OUT OF MEMORY, BUT THAT TIME IS PAST FOREVER NOW! YOU WISH LINARIAN DEAD, THEN SO BE IT! THERE IS NO TIE BETWEEN US!

"Was there *ever*?" Rathma shouted back, ivory dagger held before him like the strongest of shields. Mendeln followed suit, hoping that it was not a futile gesture.

THE STONE AWAITS ME . . . Inarius gestured. *AND I AM DONE WITH YOU!*

The mountaintop exploded.

The force unleashed by the angel ripped up snow, ice, and rock in great chunks. Mendeln expected to be tossed away with them, but for the moment, the area around him and Rathma remained intact. Not much else did, however. Dirt and snow flew everywhere and Mendeln likely would have been crushed if his own weapon had not suddenly emitted a pale light that now enveloped him. He glanced at his companion and saw that Rathma was likewise protected.

But with rock and snow crashing about him, Mendeln did not know how much longer the two would be safe. Above them, Inarius pointed with his other hand—and Mendeln felt the ground beneath him collapse.

"Remember what you have been shown!" shouted Rathma.

But all Mendeln could think about was that he no longer had any footing. His fear of falling had at last become a reality. Rathma vanished from his sight, the other's footing also torn out from under him.

As he fell, Mendeln caught sight of Inarius, the angel watching the destruction with what could only be called detachment. Even his own offspring was of no consequence to the winged being. After all, Rathma had committed the ultimate sin; he had defied his father.

Clutching the dagger tight, Mendeln sought some way to save himself. Then, a hand clutched his collar, slowing his descent. He knew instantly that it was Rathma.

As the avalanche continued, Rathma set him down on a small outcropping still holding. The shrouded figure then alighted next to him.

"This is not over!" he called.

Not at all surprised, Mendeln prepared himself for the worst. Inarius would not leave this task incomplete.

And sure enough, the winged warrior fluttered into sight. Inarius—his face more of a brilliant armored mask—inspected the two.

Mendeln felt the angel focus on him. He prepared for the end—

WHAT HAS HE DONE? demanded Inarius. *WHAT HAS HE DONE . . . AND HOW?*

Only after a moment did Mendeln realize that Inarius spoke of *Uldyssian*. He had no idea just what about his sibling so concerned the angel, but suddenly feared anew for Uldyssian's life.

WHAT HAS HE DONE? Inarius repeated. *WHAT HAS HE DONE TO THE STONE?*

From behind Mendeln, Rathma shouted, "He has done the undoable, Inarius! He has done the undoable!"

The angel hovered in silence for a moment. He started to gesture at the pair, then lowered his hand. *THEN . . . HE MAY HAVE CONDEMNED YOU ALL . . .*

And with that, the winged being soared high into the sky, dwindling to a dot in less time than Mendeln could count to the number one. Then, in a flash of light so brilliant it momentarily blinded the human . . . Inarius disappeared.

The devastation wrought by Rathma's father—so *easily,* Mendeln dourly thought—began to settle around them. The entire top of the peak had been radically altered. Now, it looked as if the mountain had grown a giant, three-fingered paw with jagged claws on two of the digits. He and Rathma stood on the outer edge of the third, a drop of well over a thousand feet merely one step away.

One question burned to be spoken by Mendeln. "Why do we live? We were clearly nothing to him, whatever your beliefs before we came here! Why do we live?"

"We were not nothing to him, son of Diomedes," the ancient figure responded, dusting off bits of dirt and snow. "If we had been, we would have been dead without ever knowing he had arrived. It is because of what we—and your brother most of all—represent, that my dear father paused to speak at all. Certainly not for me alone, as we have spoken all we can, lo, these many centuries past. He also came in part out of curiosity surrounding you, Mendeln ul-Diomed, and what a jest it was when he found that he could not bend your knee to him . . ."

"Could not—" Mendeln felt queasy in his stomach. He had *defied* the angel's will?

"Did you not know that? I thought you aware."

Seeking not to think about the subject anymore, Mendeln asked, "What is it that he kept mentioning? Did I hear him say the *Worldstone*? I know that it was mentioned by you or Uldyssian when the pair of you returned, but I never understood completely about it! Just what did Uldyssian do that so—so—*shocked*—him?"

Rathma's expression darkened. "That will take a bit more explaining. Suffice to say, we are near that which is vital to the conclusion—whatever that conclusion will be—of our struggle. The Worldstone is a thing that only one like my father should be able to alter in even the least way—and, therefore, could my mother—yet your brother did just that! The Worldstone is different now, in even a manner Inarius cannot believe, hence his reaction."

At first, Mendeln took hope from this, but then he recalled the angel's parting words. *Then, he may have condemned you all . . .*

Mendeln surveyed what even the least of Inarius's fury had done to a gigantic mountaintop and shuddered. "Rathma, what does he mean by his last?"

Lilith's son held his dagger high, as if using it to search for something. Mendeln waited impatiently as the tall figure first turned in a circle, then replaced the otherworldly weapon in the vast confines of his cloak.

"What he means has to do with the same reason that we, who could not make the stand that I hoped—and evidently did not need to since Inarius made no adjustment to the stone that I can divine—are still alive. Why should he bother with two paltry deaths when, if he reaches the conclusion to which I sense he is leaning, he will then remove *everything* at once and start his Sanctuary anew?"

Only now did Mendeln truly grasp what he realized Rathma and Trag'Oul had been saying all along. "Rather than . . . rather than allowing Lilith . . . or humans . . . to act beyond his dictates . . . you are saying that the angel could . . . would utterly destroy our world?"

"And then build anew to suit his megalomania, yes."

Mendeln could not even imagine such power in one being's control. "He can . . . *do* this?"

"He can." Rathma began drawing a circle in the air, a circle that expanded instantly. As it did, Mendeln saw that within it was utter darkness . . . the path, he knew, to Trag'Oul's realm. "He has that power . . ." the angel's son continued, sounding for the first time very, very weary. "He has that power a thousand times over . . . and will be more than willing to use it . . ."

Lilith materialized on the throne, her image only briefly that of herself before she cast the illusion of the Primus over her. The demoness sat in the darkness, utterly silent. Had any been there and able to gaze upon the face she now wore, they would have come away unable to read the emotions coursing through her.

After several minutes, she suddenly rose and departed the Primus's personal chambers. The guards outside jolted to attention. Although they had been at their positions as demanded, they had assumed—rightly—that their master had *not* been inside. Still, none questioned this miraculous appearance . . . for this *was* the Primus, after all.

At least, to their eyes.

Lilith remained expressionless as she strode throughout the vast temple. There seemed no rhyme or reason to her path. Priests, guards, novices, and other acolytes paid homage to her along the way, each seeming to try to bow or kneel lower than those before.

Then, in the great hall where the statues of Mefis, Dialon, and Bala stood, she paused. Around her, more of the faithful hesitated in their own tasks, cautiously wondering just what the Primus did.

She looked up at each of the statues . . . her eyes lingering longest on that of Mefis.

And then . . . after staring at the spirit's vaguely crafted visage, Lilith allowed the Primus's own to smile ever so slightly.

"Yes," she murmured. "Yes, that'll be the way of it. Oh, yes . . ."

One of the more daring priests stepped up to her. Hands clasped together and head low, he said, "Great Primus, is there any service I may be to you?"

Lilith glanced at him, noting his youth and good build, not to mention the fact that he had been the only one with backbone enough to approach her. "Tell me . . . what is your name again, my son?"

"Durram, Great Primus." He wore the robe of a devotee of Dialon and she already sensed that the darkness of the Lord of Terror had touched Durram despite his humble facade. He was ambitious.

"I will summon you to my chambers later to speak with you," she told him, forcing herself not to give him a beguiling smile. Lilith had a need to burn off certain frustrations and Durram looked just perfect for the task, not that he would know until it was too late.

The priest bowed lower than any of the others. Inside, the demoness sensed he was congratulating himself on his daring. She wondered how he would feel after their "discussion."

But minor pleasures had to be pushed aside for the moment. Having come to a decision, Lilith was eager to implement it. Once again, the proverbial closing of one door had led to another opening.

"I must go," she informed Durram.

"I will await your summons, Great Primus."

Lilith could not forgo a brief feminine chuckle, but Durram did not hear it. As she passed the bowing priest, she blithely commented, "Durram. Clear the vicinity. An accident is about to happen."

To his credit, Durram was quick to obey. As he shouted the warning, Lilith strode off. She waited until she had reached the corridor leading back to the Primus's chambers, then glanced over her shoulder.

There was a resounding crack—and the statue of Mefis suddenly toppled from its high perch.

Had it fallen moments earlier, at least a score of humans would have been crushed or badly injured. As it was, the statue's collision with the marble floor sent huge chunks flying in every direction. Durram had done well in directing the others away, but a few were still within range of the deadly missiles.

The demoness gestured—making certain that some of the guards and others nearby noticed—and those who were about to be struck were saved. The pieces turned to light ash, then faded, not even leaving a trace upon their supposed victims.

The dust began to settle. To one of the guards, Lilith commanded, "All are well. It remains only to clear the rubble. The priest Durram will oversee it."

The awed guard nodded. "Yes, Great Primus!"

"I must go and meditate on this event . . . and consider what form the new image of Mefis must take."

No one questioned her. In fact, she knew that word was already spreading—with Durram's aid—of the Primus's holy warning that had saved so many. Once again, they had witnessed a miracle.

But Lilith had not warned them for their sake. After all, she had been the cause of the statue's collapse. She had been simply reassuring the Primus's grand status in the temple, for what she planned soon would push these humans to the limits of their wills . . . and likely cost many their lives. Of course, as they would have willingly given those lives for their Primus and she was now *him,* that was a negligible point.

The demoness took one last look at the statue. Turning from her followers, she allowed herself a slight smirk, then whispered, "So *sorry,* Father . . ."

The Prime Evils—especially Mephisto—would be helpless to do anything against her. They so feared the High Heavens discovering Sanctuary that they would let it fall into her claws. No doubt they would think that they could retake it later, but Lilith understood the Worldstone well enough to make that an impossibility. With a world of suddenly vibrant nephalem at her command, the demon lords would discover that they had best worry about saving their *own* realm.

Yes, first the Burning Hells and then the High Heavens.

That made her think of Inarius, always skulking about. She knew his weaknesses as well. There was nothing to fear from him . . .

Still clad as the Primus, she returned to the darkened chambers. Once there, she paused. Despite the lack of light, the demoness could sense traces of webbing in the room. Someone had been here during her absence, someone who should have known better. She had actually noted some of the traces earlier, but her mind had been concerned with weightier matters. Now, though . . .

"Astrogha!" Lilith called in Lucion's powerful voice. "Get in here, you damned spider!"

"This one is here," retorted the arachnid a breath later from the shadows above. "What is it the great Lucion wants?"

There was a change in the other demon's tone that Lilith did not appreciate, a defiance. "You have been misbehaving. You have been masquerading."

"This one has been taking up the mantle that the great Lucion has forgone too much of late . . . so much so, in fact, that *others* insisted that Astrogha fill the void."

She knew exactly what the spider had been up to. Lilith was concerned with only one thing, even more so considering the shift in the other demon's mood. Astrogha represented the only impediment still existing in the Triune. It had been the demoness's hope that Uldyssian would have removed him at the same time as he had the foolish Gulag, but Astrogha had proven wilier.

"And filled it like a rabbit pretending to be a lion. There were plans in place that Astrogha did not need to know, but that his interference utterly disrupted! How would the Three consider *that*?"

There was shuffling from the shadows. Glimpses of the other demon became apparent. "That, a fair question might be, great Lucion . . . a question this one would not be above asking himself to them . . ."

Which meant that Astrogha had already survived interrogation by one of the Prime Evils, no doubt his own lord and master, Diablo.

"There can be only one Primus, one master of the Cult of the Three, spider . . ."

"Yesss . . . this one agrees . . . and only awaited your return to resolve that . . . *Lilith.*"

True spiders did not spit webbing from their mouths, but, then, Astrogha's form was but an aspect. He was no more truly one of the eight-legged creatures than Lilith had been Lylia.

The foul spray spread over the dark chamber, Astrogha seeking to assure that there would be no chance of missing his prey. When he had divined that Lilith had taken her brother's place, the demoness did not know nor did she care. She had even expected this possible scenario . . . and so, before the webbing could engulf her, created a green inferno that burned away the other demon's attack. Sharp hissing accompanied the destruction of the webbing—

But Astrogha, too, had evidently assumed removing her would demand more effort, for suddenly there were spiders *everywhere*. Even Lilith could not evade them all. They bit her wherever they could, spilling into her Astrogha's foul venom. The arachnid had learned the need for haste from his experience with the mortal, Uldyssian, but he still forgot that he dealt with no ordinary demon. This was the daughter of Mephisto . . .

With but a thought, Lilith pushed the surge of venom back into each of the spiders, then added her own to the mix. The sinister creatures began tumbling off her body in great numbers.

Astrogha hissed angrily and another wave of webbing shot forth, this time snaring Lilith's right side. However, suddenly appearing as herself, she laughed and sliced away the sticky substance with the claws of her left hand.

"I find the best way to rid a place of vermin is to burn them out," she mocked. "Don't you agree?"

The demoness snared one of the fallen tendrils. The end burst into green flames which raced up toward the shadowed Astrogha, at last revealing his macabre form to her.

Astrogha hissed and spat, seeking to douse the unnatural flames. His webbing only fueled Lilith's fire, though, and in seconds he was surrounded by it.

"This one will devour your flesh and drink your soul," he snarled. The arachnid's multiple eyes flared crimson.

Lilith faltered. There was a new presence in the chamber, one she knew too well. She almost turned to look behind her . . . then stopped.

"When next you seek to remind me of my father," she cooed, "you had best be certain you bring the real thing, not some desperate illusion, servant of Diablo . . ."

Lilith magnified the flames. Astrogha shrieked as they licked at his hairy form.

"You are a fool, Mephisto's daughter!" he declared, pulling back as best he could. "And therefore welcome to this fool's nest forged by Lucion! Savor it . . . for what little time remains . . ."

A new and utter blackness enshrouded the spider. Lilith willed the flames forward . . . but when they reached the corner, there was no longer any Astrogha.

With her mind, she searched the whole of the temple, but found no trace. Astrogha had not merely fled to safety; he had fled the Triune entirely. Lilith was not overly concerned; she should have slain Diablo's servant, but he clearly would be of no consequence, anymore. Now the Cult of the Three completely belonged to her.

No, Lilith thought with a smile as she dismissed the remnants of the struggle to oblivion and once more, as the

Primus, assumed her place on the throne. *No longer the Cult of the Three. There is only One. There is only Me.*

Feeling quite pleased with herself, she had a sudden desire for the priest Durram's company. There was time enough for a little entertainment before she dealt with dear Uldyssian. He had forced her to a decision that, in retrospect, would accelerate her dreams to fulfillment. All she needed were a few morlu . . .

Lilith giggled at her own thought. Perhaps more than *few* . . .

Astrogha had no regrets about fleeing the temple. He had not expected to be able to defeat the daughter of a Prime Evil, although his effort had allowed him to gauge her for another possible confrontation. She was welcome to the Triune and she and the mortal, Uldyssian, were welcome to the other. Astrogha had not outlived other demons by not knowing when it was best to let others deal with his problems. Let them battle it out, perhaps with the angel, Inarius, also throwing himself into the mix. The survivors—should there be any—would find themselves weakened, of that he was certain. Then . . . then the spider would pick up the pieces. The notion of a cult such as the Triune still made sense, but one more focused. On himself perhaps.

Yes, Astrogha *liked* that thought. From the ruins of this debacle, he would gather humans of his own. There were always those with an almost demonic lust for power. Unlike Lucion, though, Astrogha would maintain tight control over his minions. That had been the trouble; Lucion had lost order, had allowed himself to rely too much on others. Then, when he had finally taken personal control, something had obviously gone wrong. The son of Mephisto had somehow perished.

No, Astrogha would not make Lucion's mistakes, nor Lilith's. Already he could imagine his slaves spreading out to both sides of the world, his symbol—the spider—raised over city after city. There would come the day when no one would recall the Triune or the Cathedral of Light. It would be the cult of Astrogha that finally *conquered* Sanctuary and made humans its slaves . . . all for the Prime Evils, of course, and especially, his master.

All for them . . . eventually . . .

SEVENTEEN

Although given only an instant, Uldyssian yet managed to devise a plan to readily explain the scene before his followers. Most of it involved the truth, the rest a necessary twisting of it.

But Achilios gave him no chance to even begin it. The archer threw himself toward the gathered edyrem who, stunned, reacted as people and cleared a path for the dead man. Achilios made good use of their reaction, bolting outside before any could recover.

"Achilios!" Uldyssian shouted. "Wait!"

He rushed after his childhood friend, ignoring the clamoring that began among those gathered. To them he ordered, "Get those bodies out of there and see to her! Don't move her any more than necessary but make her comfortable! Do it!"

Outside, more edyrem stood in shock, most of them still looking west. Uldyssian ran in that direction, trying to locate the incredibly swift Achilios by both eyesight and higher senses. Yet, the archer was invisible to both.

As he neared the edge of camp, Uldyssian saw a sentry turn his way. The man, a Parthan, gaped. Uldyssian seized the guard and demanded, "A pale figure! Did he run by here?"

"No, no one's come this way—Master *Uldyssian*?"

He could explain his miraculous return to the guard when he did so to the rest. Shoving aside the Parthan, Uldyssian entered the jungle. Achilios had to have gone this way, but try as he might, Uldyssian could not sense him at all.

Defeated, he finally returned to the encampment. By that time, a great mob had gathered near the sentry, who was animatedly describing his encounter with their lost leader. Everyone grew silent when Uldyssian approached, but he had no time for them yet.

Still, he had to say something. "I'll tell all later. Return to your rest."

It was very doubtful that any of them would sleep, but Uldyssian could only hope. For now, he had to concern himself with Serenthia.

Those still surrounding the ancient building scattered out of his way as he neared. Without a glance to any of them, Uldyssian entered.

Serenthia still lay on the floor, but someone had had the presence of mind to set a blanket under her head and another over her torso. Her breathing was regular, for which Uldyssian thanked the stars. Then, he recalled particular stars, those that made up the dragon, and nearly took back his silent gratitude.

Going down on one knee, Uldyssian touched Serenthia's face. It was pleasantly warm.

A slight moan escaped her. Her eyes flashed open and she attempted to rise.

"Achilios! Achilios! Don't—don't leave—" Her strength failed her. Serenthia had to lay her head down again. Despite that, though, she kept her eyes open and repeated over and over the same thing. "Achilios . . . don't leave . . . don't leave . . ."

Uldyssian was caught between relief and jealousy. Serenthia seemed mentally intact and physically unharmed, for which he was grateful, but that her first cries had been for the archer . . .

Silently berating himself for his extreme selfishness, Uldyssian leaned nearer. "Serenthia . . . Serry . . . do you hear me? How do you feel?"

"Uldyssian?" Her eyes finally focused on him. "I—I think I'm all right." She stiffened. "No! That thing! I know it!

She's coming for me! It was—" The merchant's daughter clutched his arm. "Uldyssian! Lilith! Lilith was coming for me—"

"I know. I know. Hush, Serenthia! Lilith's been sent away again—"

But she was finally beginning to register her unsettling surroundings. "Where—where are we? The last I recall, I was by the river! I sensed her nearness too late! And then it was as if—as if she were *inside* me! Where *are* we, Uldyssian? Tell me the truth!"

There was no way he could keep the truth from her. If Uldyssian even tried, Serenthia was certain to eventually learn everything from the others.

"Listen to me carefully, Serry," he murmured. "We will talk about this later—"

The fire began to return to her. "No, Uldyssian. I need to know now. Tell me."

He looked back at the others. "Leave us."

They obeyed without protest. Uldyssian used his power to seal the doors behind him, then also blocked those outside from hearing. They would know enough when the time came, but there were some things he felt should remain only between the two of them.

Someone had wisely left a water pouch near Serenthia and Uldyssian bade her drink first. She willingly swallowed a good portion of the contents, then gave him a look that suggested he stall no longer.

And so, with a deep breath, Uldyssian told her what he could and what he dared, cutting matters to the bare facts as much as possible. Serenthia listened without interruption save for the occasional gasp. Her face, though, more than once nearly caused Uldyssian to stop, especially when he had to tell the merchant's daughter what he knew of Lilith's activities. Revulsion filled Serenthia, but to her credit, she did not lose control.

Then, Uldyssian came to the moment when Achilios had reentered the situation. Here he finally stopped short, not at all certain just how to go on. Was it better to let her believe that he had been no more than a dream?

She knew that he was trying to leave something significant out of the story and so pressed him.

Surrendering to the inevitable, Uldyssian chose a different tact. "Serry," he began in his kindest tone. "Serry, do you remember what you said when you first awoke here? Do you remember at all?"

"You keep calling me 'Serry,'" she countered, her gaze narrowing. "That can only mean you've got something terrible to tell me. What can be worse than what I've heard so far and what has it to do with what I said?"

He could not turn back. "Serry. Think. What did you say? It's vital."

Her brow wrinkled. "Let me think. I was . . . I was having a dream . . . or nightmare, I can't say which. I thought I saw . . . I thought I saw *Achilios*. I must've still been dreaming when I believed I awoke, because I think what I was doing was calling out his name and . . . and . . ." Tears suddenly rolled down her cheeks. "Oh, Uldyssian . . . I thought he'd come back to me! I thought I'd been blessed with a miracle! But—but it was nothing but my imagination . . ."

Uldyssian swallowed. "No."

"What—what was that?"

"Serry . . . Serenthia . . . he was here. You didn't imagine him. Achilios was here."

She frowned at him. "Don't make a jest like that! There's nothing funny about it at all, Uldyssian! How could you do that?"

"I never would. It's not a jest. He was—"

Pulling back from Uldyssian, Serenthia covered her ears. "Stop! Stop that! Don't say such things! Achilios is *dead*! Dead!"

The building started to quake. Small bits of stone rained down on them. Driven by her grief, Serenthia's power was affecting their surroundings.

Uldyssian quickly worked to counter her. The tremor subsided, albeit reluctantly. Serenthia was nearly as strong as him.

She had not even noticed what she had done. Cyrus's daughter shook her head back and forth and tears stained her cheeks. Over and over she repeated the archer's name.

Mouth set, Uldyssian took hold of her wrists and forced her to listen. "Serenthia! It *was* Achilios you saw! It was no dream!" He could not bring himself to say that it was no *nightmare*. Even he had not quite recovered from the shock of seeing his friend. "It *was* Achilios!"

Her eyes widened and the tears lessened. Hope filled her expression. "You mean that he's—he's—alive?"

"I . . . Serenthia . . . I don't know *what* to call what he was . . . but at least he was still the Achilios we knew and loved. He charged in here when all was lost and managed somehow to stir you to waking. Only because of him, not me, were you able to force Lilith from your body."

"I—I remember hearing his voice. I remember I was in darkness. All I wanted to do was sleep . . . but his voice . . . I had to follow it! I wanted so much to see him again . . ." Wiping away a lingering tear, the dark-haired woman surveyed the chamber. "But where is he, then? Achilios!" She started to rise. "Achilios! Don't hide from me!"

She teetered. Uldyssian quickly supported her. Serenthia put an arm around his waist, her eyes yet seeking the man she loved.

"Why won't he answer me? Why's he hiding?"

"He's not. He ran off when others entered. Serry, I think he's afraid that you'll be repulsed by what he's become."

Serenthia gave him an incredulous look. "Why? He's Achilios!"

"And he should be *dead*. Dead. We buried him, remember?" Before she could suggest the obvious, Uldyssian continued, "There was no mistake! The shaft went through his throat! He should be dead!"

He felt her shiver, but realized that it was not out of fear.

"How horrible," Serenthia murmured, eyeing empty air. "How horrible for him . . ."

As she said it, Uldyssian had to admit that a part of him felt the same for his childhood friend. Achilios had obviously been tracking them for some time, perhaps even within days of his killing. Had he meant them any harm, he could have struck several times over. Thus far, Achilios had only acted like the Achilios of old, ever protective of those for whom he cared.

Especially Serenthia.

"I've got to find him," she abruptly declared. "I've got to find Achilios! He's all alone out there, fearful to be even with me!"

"Serry, he may have good reason—"

Her voice grew sharp. "That's ridiculous! There's *no* good reason for us to be apart. I won't be deterred. I'm going to find him."

Her determination in the face of such drastic events touched Uldyssian deeply. "I'll stand with you, then, Serry. You have the right of it; Achilios has always been there for us . . . even now. Whatever he must overcome, we should be there for him, too."

That made her finally smile. "Thank you . . ."

With his continued assistance, she was finally able to leave the sinister building. Outside, they were immediately surrounded by others, Saron among them. Behind the Torajian stood a group of edyrem who were apparently acting as guards to a small, surly group.

Their prisoners were the last remnants of those turned by Lilith. They were but a handful, the rest having been sacrificed to the demoness's madness. Uldyssian recognized all but two and assumed those to be Hashiri. In addition to having the bodies removed, Uldyssian had through his powers secretly passed word to those he felt certain he could trust to locate the guards Lilith had left at the edge of the encampment. From his count, his followers had managed to round up all of them.

"What shall we do with them, master?" asked Saron. His dark expression gave easy indication of what he would have liked. To the mind of most of the edyrem present, the turned were the foulest of traitors . . . even if their fall from grace was due to Lilith's seductions.

Uldyssian had been unable to save Romus or any of those inside, but he still hoped to salvage these souls. He was already sick of the rising number of dead.

Then, he recalled Serenthia. However, before he could speak, she whispered, "Go ahead. This must not wait, not even for me . . ."

With that, she pulled away so as to give him room. Uldyssian signaled two of his followers to bring the first of the turned to him. As they approached, he sensed the other edyrem managing to keep the power of the prisoner in check. He was impressed by their action, something that they had not been taught by him.

The man, a Torajian, scowled as Uldyssian leaned into him. He looked ready to spit into his former leader's face, but evidently thought better of it.

For what he planned, Uldyssian knew that he would have to touch the prisoner. That would mean more direct contact with Lilith's taint, but there was nothing that he could do to avoid that if he hoped to save the Torajian.

With a deep breath, he brought his hands up to each side of the prisoner's head. The Torajian tried to shake loose, then settled down, glaring.

Meeting that evil gaze, Uldyssian delved within. He sensed the core of what was the Torajian and how it tied to his power.

It took him no time at all to find the blackness that the demoness had stirred to raging life. It was so evil that a stunned Uldyssian nearly retreated out of repulsion. Yet, to do so would be to abandon all hope for the man before him.

After brief consideration, Uldyssian determined that his best chance lay in trying to smother or even *remove* the darkness. He imagined it like a solid object and used his mind to try to encase it. If it could be *forced* out—

Without warning, the blackness erupted into pure, monstrous fury. Uldyssian barely had a chance to withdraw his mind—

—and no opportunity at all to prevent the prisoner from tearing free from his guards as if they were nothing and clamping his hands around Uldyssian's throat.

Sharp agony filled Uldyssian as the Torajian squeezed. Intense heat wracked his throat, the escaped prisoner using his own edyrem powers in addition to his brute strength. If not for the son of Diomedes having already had some protections up, he would have been dead already.

"I will rip out your throat and drink your blood!" snarled the Torajian madly. His face distorted, his eyes bulging as if about to pop out and his mouth stretching wide. His teeth grew sharper and his tongue—now forked—darted in and out like a wild snake. "I will—"

He screamed, his hands releasing Uldyssian's throat at the same time. The Torajian took a step back, his body blazing. He attempted once to douse the mysterious but voracious flames . . . and then burned away into a pile of black ash.

From behind him, Uldyssian heard Serenthia's weary voice. "I had—to—do it. There was nothing—nothing left to save, Uldyssian."

He nodded wordlessly, then, rubbing his throat, surveyed the rest of the prisoners. They did not look at all fearful, but rather full of malice. Uldyssian contemplated searching deeper in the hope of finding *some* chance for their redemption, but recalled too well what had just happened. Lilith had taken into account that someone, perhaps even him, might seek to save those she had turned. The demoness had made that impossible.

Which left Uldyssian with only one bitter choice.

"Stand away from them," he commanded their guards.

Saron quickly protested. "Master, it might not be safe to do—"

"Stand away from them."

They obeyed, but still used their combined might to keep the prisoners at bay. Unfortunately, Uldyssian could not permit them to continue to do that, either, for fear that they might be harmed by what he planned.

"Release them," he ordered. Before Saron could speak anew, Uldyssian added, "I'll deal with the problem. Do as I say."

He sensed the moment that they obeyed and then the one when the prisoners realized that their power was theirs again. Yet, before any of them could become a threat, Uldyssian concentrated.

The turned edyrem froze. Even then, though, he could feel their evil struggles.

"Away with you," Uldyssian grimly uttered.

A wind picked up around the turned, a fierce wind that touched only them.

As if made of sand, Lilith's creatures literally *blew* away. The wind ripped up the particles and flung them high, high into the night. Uldyssian did not let his concentration falter as he made that gust throw what had once been men far from his followers. If any trace of the demoness's taint remained, he did not want it to affect anyone else.

Finally, after what he felt a safe interval and distance, he dismissed the wind. Somewhere to the west, far from where any of the edyrem would have reason to go, he let the dust finally scatter.

Would that it could be so easy with Lilith. But his treacherous lover had protected herself against him, and although he would not admit it to the others, this sort of spell, so akin to what he had done to Lucion, took much, much out of him.

So much so, in fact, that now *he* began to teeter.

"Catch him!" someone called. More than one pair of hands obeyed, Serenthia's among them.

"I'm—I'm good," he managed, straightening again. Ignoring the awed stares of the others, he turned to Serenthia. "We can—we can go after Achilios now."

"No. Neither of us is strong enough for that, no matter how much I deeply want to. He's followed us this long, Uldyssian; he'll surely be in the vicinity still."

That made sense to him, too. Achilios appeared unwilling to give up on his friends.

"For now," Serenthia continued, "we need rest." She looked down, and in a voice so soft that only he could hear it, added, "I also need . . . I need to sleep near you. *Just* sleep. I—I have to."

"I understand." She would have nightmares, Uldyssian knew, nightmares of all the things Lilith had done with and through her. From him, Serenthia sought some comfort to get her through those nightmares.

Uldyssian would gladly give her that comfort, too, and not for any other reason than that she was his friend and had been through a terrifying ordeal. More to the point, having seen Achilios reminded him of who Serenthia actually loved. What he had believed to be growing between him and her had merely been again the demoness's seductions. Small wonder that Uldyssian had fallen into the trap so easily.

But someday . . . someday he would make Lilith pay . . .

Achilios had finally stopped running. There was at least a good mile, even two, between him and the camp. Not needing to breathe, the archer had managed the distance in astounding time, even considering the dense growth around him.

As he paused, the same thoughts that had been swirling about his mind since he had begun running returned with a vengeance.

She had seen him.

Serenthia had seen him.

There had been no manner by which he could have avoided a confrontation. The demoness had made that impossible. Achilios had sensed what she had been about and that Uldyssian had been betrayed by one he trusted.

The archer felt some sympathy for Romus, but not much. Unlike Uldyssian, who generally saw the good in all men, Achilios had tended to keep a watch out for the bad, as well. True, from what he had seen through the air slit the Parthan had appeared to attempt to redeem himself, but perhaps he had merely been trying to avenge his own death. Achilios neither knew nor truly cared.

All that mattered was that Serenthia was free of her possession . . . that, and that she had seen him.

He had no idea what to do about that.

With an unearthly groan, Achilios slumped against a tree. A small lizard near his head sought to quickly scurry away, but the hunter grabbed it without even looking. The reptile squirmed as he brought it around to view. Achilios could feel its heart beating wildly as it tried in vain to escape. It was certain it was about to be eaten.

He savored the small creature's life motions, realizing that he was jealous even of it. A part of Achilios suddenly wanted to *crush* the lizard to a pulp . . . but instead he set it on the tree again and let it rush to the freedom it had been certain it had lost.

She had seen him . . .

Achilios could not get that thought out of his mind. He was haunted by it.

The archer let out a grating chuckle. He, the walking dead, was *haunted*.

"It . . . doesn't matter . . ." Achilios quietly grated. "Doesn't matter . . ."

But it did. He had taken some small comfort in being able to at least be near Serenthia, and on occasion, secretly aiding both her and Uldyssian. That would be next to impossible now.

Yet, if not to help those nearest and dearest to him, of what use was his resurrection? Perhaps he should call and call Rathma or the dragon until one of them came and put him to rest forever . . .

Despite the sense of that . . . Achilios uttered no sound.

Even this mockery of life was something, if only because Serenthia still lived.

You must make a choice! the archer berated himself. *Either stay clear forever or show yourself to her and pray that she doesn't go screaming in terror . . .*

Achilios grunted. More likely, Serenthia would deem him the abomination he was and use her new powers to do what he had just been considering asking of those who had brought him to this state.

And that settled it for him. He would go to her, to all of them, and reveal the truth. If she and only she demanded he return to the grave, then Achilios would obey.

He turned . . . and before him suddenly shone a brilliant blue light.

Achilios backed away, an arrow already drawn. A memory once hidden from him flashed through his decaying brain, a memory preceding his collapse near Hashir.

There had been a light there, too. He remembered now.

But this was not the same light, that he knew immediately. However, whatever its source, Achilios had no doubt that he would not like its presence so near.

He fired the arrow, and even as it left the bow, reached for a second.

The shaft soared into the exact center of the unsettling glow, soared into it . . . and out the other side. It struck a tree beyond with a hard thud.

Undaunted, the archer readied the second. This time, though, he waited.

Achilios was rewarded but a moment later. A shape vaguely human appeared in the mist of the blue light. With grim satisfaction, Achilios pulled. He thought that he caught a glimpse of some armor—a silver-blue breastplate—and adjusted his aim accordingly.

I HAVE NEED OF YOU . . .

The voice echoed throughout his entire rotting body in a manner akin and yet not akin to that of Trag'Oul. At the same time, Achilios's grip on his weapon weakened. In fact, no part of him seemed to want to obey his commands anymore.

Like a rag doll, the archer collapsed.

He fell face-first, making him unable to see what was happening. Achilios listened for footsteps, but heard none. Nevertheless, when the voice spoke again, he felt as if its source now hovered over his corpse.

I HAVE NEED OF YOU . . . it repeated.

And, as Achilios now also recalled what had happened last time . . . the archer blacked out.

EIGHTEEN

They did not find him. Despite their combined efforts, Uldyssian and Serenthia discovered no trace of Achilios. Refusing to give up, Uldyssian kept his followers in the same location for two extra days. However, by the end of that period, even Serenthia felt it unwise to postpone the march any longer.

"We have to move on. Achilios either is not around or he doesn't wish to be found by me . . . at least right now," she said morosely. "I've got to think it's the second reason and that, eventually, he'll come back to me."

"He can't stay away from you. I've known Achilios even longer than you, Serenthia. You'll see."

His companion nodded, glancing not for the first time out into the jungle. "Does he really think I'd be so terrified by him?"

"I told you how he looked." Uldyssian had not been graphic in his description, but he had left nothing out. Despite that, though, Serenthia's sympathy for the archer had only grown.

"And I've no doubt that I'll probably gape and gasp when I do see him, but you say it's still Achilios. How can I not love him, then?"

He had no answer to that. Besides, she was correct that they had to get moving. Lilith had surely not been standing by idly; whatever new course her plot had taken, it would not do to simply wait for it to pounce upon them.

That is, if it was not already too late.

Saron, a Hashiri named Rashim, and the Parthan

Timeon, were now the unofficial commanders of their various folk. Uldyssian had not intended each party to be divided up so, but he also did not wish to make one group seem dominant over another. It was his hope that by treating the Parthans, Hashiri, and Torajians on an equal basis, that they would further blend and eventually he could dispense with calling them anything but edyrem.

Timeon was the cousin of Jonas, one of the first of Uldyssian's converts. Jonas had always been among the first of the Parthans to volunteer for different tasks, but he had never shown any desire to act as one of Uldyssian's seconds. Still, the once-scarred man assisted his cousin in organizing their remaining comrades from the town . . . a group particularly smaller than the others now.

This must end soon, Uldyssian thought, watching those most like the people with whom he had grown up. Each time a Parthan died, more of Uldyssian's past faded away. He had to finish his struggle before all of Jonas's people were slain . . . and along with them the Hashiri and Torajians, too.

Uldyssian had not spent all of his time on Achilios. He had also explained, in an abbreviated form, his vanishing to his followers. Naturally, he had left out such fantastic details as Trag'Oul and Rathma, feeling that now was not the right time to try to explain *them.*

The edyrem marched come dawn the next day. Because of Lilith's wicked detour, they had lost three more days in addition to those spent by him and Serenthia searching for Achilios. Three more days to give the demoness time to devise their doom . . .

The jungle proved unduly quiet as they wended their way through it. A few birds could be heard in the far distance and there were always insects, but even they were less evident than normally. Uldyssian took this as an omen, but did not mention it to anyone else, not even Serenthia. Still, he kept the edyrem watchful, reminding them that their enemies were cowardly and often sprang from the shadows rather than face them directly.

When they finally reached the river—half a day earlier than he had originally hoped—Uldyssian gave thanks. Their path was now clear again. Still, despite wanting to push on for at least another hour, he knew that he had already worn out the others too much. With reluctance, Uldyssian called for a halt.

The lone benefit of Lilith's vile possession of Serenthia was that the demoness had brought with her from Hashiri charts of the regions leading to the lands surrounding the main temple. The charts were old, but they were accurate enough in identifying not only the general location of Uldyssian's adversaries, but the largest population centers between him and the Triune.

"Yes, I know of Kalinash," answered Rashim to his question as he pointed to where the city lay. The bushy-haired Hashiri had served as an apprentice to a merchant and had made the journey there more than once. "It is a little larger than where I am from and the temple there would be strong, so near Kehjan." His finger slid more north. "Of Istani, I know little, save that it is smaller than Hashiri and not so rich despite its location."

Saron acknowledged the second. "The Triune would not be so strong there. If the master wishes to reach the main temple swiftly, it would be good to take the road leading closer to there."

On the one hand, Uldyssian agreed with that logic, but on the other, he did not like leaving the Triune's supporters in Kalinash untouched, and especially at the edyrem's rear when it came time to confront the main citadel. Yet, to veer toward Kalinash would further slow the trek and cost lives; both things that would only benefit Lilith.

"How quickly can we reach Kalinash?"

After a moment's consideration, Rashim answered, "Four, five days."

"And Istani?"

"Four."

The path was quicker. More important, with a much

smaller presence of the Triune, Istani promised not to slow them in terms of struggle. Kalinash might mean many days of blood . . .

With some reluctance, Uldyssian came to a decision. "Very well. Istani, it is. But we must move with all haste."

The others nodded obediently and departed. Uldyssian looked to Serenthia for some confirmation that he had chosen wisely.

"I would've done the same," she returned. Her brow furrowed. "What else is bothering you?"

"Two things . . . or two people. Achilios, as you know . . . and Mendeln."

"Of course. I've discussed Achilios with you enough to sicken you, Uldyssian. Forgive me for not thinking about your brother. This—this Rathma. Do you think he can be trusted?"

He grunted. "I don't know. As much as any of the blood of Lilith can be . . . which I suppose includes me far, far down the generations."

"Then, Mendeln will be all right." Serenthia considered. "His path converges with yours, but I think it also diverges more and more."

"I don't care anything about that, Serry." He had returned to calling her by her childhood name, the better to keep in his head that they were friends, not lovers. Uldyssian had no desire to stomp upon the grave of his friend, especially now that he knew that grave to be empty. "I just want Mendeln safe."

"As he does you."

"But it would be good to hear some word. *Some* word."

She shifted into a sleeping position near the fire. "I know. I know."

And from her tone, Uldyssian understood that she desperately desired the same from Achilios.

Mendeln had never dreamt that he would return to Partha. That place was supposed to be far in his past. He had tried to erase his memories of the town, for in Partha had come what he felt the final severing of his life as a simple farmer and the beginning of all the cataclysmic changes for and within him. There had been no turning back after Partha, even more so than Seram, which the younger son of Diomedes was also glad to avoid.

Trag'Oul and Rathma had sent him here alone . . . for some final test, they said. As usual, their replies to his questions were murky. In the end, with the promise that he could rejoin his brother if he finished this task, Mendeln had agreed to return to the town.

And only after arriving had he realized that Trag'Oul had used the word "if" . . .

He did not actually stand in the town itself. No, Mendeln sensed that what he sought was far outside the town walls. Very close to where the Parthans disposed of their refuse. A faint hint of decay already indicated that he was near the spot.

There was no one else about. Those still living in the town—which surely had to be more than half-empty—were likely asleep. The few guards would not be bothering with this area; who would be interested in their trash?

Mendeln certainly was not. He was only here because this also happened to be where the burning had taken place. According to Rathma, it was the best location to make the summoning.

Uldyssian's brother had little desire to cast the spell, but his mentors insisted that it was necessary. He had the feeling that they were not telling him something . . . not at all a surprise. Their methods of teaching, especially that of Lilith's son, left much to be desired.

The confrontation with Inarius had influenced this event. Of that, Mendeln was certain. After bringing him back to the dragon's realm, Rathma had requested a private audience with the celestial beast. The first announcement after their discussion had been the requirement that Mendeln do this.

I should have refused, he told himself for the dozenth time. *I should have demanded that they send me back to Uldyssian.*

Somehow, though, even if he had, Mendeln knew that he would have ended up back in Partha.

From his robes, he removed his dagger. It would guide him to the exact location, so Rathma had said.

As soon as he held it up, it glowed. Mendeln turned, noting when the dagger flared brighter. Yes, he recalled the area well, recalled all the grisly events.

Here they and the Parthans had unceremoniously burned the bodies of the high priest Malic and his morlus.

Mendeln still recalled the man with a shiver. He was not afraid of Malic, but of his evil. How any man could give himself to such darkness was beyond him. The mere thought of Malic repulsed Mendeln so much that he wanted to turn around and leave.

But Rathma had insisted that he needed to do this.

Taking a deep breath, Uldyssian's brother tried to summon the feeling of calm determination that the dragon had taught to him. In order to best serve the Balance . . . and, therefore, Sanctuary and Humanity . . . Mendeln had to learn to see things in a more clinical manner. Emotion was not forbidden, for even Rathma clearly fell prey to it, but that emotion had to be kept in check, for the forces with which Mendeln dealt could be very dangerous.

As ready as he knew he could ever be, Mendeln knelt down and began sketching patterns designed to amplify his efforts. They were based on the very energies binding not only his world together, but all that beyond Sanctuary. The patterns pulled to them some element of those energies, bringing them to the location of the summoning.

With that accomplished, Uldyssian's brother held the dagger over the center. He did not have to draw blood for this, although there remained the possibility that he might have to at a later point. Now, all that mattered were the words, which themselves were parts of the energies keeping all things together.

In a low tone, Mendeln uttered one word of power after another. With each syllable, he sensed the forces swirling into place. An ominous presence began to coalesce within the area of the patterns.

Mendeln repeated everything that he had been told to say in such a situation, repeated all of it over and over. Each time, he added emphasis to a different part, in this way strengthening every aspect of the summoning.

Something drifted past his face, so very gently rubbing against his right cheek. A gauzy wisp of smoke drifted in from the direction of the town. As Mendeln continued, these and similar sights began to move around and around him like small children seeking attention.

Rathma had warned him that, until he learned to focus better, others would come in the mistaken belief that he had summoned them. There was nothing he could do right now save ignore the uninvited spirits; to dismiss any would mean to lose concentration at the most vital moment.

Yes, he could sense the dark presence gathering strength. It was in conflict, on the one side not desiring to be stirred up, on the other eager to see if somehow this could be used to its advantage.

Mendeln gripped the dagger tighter, aware that he could not let the latter happen. The dragon had warned him of the potential repercussions should that terrible thing come to pass.

And then . . . a black form arose above the spot, a sinister form quickly swelling to the height of a tall man. Still muttering, Mendeln cautiously stepped back. So long as the patterns he had drawn remained whole, the spirit could not escape them without his assistance.

The shadow solidified, taking on the vague appearance of a particular figure. Tall, pale, and bearded.

The high priest of the order of Mefis—or Mephisto—*Malic* himself.

Grimly satisfied, Uldyssian's brother met the dire spirit's

unblinking gaze. Malic recognized him; that much was immediately clear. Mendeln could sense the smoldering hatred behind the emotionless face and saw the shadow of a hand—an inhuman hand—briefly emerge from the misty, translucent robes.

Whether or not the ghost could strip Mendeln's flesh from his bones—as Malic had done to Master Ethon when alive—the son of Diomedes did not know. He did not intend to give the specter the chance to test that.

"You know who I am, priest," Mendeln muttered. "You know that you are not permitted to act or speak in any manner without my permission or guidance. Nod your understanding."

Malic slowly did, his eyes never leaving his summoner's.

Satisfied thus far, Mendeln turned to the purpose of his having called up this ghoulish figure. "Malic . . . your master is no more . . ."

For the first time, he registered a brief reaction. The spirit flickered out of and back into existence with a swiftness that the untrained eye would not have noticed. There was also a momentary shift of the dead eyes.

"Yes, priest, Lucion is dead." Not exactly true. Uldyssian had caused the demon to cease to exist. According to Rathma, there was something different about such a fate, although Mendeln did not yet understand the vagaries of such things. "And do you know who now sits in his place? Do you know?"

The ghost was utterly motionless. Mendeln frowned, having expected much more from Malic. Trag'Oul had warned him that those existing in the "afterdeath" state were not necessarily averse to attempting to cross back over or seek vengeance on those whom they hated. Malic knew him, knew that he was Uldyssian's brother.

The sooner Mendeln was able to judge if Malic could be of use, the better. "It is *Lilith,* his sister," he informed the specter. "You may recall her in another guise, priest, that of the lady Lylia."

This time, the ghostly figure wavered and his eyes widened beyond human ability. His mouth opened . . . and *continued* to open, stretching more than a foot down. Mention of Lilith, especially her mortal guise, had finally done the trick. After all, it was *she* who had actually slain the priest.

Mendeln was astonished by the ghost's continued violent reshaping. He had been forewarned by his mentors that spirits were not bound by their mortal states, that they could appear in a variety of twisted forms attesting to their deaths, their anger, or their intentions—

Intentions . . .

Mendeln spun around, already mouthing new words, those given to him as a quick defense against the unthinkable. At the same time, he thrust the dagger as far ahead of him as he could, drawing sharp slashes in the air.

With a frustrated hiss, the shadow of a morlu collapsed to dust. A second of the creatures, made the more macabre by this fiendish reconstruction of burnt ash and dirt, nearly had its fleshless hands upon him. Mendeln turned the dagger around for use as a weapon and touched the chest of the undead.

The second morlu also collapsed back into dust.

But the third struck him hard on the shoulder with a piece of rotting timber. Mendeln grunted and fell back out of reach. The morlu stumbled forward, bits of it flaking off as it moved.

These were not truly the monstrous warriors who had accompanied the high priest, for Mendeln himself had made certain that the creatures could never be raised to fight again. No, what stood before him were constructs animated by Malic's evil. Still, even if only that, this morlu had the brute force not only with which to slay Uldyssian's brother, but then assist its creator in enabling the ghost to free himself.

And if that happened, Partha would be only the first of many places to suffer horribly . . .

The morlu swung, but his aim was erratic. Mendeln leapt

to the side, easily evading it. If that was the best the beast could do—

Then, Mendeln recalled just where Malic's ghost stood in relation to him. As the morlu attacked again, the son of Diomedes threw himself in an entirely different direction. It meant landing hard on congealing trash, but that was a small price to pay to keep the priest's plan from succeeding.

Indeed, Malic had come within *inches* of freeing his spirit. Had Mendeln been herded just a little more in the previous direction, then his boot would have scraped away a part of the patterns securing the specter.

The morlu loomed over his intended victim, but now Mendeln had his bearings. He held fast the dagger point down and cried the words of banishment that the dragon had taught him.

The last of Malic's puppets crumbled. The timber clattered next to Mendeln's head.

Rising, Mendeln turned back to face the high priest. "No more of such tricks!" he commanded. "Raise up another and I will cast you to a place that will make your violent death seem so pleasant by comparison!"

It was an exaggeration, Mendeln not having learned how to do any such thing, but if worst came to worst, he could at least dismiss the shade.

Malic, his appearance once more "normal," wavered. At last, the ghost dipped his head once. Mendeln silently cursed himself for having fallen for the priest's diabolical distraction. While Rathma and Trag'Oul had warned him that a powerful priest such as Malic might be able to circumvent the rules of the summoning, Mendeln doubted that even they had expected such a startling maneuver. Great had been the power granted Mephisto's high priest, even in death.

But Mendeln would have no repeat of that. As the ghost hovered, Uldyssian's brother bent low and made corrections to the patterns. He then repeated other words given to him by Trag'Oul and—on a hunch—altered some others to further add to what he believed a better spell.

Rising, Mendeln addressed the spirit again. "Malic, you heard what I said. She who slew you is not masquerading as the Primus. You are eager for revenge; why not toward her?"

It was no difficult matter to feel the priest's abrupt interest. Mendeln decided that it was time to permit the ghost to speak.

"Well?" he asked of Malic.

The high priest's voice came out as a vicious rasp that made Achilios's so much more alive by comparison. "Brother . . . of Uldyssian ul-Diomed . . . what will you . . . have of me?"

"Knowledge of the temple near the capital. Its dangers and hidden secrets. Those things that Lucion made that Lilith now controls . . ."

The ghost laughed, a jarring cough with no humor in it. "Brother of Uldyssian ul-Diomed . . . you ask more than . . . can be told . . ." The translucent figure gave a smile. " . . . but it can be *shown* . . ."

This was not part of what the dragon and Rathma had discussed with Mendeln. There had been no explanation of what to do if Malic sought to *accompany* his summoner. Still . . . now that he had the specter under control, Mendeln saw the value in having the priest for constant questioning.

The only trouble was . . . how to accomplish this. He did not want to go back and ask the others. Mendeln considered for a moment, then turned the dagger to where the pyre had burned strongest. He focused on what it was he desired, willing the dagger to draw it to him.

The blackened ground underneath Malic's vague form shook as if the body of the priest himself were about to rise up from the ashes like the morlu. Instead, though, what at last erupted to the surface was a small, white fragment like a pebble. It paused once it was free of the soil, then rolled directly to Mendeln's waiting hand.

He straightened, studying the object. The largest bone fragment remaining of the high priest.

Mendeln touched the blade's tip to the bone. He then muttered a binding spell akin to what he had utilized to keep Malic sealed within the patterns. The words used were again Mendeln's own combinations, but something just felt right about them.

He prayed that he had not made a fatal mistake.

Clutching the fragment, Uldyssian's brother studied the patterns on the ground. Then, with one quick sweep of his foot, he destroyed them.

The ghost let out a sigh. He lost all form. Now no more than mist, Malic suddenly swirled into the bone fragment. Once he was within, the fragment flared bright once, then returned to its normal state.

Mendeln carefully checked to make certain that Malic had done nothing sinister. Detecting no fault in his spell-work, he finally exhaled in relief.

But before he could actually relax, from the direction of the town there came excited cries. Whether or not they concerned Mendeln, he did not wish to discover. His task here was at an end. As Trag'Oul had previously instructed, Mendeln used the dagger to draw a circle in the air, then two small symbols within.

Yes, I sense you . . . came the dragon's voice.

The next moment, Mendeln stood in the familiar darkness. He was surprised to not see Rathma.

"I've done all you asked," he told the stars.

They changed position briefly, then, as ever, became the half-seen leviathan. *Yes . . . all that was asked . . . and much that was not expected . . .*

"What do you mean?" Mendeln could think of only one thing. He produced the bone fragment. "I know that you only sought information from the priest's shade, but I realized that questioning him would take too long and there might be other points that would come up later, when it was too late. I judged that the best course was to risk taking him with me. Was I wrong to think so?"

Whether you are wrong, the Balance shall show, responded Trag'Oul calmly. *But how you managed the feat is what most interests me . . .*

"I merely followed the teaching of both you and Rathma and adjusted as I believed would work. Thankfully, I was not wrong." Mendeln frowned. "Did I do wrong?"

Rather, it should be said that you did the impossible . . . but then, the brothers ul-Diomed have been revising the meaning of that word over and over . . .

Mendeln did not understand. All he had done was attempt to follow through a logical procession. Why would Trag'Oul, to whom so much was possible, say otherwise?

Nevertheless, the dragon went on. *You offer new hopes and potential with this direction you have taken. I have observed the binding on the stone; I cannot foresee the priest's ghost freeing himself.*

"I am glad to hear that—"

But do not mistake his alliance for obedience. The shade will seek to undermine, if he can, for his own ends . . .

There was no opportunity for Mendeln to reply, for Rathma materialized next to him, the demoness's son fighting to keep his normally disinterested expression intact. Mendeln had become experienced enough reading the ancient spellcaster to know that what news he brought was not good.

"He is nowhere to be found," Rathma reported, more to Trag'Oul than to Mendeln.

You have gazed upon all planes?

"Naturally. I have also summoned him in a hundred manners, some of which put me at risk. It was necessary to do so, though the results were not as I wished."

The dragon was oddly silent for a time. Then, *You realize, my friend, that there are few other paths . . .*

Rathma nodded. "Yes, the most preferable one is that

somehow he has passed on to that place from which even you could not summon him back. Certainly, it would be his reward for what he had so far done."

His reward . . . yes . . . that would be the best hope . . .

"But you find that as unlikely as I do."

Mendeln had listened to their back-and-forth long enough. "Who? Is my brother in danger? Is that of whom you speak?"

Rathma's aspect grew as grim as Mendeln had ever seen it. "No. It is your friend, Achilios. I can find no trace of him. None."

"Is that possible?"

"Possible . . . barely. Potentially devastating, definitely."

"Does Lilith have him?" Mendeln's mind raced as he attempted unsuccessfully to determine just what the demoness would do with the archer.

"If that were so, I would be much relieved," her son replied frankly. "No, Mendeln, I fear someone else has him and it *may* be my father."

"Inarius?" But the moment after he spouted the angel's name, Mendeln recalled the odd inflection in Rathma's voice when uttering one word. "But wait! What did you mean by 'may'?"

There was silence, made the more ominous by the stirring of the stars above them. Whatever Rathma had hinted at, Trag'Oul understood exactly and did not like.

And if it so disturbed even the timeless entity, it meant ill for not only Uldyssian, but likely all of Sanctuary.

"I mean . . ." Rathma began slowly, looking very weary. "I have charted path after path concerning my father and cannot fathom any reason that he would take your Achilios so blatantly. His presence would explain one short period of mystery, but certainly not this. This is not how Inarius works . . ."

Even though Trag'Oul was stable, he yet radiated his concern, too. *No . . . it is not . . .*

"And if that is the case, it may be that we are all already

doomed." The son of Lilith declared the end of Sanctuary with barely any inflection. "For if it is not Inarius who has taken Achilios . . . then I fear that it was another angel . . ."

"Another angel? Surely, a demon instead!"

"No. That I have made certain of. No denizen of the Burning Hells could have taken him without leaving their foul touch behind. Only with my father have I seen such absence of signs."

The stars that were Trag'Oul grew more and more agitated, as did Mendeln. They all knew what it meant if another angel was present.

The High Heavens had discovered Sanctuary.

The end of the world was imminent.

NINETEEN

There was no word from Mendeln and certainly none from Achilios. Uldyssian feared for both of them, but could not let their absences hinder him any longer.

The edyrem marched. Marched in the direction of Istani. The closer they got to the smaller city, the more Uldyssian took precautions, especially when it came to scouting. Not only did he stretch his abilities to their utmost, but for the first time he dared send out others even farther beyond. They, in turn, maintained contact with him and those nearest, creating a sweeping field that, besides its main function, Uldyssian also hoped would keep any of those who had volunteered from suddenly vanishing or being attacked.

With barely a day more to Istani, Uldyssian remained tense. The supreme temple lay not all that much farther away; he had no doubt that they were already preparing for his coming. The sooner the edyrem finished with Istani, the better.

Serenthia joined him at the lead. "Should we even stop? I know that you've gone back and forth about it since we began moving again, but the main temple is so close . . ."

"I know. I've been considering something." Uldyssian finally summoned Rashim to him. "I've a mission for you, if you will accept it."

"Of course, master!" the Hashiri eagerly replied.

Wincing at the man's willingness to take on what might be a deadly task, Uldyssian explained, "I want you to find four others and race as quickly as you can toward Kalinash."

This startled both Rashim and Serenthia. "Kalinash, master?" the Hashiri repeated. "Surely *Istani*?"

"No. Kalinash. Ride for a full day and keep seeking with your mind as I've shown. I want to know if there's any movement at all from that direction."

Understanding now came to the others. "Aaah, yes, master," Rashim replied. "I will pick the others and be gone as quickly as the wind!"

"Rashim . . . always take care. Return as soon as you can. Don't go any farther."

"I will obey, master."

Serenthia nodded in approval. "You fear a trap."

"They know that we're coming. There could already be an army or worse heading toward us from the south. Why else wait until we're pounding at the gates?"

She mulled this over for a moment, then answered, "Because they have something even more terrible awaiting us *there*?"

"That may very well be the case," Uldyssian agreed, "but I can't take the chance that we're being outflanked."

"No . . . you're right. Rashim is good; if there's anyone coming, he'll definitely alert us, Uldyssian."

"That's what I hope."

True to his word, Rashim and his chosen set off but minutes later. Uldyssian had not allowed the rest of his followers to even slow during that time. The mass of bodies was so great that they stretched for a mile in the jungle and for the first time, Uldyssian formally thought of them as an army, too. The term had drifted into and out of his mind over the course of events, but with the confrontation with the Triune close at hand, he decided that he had to treat them as such. Discipline had to be at its utmost; otherwise, even with the advances made lately by many—including the newest converts—the edyrem's combined powers might not yet be enough to defeat Lilith and her pawns.

Not that Uldyssian was all that certain that victory was assured even if they were.

The day wore on. He sensed Rashim now and then, a simple touch from the Hashiri's mind enough to let Uldyssian know that all was well with the scouting party and that nothing had so far been detected. It was very possible that Kalinash was entirely ignorant of events. Uldyssian certainly hoped so.

When evening came and the edyrem halted, he summoned Saron, Timeon, Jonas, and all the others who had some sort of commanding role and reemphasized the importance of coordinating every aspect of their journey from this point on. For the first time, the children and weaker among them were slowly being ushered to the rear, where a select group of the stronger would assist in protecting them. The rest of the edyrem were divided under Uldyssian's most trusted.

Only Serenthia and he had no one personally under them, they being the two to coordinate most of the potential action. It still surprised him that the merchant's daughter had become second only to him; this was not a Serenthia he could have earlier in his life ever imagined knowing.

But without her, Uldyssian could not have imagined now leading such a vast force.

Shortly before daybreak, he awoke to the sense that Rashim was trying to contact him. At first, Uldyssian expected to hear the worst, but the Hashiri had only sought to tell them that he and his companions were beginning their return. There had been no hint of danger emerging from Kalinash; the city appeared entirely oblivious to the edyrem's movements.

That gave Uldyssian tremendous relief. He alerted Serenthia and the others. Then, as soon as everyone had eaten, he ordered the edyrem on their trek again.

And barely three hours into the day, they sighted the towers of Istani in the distance.

Istani might have been smaller than Hashiri or Toraja, but it still appeared much larger than Partha. Uldyssian made an estimate as to the size of the temple based on what he had seen in the previous cities. Not very large, but with the potential to cause enough of a delay to jeopardize their chances of reaching their ultimate destination before Lilith could plot anew.

He decided that there would be no preliminary introduction to the citizenry, as he had done each time in the past; Uldyssian would strike directly at the temple the moment he could and pray that he would be able to make the rest of the Istanians understand that he had done it in part for their sakes.

Aware that the priests might be scrying for any trouble and certain that the edyrem could not remain entirely hidden, Uldyssian sought out the most open path to the city. Speed was essential.

Rashim and the others were not yet back, but Uldyssian could not wait for them. He had the rest of the edyrem spread out as they neared the thinning jungle. Soon, very soon, the gates of Istani would stand before them—

He straightened. For just the slightest of moments, Uldyssian could have sworn that he had felt . . .

But no . . . it had to be his anxiety. It had to be.

"Serry," Uldyssian murmured. "Stand next to me and follow my will."

She did not question why, trusting in him as always. Once Serenthia was ready, Uldyssian guided her mind to where he wanted her to focus.

"Do you see or sense *anything*?" he asked.

"No—for a moment, I thought—but no—"

It was the answer that Uldyssian expected and receiving it only made him more suspicious. "Serry, will you let me try something?"

"Together, you mean?" She knew about the spellwork that Lilith had shown Uldyssian while pretending to be her. "If you think it worth to try, then I'll do it."

Rather than position themselves as he and Lilith had, Uldyssian simply stood next to Serenthia. They shut their eyes and concentrated on reaching out to one another . . .

The results were as swift as they were remarkable. The ease with which the two managed to link pleased Uldyssian, who had, in truth, feared complete failure.

There was only one trouble with the link and that was the incredible closeness it created between Uldyssian and Serenthia. To prevent any stirring of his feelings, he quickly guided her mind out in the direction he wished to survey.

However, even after the two of them completed what he felt a thorough search, Uldyssian came away with nothing. He did not even detect what had earlier disturbed him and knew that neither had Serenthia. After a few more minutes of futile hunting, Uldyssian ceased the effort.

"I was wrong," he muttered. "Merely my imagination."

"That's better than *another* threat, isn't it?"

Uldyssian nodded. "Just so long as I don't start seeing shadows everywhere. It'll become that much harder to tell when a real danger rears its head . . ."

The edyrem progressed. Uldyssian watched as Istani became an actual city, not merely a few structures above the treetops. He drew in his scouts, wanting no one cut off from the rest. That left only Rashim and his party, who he knew would catch up while Uldyssian was dealing with the local temple.

But to his surprise, before he and his followers could reach the city gates, a contingent from Istani rode out to meet them. There were twenty-five in all, most of them guards. A handful of officials led by a middle-aged, plump figure in rich blue and green silk robes confronted the son of Diomedes.

"We have come to speak with the leader of this army," the plump man said. He wore an elaborate silver nose ring that itself was encrusted with tiny rubies.

Uldyssian strode forward. He did not care that the Istanian, being mounted, had the advantage in terms of eye level; the official would soon learn who truly held the power in this conversation, especially if he sought to protect the Triune.

"I'm who you seek," he told the rider. "I am Uldyssian ul-Diomed." As the official started to speak again, Uldyssian raised his hand. "And I have only one thing to say. You and yours have nothing to fear from us. It's only the Triune. Stand out of our way and the evil truth about them will be revealed soon enough."

The rider fidgeted throughout his speech. Finally, the moment that Uldyssian stopped, he blurted, "But that is why we have come to you, Master Uldyssian! There is no need to enter Instani! The Triune . . . they have fled!"

As Uldyssian stared at the man in disbelief, excited voices broke out among the edyrem.

"What do you mean by that?" he demanded. "When?"

There was that in Uldyssian's tone that evidently cowed the official further. He bent low in the saddle, hastily explaining, "It was but two days ago, Master Uldyssian! Without word, the priests, the guards—all within the temple—they did vanish during the night! It was noticed by the sentries and the people the next day, and when we went inside to seek the high priest, we found his chamber empty, too!"

"Do you think they're lying?" murmured Serenthia, a step behind him.

Uldyssian did not answer, for he had already begun finding out on his own the answer to that question. He sensed no guile on the part of the Istanians—in fact, they were afraid of angering him with this news. Satisfied as to them, Uldyssian then reached out to the city itself, seeking the taint of the Triune.

He found traces, but nothing more. The temple was, as the official had insisted, entirely abandoned. Uldyssian's mind swept over the three-towered edifice, searching for any clue, but the priests had been very thorough in clearing out their rooms.

Seeking their trail, he located, as in Hashir, a secondary city gate near the temple. There were only a few guards manning it and it did not take the son of Diomedes much guesswork to assume that those sentries had been mystically blinded to the departure.

Once into the jungle, the trail quickly faded, the priests having strived hard to avoid detection. However, what little was evident indicated a route heading directly toward the supreme temple.

While Uldyssian had been doing all this, the Istanians had grown more and more anxious. They could not know what the foreigner was doing standing there as if asleep. The lead official kept glancing back at his counterparts, likely begging for some advice. However, they remained silent, none wishing to be drawn into the talks. Clearly, if there proved to be any violence, the blame would all fall upon the spokesman, who likely had been chosen for this task against his liking.

Withdrawing from his search, Uldyssian exhaled, then met the first rider's wide-eyed gaze. "You speak the truth."

This brought renewed excitement from the edyrem. Their master's enemies were running scared. Victory was surely at hand . . .

Uldyssian dared not get his own hopes up. Still, this reprieve meant that less time would be lost in this area. If they left in the morning, they could reach the supreme temple two days earlier than planned.

"You speak the truth," he repeated, "and so there remains only one thing for us before we leave your domain."

The Istani leaders all looked sick. They no doubt expected either some reprisal or some great demand for riches.

"We've need of some food and fresh water. In addition, we must make camp nearby. Any of your people are welcome to trade with us, to learn about us." Because of the shortness of time, Uldyssian could not enter Istani and preach to the locals. That would come later, supposing that he survived his confrontation with Lilith.

A hint of relief spread through the locals. The lead official nodded several times. "Food and water can be provided, yes, Master Uldyssian! There are those who will trade with you also, yes!" He leaned back. "Barenji! See to it, yes?"

One of the other officials nodded once, then turned his horse around and rode off as if on fire.

Uldyssian indicated his gratitude. "That's all, then. If any of you have other questions, I'll answer them; if not, then I wish the wise people of Instani good health and thank them for their efforts."

It was not exactly the formal greeting that he had learned for Hashir, but it was satisfactory. With many bows, the contingent turned and rode back to the city.

"Can they be trusted with the food and water?" asked Timeon. "They may seek to poison it . . ."

That was highly doubtful to Uldyssian, but he had already considered what to do. "Nothing'll be distributed until I've looked it over."

His answer was, of course, enough to satisfy the others. They had full trust in him, which Uldyssian appreciated. He prayed that he would not let them down.

With the guidance of those among the edyrem who understood the territory best, Uldyssian chose a place to camp for the night. Even before his followers had settled down, the Istani began to bring foodstuff for them. The articles came in wagons drawn by both oxen and more of the huge beasts used in the lowlands. Saron called them *pachyshon,* which meant "long-nosed brothers." The pachyshon made delivering the food a quicker operation, for they used their flexible snouts to reach baskets down to where Uldyssian awaited. Once he made certain that there was no poison or other threat, Saron, Timeon, and others began passing the supplies around.

The Istanians treated them with the utmost regard, almost falling over themselves to please. Uldyssian did not expect any of the locals to come to hear about the edyrem, but a large handful did. He welcomed them and spoke to all as he had times previous. Some of the Istani departed after his speech, but more stayed. To the latter, Uldyssian offered to reveal their own gifts.

This time, he did one other thing as he stirred the latent powers to life. Within each, Uldyssian sought out as best he could any kernel of darkness that he could find and crushed it utterly. There would be no repeat of Lilith's foul work with Romus and the other unfortunates.

And then, before he knew it, the sun had risen again. There was indeed no more reason for staying. From the officials, who obviously wanted to do their best to see the intruders depart as quickly and peacefully as possible, he received updated information on the path leading to the Triune's supreme temple. A couple of the newest converts verified the charts and directions. Uldyssian thanked his reluctant hosts, then led his army on again.

And now . . . there were no more distractions. Only their goal lay ahead.

Rashim and the other scouts were closer than before, but, as Uldyssian had realized, the swift departure from Istani meant that they were now a day or two again from reuniting with the rest. With Lilith just ahead, Uldyssian could not focus on the small band constantly; instead, he sought out the scouts during each pause. Satisfied that they were still all right, he then returned to constantly attempting to analyze just what the demoness might have in store. But although he thought of a thousand nightmares, Uldyssian doubted that any of them would match her true plan.

The edyrem moved on through the jungle, becoming quieter as they ate away at the miles. It was as if a shroud had fallen over them; for the first time, they became aware of the monumental task quickly approaching.

And then . . . and then something touched Uldyssian's very soul. A gnawing darkness that grew with each step.

"We're close," he finally muttered to Serenthia. "We're so close . . ."

She only nodded. Uldyssian doubled his precautions.

For him, the Triune was no longer hiding what it was. They—under Lilith's guidance—were trying to undermine the edyrem's confidence.

Uldyssian's mind swept over his followers, reassuring them of their intentions. This new and subtle ploy would fail his enemies, of that he swore.

He wished that Mendeln and Achilios were with him. That he had seen nothing of either bothered Uldyssian, for surely at least his brother would have tried to be there. As for the archer, it was possible that Achilios *was* nearby, but if so, why had he not at least given some sign?

Uldyssian decided that he could not rely on their assistance. It was up to him and those who stood with him to survive this struggle.

Night came again, the last night, by his calculation, before they would sight the lands surrounding their target. Somewhere to the northeast—so he was told by one of the Hashiri—stood the vast capital. As Uldyssian sat down by one of the low fires, he marveled that its masters outwardly appeared oblivious or unconcerned about the struggle going on. Uldyssian knew that such could not be the case, that they were actually keeping avid watch to see if the victor in this conflict would then be vulnerable.

So much blood . . . it won't end here . . . it'll go on and on and on . . . He wondered if he should just seek out the angel Inarius and ask him to start the world all over. Maybe that was the best course after all . . .

Ulydssian shook like a dog, trying to jar loose such vile thoughts. He felt ashamed for having even wildly considered them.

Serenthia joined him by the fire. "Are you all right?"

"No," he returned bluntly. "But that never matters."

She was taken aback by his reply. "Uldyssian—"

"Forgive me, Serry. It's nothing. It'll pass. It'll—"

Uldyssian leapt to his feet. Once more, he had that sense that there was something not quite right in the vicinity. He turned in a circle, studying each direction carefully.

Back along their trail, Uldyssian almost thought that he noticed something . . . but then did not.

Coming to his side, Serenthia asked, "What's wrong? What happened?"

He did not answer, instead considering the facts. They were within striking distance of the main temple. The Triune certainly had to know that their arrival was imminent and that there would be no negotiation. Lilith wanted this confrontation. The Triune had even entirely abandoned Istani, where he would have expected that Lilith would have at least forced him to spill more blood before reaching her.

She still wanted the edyrem. That was also a fact. Uldyssian and his followers would face no ordinary battle. Lilith would have something particular in mind . . .

Once more he checked the region surrounding them. Yet, again, there was nothing.

But what if *nothing* was more than it seemed?

"Serry . . . the others need to be alert. Please tell them to be prepared for my command . . ."

"For what?"

"I don't know."

She asked no more questions, instead turning to silently spread the word. As Serenthia reached out to the others, Uldyssian concentrated on the general area where he had momentarily believed that he had sensed a presence.

There had to be something wrong. There had to be a reason for his wariness. It was more than merely nerves.

He focused hard, trying to draw his will into the task as much as possible. This time, Uldyssian could not simply give up. He had to keep searching, even if it took him all night.

Perhaps that was what Lilith wanted. Perhaps she desired Uldyssian so exhausted that he would make crucial mistakes. Maybe all he sought out beyond the camp was one of her illusions.

No, it has to be more . . . Uldyssian sweated as he pushed himself harder. There was something out there, something worth much effort in hiding—

And suddenly, it was all there to see.

As if a vast blanket swept back by a powerful wind, the truth revealed itself in one rapid layer after another. Through his mind, Uldyssian saw a row of familiar armed figures slowly but relentlessly wending their way toward the encampment through the thick underbrush. Behind them materialized another row and another and another . . . and on until it became clear that an army had been secreted from him.

Peace Warders . . .

The Triune's soldiers were not alone, either. Uldyssian noted priests among them, priests of all three orders. They were the ones casting the elaborate cloaking spell, but he sensed Lilith's hand in its making. Such a casting was far too advanced even for these senior acolytes.

So at last the truth about Istani was known. Lilith had arranged their vanishing, only to have them—and surely warriors from Kalinash and perhaps even the supreme temple—gather nearby. While Uldyssian's concentration had been upon the enemy ahead—even with his attempts to sweep the trail behind the edyrem—they had followed, awaiting the moment to strike.

That moment, it appeared was to be tonight.

Serenthia! Uldyssian silently called. She answered with a questioning note. He quickly filled her in.

But as he did, the son of Diomedes discovered that he had erred. Within the invisible ranks, a priest's mind abruptly closed itself from him.

Instantly, the entire army vanished from Uldyssian's second sight. He had just enough of a last glimpse to see the Peace Warders pick up their pace.

They had noticed him. The attack was coming.

The enemy is behind us! he told not just Serenthia, but everyone. *Behind us! Ready yourselves!*

It should have made absolute sense to Uldyssian that Lilith would send her forces against him at night, not daylight, when most would attack. Worse was the veil of invisibility that added to the darkness. The edyrem could defeat this foe, but they would need to be able to see them in some manner.

Or did they? Uldyssian knew the approximate location of the Peace Warders. That, in truth, was enough with which to start . . .

He had no time to summon the aid of the others. Uldyssian clapped his hands together. As he had done once before, what sounded like thunder rolled forward. This thunder, though, was a sound wave so powerful that it tore the nearest trees from their roots and sent leaves and vines scattering.

It also, he knew even without seeing, struck the first ranks of the Peace Warders with equal force.

Once again, the blanket blew back. The Triune's minions were revealed to him. The first row lay completely scattered, the two behind it in various levels of disarray. Yet, those farther back, those who had not fallen, only looked more determined, more ready to spill the blood of their master's enemies. Charging past the fallen, the temple's servants waved their weapons . . .

But they would find themselves a foe more than ready for them now. He felt Serenthia, Timeon, and the other "commanders" of his army letting him know that those in their charge merely awaited his word. However, just as Uldyssian was about to give orders, he felt another presence. Rashim's distant mind reached out to him, the Hashiri's thoughts desperate.

Beware, master! Rashim called. *Beware! They march from the main temple! Look ahead!*

With the Peace Warders almost upon them, Uldyssian dared not take the time to question Rashim further. Instead, he tore his thoughts from the oncoming attackers to the direction in which the edyrem had been marching . . . the direction in which lay the supreme temple and Lilith.

There, he saw with dread that the Hashiri had been speaking the truth. Like those who had followed the edyrem, these, too, had been expertly hidden from even his sight until now . . .

There was *another* army—several times larger than that they were about to face—sweeping toward them, an army composed of many Peace Warders and priests, yes . . . but also something more terrible.

Morlu . . . hundreds and hundreds of morlu . . .

TWENTY

"We have lost . . ." Rathma uttered again. "We have lost . . ."

Trag'Oul was oddly silent. The glittering stars shifted this way and that and in their centers a brooding Mendeln caught glimpses of a multitude of lives. Some were of the past, others of the present. Whether any were of the future, the dragon would not say.

And that boded ill, too . . .

Uldyssian's brother finally had to speak. "Surely, there is *something* we can do! The angels have not alighted unto Sanctuary nor have the demons risen out of the black depths onto its surface! There must still be hope!"

"I had always thought that," returned Lilith's son. "because I knew that the Burning Hells would do all that they could to keep the secret and thus move at a slow, deliberate pace that I could counter. I knew that my father, too, would not rush matters, for he has no desire to reveal his paradise to his brethren nor face their stern justice for his crimes."

"And so?"

Rathma frowned. He suddenly looked his centuries of age. "And so, it all would have gone on as before, perhaps for a hundred lifetimes more still. Yet, now that the High Heavens are aware, there is nothing we can do."

Turning on Trag'Oul, Mendeln blurted, "And you think this also?"

It is not what I think or believe, but what the Balance will demand, son of Diomedes . . .

"And what does the Balance demand? Tell me!"

The dragon re-formed. The eyes stared deep into the human's own. *It is for you to tell me . . .*

But all Mendeln could think about in the face of Rathma's declarations of doom was his brother. If Sanctuary was to end, he should be there at Uldyssian's side. They had always sworn to do that, to protect one another. They were the last of their family . . .

"I want to go to my brother!" Mendeln demanded. "I want to go now!"

He vanished.

Rathma stood silent for a moment, then also looked up at Trag'Oul. "His choice is made."

As the Balance will determine . . .

"We are bringing the elements together. If they can survive my mother, perhaps there is hope against my father."

Perhaps . . . your chosen successor was not even defeated by your talk about what will be if the High Heavens and Burning Hells do indeed meet in Sanctuary . . .

"No . . . and that with me believing much of it myself, when I spoke it. In truth, Trag, this does likely mean that all is for naught."

If it is to be, it will be. Does that mean that you will do nothing more, as you pretended to him?

Rathma straightened. "Of course not."

The dragon made a sound much like a relieved sigh. *And so, even in our hopelessness, there is hope . . .*

Here it was, then. Lilith's plan revealed. Once again, he had underestimated her power and cunning.

If not for Rashim's desperate call, there would have been no hope for the edyrem. They would have focused on the Peace Warders approaching from the rear, remaining unaware of the other cloaked force until it was upon them.

Whether the demoness desired to capture most of Uldyssian's followers or slay them and start anew was a moot point. If it ended here one way or another for

Uldyssian's dreams, then Sanctuary was lost to either her or Inarius. They would transform Humanity to their wishes—a monstrous army for Lilith or crawling worshippers for the angel.

Uldyssian reacted quickly to the warning, spreading the word to the others. He urged Serenthia and Timeon to him, at the same time ordering the rest to turn around to face the new danger.

They and those with them reached him but a moment later—and barely a breath ahead of the Peace Warders Uldyssian had already confronted.

With wild howls, the servants of the Triune leapt toward the line of edyrem. Uldyssian maintained a calm in the minds of those near him, guiding their initial efforts.

But two of his followers suddenly collapsed, writhing in agony for brief seconds before stilling. Uldyssian sensed the spellwork of the priests and struck back at them. With grim satisfaction, he crushed their hearts from within. The three fell, already dead.

The edyrem were not merely armed with their abilities. Uldyssian was well aware that many were not capable of continuous effort in that respect. They wielded swords, pitchforks, and whatever tool they were familiar with that could be easily turned into a weapon.

The first line of Peace Warders collided with an invisible wall guided by Serenthia's will. However, those that followed pressed at it and so it became necessary to add attack to defense. For the edyrem, Uldyssian first suggested the most simple of spells. A series of fireballs bombarded the breastplated warriors. Several screamed as they attempted to douse flames that could *not* be doused. The Peace Warders' advance faltered.

Pleased by this turn, Uldyssian sought out Serenthia. She knew immediately what he wanted of her.

Go! she encouraged him. *Go! The others need you! We'll deal with these!*

As if to emphasize her confidence, the merchant's

daughter raised her spear and threw it at an approaching foe. Fueled by her power, it not only impaled the Peace Warder, but dragged his body back until it reached a second warrior who, although wearing a breastplate just as the first had, died much the same. The two bodies tumbled down.

Serenthia held out her hand and the spear dislodged itself, then flew back to her grip.

Go! she repeated with a smile.

Nodding, he turned and ran to where Saron and others had already arranged the most powerful of their edyrem for maximum effect and protection. In the center of the camp stood the youngest and the weakest, but as always, Uldyssian had not left them unprotected. Not only did those among them that had the ability work to shield all, but stronger edyrem stil kept watch, too. Uldyssian did not want the priests' spells striking at those least able to defend themselves.

Saron looked very grateful for his arrival. "Master Uldyssian! We have tried and we have tried but we cannot sense those you say approach! Is it possible that Rashim is wrong? He is so far away!"

Uldyssian had not had time to consider the last point, especially since the warning had proven accurate. "They're coming all right, Saron! Everyone needs to be prepared! There are many morlu among them and they will be harder to stop than Peace Warders . . ."

The Torajian turned bitter. "Yes, Master Uldyssian. I know. It was one of those fiends who slew Tomo."

Having never heard exactly what had happened to Saron's cousin, Uldyssian was momentarily at a loss for words. Then, he suddenly felt the wave of unnatural evil all but at the camp.

"Make no mistake, Saron; they're almost upon us!" Uldyssian sent out the warning to the others, then positioned himself near the lead. He spread his arms, ready to do as he had against the other attackers.

But before he could, there came a sinister buzzing.

Several in the lines looked up in puzzlement. Too late Uldyssian remembered what that ominous sound presaged.

"Keep your shields strong!" he warned.

Dark shapes the size of birds of prey flew out of the shadowy jungle. The buzzing came from them, growing louder and more frightening with nearness.

One man screamed as one of the shapes collided with his chest. The angular object had buried itself deep. Two others also fell, struck down as if by lightning. Uldyssian recognized the vicious weapons that the Peace Warders had once tried to use to assassinate him. The toothlike blades on the edges were designed for maximum carnage. Blood soaked the bodies of the victims.

But most of the remaining weapons in flight collided with air, then went spinning harmlessly away. Still, Uldyssian could sense how unnerved many around him had become. Lilith was doing all she could to undermine their confidence and, thus, their powers.

No sooner had the bladed weapons come flying than Uldyssian sensed the attackers flow forward. At the very last moment, as they surged within striking distance, the spell keeping them unseen fell away.

A gasp arose from many in the forefront as the edyrem beheld the awful sight. More than one of Uldyssian's followers fell back in fear. Uldyssian tried to boost their confidence with his own, but it was a difficult task in the face of such monstrous foes.

The Peace Warders made up the Triune's first lines, but they were not the bulk of the threat. That fell to the morlu, seen in such numbers as even Uldyssian could not have believed. He could not say what was worse, that so many existed or that they all looked and moved like the same beast replicated hundreds of times over. Even more than the Peace Warders, the unliving warriors were driven by one urge . . . to soak their weapons in the blood of their victims.

But neither they nor the Peace Warders were the first to strike. That dark honor went to the priests. Uldyssian sensed their spells and gave warning, but even then, some of his people were not strong enough. Their wills—and thus their shields—were broken. Peace Warders, obviously alerted by the priests, immediately leapt at those vulnerable. For the first time came the clash of arms.

Uldyssian sighted two Peace Warders who had broken through the wall of edyrem. At his command, the first warrior's weapon turned on its wielder, gutting the man. Uldyssian sent his second foe flying back over his followers and into the vicious throng from which he had come, using the Peace Warder as an effective missile that bowled over a dozen other fighters.

The edyrem were being assailed on all sides, but they were, for the most part, holding their own. The morlu had yet to join the combat, but would so very soon. Still, Uldyssian had expected more from Lilith—

And at that moment, the ground to his left erupted in a mass of horrific tentacles that reached out and grabbed people in every direction. Two of the victims were immediately squeezed to death with such force that they nearly snapped in two. Another was raised up and thrust hard to the ground again, his bones cracking audibly.

Cursing, Uldyssian had to abandon the front lines. He knew that he played into Lilith's hands, but had no choice. He was not even certain himself how to handle the beast, but his powers were the best hope of defeating it before it killed again.

Rather than seek to deal with every individual tentacle, Uldyssian focused on the area from which they had sprouted. The demon—for what else could it be?—had to lurk just below the surface. He could not imagine its size based on all the tentacles and their length, but it had to be enormous.

Lilith had outplayed him yet again. Each of her attacks had been shrouded well. The effort had surely cost her and the priests, but it had served her. He had noticed the one, been warned of the other . . . but those two had kept him from ever conceiving of an attack from *underneath*.

Uldyssian had no notion as to the demon's weaknesses, but he attacked with the one most sensible. Raging flame suddenly burst at the point nearest to where he thought the tentacles originated. The fire burned not only above the surface, but also directly below.

It had effect. The sinewy appendages flailed, flinging the creature's victims everywhere. Uldyssian instantly spread his powers as wide as he could, creating an invisible net that caught each and every one of them. The effort left Uldyssian panting. Sweat poured over his body as he sought to lower the edyrem to safety.

Just as he was nearly able to accomplish that, something jerked him from his feet. Uldyssian yet managed to keep his net working until he was certain that his followers would not be injured by the remaining drop, then ceased that spell.

One tentacle had his left leg, another seized his waist.

In his head, he heard Lilith.

If you no longer desire my embrace, dear Uldyssian, perhaps you will enjoy that of the Thonos . . .

She ended the comment with a throaty chuckle. Uldyssian swore at her, but the demoness had already severed contact. He felt the tentacle crushing his leg and focused on his adversary. The Thonos was obviously an instinctive thing, not a cunning being such as Lilith or her brother or even the demon Gulag. What fought with Uldyssian was truly a beast, which gave him hope that he could outthink it.

But first, he had to free himself. As more of the savage appendages turned his way, Uldyssian noted that at least one had, at some point in the recent past, been cut off. The stub was still dangerous, but lacked the tapering end. That gave him a desperate idea. Uldyssian reached with his free hand to his side—where he kept a long knife—only to have the knife snared by a smaller tentacle. That did not stop him, though. Instead, Uldyssian's mind seized the weapon of the dead Peace Warder, raised it high in the air, and flung it at the foremost tentacle.

Energized by his will, the curved sword made short work of the Thonos's limb.

There came a deep roar and a tremor that sent both edyrem and Peace Warders toppling. Not only did the ruined tentacle go flying back below the surface, but so did the *rest*.

Exhaling, Uldyssian started to rise—

The entire area around him—nearly a quarter of the area of the encampment—exploded as a giant shape shot up from the depths. Screams arose as those nearest fled.

The Thonos did not merely have many tentacles . . . it *was* tentacles. They all originated from an oval mass at the center, a mass equal to perhaps a dozen Uldyssians. From every part of it sprung limbs of various sizes and lengths, more than a hundred, if Uldyssian could believe his eyes.

And in terms of eyes, the Thonos was also nightmarish. Over those parts of its body that were clear of tentacles were *eyes*, very human eyes. Most were larger than a man's head and all were not only fixed upon Uldyssian, but doing so with deep malice.

A score of limbs shot at him. Uldyssian shoved his palm forward and deflected most, then had to leap out of the way when two others nearly caught him. He summoned the Peace Warder's sword to his hand and slashed at one, but the Thonos moved it out of reach.

The gargantuan demon rushed him, moving swiftly on more than twenty other tentacles. From somewhere, it emitted another deep roar. Uldyssian could spot no mouth and hoped that he would never come near enough to find it.

Lilith's face suddenly formed before the Thonos's macabre body.

All is lost, my love . . . she mocked. *Look about! Your precious followers are falling to my puppets! See?*

He would not have even deigned to look, for certainly it

sounded as if the demoness sought to distract him further, but the Thonos stilled as if hypnotized. A simple-minded thing of destruction, it no doubt lived simply to obey what it thought was Lucion. Uldyssian wished he could have revealed to it otherwise, but even then the creature might not have ceased its rampage.

Lilith continued to hold the Thonos in check. Uldyssian finally did as she suggested . . . and saw that, for once, his former lover did not lie. The Thonos's rise to the surface had set into motion chaos among the edyrem, who thought—perhaps rightly—that they now had to fear a terrible danger looming behind them as well as the relentless threat still flowing in from the jungle.

Serenthia's position was the most stable, but even she was hard-pressed. He dared not distract the merchant's daughter by contacting her, for already she fought against more than one Peace Warder herself.

Those battling Lilith's second army were in the most dire straits. The morlu had reached the struggle and were shoving past their living allies in their hunger for edyrem blood. In the face of such evil and aware of the terrifying fiend in their midst, the edyrem were not only losing ground, but losing faith in their own abilities. More and more were resorting strictly to physical weapons and defenses, weapons and defenses that, against morlu, put them at a severe disadvantage.

You see? said Lilith, drawing attention back to her and the Thonos. *Would I lie to you? You've led these poor fools to their deaths. They will be slaughtered and all because of you . . . unless . . .*

He could not help but wait for her to continue. Lilith did not disappoint him.

You can still surrender them, my love . . . surrender them to me and I will call off the Triune . . . and my little pet, here . . .

Surrender them . . . so that they would be taken to her and converted to her evil crusade. The myriad layers of her plot continued to peel away. Uldyssian had no doubt that the demoness would also continue the slaughter until he finally acquiesced.

For a moment, he considered her demands. So many lives would be saved. There would be no more blood—

But only for the moment.

He had only one answer for her. "Better that we all die, Lilith, than kneel to you even once."

And with that, he thrust out his hand, aiming for the eye most dominating this side of the Thonos.

What began as a stream of light shot through Lilith's smiling countenance, which vanished in its wake. Before the light reached the monstrous demon, it transformed, solidifying into a gleaming lance.

The point buried itself in the pupil. A yellow pus burst from the eye and the Thonos roared anew.

Scores of tentacles sought for Uldyssian, who had to fight with all his wit and agility to avoid them. Some were so heavy that if they had reached the son of Diomedes they would have surely crushed him; others were so fine that he suspected the Thonos of using them like whips or nooses. Either way, Uldyssian dared not let any get through to him.

If there was any consolation in his desperate situation, it was that the beast was now obsessed only with him. It utterly ignored the edyrem, a fortunate thing in that they were already struggling merely to survive. The morlu had begun cutting a bloody swathe through the left flank, their laughter chilling even Uldyssian's heart.

He knew that he could have helped turn or at least stem the tide, but only if the Thonos was defeated. Yet that in itself would take far too long . . . if it was even possible. The loss of its eye had more angered the demon than it had injured it. It was just as likely, perhaps even more so, that Uldyssian would soon perish.

But he continued to dodge and deflect the tentacles, amazed for each second that he managed to avoid them. The Thonos roared over and over, its tone almost suggesting that it was becoming annoyed at this gnat's persistence.

Then, without warning, he was grabbed at the ankle. Uldyssian toppled. A smaller tentacle had risen out of the ground, rising up like a serpent from its nest to encircle his lower leg. Uldyssian had underestimated the monster's intelligence, perhaps fatally.

He moved to slice at the appendage, but another tentacle caught his wrist while a third tore the sword away. A fourth pummeled his chest, forcing the air from his lungs . . .

Uldyssian nearly blacked out. A part of him wondered if that might be for the best; what was left but for him to witness the destruction of the edyrem and his own grisly demise?

Yet, he struggled, albeit feebly. Uldyssian could not regain his breath and, thus, enough wit to use his powers. He felt the Thonos drag him toward it. Through blurry eyes, Uldyssian finally caught sight of the mouth, a menacing beaklike projection underneath the demon's body. A thick tongue dripping with saliva thrust out of the mouth, seeking him.

Stirred by the sight, Uldyssian managed to send a bolt of pure force at the mouth. It struck the tongue, searing it.

Letting loose an ear-pounding sound, the demon pulled back its tongue, then shut its mouth. The tentacles holding Uldyssian tightened painfully. If it could not eat the human, the Thonos evidently would be satisfied with crushing him.

Then, Uldyssian sensed a figure near him. His mind flashed back to the jungle, when Mendeln had come to his rescue against the ancient demonic presence. He had wondered where his brother was in all this; should not the fate of the edyrem have been integral to Rathma and the dragon? Would not Mendeln himself have sought to come to his sibling, just as Uldyssian would have come to him?

Something happened, but what it was, a weary Uldyssian could not say immediately. He only knew that the tentacles abandoned him. Air filled his lungs. The Thonos bellowed angrily—

"Mendeln . . ." Uldyssian managed, shaking his head to clear both it and his vision. "Mendeln, I knew you'd—"

It was not Mendeln.

Achilios stood next to him, firing one arrow in rapid succession after another. Those bolts, those seemingly insignificant bolts, struck true against each of the visible orbs of the demon.

But more to the point, after they hit . . . they dissolved in an explosion of energies far more deadly than the point of an arrow.

Six eyes were ruined and blue lightning crackled from each. The Thonos shivered and many of its limbs flailed about without reason. Achilios, standing like some dread guardian, pulled arrow after arrow out of his quiver . . . and never seemed in danger of running out.

Recovering from his shock, Uldyssian called out, "Achilios! What—"

Without missing a shot, the archer turned his gaze to his old friend.

Achilios's eyes blazed white. Expressionless, he said, "Go, Uldyssian. You are needed."

With that, the blond figure returned to firing. For the first time, the Thonos showed some hesitation. Several tentacles wiped at the eyes already targeted. Others began churning up the ground.

Uldyssian, still uncertain as to whether to leave Achilios alone against this behemoth, recognized immediately what the Thonos was doing.

"It's going to burrow!" he shouted to the hunter. "It's going to attack from underneath!"

To this, Achilios remarked in the same monotone voice as before, "No. It will not. Go now, Uldyssian."

This time, Uldyssian listened. He did not understand this latest face of his childhood friend, but what mattered was that Achilios did appear to be holding the Thonos at bay.

At the very least, Uldyssian hoped to salvage the edyrem and then return to help the archer.

If all of that was yet possible . . .

The struggle with the morlu had turned very desperate. The one beacon of hope centered around Saron. The Torajian, looking almost as fierce as the helmed warriors, wielded a long, slim sword and at first appeared to be simply using skill against his insidious adversaries. However, each time the sword hit, a flash of blue accompanied the slice. In this particular case, the result was the toppling of a morlu's head the next moment.

But other than those surrounding Saron, the edyrem were in retreat. The morlu and surviving Peace Warders trod over the bodies of the dead, eager for more victims.

Pausing to catch his breath again, Uldyssian glared at the encroaching villains. He spied a morlu about to slay a Torajian and fury took over.

The morlu let out a hiss as the blade in its hand melted. That hiss turned to a howl as the creature's gauntleted hand followed. Uldyssian did not stop until he had reduced the morlu to a bubbling mass, an act that took him all of three breaths.

The edyrem realized that he was with them again. Their confidence visibly rose. Under Uldyssian's guidance, the line began to strengthen, even push back in some places the servants of the temple.

Then, a Parthan whom Uldyssian had thought slain rose up again, ax in hand. Next to the man, a Torajian also stood. Uldyssian cheered at this sight . . . until a Peace Warder whose throat was a bloody tangle of sliced flesh and sinew joined them.

All three turned to face the defenders . . . and all three began attacking.

All three were dead . . .

Serenthia's anxious voice filled his head. *Uldyssian! The slain! Theirs and ours! They're rising! All of them! They're rising!*

They were indeed. Everywhere that he looked, Uldyssian saw that those who had been killed were now standing. Some of them lacked limbs, even heads. Whether edyrem, Peace Warders, priests, or morlu, those still intact enough were now back on their feet.

And all now marched with the rest of Lilith's servants against Uldyssian and his followers.

TWENTY-ONE

He could hear her laughter again. Lilith's triumphant laughter. Each time, she stole hope away from him.

But if she thought that this would finally break him, finally make Uldyssian surrender the souls of the edyrem to her, than the demoness was sorely mistaken.

The corpses shambling toward his people were no more than shells. The spirits of the men and women they had once been had moved on. That was made even more evident by the fact that none of the resurrected edyrem used their powers. All kept to the weapons at hand. When Uldyssian probed one of the figures, he sensed nothing living.

That settled it for him. Feeling no regret for what he had to do, Uldyssian waved his hand toward the first several walking dead. They immediately collapsed. However, before he could sigh in relief, the bodies stumbled to their feet again, weapons once more ready to add the living to their ranks.

As powerful as he was, Uldyssian could not play this endless game against Lilith and the priests. He would have to destroy her creatures en mass, but that risked him injuring or even slaying his followers in the process.

But there was no other choice. Each moment that he hesitated, more of those who had put their lives in his hands fell victim . . . and then rose to add others.

He had only one hope, but it risked everything.

Then again, the battle was already beyond concerning himself about that.

Pull back . . . he commanded the edyrem in front of him. *Quickly! Those that can, create a shield! Separate us from them, if only for a few feet!*

They obeyed without question, which made him cringe inside. In their minds, Uldyssian had come to save them again. However, he could no longer promise that would be the case.

His heart beat as he waited for them to do as he said. Yet, although in some places they managed to succeed, in others it proved impossible to disengage with the morlu and the Peace Warders. Uldyssian could wait no longer. He prayed that he could control his powers enough to keep from adding too many of his companions to the casualties. Worse, he did not even know if what he planned would accomplish anything accept delay defeat.

He focused on the mass of bodies—

The resurrected dead suddenly began falling. Not merely those of the dead edyrem and Peace Warders, but also the slain morlu. They simply collapsed as if a gust of wind had blown all of them over.

But this miracle was not due to Uldyssian. Startled, he looked around for the source, but could not find it.

Then, it occurred to him not to waste this moment.

Strike! he ordered the others. *Strike before they recover!*

To their credit, the edyrem reorganized immediately. Saron and the other commanders led them forward. The surviving Peace Warders and morlu readied themselves for what was surely the last confrontation. They had every confidence in their might despite this abrupt turnaround.

But then a voice called out in a language that Uldyssian did not understand. He did recognize that voice though, and his heart leapt at its sound.

A figure in black, one hand holding high a gleaming white dagger, shouted again in the direction of the attackers. Mendeln, his pale face drawn and his voice strained, repeated the same words over and over.

And as Uldyssian watched, in the front line one morlu

after another let out hisses of dismay . . . and fell as dead as the once animated bodies.

The Peace Warders and priests faltered, stunned as their most potent weapon proved vulnerable. Those morlu behind also slowed, for the first time their movements showing uncertainty and even, perhaps, a little anxiousness.

Uldyssian glanced around quickly and saw that nearly everywhere the foremost morlu had collapsed. He immediately urged the edyrem to press the fight harder and they answered his call. Peace Warders and morlu who dared to push forward found their advance blocked by the invisible barriers. Balls of energy flew at the ranks of the Triune, downing more than one foe. Uldyssian directed the efforts of his best converts against the priests, harrying the robed figures to such a point that some started to retreat.

But those who did were not allowed to get very far. One screamed as thorns burst out over all parts of his body. He toppled into one of his fellows, who pulled back with blood from two puncture wounds staining the side of his garments.

It had been through no effort of the edyrem that this had happened. Uldyssian sensed Lilith's anger, as, of course, did the priests. Out of fear of their supposed Primus, they returned to the struggle.

Uldyssian rewarded their decision with a net of vines that dropped down and roped the necks and limbs of three. Using the Thonos for his inspiration, he had the vines tightened until they strangled his adversaries.

As if thought of it had somehow caught the demon's attention, the Thonos let out a roar so loud that Uldyssian knew that it had to be right behind him. He barely scattered out of the way as the behemoth *staggered* past. Many of its tentacles hung limp and there were burning sores where most of the eyes had been. Arrows pincushioned the beast, each having struck a vital part.

Of Achilios, there was no sign, but Uldyssian could not

concern himself with the archer, for the Thonos, each step more ragged than the previous, began listing dangerously. Uldyssian calculated its path and quickly warned those in the way.

Move! Move now! he repeated over and over until the last edyrem had managed to leap aside.

The Thonos unleashed a last, drawn-out roar . . . and tumbled over. Uldyssian did what he could to adjust the giant demon's descent.

Their ranks tight, the Triune's minions could not clear out of the way. Some did manage to flee, but most were caught under the falling behemoth. Hardened Peace Warders cried out in panic, then were crushed beneath the massive body. Other warriors escaped the corpse, but were batted aside by the many flailing limbs that followed. Even the morlu did not escape, several of them tossed like leaves.

With gusto, the edyrem charged back into the area. Only the morlu there still had any fight left in them, but their numbers kept dwindling as Mendeln shouted out the mysterious words at the top of his voice.

Then, a familiar buzzing sound filled the air. Uldyssian let out a gasp and reached out, but his reaction was too slow. The deadly Peace Warder weapon flew at his brother, its thrower expertly aiming for Mendeln's chest.

At the last moment, Mendeln twisted, his free arm blocking the way. Unfortunately, flesh and bone were not enough armor against such a sinister weapon. The spinning blades cut *through* his arm midway between the shoulder and the elbow. Mendeln's arm literally dropped off.

The blades cut through his garments and left a shallow cut along his side, but that was finally the end of it. It said something for Mendeln's stamina that he still stood even as blood poured from the ruined arm. Uldyssian's brother gazed down at the lost limb, then touched what was left near his shoulder.

The bleeding halted just as Uldyssian joined him. "Let me help you with that!"

"There is no time!" Mendeln argued. His pale face had grown even more so, but otherwise he seemed himself. The massive wound looked half-healed already. "We must press! We must end this here!"

But it'll not end here! Uldyssian realized. *It'll go on as long as Lilith continues to haunt us!*

Nevertheless, he let Mendeln have his way. Once again holding high the unsettling blade, Uldyssian's younger sibling renewed his chant. More and more morlu toppled over, the demonic strings guiding them severed forever.

Uldyssian turned to seek Achilios, but still his friend was nowhere to be found. There *was* Serenthia, however. She utilized her spear and her powers as if born to them. Each time a Peace Warder or some other adversary perished at the point of the weapon, another fell to a fire ball, a storm of dust, or some other conjuration.

Serenthia! he called. *Where is Timeon?* Like Achilios, there was no trace of him.

Dead! A morlu caught his eyes turned elsewhere and his powers defending another!

The Parthans were growing fewer and fewer and even though this night had witnessed both his brother and his childhood comrade return to his side, the loss of Timeon only emphasized again how Uldyssian's past was being eaten away. It did not help that he saw Jonas—once scarred Jonas—commanding others in the name of his only blood relation.

Damn you, Lilith! he silently swore. No, this would never end! If she could not use the Triune, the demoness would slip away to find some other method by which to seize the edyrem . . . seize *all* of Humanity for her own.

He could not let her. He could not let her continue. Uldyssian imagined her before him, imagined her in his grip—

And so she *was*.

The daughter of Mephisto stood right in front of Uldyssian, her expression as wide-eyed and wondering as his. She wore no guise, appearing before him as the reptilian temptress he had last seen. Uldyssian did indeed hold her as he imagined, hands clamped painfully tight around her upper arms. Their faces were less than a foot apart.

Unfortunately, it was Lilith who recovered first. Her gaping mouth transformed into the familiar, beguiling smile with which as Lylia she had first captured his heart.

"Why, Uldyssian, my love! If you wanted me in your arms again, you should've just told me."

Something snared him around the throat, constricting like a serpent. Too late he recognized it as her tail.

"We should go to somewhere more private, don't you think?"

They vanished from the battle.

Serenthia felt Uldyssian's surprise and his subsequent dismay, but the struggle against the Triune prevented her from coming to his aid. She sensed Lilith's awful presence and almost screamed in horror when both he and the demoness disappeared.

But even then there was nothing that the merchant's daughter could do, nothing but continue to fight and kill Peace Warders, priests, and morlu, each of whom seemed immediately replaced by two more. That Mendeln had returned and had stripped many of the morlu of their parody of life had helped stave off the onslaught, but that was all. The servants of the temple were better trained for this chaos; Uldyssian's followers were still, for the most part, farmers, merchants, and the like.

Yet they fought with far greater determination and skill than even she could have imagined . . . but would it be enough?

Two morlu converged on her. However, before Serenthia could deal with them, a succession of arrows caught the pair in both their eyes and their throats. Each strike was accompanied by a flash of energy.

The morlu dropped.

"Achilios?" she blurted. Through Uldyssian, Serenthia had been alerted to the archer's presence, but unable to sense him herself, she had only half-believed. Now . . .

Now the dark-haired woman fought harder. Achilios was with her, even if she had yet to actually see him. He was with her. Whatever the outcome, victory or defeat, they would be together.

Whether in life or in death, they would be together . . .

Had someone informed Mendeln that he would have the wherewithal to not only survive the severing of his arm but go on as if nothing had happened, he would have thought them mad. Now, he thought *himself* mad . . . but did not care. Uldyssian was gone, taken by the demoness. Mendeln could not tell what was at this moment happening to his brother, but it could be nothing good. Lilith had surely had enough of his defiance; she would see to it that he would pay for it and pay dearly.

I wanted to stand at his side, Mendeln bitterly thought. *A short time that certainly was . . .*

He considered calling to Rathma and Trag'Oul, but for reasons that he could not explain, held back. Instead, he used his wound and his bitterness to power his work. One morlu after another morlu—the fiends bereft of the demonic essence that animated them—dropped before him. Each casting took its toll upon him, though, something he did not outwardly show. Yet, there were still morlu, too many morlu, and their savage blades continued to get through some edyrem's shield, splattering the innards of that hapless person over other defenders.

They must all be cast out if we are to win . . . or even survive . . . they must be!

A morlu broke through. Rather than attack from behind those battling the Triune, the bestial warrior headed for the children and weaker within the circle. A monstrous grin stretched across the fiend's unnatural countenance. At the same time, two more slipped through other cracks in the ranks of Uldyssian's followers. The edyrem had proven themselves several times over; they were just outnumbered and lacked the foul expertise of their foes.

They must be cast out! But he was the only one with that ability and had so far proven wanting. All that the dragon and Rathma had shown or taught him meant nothing. None of their methods or spells had focused on such a monumental and desperate task.

Yet, Mendeln had to try. It still did not mean that the edyrem would be saved, but to simply give up . . .

And that suddenly gave him an idea of how to come to his brother's aid. It, too, was a desperate notion . . .

He pulled the small bone fragment from his pocket. Without hesitation, he said to it, "To my brother. To help him against Lilith."

The fragment vanished. Mendeln hoped that he had not just made a terrible mistake, but he had not had any other choice.

That left the morlu with which to deal. Bracing himself, Mendeln ran through the words in his head. They had to be arranged just so. He no longer followed his mentors' examples, but his own.

If the Balance decrees it, Uldyssian's brother thought. *Then it will work . . .*

And if the Balance did not . . . Mendeln did not want to think about it.

He held the dagger up and began shouting. His spell was his own variation of what he had used already, but now amplified. Yet it was not the words of power alone that he needed. Mendeln threw his will into it, threw everything that he was into it. The morlu were an abomination; they had to be cast out . . .

From the dagger burst a blinding light which caused Mendeln himself to cry out in surprise. He staggered, suddenly feeling as if his very life were draining from him.

The light spread out among the edyrem and then

their enemies. Mendeln watched with hope, with anxiousness, waiting for something to happen. When nothing did, he nearly gave in to his growing weakness.

But then, a morlu flung back his helmet. The ghoulish warrior, his horrific, scarred face fully revealed, took an awkward step in Mendeln's direction . . . and then spun around and crashed to the ground.

The one next to the first fell over. A third followed suit.

It is happening! Mendeln cheered. *It is happening!*

However, it was still happening too slow and the stress on him was becoming overwhelming. He fell to one knee even as an entire row of morlu simply collapsed.

Mendeln cursed his failing body. He also cursed Rathma and Trag'Oul for leaving all of this to him. They spoke of the need to maintain the Balance, but how could that happen if the edyrem were slaughtered here? Of what use was the Balance, then? Why could the dragon not once come out of hiding and act, rather than endlessly preach what others should do?

You speak the truth, came the familiar voice suddenly. *You speak the truth, Mendel ul-Diomed . . .*

It was as if Uldyssian's brother had been asleep all his life and only now had awakened to the forces with which the dragon—and Rathma, Mendeln sensed—filled him to overflowing. Mendeln rose full of hope, full of power.

Power which he focused on the dagger . . . and his spell.

The light shone so bright that surely even those awake in the capital should have seen it. All around him, the combatants froze in astonishment.

And the morlu—all the morlu—finally died . . . again.

They fell by the dozens, by the scores, and Mendeln was certain, by the hundreds. As he turned around, he saw only their corpses littering the already blood-soaked jungle. Thankfully, he knew that these beasts would not rise again, for he had taken that into account when he had derived his own spell.

They are all finished, Trag'Oul declared. *They are no more . . .*

The dragon and Rathma withdrew from him. Mendeln teetered, then dropped to both knees. His arm fell to his side and as it did the incredible illumination cast by his dagger vanished.

Another voice entered his thoughts, yet one that he welcomed, for it did not speak to him alone, but *all* the defenders.

Have at them! Serenthia commanded. *They're confused! Lost! Now's the time to strike—for Uldyssian!*

A spontaneous cheer arose from among his brother's followers and even Mendeln added his own ragged cry to it. The edyrem swept out toward their adversaries, beating back the Peace Warders and countering the spells of the priests. In addition to the clash of arms, there were balls of energy, feats of enhanced strength, and more. The once invincible ranks of the Triune splintered. Peace Warders fought, but not with much hope.

Mendeln wanted to do nothing more than sleep, but he fought to his feet. Sleep could only come when—assuming no new horror reared its ugly head—Lilith's minions were utterly broken. Only then . . .

He sensed a priest casting. Mendeln shoved the dagger forward and muttered. In his mind, he saw the priest's spell turn on the man. A dark shadow enveloped the caster, a shadow that literally ate away at him until nothing remained. The priest did not even have time to scream.

There were still many to fight, but the odds were now with the edyrem. Their confidence continued to swell—that, and the fact that they knew in their hearts that this was the decisive moment.

And so they fought. Mendeln, aware that he could do no more for his brother, fought with them. At that moment, he both respected and hated the Balance, for he knew very well that the edyrem needed to win, even if it meant losing Uldyssian. Sanctuary could survive without his brother.

Mendeln could only hope that by sending the bone fragment to wherever his sibling was that it would help Uldyssian survive.

Of course, considering just what the piece contained, considering the potential for evil within it, it was also possible that Mendeln had done just the opposite . . .

TWENTY-TWO

Uldyssian stood in a maze.

He knew that this was some part of the supreme temple, but other than that he was entirely without a clue. Each time he used his powers to try to escape, nothing happened. He did not appear somewhere else, and this time, he could not summon Lilith to him. Why that was, the son of Diomedes did not know, but it boded ill for his efforts against her.

With nothing else left to him, Uldyssian continued down the stark, stone corridor. Torches in the walls lit the way, not that there was anything to see. Still, with memories of his encounters in the temple in Toraja still fresh, he kept a wary eye on the ceiling, the floor, and the walls. Uldyssian knew that such distraction only worked in the demoness's favor, but could do nothing about it.

The corridor ended at another one that gave him the choice of turning left or right. Having already chosen the right at the last intersection upon which he had come, Uldyssian picked the left this time. In truth, a part of him was suspicious that he would end up in the same place regardless of which direction taken. There was something entirely unnatural about this maze, not at all surprising since it was demonic in origin. While it reminded him of Lilith, it was very likely that it had been designed by her brother, Lucion.

After only a few steps down the new hall, Uldyssian suddenly turned and swung his fist into the nearest wall. Both shielded and powered by his gifts, his fist slammed a tremendous hole in the stone. Cracks spread from the broken gap along much of the nearby area. Uldyssian pulled back his hand to inspect the damage he had created—

And the wall mended itself. The stones shoved back in place and the cracks sealed over. In less time than it had taken him to do the deed, all trace had disappeared.

He swore. Uldyssian had thought that perhaps by taking an impulsive action he would catch Lilith by surprise. Her trap, though, was proving very, very intricate.

Uldyssian had immediately materialized in this place, his former lover nowhere to be seen or sensed. He still berated himself for having reacted too slowly to her sudden materialization. After all, he had been the one who had so much wanted her there . . .

Try as he might, Uldyssian could not repeat that act. Again, he did not understand why. Lilith had to have done *something* to him—

There was a clatter just ahead.

It sounded as if someone had dropped a small object. The clatter echoed for a brief time, then silence reigned once more. Uldyssian could see nothing, though. Was this a new torture of Lilith's? Did she plan to keep him distracted with sudden, random sounds? Judging by the way his heart beat now, Uldyssian thought that perhaps the demoness had a good point.

He took a few tentative steps toward where he had heard the noise. Uldyssian did not notice anything different at first, but then he saw a small, oddly pale stone lying against one of the walls. For some reason, Mendeln came to mind. Despite not trusting why that should be so, Uldyssian bent down to take the piece.

There was a coldness to the odd stone that nearly made him drop it. Yet, again he felt that his brother had some sort of tie to this find. Straightening, Uldyssian inspected it.

The way you seek is behind you . . .

Uldyssian smothered a gasp. He *knew* that voice, knew it

so very well. Never had he expected to hear it again, especially emanating from a stone.

No . . . he saw it for what it actually was. As a farmer raising animals, he should have recognized it instantly. It was a bone.

And the voice had belonged to dread Malic.

The way you seek is behind you . . . the voice repeated.

On a hunch, Uldyssian muttered, "Why are you here, priest?"

At the command of your brother . . . and the pleasure of vengeance . . .

The first part Uldyssian understood, the second confused him at first. He could not see why Mendeln would send the spirit of Malic after him if all the latter desired was retribution against Uldyssian. Then, the son of Diomedes remembered just *who* had been responsible for the man's death.

"So, it's Lilith you're after . . ."

The way you seek is behind you . . .

Malic's cryptic response made Uldyssian frown. He did not entirely trust this ghost, even if Mendeln *had* been the one to send him. Still, he had no other choice than to believe the instructions . . . for the moment.

Returning to the previous intersection, Uldyssian headed in the direction that he had rejected. There was no further contact by the priest's specter and so Uldyssian assumed that he should keep walking until it said something.

Indeed, the voice arose at the next junction. *To the left you must go . . .*

"How long is this going to take?"

The distance shortens, Uldyssian ul-Diomed, even if the danger also heightens . . .

"Which means?"

This was the plaything of my lord Lucion . . . a wrong step, a wrong turn . . . and you will have your hands full . . . The voice went silent after that and Uldyssian decided not to bother seeking more. Other than the directions, all Malic offered were riddles. Again, Uldyssian vowed to remain wary of the ghost.

Malic did not speak again until they had reached another corridor. Uldyssian followed the new path and after a few minutes noticed that the way was growing darker. In addition, a sense of claustrophobia took hold of him.

Recalling the tricks of the Worldstone's cavern, Uldyssian rejected the feeling. As the torches grew farther and farther apart, he summoned a light of his own.

The changes in his surroundings did not bode well. He resorted to the bone fragment for answers. "What goes on here, priest?"

Remain steady on the path, the ghost replied very succinctly. It was almost as if Malic stood next to him. *Touch not the walls, whatever the need . . .*

While he was certainly willing to obey, Uldyssian wanted a reason. "Why? What'll happen if I—"

The stone floor tilted, sending him sliding to the left.

Beware! The wall!

Still clutching the fragment, Uldyssian grasped with his free hand a depression between two stones in the floor. His momentum ceased. He held on tight. Oddly, the path behind him looked absolutely normal. With the utmost caution Uldyssian pulled himself toward it.

The floor shifted, sending him rolling on into the darkened areas. This was not some clever use of mechanisms; the only manner by which the floor could move in so many directions was magic.

He concentrated, willing the floor to become even again. The angle at which he tumbled lessened, then disappeared altogether.

Uldyssian paused to catch his breath.

The floor shifted to his right.

The wall, fool! Beware the—

It was too late. Uldyssian, already near one side of the

corridor, had no chance to react before his shoulder slammed into the wall. The stone there gave way. He dropped into emptiness . . .

And a moment later, landed on a harsh, slick surface.

Rise up! Rise up, you dolt! Malic all but shouted in his head. *They come! They come!*

Savage grunting filled Uldyssian's ears. On instinct, he rolled away from their source.

A heavy battle-ax chopped into the ground near his head.

Ending on his back, Uldyssian stared up into the black pits that were the eyes of a morlu.

Uldyssian thrust his hand toward the monstrous figure. With a roar of anger, the morlu went flying back, finally crashing into a jagged wall far away. The body fell several dozen yards before hitting the bottom.

But as Uldyssian rose from dealing with this threat, he saw that Malic had been correct when the ghost had used the word "they."

He was in a vast underground chamber filled with morlu.

Uldyssian had been certain that Lilith had thrown all her resources into attacking the edyrem. He would have never believed that she had kept so many of these hideous creatures at hand should Uldyssian escape her trap. Then again, perhaps she had merely held on to this band for other ventures, such as against Inarius, conspicuously absent in all this struggle.

Whatever the reason, the morlu howled at the sight of Uldyssian and charged him. Like ants, they flowed toward the intruder from every direction. Some waved weapons, others merely sought to tear him apart with their hands.

He thrust the fragment into his shirt and then met the first of his attackers. Uldyssian grappled with the morlu just long enough to gain a hold, then twisted the warrior around in time for the ax of another to bury itself deep in the first's chest regardless of the armor.

Tossing aside the body, Uldyssian sent a ball of fire at the second attacker. Perhaps because of the morlu's undead nature, the creature immediately became an inferno. Uldyssian kicked him into another, then turned to his left, where his most imminent foe now stood.

That morlu received what the initial one had. Driven by the human's powers, the armored beast flew up, then dropped over a lava flow Uldyssian had spotted. The morlu sank out of sight, the lava sizzling loud.

But even with such success, the horde was pressing him harder. With a cry of defiance, Uldyssian swept his arm across the chamber. The ground around him exploded and morlu by the scores were ripped apart or tossed far away. Uldyssian did the same with his other arm, with just as dramatic results. He continued this twice more, clearing for a great distance the ground around him.

Morlu bodies and parts lay scattered everywhere. Driven by his frustration and fury and not having to fear harming friends, Uldyssian had been able to take down nearly as many of the creatures as had been part of the entire attack on his followers. He did not fear the survivors; all Uldyssian wanted was a moment to catch his breath and then he would rid this place of the last of the vermin.

But then he saw an arm lying over one body slide off that and roll to its former wielder. Once there, it reattached itself. Uldyssian looked to the other side and beheld the ruined throat of another heal itself.

As that happened, something emerged from the lava. Armor blazing red and flesh seared, the morlu he had tossed into the flow also stalked toward him.

Everywhere, the demonic warriors healed and rose. It was an even more horrible tableau than that from the battle, yet Uldyssian knew that it had to be related.

It is the Kiss of Mephisto that raises them, but the demoness has amplified its powers, came Malic's voice. *Seek the black gemstone in the center! Seek it!*

Morlu blocked his view in that direction. Inhaling, Uldyssian clapped his hands together. The crashing sound bowled over his foes . . .

There, at last revealed, was what Malic claimed the source of the warriors' regeneration. A gleaming black gemstone nearly as tall as him and embedded in a triangular column of red-streaked marble.

That is it! It must be destroyed! Quickly!

But the morlu perhaps understood what he intended, for they came at him in a frenzy, screaming and leaping and swinging whatever weapons they carried. They converged on Uldyssian from all sides.

Despite that, he concentrated only on the huge gem. Compared to the Worldstone, the task proved easier. Uldyssian located within it a fault and threw all his will into that one place—

With a shattering sound worthy of the colliding Shards of the Worldstone, the Kiss of Mephisto was no more.

The morlu did not slow even then. Their hatred for him was absolute. Foam splattered the mouths of many and their shrieks would have frightened the dead. The morlu lived only for his utter annihilation.

Just as he had done before, a grim Uldyssian waved his arm across his view. He threw morlu left and right, into walls and into the lava flows. Those that got closer he burned with flame or speared with solid light. When even that did not halt the tide, Uldyssian seized one morlu after another and crushed their throats or broke their necks or backs. Blades cut wounds in him that he forced to heal. Gauntleted hands grasping for his limbs or neck slid off as if seeking to hold oil.

Uldyssian pictured Lilith in his mind as he tore through the ranks of the morlu. Each one slain was her.

And then . . . and then there *were* no more morlu to fight.

It took Uldyssian nearly a minute to register this astounding fact. Around him lay the bodies. No part of the floor of the cavern seemed untouched by corpses or blood. Yet, the beasts of the temple did not rise to fight him again. The morlu were dead, this time forever.

Well played . . . Uldyssian ul-Diomed.

Uldyssian grunted, this the first time that he could sense respect in Malic's voice. However, there was no time for congratulations. There was only the hunt for Lilith.

Seek above, to your right. There you will find the way . . .

Malic's directions led Uldyssian to a door. No longer concerned about stealth, Uldyssian sent the door flying inward.

He found two more morlu within, both slain by the door's explosion. Uldyssian trod over their bodies, already sensing that Lilith was close at hand.

With the aid of Malic's ghost, Uldyssian emerged into what the spirit indicated was the Primus's personal chambers. There was not much to see other than the elegant throne in the first and innermost chamber. The Primus, after all, had been only a facade for Lucion and his sister.

He reached the doorway leading out, but there Malic suddenly spoke again. *Hold the bone high and ready!* the ghost demanded. *And be prepared to throw!*

Uldyssian tensed. This extreme difference from previous instructions told him that Malic knew of some powerful threat without that even the son of Diomedes could not sense.

With his thoughts, Uldyssian flung open the doors—

Throw! commanded Malic urgently.

Guided by his power as well as his arm, Uldyssian unleashed the bone. It soared out of the Primus's chambers and down the darkened corridor beyond. Then, just as Uldyssian was about to lose sight of it, the piece abruptly veered to the right.

He heard the bone strike something, followed immediately by a pained grunt. That, in turn, was followed by a heavy thud that Uldyssian recognized all too well.

Darting out, he sought for the location. Sure enough, a

figure clad in the robes of a Dialon lay sprawled in the corner. Blood from a wound to his forehead marked where the fragment had hit.

Uldyssian started to reach for the bone—and then straightened. She was *here*.

"Poor, poor darling Durram! He so wanted to be of assistance to his Primus!"

Forgetting the fragment, he looked around. Try as he might, though, Uldyssian could not pinpoint exactly where she was. However, he finally thought he knew why. This was the main temple of the Triune, designed and built to Lucion's expectations. Surely, like the ancient structure in which Lilith had planned to turn all the edyrem, this place was situated on a *nexus*, one of the points where the angels and demons had first begun to create the world. Lucion had usurped the forces of that nexus for his temple and manipulated them to mask the evil inherent in this place.

And in masking the evil of the Burning Hells, those forces now also masked Lilith from him.

"Ah, my dear, sweet Uldyssian!" the demoness mocked. "Always so near victory, always so willing to let it slip away from you . . ."

"Not this time, Lilith!" he returned, pushing his will to the limits in order to find her. "Not this time!"

"But, my love! Your brother and your friends are dead and your precious edyrem are even now being marched back here! How much greater a defeat can there be?"

For a moment, her words sparked fear and despair in him, but then Uldyssian recalled just who spoke. "No more of your lies. No more of your games."

With that, he plunged toward where he believed she was.

Suddenly, there were heavy doors in his path. Uldyssian, prepared for any barrier, threw his power into a blast that decimated them. His momentum sent him through a second later.

He landed on all fours much like a cat . . . and then stared wide-eyed.

Uldyssian crouched in one of the entrances to the huge chamber where the faithful gathered prior to the sermons of their respective priests. He knew the design of the other temples enough to know that he should not have yet reached this place. Once again, Lilith had played him.

The towering statues of two of the false spirits loomed over him. That of Mefis—Lilith's father, Mephisto—was oddly absent. The pedestal gave some indication that the statue had broken off at some point. Somehow, Uldyssian doubted that it had been an accident.

Recalling Toraja, he kept a wary eye on the remaining two figures. Lilith wanted him in this chamber for a reason. Therefore, everything within was suspect.

And just then, her laughter filled the room.

"The game is done, my dear, sweet Uldyssian!" she called from everywhere and nowhere. "You *have* been a marvel and all that I imagined you'd be, but I would be finished with this, for I've *so* much more to do!"

She was here . . . and yet, she was not. Uldyssian probed every direction. Each time, he felt that he had found her, but then some other location would then take prominence.

"Show yourself," he growled. "Show me where you are!"

"Why, I am right here, my love."

Lilith appeared . . . and appeared . . . and appeared over and over and over. A hundred visions of the demoness materialized, followed by hundreds more.

That they were merely illusion was the obvious thought to Uldyssian. Yet, when he sought to tell the true from the false, *all* of the figures seemed to him as the former. None were merely figments . . .

"Hold me in your arms one last time," they mocked in unison. A thousand Lilith's pursed their lips. "Kiss me one last time, my love." They started toward him, hips swinging, bodies moving suggestively. "Come lay with me one more time . . ."

They could not all be real, yet they were. Uldyssian tried to focus, but the battle, his personal fight with the morlu . . .

so much had happened to drain away his strength and concentration. He knew that the demoness had planned this. A weakened Uldyssian was less a threat to her and possibly, in her mind, more manageable. After all, she still wanted his edyrem and he was the easiest path to that.

Then, Uldyssian thought about the fact that Lilith had gone to the trouble of sending him through the maze and against the morlu below. She had expected him to somehow survive. He felt certain of it. That, and her shock when she had first materialized in the midst of the jungle battle, revealed to him that the demoness respected his abilities more than she let on. In fact, Uldyssian suddenly believed that she was even a little frightened. Why else go through all this elaborate spellwork? Could Lilith not have done with him as she wished after stealing him from the others?

Perhaps not . . . perhaps she had indeed needed him *much* weakened first . . .

The horde of Liliths converged upon him, all with arms outstretched. Uldyssian suspected that if he fell prey to her here, he was lost forever. Somehow, he had to find the one and only Lilith . . .

In his fogged mind, a question arose. This was the supreme temple, the focus for the life of the sect.

Where, then, were all those who should have been within? Lilith had sent only lesser priests, Peace Warders, and morlu into the jungle. Where were the acolytes, the high priests, the guards, and all the rest that kept the temple functioning but of whom many were not trained warriors? The only one that he had seen had been the one Malic's bone had brought down.

He suddenly knew.

And knowing it, Uldyssian *demanded* in his mind to see the reality.

The Liliths melted away. In their place stood the faithful. Priests, priestesses, acolytes, Peace Warders, and more. The whole of the sect was represented.

But Lilith was not among them.

She had to be here. Uldyssian reminded himself just who he was hunting. It would not be impossible for her to transform herself at the same time that he was ripping away her other illusion.

The servants of the Triune must have realized, too, that they were no longer disguised, for they came at him like a maddened mob. In their minds, they still served the Primus and Uldyssian knew that nothing he said would shake their faith in that knowledge.

But then, there were none here who did not know what the sect truly was, that it was actually a cult following the monstrous dictates of the lords of the Burning Hells. All concern for these fellow men and women abruptly faded. They cared nothing for the lives of his followers nor the innocents who came to listen to the "holy" sermons.

As he had done with the morlu, Uldyssian swept away the ranks of the faithful. Screams echoed throughout the vast chamber as bodies went flying in all directions. Several flew high in the air, others crashed against the walls. Uldyssian left no direction unscathed. All those serving the Three were tossed aside like the refuse that they were.

And that left one figure still standing. A nondescript follower in robes of gray and brown.

"Hello, Lilith," Uldyssian remarked.

Her instinct for defense had this time played against her, but only momentarily. The human guise vanished, the demoness now in her full glory. She leapt up into the air, hovering momentarily.

"My dear, sweet darling," Lilith cooed. "You must be *so* weary! It's a wonder that you can even stand . . ."

In truth, he was *very* tired. Even the last spell had taxed him too much. Lilith, on the other hand, appeared strong and fresh.

"I will miss you, my love," she continued. "But all things must come to an end! I—"

"Be silent, Lilith."

"Now, Uldyssian . . ." The demoness's aspect grew dark.

"That is no way to talk to me. I fear that this time I must truly punish you . . ."

And suddenly, she stood before him, claws out and tail whipping. One pair of claws tore through his ruined garments and his flesh and this time Uldyssian could not entirely heal those wounds. He wanted to fall over, but knew he could not.

His hand caught her wrist just before the second pair of claws would have raked his throat. He twisted Lilith around and threw her high into the air toward the statue of Bala. Lilith struck the top hard, cracking the head off.

But even as the huge chunk of marble crashed to the floor, the demoness vanished, reappearing behind Uldyssian. Both her hands thrust forward, seeking his spine.

However, Uldyssian had already sensed where she planned to materialize and so turned before that. He seized her hands in his own, clamping them together before sliding down to take the wrists tight.

"It ends now, Lilith," he stated flatly.

A rumbling arose, one that shook the entire temple. Those followers of the cult who were still conscious and able to move began fleeing through the exits. They had no more reason to stay, after all. There was no sign of the true Primus, and Lilith had at last been revealed as their manipulator.

"Now dear, sweet Uldyssian—"

She got no further. A huge, marble hand grasped her, pulling her arms to the side and against her body. She squirmed and wriggled, but could neither vanish nor escape. Uldyssian dared not permit that to happen again.

His breathing grew more ragged. This had to be done quickly. Uldyssian even had his doubts that he would be able to save himself, but that would be a small price to pay.

The hand pulled the demoness high above him. Another joined it, grasping over the first. The two remaining statues had the demoness imprisoned.

"It ends now," Uldyssian repeated to her.

Lilith bowed her head in defeat . . . and more than a dozen of the quills that were her tresses shot forth.

Already teetering, Uldyssian allowed his powers to guide him. Almost of its own accord, his hand came up. A golden light formed in front of him.

Borrowing from the evil of her brother, Uldyssian sent the quills back. Lilith could do nothing. Wherever she was visible, they pierced her scaled hide. Two in her stomach, three in her chest, more in her shoulders. Even her throat.

A green ichor splattered the statues' hands. Lilith let out a gurgling gasp, yet even then she still did not perish.

"My sweet Uldyssian . . ." the demoness called out. "Think what you'll do without my . . . my embraces . . ."

His expression did not change. "I already do."

A fierce tremor shook the temple. Many of the Triune had already fled, but others still fought their way out. What neither they nor those who had already left had yet to realize was that all outer entrances had been sealed off.

"Do you recall the last time we were in such a place, Lilith?" he managed to say without once pausing for a desperately needed breath. "Do you remember?"

She said nothing, but her eyes burned with hatred. Her tail weaved back and forth, a sign to Uldyssian that, despite her own condition, she was very much a danger yet.

"The last time, it was only by the strongest will on my part that the building held long enough for my people to escape."

By now, he could hear some of those beyond the chamber shouting and clamoring for anyone to let them out of the temple. They would shout to no avail. Uldyssian had made certain that no one could come to their aid.

He took a very deep breath. "Now, even if it's the last thing I can manage, I'm going to bring this one down."

The rumbling magnified a thousandfold. Veins spread like fire over all the walls, the ceiling, and even the marble floor. Great chunks started to fall.

"Goodbye, Lilith. For the very last time."

She hissed.

Her tail, stretching impossibly, reached all the way down to snare him. Caught unaware, Uldyssian fell on his back.

But his own spell had already come to fruition. The entire roof—and all three towers, Uldyssian knew—collapsed. Hundreds of thousands of tons of stone and wood fell upon the chamber and all else. The shrieks of the faithful momentarily outdid even the roar of the collapse.

Lilith, too, shrieked, as Bala and Dialon tumbled into one another . . . and on top of her in the process. Her tail unwound from around Uldyssian, flopping madly before vanishing into the rubble left in the wake of the demoness's destruction.

Uldyssian could pay no more mind to her fate. He struggled only to keep himself alive. Even as marble pieces ten and twenty times his size sought to crush him, he fought with all he could to keep a shield all around him.

But the stone kept pressing and pressing and Lilith's deeds had sapped him of more strength than he had let on to her. The effort of bringing down the gigantic structure was too much. Uldyssian felt the stone pushing closer, tighter—

And then . . . the pressure eased. Uldyssian took advantage of that easing, straining to make his shield stronger, larger. Despite his body screaming to let it lie there, he shoved himself to his knees, then, when that worked, to his feet.

Only then did it come to him that, other than the dust, the collapse was over.

The ruins lay sprawled for as far as he could see. The dust made it impossible to know more about the destruction he had caused, but Uldyssian sensed a wave of emotions coming from the north. The capital, just beyond his physical view, had felt the collapse and now, no doubt, saw the cloud rising above to obscure the stars. It would not take long for riders to come out to see what had happened. The mage clans likely already knew.

Uldyssian's legs almost gave way. Fearful that he would leave matters incomplete, he quickly surveyed the area for any living sign of Lilith. After a moment, he sensed her trace some distance from him . . . a trace that faded away as Uldyssian monitored it.

She was *dead*.

It was over.

The son of Diomedes let out a sigh . . . and fell. As he did, his fading mind wished that somehow he could return to the others. That was all that mattered, returning to them.

And so you shall . . . came the voice of Trag'Oul. *And so you shall* . . .

TWENTY-THREE

There had been many losses, but many more lived who should not have. Mendeln and Serenthia saw to the comfort of all the edyrem, feeling that, in Uldyssian's absence, they should do whatever they could.

Despite the blood, despite the losses, there was an aura of joy among those there. They had vanquished their enemies. The few Peace Warders and priests to survive had fled into the deep jungles, their wills broken. They had nowhere to go, for everyone had felt the sudden destruction of the great temple. Jonas, climbing up a tree, claimed to have seen a dark cloud obscuring part of the sky in that direction. Daylight was coming soon, but no one needed to verify his claim . . . for suddenly Uldyssian himself was back among them.

Although Uldyssian appeared alone, Mendeln knew that the dragon had lent his brother aid in the return, a second startling act by a being who insisted on complete secrecy when it came to his existence. Truly, Mendeln thought then, the Balance must have seen the good need for Uldyssian.

He and Serenthia came to Uldyssian's side. The merchant's daughter brought Mendeln's brother something to drink. Uldyssian nodded his thanks, then, when he had taken as much as he could, he eyed the two and said, "You know?"

"Yes . . ." answered Mendeln. "You are free of her."

But Uldyssian shook his head. "Never." He suddenly looked around. "Achilios?"

It was Serenthia who responded to this. "He was here . . . and then he was gone. None of us saw when he left."

Mendeln remained quiet.

Nodding, Uldyssian reached for a helping hand. With their assistance, he stood. Around the trio, the edyrem—summoned silently by Uldyssian—gathered.

"The Triune is crushed," he stated bluntly. There still existed some minor temples, but the cult had depended upon the main temple for their influence. Well aware now how things worked, Uldyssian knew that what little remained would fade away.

"The Triune is crushed . . . and now the Cathedral awaits."

No one cheered. No one lamented. They accepted both parts as fact, nothing more. Whatever Uldyssian wanted of them, they would do their best to achieve.

"Clear the dead away and send to me the wounded," he next ordered. "Then, everyone sleeps." As they left to obey, Uldyssian looked at his brother. His eyes went to the wounded arm.

An arm Mendeln again wore whole.

"It shall be explained," replied the younger brother.

"The dragon?"

"Rathma."

Nodding, Uldyssian asked, "Will they help us more? Or is it just us, again?"

Mendeln considered before answering. "I believe that they have seen that they must. I believe that the scales tip in favor of our needs. The Balance will demand it of them, just as it demands much of us."

That satisfied Uldyssian, even if all his brother had said was not exactly clear to him. "Then, tomorrow we march."

Both his brother and Serenthia bowed their heads in agreement.

"Tomorrow," they repeated.

With that Uldyssian turned to help his people, but although his face showed only pride and concern for those who had followed him . . . it was the face of Lilith that would burn forevermore in his mind.

And in that, at least, the demoness had triumphed.

Rathma materialized atop the rubble that had been the temple. He had come to determine the truth as to whether or not his mother was actually dead. More than most, Rathma knew Lilith to be a cunning vixen. She might fool Uldyssian into believing her no more, but he did not believe that she could do so with her own son.

Yet as he looked over the ruins, he found nothing more than the mortal had. Rathma located where Lilith should have been buried and when he probed, he found a still corpse. Not much was left of it and by the time this land was cleared—assuming that Sanctuary would still exist—there would be nothing recognizable as inhuman.

"So it is very much farewell this time," he murmured. "I would say I am sorry, Mother . . . but we know the truth."

With that, he disappeared. There was no time to mourn the dead, especially the dead who did not deserve it. Rathma had other concerns.

He still had a father, after all . . .

He was gone. She had fooled even her ungrateful wretch of a child. Despite her horrific wounds, Lilith managed a smile.

The body that he and Uldyssian believed hers had been that of a minor priestess. Lilith had managed to save herself at the very last moment; then, with her will pushed to its limits to shield her, the demoness had managed to crawl free of the devastation. Still, even she was willing to admit to herself that it had been luck for her to survive, much less keep the two from noticing her.

But Lilith would turn that luck back in her favor. She would regain her strength and this time she would repay Uldyssian and his companions with the most insidious tortures. Even her son would learn what it was to earn her wrath—

A shadow fell across her . . . a shadow that made the demoness start, for she had sensed nothing. Yet, Lilith knew exactly to whom that shadow belonged.

She tried to move, tried to escape . . . but his power held her fast.

"Release me!" Lilith hissed. "Release me . . . Inarius!"

AFTER I HAVE DONE SO MUCH TO SAVE YOU?

"Save me? Ha!" But even as she sought to deny it, the demoness realized that he spoke the truth. All her good fortune made terrible sense. Lilith had believed herself responsible, but no . . .

The angel stood above her in all his glory. Lilith both hated and desired him. *YES, SAVED YOU, MY ONCE LOVE! I DID PROMISE, THOSE MANY CENTURIES AGO, THAT I WOULD NEVER STRIKE YOU DOWN NOR LET ANOTHER DO SO!*

Yet, he had done even worse, in her opinion. Lilith vividly recalled the emptiness, the void in which she had been sentenced until her fortunate escape.

Hissing, the demoness tried to attack, but it was like a fly seeking to batter a horse. Inarius dismissed her weakened assaults as less than nothing.

I WOULD NOT EVEN LET OUR OFFSPRING FIND YOU, FOR HE WOULD HAVE FELT OBLIGATED TO FINISH WHAT THE HUMAN THOUGHT DONE! The hood shook back and forth. *NO CHILD SHOULD SLAY HIS MOTHER, NO MATTER HOW UNGRATEFUL THAT CHILD NOR HOW EVIL THAT MOTHER . . . NO, IT IS ONLY I, ALWAYS, WHO MUST METE OUT JUSTICE WHERE YOU ARE CONCERNED . . . JUSTICE WITHOUT DEATH, OF COURSE, AS I PROMISED!*

"S-Spare me your sermons—"

AS YOU WISH. Inarius raised one palm. In it formed a gleaming sphere so transparent that it was almost invisible.

The demoness's expression turned to horror. "No! Inarius! Don't—"

But in the next second, Lilith floated inside the tiny sphere, her size reduced accordingly.

I HAVE REMEDIED WHAT WAS DONE INADEQUATELY BEFORE, the winged being said without emotion. *THE MISTAKE SHALL NOT BE REPEATED. GOODBYE, MY ONCE LOVE.*

She spat at him although the sphere prevented it from having any result. "You think Sanctuary yours? You see what this human has wrought! He'll bring you down, too, Inarius!"

HE WILL NOT, FOR IT IS THROUGH MY EFFORTS THAT HE HAS DONE YOU IN. Before she could argue more, Inarius added, *FAREWELL, MY ONCE LOVE . . . FAREWELL . . .*

Lilith screamed and cursed, but her voice—as well as she—grew tinier and tinier. The sphere became a marble, then the size of a pea.

And then, for all mortal purposes, shrank so tiny as to become nothing.

CONSIDER YOUR FATE FORTUNATE, MY ONCE LOVE, Inarius said to the emptiness. *CONSIDER IT FORTUNATE, COMPARED WITH THAT AWAITING THE MORTALS WHO WOULD DARE THINK THEMSELVES MORE THAN THEY ARE!* He spread his astonishing wings wide and took to the air, staying above the wreckage of the temple only long enough to peer in the direction of the mortal, Uldyssian ul-Diomed, and his naive supporters.

THEY WILL FIND OUT THAT NOTHING HAS GONE ON THAT I HAVE NOT COMMANDED . . . BUT THEY, LIKE YOU, WILL FIND THAT OUT ALL TOO LATE . . .

And with that, he soared off, unseen, to his sanctum, to decide the fate of his world.

The Sin War
Continues in
The Veiled Prophet

About the Author

Richard A. Knaak is the *New York Times* and *USA Today* bestselling author of some fifty novels and numerous shorter works. He has written for such well-known series as WORLD OF WARCRAFT, DIABLO, DRAGONLANCE, CONAN, and PATHFINDER and is the creator of the long-running, popular epic fantasy saga THE DRAGONREALM. He has also written comic, manga, and gaming material, and his works have been translated worldwide.